# MAILBOAT V

## DANIELLE LINCOLN HANNA

**HHP**

HEARTH & HOMICIDE PRESS, LLC

Cover photography by Matt Mason Photography
www.MattMasonPhotography.com

Cover design by MaryDes
MaryDes.eu

Paperback: ISBN 978-1-7373962-1-5
Ebook:     ISBN 978-1-7373962-6-0
Hardcover: ISBN 978-1-7376089-1-2

# BOOKS BY DANIELLE LINCOLN HANNA

## The Mailboat Suspense Series

The Girl on the Boat: A Prequel Novella
Mailboat I: The End of the Pier
Mailboat II: The Silver Helm
Mailboat III: The Captain's Tale
Mailboat IV: The Shift in the Wind
Mailboat V: The End of Summer
Mailboat VI: *coming soon*
DanielleLincolnHanna.com/shopnow

# LAST TIME IN LAKE GENEVA

Mailboat Captain Tommy Tomlin is finally on the mend after his shooting. During his recovery at a friend's house, one thought weighs on his mind: He told his sixteen-year-old mail jumper Bailey Johnson that he's her grandfather—and hasn't heard from her since.

But after spending most of her life in foster care, bouncing from one home to another, Bailey can't bring herself to believe that someone might finally be there for her. Terrified to finally trust someone, she leaves all of Tommy's efforts to reach her unanswered.

Meanwhile, Patrol Officer Ryan Brandt has figured something out: While he never meant to end up in his hometown department again with his ex, Detective Monica Steele, he's still madly in love with her. The question is whether she can ever forgive him for cheating on her ten years ago, breaking up their marriage. For Monica, it's an entirely different question: Would Ryan forgive her if he learned that she aborted their baby?

The personal tensions challenge their ability to concentrate on a case that's rocking Lake Geneva to its foundations: Several homicides, a bombing, and a shooting, all linked to a long-ago crew of high-end bank burglars known as The Markham Ring. But the veiled mastermind behind the violence, an individual calling himself The Man Upstairs, suggests to Monica that he knows more than her personal phone number; he knows about her secret abortion.

Monica and Ryan aren't the only ones pursuing an investigation. Angelica Read, widow of the first homicide victim in this summer of terror, has come to Lake Geneva intent on learning the truth about the man she married. She never knew he was one of the members of the Markham Ring. She meets Roland Markham, bereaved father of the ring's namesake, and together they explore the case. From what Roland says, she wonders if now-Police Chief Wade Erickson should in fact be credited with breaking up the ring—or if he was in on it, and is now eradicating anyone who had connections to it.

However, her search for information hits nothing but dead ends, the evidence under legal locks and keys. At last, Angelica's mother insists she come home to California. Her two sons are struggling with the murder of their father, and now the absence of their mother. Angelica leaves, but promises Roland to stay on the case and return if she can.

Monica Steele spies Roland and Angelica at their parting meeting, and her suspicions are aroused. She had interviewed Angelica as part of the murder investigation, and still can't bring herself to believe that Angelica was married to a member of the Markham Ring for fifteen years, and never knew. What is she doing in Lake Geneva now? She determines to keep an eye on the mysterious woman.

But Monica isn't the only one who's taken an interest in Angelica Read; The Man Upstairs has, too. He assigns one of his agents, Skull, to tail her.

Ryan Brandt, meanwhile, is trying to get Bailey Johnson out of her abusive foster home. But Ryan can pin nothing on her foster dad, Bud Weber. Nor can he get Bailey re-homed; the foster system is overburdened, and there's nowhere for her to go.

Bud is none too happy with the police pressure, and he's downright furious with his ex-employer, The Man Upstairs, for trying to have him killed. Bud determines to confront The Man and exact his revenge.

At the same time, The Man is convinced his plans are maturing nicely. He green-lights Skull to initiate the secretive "next phase."

That stormy night, two men skulk in the shadows on two separate missions—Skull to further The Man's plot, Bud to secure The Man's demise.

At Chief Wade Erickson's house, Tommy awakens to the sound of someone trying to break in. Wade goes outside to investigate, and comes back with a bloody hand and a made-up story about a squirrel trying to burrow into the siding.

At Roland's house, a different figure lurks in the shadows, then shatters a French door with the grip of a handgun. A shard of glass gives Roland a nasty cut to the head.

Skull later calls The Man Upstairs to report that all went according to plan. The Man, however, sounds upset, or possibly unwell.

For Bud, however, nothing turned out as he intended. He had a gun to The Man's head—and with nothing but words, The Man manipulated Bud out of murdering him. Worse, The Man revealed that he knows Bud's deepest secret: His romance with a man named Zayne Mars. Bud flees into the night, distressed by the memories of losing his only love to a hate crime murder.

Two break-ins, two purposes, two victims injured. Only one of them can be The Man Upstairs...

# MAILBOAT

# FRIDAY, JULY 18, 2014

# Chapter One

# ROLAND

A muffled voice pushed into Roland's consciousness.

"Sir? Sir, can you hear me? We need you to wake up."

A male voice. Young. Brisk. Professional. If he had been applying for a position at Roland's bank, Roland would have asked what the competition was offering, added ten percent, and shaken his hand on the spot.

Never mind he was retired from banking. Never mind he couldn't move his hand right now. Or anything.

A sharp pain stung his left temple. The side of his face felt wet and sticky. Something in his mouth tasted like old copper pennies.

Plastic ripped and someone—presumably the promising young man—pressed a cloud of cotton into the source of the pain.

Roland flinched. Unbidden, a moan escaped his lips.

"Sorry, sir," said the young man. "You've lost some blood. Just trying to slow it down a bit."

Far from reassuring him, the chipper, off-handed tone implied the situation was, in fact, more dire than implied.

Roland blinked. Dried blood crackled around his left eye. A few flakes needled their way in, stinging, eliciting tears in response.

Through the blur, he observed the elaborately moulded ceiling of his own library. His grandfather had brought in plasterers from Italy to craft that masterpiece, never to be fully appreciated unless, like now, one was lying flat on one's back, bleeding from the temple onto the Persian rug. The intricate curlicues of the molding were bathed in soft yellow light. From the corner of his eye, he noted that the reading lamp beside his armchair was still on. No doubt, *Anna Karenina* was lying around somewhere. Hopefully, he'd remembered to put in the bookmark.

From this same view, he noted that the French doors to the stone patio stood ajar, one of them shattered and hanging from a single hinge. Lightening flickered between heavy black clouds, hanging low over Geneva Lake, the unsettled waves crashing against the shore.

The broken doors. Yes, he remembered. The shadowy figure outside. The outline of the gun in the man's hand. He had used it to smash in the door. The glass had exploded. The shards had flown towards him, and—

And that was the last thing he remembered, besides coming to long enough to call 911.

"Do you have any other injuries, sir?"

Did he? Had the intruder used his gun on anything but the door? But the only pain he registered was from his head. "N-no. No."

"What's your name?" The young man began to secure the cotton pad with a bandage. Roland could see now that the boy had neatly trimmed black hair and a chinstrap beard. He was dressed in an EMT's uniform.

"Markham," Roland said, his mouth moving stiffly. "Roland Markham."

"Were you the one who called 911?"

"Y-yes."

"You said there was a break-in?"

"Yes."

"The police have already cleared your house, sir. Whoever was here, they're gone."

The police were here? "Monica...?" Roland muttered.

"Monica? Detective Steele, you mean?"

Roland nodded, then winced with the movement. Monica Steele was investigating the murders and other violent doings that had rocked Lake Geneva this strange summer. Never mind that Roland's son had died by police gunfire seventeen years ago—his evil deeds were creating ripples even now, and a shocking number of people had paid for it.

"She's not here yet," said the EMT. "She's on her way. But we're taking you to the hospital, Mr. Markham. I'm sure she'll want to chat with you later."

Chat? Roland closed his eyes and groaned. His next conversation with Monica Steele would most certainly open with her saying, "I told you so," and end with a vigorous tongue lashing.

She had insisted all along he was next on the killer's list.

# CHAPTER TWO

# MONICA

As I breezed down the hospital hallway, I ran my hands over my face, trying to stimulate my nerve endings, trying to keep awake and alert. Pulling an all-nighter wasn't as easy as it used to be, though I hoped that had more to do with the insanity that was this summer and not passing my tenth anniversary of turning thirty. One hand found the end of my long, dark brown ponytail and, impulsively, I flipped it upwards to look. Big mistake. There were more gray hairs than I remembered.

I flung it back over my shoulder. Screw this shit.

When I found Roland Markham's room, I marched in like Joan of Arc rebuffing the English. Nestled in pillows, Roland sat upright in bed, eyes closed, hands folded in his lap. With the morning sunshine bathing his face, he looked peaceful—prayerful, even, despite the bandage wrapped around his head and the evidence of some impressive bruising underneath. I hated that his mood didn't match mine.

I planted one hand on my belt, the other on the grip of my service weapon. "Jesus Christ, Markham."

He opened his eyes, looked at me, then dropped his head sheepishly and tapped his thumbs together.

It dawned on me that the all-nighter wasn't the only thing that had me run down. Exasperated, I flung a hand at him. "What am I supposed to do with you? It's like raising a teenager." I shifted an eyebrow. "Can I say it finally? Can I say it?" I planted both hands on the plastic footboard and leaned in. "I told you so."

He offered a watery smile. "At least you can't say Angelica Read had anything to do with it."

I rolled my eyes. Angelica Read. Her husband's murder at the beginning of the summer had merely been the ripple on the surface of the lake, foretelling the storm to come. I still wasn't convinced the woman was ignorant of her husband's criminal past. Why had she wormed her way into Roland's confidence? What was her angle?

"I checked her flight to LA," I said. "She was definitely on it. So no, Angelica Read wasn't the one who busted down your door and knocked you out."

Roland laughed. "I'm delighted her whereabouts were the first thing you looked into. I imagine you've already helped yourself to my security camera footage?"

"Yes," I admitted, then shrugged. "I made myself coffee, too." I still felt a little guilty about breaking into his kitchen cupboards, but he owed me one for getting me out of bed in the middle of the night. "That dark roast of yours is pretty good."

Roland smiled and shrugged. "Brazil. It's organic. I'll get you a bag."

"Thanks." We'd been working together so frequently this summer, this conversation wasn't even weird. "By the way, fire whatever handyman fixed your cameras."

He looked at me, surprised. "Why?"

"One of them wasn't hooked up properly. The one overlooking your patio door." I shrugged as if it were no big deal. "You know. The one that mattered."

Roland looked down and tapped his thumbs again. "Oh."

I drummed the plastic railing and squared my jaw. "So. I don't have footage of what happened. I don't have a face." I closed my eyes, saint-like, smoothing a hand through the air. "Neither of these facts pisses me off. At. All."

Roland laughed, but quietly. He knew he was treading on the eggshells of my patience.

"So, what can you tell me?"

Roland sighed. "Well... he was a tall fellow. Dressed in black. He was carrying a gun. I believe that's what he used to break the window."

"What kind of gun?"

He laughed. "I don't know firearms at all."

"Handgun?"

"Well, yes. It would have been a handgun. He broke the glass with the butt of it. That's what it's called, yes?"

I nodded, impressing myself with my own patience regarding the disparity in our firearms knowledge. Did he know what a bullet was, and the risk it posed to him as next-of-kin to the Markham Ring?

I tapped my forehead, mirroring where the bandage was on his own. "It was the glass that cut you? He didn't get a shot off?"

"That's right. The shards just... went flying." He demonstrated an explosion with his hands, fingers splayed. He shook his head mournfully. "That door was original to the house."

"Sorry for your loss." My voice lacked compassion. "And the intruder just left you there, passed out?"

He looked up vaguely, as if still broken up about the door. "Yes. Yes, that's correct. I came to later and called the ambulance."

"You put in that call at 11:45. At what time did the break-in itself happen?"

Roland frowned and twirled his thumbs. "I don't know precisely."

"I'll settle for approximately."

"Eleven thirty?"

I lowered my brows, concerned. "You were out cold for fifteen minutes?" A loss of consciousness that lengthy could result in brain damage—and most days, I already worried about the state of his head.

"Well, no. I came and went a bit."

I nodded. Odds were, the doctors weren't letting him go anytime soon. "So, eleven thirty. That's your best guess?"

"Yes. Is it important?"

I bit my lips together and rocked back and forth on my toes, looking to relieve the stress coming at me from an entirely separate angle. Roland wasn't the only one who could have been murdered last night. "Someone tried to break into Wade's house, too."

I'd seen Wade Erickson, the chief of police, briefly at the station before coming to the hospital. His hand had been wrapped in a bandage. He said he'd cut himself on a scrap of plastic the perpetrator had tried to use to force the lock. He also said he'd searched his yard for the intruder—unsuccessfully—and it crossed my mind, after so many homicides this summer, that he was lucky to get away with a cut hand. While I liked to think of my mentor as a tough old scrap of leather, I had to admit, he was getting up in years.

At the mention of his name, Roland's eyebrows lifted. I was never sure if I should bring my boss up in front of him. Seventeen years ago, Wade had shot and killed Roland's son, Bobby. Blind-sided as Roland had been by his son's secret life of elaborate bank heists, he had nonetheless never forgiven Wade. The bad blood ran deep.

"Based on the timeline," I went on, "we're looking at two sep-arate perpetrators, entering both houses simultaneously." Why was it that every new development only made this case bigger in scale, not smaller?

Roland's eyes flashed with insight. "Tommy—?"

"He's fine," I rushed to assure him. "The intruder never got in."

Roland settled back into his pillows, looking relieved, a senti-ment I shared. I'd worked on the lakeside tour boats with Tommy Thomlin when I was a teen, and for all intents and purposes, he'd been a second dad to me. My heart had already stopped once this summer when someone had put a bullet in him. He was spending his recovery with Wade, his best friend. I didn't like it one bit that someone may have intended to come at him a second time.

I drummed my fingers on the footboard. "Roland, it wasn't good enough to wipe out the members of Bobby's ring. Whoever's behind this, they're after next-of-kin as well. You and Tommy."

"They're doing a shoddy job of it."

I raised an eyebrow and pointedly eyed his hospital bed.

He jutted his head forward. "I'm alive, Monica. Whoever broke into my house, he had all the opportunity in the world to 'finish me off,' as the saying goes. But he didn't."

I considered that and nodded. "In that case, you either have something or know something that the killer wants. Have you told me everything, Roland? Everything about Bobby and the other two boys in his ring?"

Roland spread his hands. "I am an open book, Monica. To dig anything more out of my gray cells would require a brain scan, a scalpel, or a very good hypnotist." He grinned. "I've already had the brain scan today. I'll get you the results, if you like."

I allowed a smile at his paltry humor. "Then there's something in your house. Something the perp may or may not have found last night."

Roland tucked his chin into his chest and thought, tapping his thumbs furiously. "Well, the boys could have left practically anything behind. They were all over my house, well into their adult years."

"They had dinner with you the night Bobby died."

"They did."

"They might have left something someone wants. Did they have a secret stash?"

"Do you know, they always implied they did, but I never found it. It must have been a different hidey-hole from the one I discovered when I was a lad." His eyes lit up and he gestured something rectangular with his hands. "There's a loose bit of panel in the formal dining room. I used to keep my baseball cards in there—"

I sighed and eyed the gray walls of the room. "When are they busting you out of here?"

He let his hands rest in his lap again. "Not for a couple of days." He fingered his bandage. "The cut's all right, but apparently they increase your sentence for passing out from blood loss." He sighed mournfully. "Of course, I forgot to bring my book when the ambulance came."

I cocked my head at the TV and raised my eyebrows, implying the obvious solution.

"Yes, but there's never anything good on, is there?"

I nodded his point. "Well. Once you do get out, you'll wish you were back in." I pointed a finger at him. "Because as soon as you're home, you and I are combing over every inch of that house until we figure out what's missing or if there are any stashes that look like they've been raided."

Roland looked as if he were mildly horrified, while trying not to laugh at the absurdity of my statement. "Markwood Estate is a veritable museum, Monica. Thirty-five rooms. Four generations of Markham history... I couldn't begin to tell you if something were missing. And as noted, I've lived there over seventy years and never found the stash that Bobby and the boys had."

I gaped at him. "You literally don't know what's in your own house?"

He shrugged and shook his head.

I groaned and ran a hand over my face. My nerve endings were fritzing out again. "Oh, God." I stared at the ceiling, then sighed and shook my head. "We'll just do our best. Okay?"

Roland smiled and nodded gamely.

"Okay. Great. Give me a call when you're out of here. I'll give you a ride." I made for the door, then stopped, leaned on the frame, and jabbed a thumb at the TV. "Try PBS. Probably up your alley."

"Ah!" Roland's face lit up. "Good idea." He reached for the remote on his bedside table.

I smiled, shook my head and walked away. I was pretty sure there was no hope for Roland Markham, but I was also okay that I wasn't currently investigating his murder.

I breathed deeply to steady myself. Roland, Wade, Tommy—all three of them could have been killed last night. I'd always prided myself on my nerves of steel, but anymore those nerves resembled a pile of fine-grade steel wool, ready to crumble and burn at the slightest ember.

*It's a game, Monica.* The unearthly voice of The Man Upstairs rasped in my memory.

I ground my teeth. The fate of my town and the people I cared about were nothing but a game to whoever was behind this summer of horrors. I'd never let him win.

And yet at every turn, he proved he was a step ahead of me.

# CHAPTER THREE

# BAILEY

I threw down my bike in the weeds behind my foster dad's restaurant, dropped my helmet on top of it, and pushed through the door into the kitchen. A tiny voice insisted there was something off here today—like maybe there was a kitten in the corner, or the floor was suddenly blue instead of brown, or time had warped in this location specifically and I was suddenly seventeen instead of sixteen—but I ignored the little voice. A much louder one was screaming that I was late for dishwashing duty, and if Bud Weber, my foster dad, caught me, he'd be mad. It had been weeks since the last time he'd belted me, and frankly, not having to hide my bruises was really nice.

Pushing stray hair out of my face, I whipped my time card out of the holder and used the door frame to Bud's office as a writing surface.

A heavy sob came from beyond the door.

I froze, pen hovering over paper. That's when I realized what the tiny voice had been trying to tell me. The kitchen was cold. There was no smell of fresh-baked buns, the daily soup special, or roast pork. Nothing boiled, simmered, or sputtered. Bud had been here since the crack of dawn or earlier, yet his kitchen was empty, silent.

The door to his office stood open a crack. Cold fluorescent light peeked out. I slid my time card back into its slot. Laid my hand on the door. Asked myself what I was doing. Then pushed it open.

The tiny, windowless office was strewn with junk. In the middle, Bud slouched at his desk, the worn-out office chair fighting to contain his bulk, his head in his hand, an open bottle of whiskey within reach. So far, nothing weird. Except for the tears rolling down his cheeks. I mean, like, actual tears. Big ones. A lot of them. And in the middle of his desk, on top of a mess of paperwork, sat a gun.

Cold fear trickled down my spine. I knew Bud had guns, but I had rarely ever seen them. The sight jerked me back to that night a few weeks ago. Flashes of light popping in the darkness. A man gunned down in the street. A man who, a few minutes before that, had tipped me a hundred dollars.

The man who Tommy said had been my real dad.

Bud hadn't noticed me yet. I backed away. I could pretend I'd never been there. Never seen anything. I didn't know what was wrong with him, but I could almost glimpse his mind—what he was thinking about doing with that gun. I was pretty sure I didn't want to be around when he shot himself. Neither did I want to piss him off somehow and get shot myself. Beatings, I could take. Him forcing himself on me, that was old news by now, something I had learned to blank out when it happened, to simply not be there.

But gunfire now echoed in my dreams at night. I saw the man I hadn't known was my dad lying dead, his chest riddled with bullets. I saw Tommy sprawled on the deck of the Mailboat, blood seeping from a wound in his side. I tasted the terror of the fear of losing him all over again—and that was before I'd even known he was my grandpa.

The weapon on Bud's desk threatened to yank me into a whirlpool of images I didn't want and couldn't get rid of. My feet pulled me back from the doorway.

And then I glimpsed Bud's eyes. They were all big and empty, staring not at the gun or the whiskey, but at a void with no end. His mouth hung open as if his very soul were slipping out between his lips. His eyebrows were all up high and twisty like confused tumbleweeds.

I stopped. I'd seen that look before. Not on Bud. On me. In the mirror. My whole life. A sadness so deep you knew there wasn't a bottom, even when you believed things couldn't get any lower. You pretended you had things put together so you could walk on a little longer, smiling for the world. But this—this was what your life was really like, your soul slipping out through your mouth and your brows twisted up like tumbleweeds.

In a moment, I forgot everything I thought I knew about him. I explained away every time he'd raised a belt against me—if I'd been a little more careful to keep him happy, maybe I could have avoided it. I forgave the things he did to me in secret; he was probably right that I wasn't good for much else anyway.

Maybe I was wrong about him. Maybe he wasn't so bad. Maybe he was just sad and confused about life and everything in it, like me.

Maybe if I just tried to talk with him...

"Bud?" My voice was tiny. But against the backdrop of the silent kitchen, it rang like a bell.

"Shove off," he said, the words dropping from between his lips, barely audible, barely human.

Okay, yep. What else had I expected him to say, really? My brain played through the scenario of me deciding to walk away, closing the door behind me. In my mind, that scenario ended with a shot exploding seconds later. It teased me with images of blood splattered against the walls and soaking into the paperwork. Images of Bud's lifeless body slumped over the desk. I thought of adding that picture to the collection already stuck in my head. These were the images that made up my life now. I really didn't want a fresh new one, even if it was Bud.

He'd been my placement for two years now—a crazy long time in foster care. And badly as I hated him, I wasn't really sure anymore what life looked like without him. I'd forgotten. Where would I go next? Would it be better? Would it be worse? At least I'd figured out how to navigate Bud's particular brand of insanity.

And in a messed-up way, I had something to thank him for. After all, if I'd never been fostered with Bud Weber in Lake Geneva, I never would have become a mail jumper. I never would have met Tommy. I never would have known I actually had a grandpa in the world.

Never mind I still didn't know what I meant to do with that information.

I lifted my chin. "No," I said. I wasn't leaving. We were going to talk this time. For the first time ever. My jaw trembled. This was also the first time I'd ever defied him to his face.

Bud swept the gun off the desk. Pointed it at me. "I said, shove off!" His face turned red. The cords stood out in his neck and hands. I could count his racing heartbeats in the blood vessels in his temples.

The cold black circle stared at me—the mouth of the gun. My hand tightened on the doorknob. I told myself I wasn't scared. I could fix this. I could make him see. Make him listen. I could make the nightmares go away.

But that was a gun he was pointing at me. I saw my dad lying dead in the street. Tommy bleeding on the deck of the Mailboat.

I turned and ran to the dish room. Grabbed a pot and threw it into the sink. Blasted it with the faucet. The dampness on my face wasn't water. I waited for the gun to go off back in the office, for the cold silence of the Geneva Bar and Grill to become permanent. But it never did. Maybe Bud wasn't going to kill himself. Not this time.

It wasn't until a full five minutes later that my legs began to shake. My arms. My whole body. That's how long it took my subconscious to tell my conscious that I actually *wasn't* okay with what just happened.

I half leaned, half fell against the metal countertop behind me, drying away the tears on my sleeve. Why was I crying? Was I this scared? I'd always known Bud could kill me. So could have a lot of people. My mom's boyfriends. That one boy I'd shared a foster home with. The near misses I'd had this summer. Why was I breaking down now? Whatever inner fiber had carried me through all these years, was I finally running out of it? Was it too much to ask if I could just fall asleep at night without being afraid?

Or did my own life finally feel worth something—like, worth crying about, even—now that I knew there was someone on the face of this earth who actually gave a rip about me? My own grandpa...

What had I been thinking, trying to confront Bud? Had I actually believed for two cotton-candy seconds that he would melt into something capable of feeling? Something human? Did I still entertain a fantasy of one of my foster families caring about me? Why did I look to Bud for acceptance, when far better people were desperate to help me? Like Tommy. Like Ryan, the cop who was so determined to get me out of Bud's home. Why did I push them away? Why did the mere thought of the words, *You're worth something,* hurt like knives? Was I that broken? Did I even know what goodness and happiness and light looked like?

No. Clearly, I didn't. And that's why fixing Bud Weber seemed so much more reasonable than simply answering Tommy's phone calls.

If there was a way out of my current life, I didn't know what it was or how to find it.

No, that was a lie. I knew the way out. Trusting Tommy. Trusting Ryan. Letting them fix everything for me.

But letting go and trying something so radical felt like free-falling from the top of a cliff into absolute blackness, unsure if there was hard pavement at the bottom, or daggers stuck handle-first into the ground, or angry, chomping waves—and somehow deciding to throw myself from that cliff on purpose.

Hard as I thought about jumping... I didn't know how to do it. How to just step over the edge. How to go weightless for that terrifying eternal moment.

How to trust that someone might even be there to catch me.

# CHAPTER FOUR

# BUD

Bud kept pointing the gun at the door, even after it was closed, and Bailey was gone. He could still do it. He could pull the trigger and let the .22 splinter through the flimsy wood before sinking into her slender body. He could shoot her with the same gun he'd used on that beloved boat captain of hers. Wouldn't that be poetic?

He tried to squeeze the trigger, but his hand trembled. Tears blurred his vision, making it hard to see the gun sights—or the door, for that matter. With a choked sob, he threw the gun down on the desk.

He couldn't do it. He couldn't hurt his Bailey. Not anymore. Not after what The Man Upstairs had done to him.

Bud had meant to kill him. Last night. At The Man's house. He'd had the gun right up against his frickin' head—but then, just like now, he'd failed to pull the trigger. Maybe there was something to the name. Maybe the bastard really was God. How else did you explain how The Man had turned everything upside-down? Instead of filling the double-crossing jerk full of bullets, Bud had found himself bawling into his shoulder like some kid who thought he was the shit, until his old man caught him with the key to the gun safe.

What... what had happened? That freak wasn't human. Cornered and bleeding, The Man Upstairs saved his own ass with nothing but flippin' words. And now he'd reduced Bud to... to *this*. A killing machine who couldn't kill.

All The Man had to do was remind Bud of a single name.

Bud shifted aside the whiskey bottle. Behind it sat a pewter beer stein, enameled with the Weber family coat of arms. He'd bought it off eBay. His family name had never meant shit to him. He just liked the mug. Seemed like the kind of thing he oughta add to his collection.

He lifted the cover and pulled out an eight-sided onyx locket. A silver spider adorned the lid, its filigree legs splayed, clutching.

Bud sighed and sprang the locket open.

A photo of himself stared back, twenty years younger, a stocky blond with his arms crossed over his chest and a lopsided grin on his face. If you looked close—real close—there was a glint in his eye. The kind of spark of life and humanity like his mirror wouldn't recognize anymore.

Sharing the tiny frame with him, a young man hung off Bud's shoulders, leaning into the camera, mouth laughing, eyebrows raised in a crazy, flirty expression.

Zayne Mars.

You'd never know it from the goth girl look—the fishnet top, the feathered black hair, the perfectly executed wingtip eyeliner—but Zayne had always been the stable one in the relationship.

Bud could almost feel his presence in the room now, soaking in the disaster of his office, the visual representation of everything Bud had become: The overflowing trash can. The drifts of years-old paperwork. The near-empty bottle of whiskey.

The gun.

He could hear Zayne's voice, heavy and heartbroken and disappointed. "Oh, Bud. Baby. What's happened to you?"

But Zayne wouldn't have needed to ask. None of this represented a fall from grace—just a return to Bud's roots.

He snapped the locket shut. Zayne had put too much faith in him. In his ability to change. To silence the demons of his past. The short-lived glint that had found its way into Bud's eyes had been a lie. There was nothing here worth saving.

Ever since Zayne's death, he'd gone out of his way to prove it.

# MONDAY JULY 21, 2014

# CHAPTER FIVE

# ANGELICA

Angelica Read's mother could crush her with love just as well over the phone as she could in person. "You shouldn't work so hard, *mi niña*," she said, conversing in Spanish. "You fly back from Chicago on Friday, you show houses all weekend, and you go to the office today. What's wrong with you?"

Angelica sighed and laid her laptop case on the white marble countertop in her kitchen—part of an open floorplan with a flying ceiling, skylights, and a panoramic view of the back yard, the swimming pool, and, in the distance, the Malibu coast. "Mamá, I'm a real estate agent. I show houses on the weekends. That's my job. What am I supposed to do, lie in bed all the time?"

"Give her some space, Martina," said her papá. Apparently they were on speaker phone. "She's a grown woman. She can live her own life."

Her mamá huffed. "I *am* giving her space, Javier. I'm trying to *help* her give herself space. She shouldn't work so much." She spoke into the phone again, accusation putting an edge to her tone. "Especially when she came home early to be with her *boys*."

Angelica rolled her eyes and threw her hand. "Mamá, I showed two houses. Every other minute, I spent with Kaydon and Mason. I promise." Angelica shifted her jaw and tapped the counter. "You're just upset I didn't spend my time with *you*."

"Oh, shush, *mija*. We'll discuss this later." Her mamá's voice grew cozy and conspiratorial. "Angelica, did you meet anyone nice while you were in Chicago?"

"¡Dios mío! Por favor, Martina," her papá exclaimed, his voice trailing away as if he'd left the room, unable to take the conversation anymore.

Her mamá ignored his swearing. "Did you, mija?"

Angelica rolled her eyes and kicked off her wedge sandals. Her mamá had loved Angelica's husband, Will Read, for his money more than anything else. But now that he was dead, with a criminal past none of them had known about, she had no love for him at all. Still, Angelica couldn't believe how fast her mother was trying to pair her with eligible bachelors. "Sí, Mamá, I met someone," she said, placing her shoes in the closet in the rear hall.

Her mamá gasped, long and loud. Angelica could picture her pressing a hand to her chest. "Who?"

Angelica walked barefoot across the terracotta tiles, smiling at her own joke. "He is very rich and he lives in a mansion on the lake."

"Lake Michigan?"

Her papá's voice came back into range. "No, Martina. Lake Geneva."

"Where?"

"It's where she went!" His hands sounded like they clapped on his thighs after what was likely an exasperated gesture.

"Don't be ridiculous, Javier. She went to Chicago."

"Ay ay ay..." His voice, pained, trailed off again.

Angelica rolled her eyes. Lake Geneva was just ninety minutes north of Chicago. She'd tried multiple times to explain this to her mother, but apparently it still hadn't stuck.

Her mamá humphed, but otherwise ignored her husband. With the phone to herself again, she delved into the juicy details. "Angelica, mi amor, what's he like, this man you met?" Angelica imagined her mamá was nibbling the end of a bright red thumbnail.

Angelica popped open the fridge and reached for the lemonade. "Very kind. A gentleman. Mmm, a bit old-fashioned, but he's older than me."

"Phbbbt, age doesn't matter. How old?"

Phone tucked between her ear and her shoulder, Angelica shrugged and pulled the lid off the glass pitcher. "Seventy? Seventy-five?"

There was dead silence on the other end of the line and Angelica knew her joke had hit home. Roland Markham was older than her parents by a decade.

Her papá burst out laughing. Apparently he was still in the room. "¡Ay ay ay! If you could see your mamá's face right now. Hehe!"

Angelica grinned. Payoff.

"So who is your friend really, *princessa*?" he asked, his voice close to the phone again.

Angelica poured the lemonade into a glass, watching it swirl. There was nothing she could hide from her papá. Or her mamá, come to think of it, but it was different somehow. She laid humor aside. Her parents really did need to know what had happened in Lake Geneva. "He knew Will when he was a boy."

"Oh-h-h," her papá said, his voice rumbling deep and low. "You had much to talk about."

The simple insight hit home deeply. Angelica tilted her head back, blinking away tears that had come out of nowhere. Tears for Will. Tears for the trove of childhood memories she had only just discovered with the help of Roland. Tears for the way her husband had betrayed her—building a beautiful life with her and their sons while hiding the truth of his past, right down to his real name—not Will Read, but Fritz Geissler. He had never told her of the bank heists. Of the Markham Ring. Of Lake Geneva. He had never told her *who he was*, and she had no idea if she could ever forgive him.

To her surprise, some of her tears were for the lake she had only just discovered and was shocked to have fallen in love with. How could a place be so utterly meditative—filled with a silence that resonated above the noise of the tourists who flocked to it? How did it cling to its small-town charm, blissfully deaf to the clamor that pushed down on it every weekend? No matter how you tried to reform it, the lake always trickled back to its original state, a glittering sapphire in the woods, unaware that it had ever been discovered as a go-to destination. She missed it so much already, like a second home she'd never known she had.

She could at least thank Will for bringing her there—the place where his twisted, pain-wracking story somehow began.

"Sí," was all she managed to say, and that in a whisper.

"*Dios mío*," her papá grumbled, "why are we talking about this over the phone, eh? You and Kaydon and Mason need to come over for dinner tonight. Tell them Abuela is making chicken tortilla soup."

Angelica tapped a fingernail on the side of her glass. Did she want to come? No. In all likelihood, her brothers and sisters would somehow show up, too. Maybe even her aunt and uncle and cousins, not to mention all the children. Word traveled fast in the Moreno family and her mamá was a master at stretching a meal for two into a feast for twenty at a moment's notice. Angelica would be interrogated by each member of the family until not one fact remained untold. She wasn't sure she had the strength for that tonight. Did she want them to know that she had resorted to investigating her husband's murder personally? They would be against it. They would say it was dangerous.

But to Angelica's mind, the case was half-solved already. She had discovered too many coincidences tying now-Police Chief Wade Erickson to the Markham Ring. For instance, why had Erickson been investigating the multi-million-dollar burglaries cropping up in Chicago, Madison, and Milwaukee, looking for connections, when those cities weren't his jurisdiction? What on earth could have led him to believe that his friends' sons were involved? Why had the boys chosen a bank in Lake Geneva, their own hometown, for their final, fateful job? Was it because they had been led there?

So far as Angelica was concerned, only one answer explained everything: Wade Erickson *was* the theorized fourth member of the Markham Ring, and he had betrayed the boys.

The problem was, she had no evidence.

Her father's voice brought her back to the present. "What do you say, *princessa*?" he prodded. "Will you come?"

Angelica sighed. It was fruitless to say no to her parents. They would wheedle and cajole until she gave in, or if that didn't work, they'd enlist the others to call her and ask why she wasn't coming to the family dinner.

"Seven o'clock?" she asked.

"Sí," her papá confirmed.

"Okay. I'll bring the tortilla chips."

"That's my girl," her papá said, his voice smiling.

"We love you, *mi amor*," her mamá said, her voice a warm hug over the phone.

"Love you, too, Mamá. See you soon."

Her parents continued sending their goodbyes, even as Angelica hung up. She sighed and stared at her glass of lemonade. Exhausting as her family was, each armed with their own bull-headed opinion, she could never say they didn't love her. Even if she made up her own mind about things—like marrying Will or traveling to Lake Geneva or working part of the weekend after her trip—they were still there for her, no matter what, and always would be. In the end, they would accept that Angelica needed to find the truth in her own way.

She glanced at the time on her cell phone. Kaydon and Mason were down the street at a neighbor's, where they'd been since she'd left for work. With rush hour traffic glutting the arteries of the city, she should call them home now and get them in the car. But to be honest, she needed a moment of peace before subjecting herself to the upcoming battle.

She eyed a bottle of Bacardi at the end of the counter, then grabbed it, twisted off the lid, and added a splash to her lemonade. She tried a sip. Mmm, much better.

Carrying her spiked lemonade, she moved into the living room, curled up on the white leather sofa, and picked up her tablet from the glass coffee table. She sipped with one hand and logged into the *Lake Geneva Regional News* website with the other. While waiting for her flight out of Chicago, she'd bought a subscription, just so she could keep in touch with this lake two thousand miles away.

The website loaded. She skimmed the headlines and their accompanying photos. One picture leapt out at her, staying her hand from scrolling any further. It was a picture of Roland's house, strung with yellow police tape. *Lakeside Resident Attacked in Home.*

Her stomach lurched. Hurriedly, she tapped on the article.

*A home on the 900 block of South Lake Shore Drive was broken into and the homeowner attacked Thursday night, police say. No arrests have been made.*

Angelica's blood froze. She set her glass on the coffee table and gripped the tablet with both hands.

*"We do not believe the public is currently in any danger," said Detective Sergeant Stan Lehman of the Lake Geneva Police Department. "But we do advise the public to lock their doors and check that any security cameras and yard lights are operational."*

*On June 16th, the body of Fritz Geissler, 45, a former member of the Markham Ring, was found at the same address.*

*The police are requesting information from the public. If you have any information, please call the Lake Geneva Police Department and ask for Detective Sergeant Stan Lehman.*

Angelica threw down her tablet and stormed back into the kitchen where she'd left her phone. She pulled Roland up in her contacts and dialed. It rang five times before it was answered.

"Well, hello!" Roland chirped. "I didn't expect to hear from you so soon. How was your flight?"

His cheerfulness annoyed her. "Roland, what is going on over there?"

He laughed quietly. "Oh. You heard."

She paced her kitchen. "I read it in the news. What happened?"

"I'm fine, my dear. It was just a bit of a mishap."

"Are you in the hospital? Where are you?"

"No, no. They released me earlier today. I'm home now. We're looking for evidence."

"'We'?" Angelica slitted her eyes. "You and who else?"

"Er..." When he paused, she knew the answer. "Monica Steele."

Angelica sighed. She had told him she didn't trust Detective Steele. "Does she know you and I met?"

Another pause. "She knows."

Angelica rolled her head and pushed her hand through her hair. "You told her?"

"She saw us. At breakfast before you left."

Angelica's blood was coming to a slow simmer. She forced herself to breathe deeply. "You told her what I think about her boss?"

"No, no, no. Not at all. I gave you my word."

Angelica sighed. She was upset, but at least Roland hadn't spilled everything, thank God. Roland swore that Steele was the cop they needed on their side, but Angelica wasn't convinced. For love, fear, or money, would she protect Wade Erickson? All she knew was that Steele had about as much human sympathy as a doormat. The detective had come here, pretending to be sensitive to Angelica's grief after Will's death—then stabbed her with the news of his criminal past and grilled her for details. Try as she might, Angelica had failed to convince the woman that she was hearing it all for the first time.

Angelica planted both elbows on the kitchen counter and cupped her hands around the phone, as if doing so would guarantee that Steele wouldn't overhear. "Roland, where is she right now? Can she hear us?"

"No. She's upstairs."

"Good. Did you see the person who attacked you?"

"Not very well, I'm afraid. My dear, I assure you, Monica's already asked—"

"Shush!" Angelica bit him off. "Was it a man? Was it a woman?"

Roland sighed before replying dutifully. "A man."

"Do you have security cameras?"

"There was a bit of a technical issue. The one that mattered didn't record anything."

Interesting. There were no cameras the night Bobby died, either. The Markham Ring had known how to disable any kind of security measure. She imagined Wade Erickson was well-versed, as well. But why would he enter Roland's house? Why attack him, but not kill him? Why would Monica Steele be there now, combing over the house in detail? Why—?

Understanding flickered.

"Roland, what room is Monica in?"

"We were going over Bobby's old room." He chuckled. "A lot of memories in there."

Angelica gripped the edge of the counter. "Roland, you have to get back there. Don't leave her alone in Bobby's room—or anywhere in the house."

"Why ever not?"

Angelica rolled her eyes in impatience. "Wade wants something in your house. Don't you see? Something Bobby or Jason or Will left behind. Evidence that would implicate him. Or—or money. Maybe Bobby hid money that was supposed to go to Wade."

"Angelica." Roland's voice was sharp, like the period at the end of a sentence. "I will be the first to admit, anything could be hidden in this house, from a missing fortune to a three-ring circus, and I would be the last to know it. But I really do think you're getting carried away. I've already gone to bat for you on this—I've asked my reporter friend to try to access any police records at the station, and I haven't mentioned a word about that to Monica. But for the time being, you have no evidence."

Angelica clenched her jaw and sighed in the back of her throat. She had no evidence *yet*. "Did you talk to Tommy Thomlin?" She'd never met the man, but he was chin-deep in everything that was going on. His son Jason, another member of the ring, had been murdered not long after Will. Then Thomlin himself had been shot, and the perpetrator was still at large. Now the boat captain was recovering at Erickson's house, a fact that ate at Angelica's psyche.

"Yes, yes," said Roland, "I've spoken to him."

"And?"

"Eh... I believe I mentioned that conversation might not go well..."

"He doesn't believe you?"

"No. Not at all."

Angelica ground the side of her fist into the countertop. None of this was going well. "Please, just... keep an eye on Steele. I don't like her in your house."

"I'll go straight upstairs, the minute I hang up the phone."

She worked her jaw unhappily, knowing there was little more she could say. "You'll be careful, yes?"

"Careful shall be my middle name."

"And you'll call me if anything happens?" She jabbed her finger into the marble. "I mean it. You hear a leaf move in the yard, you give me a call. Okay?" *Dios*, she was sounding just like her parents.

Roland chuckled. "Agreed. Angelica? Thank you. Your concern really does mean a lot to me."

She nodded to herself, wishing she were still in Lake Geneva. The reasons to go back seemed to be piling up, not least of which was to keep an eye on Roland Markham. "Don't mention it," she said, waving her hand, even though he couldn't see it. How long had she been on the phone? She needed to round up the boys so they could go to her parents'. "Okay, I'll talk to you later."

"Yes, we'll talk later."

Angelica hung up and stared out the patio windows over-looking the pool and the backyard. She didn't like any of this. What was happening? Was Roland really safe? Was *she* safe? Had she stuck her neck out by showing up in Lake Geneva? Asking questions about her husband? Had she painted a target on her back? On her boys?

Her eyes flashed open. Her boys...

She grabbed her phone again and dialed her neighbor. The longer it rang, the faster her heart pounded and the more vivid the horrific possibilities evolved in her mind.

Jessie finally picked up. "Hey, Angie. Time to send the boys home?"

"Where are they?" Angelica bit out.

Jessie paused as if taken aback. "In the yard. Why?"

"Can you see them?"

"Yes, I'm looking at them. Angelica, what's wrong?"

She took a deep breath to steady her nerves. God, she was becoming paranoid. She needed to get a grip. Whoever attacked Roland, they were in Lake Geneva, Wisconsin, not Malibu, California.

She rubbed a hand across her temple. "Nothing, Jessie. I'm sorry. I just..." She leaned on the counter and propped her forehead against her fingertips. "Would you tell them to come home, please? We're going to their grandparents' for dinner."

"Of course." Jessie paused. "Honey, do you need anything?"

"No." More rum, maybe. Something to remove this black root that had pushed its way into her soul. "I'm sorry, Jessie. You know, just mom intuitions going haywire." She trilled a laugh, trying to sound light-hearted and not nervous.

"Oh, honey, who can blame you?" The tone of her voice said she was thinking of Will's murder, and she wasn't fooled at all. "I'll walk them home for you."

"There's no need." Really, there wasn't. This was a gated community. No one came in without either a passcode or a homeowner buzzing them through. She should have thought of that before calling Jessie. The boys were fine.

"Oh, hush now. I'll see you in ten minutes."

Angelica grinned acceptance. "Okay. Thank you."

They hung up. Exhausted, Angelica let her phone fall to the counter with a thud. She glanced around her sunlit kitchen. Looked over the backyard with the lush palms, the high fence, the Pacific Ocean glittering beyond. It was quiet. Everything was fine. They were safe here.

So why did that black root curl tighter around her heart?

# CHAPTER SIX

# ROLAND

One hand on the polished cherry banister, Roland climbed the grand stair, then paused on the upper landing to catch his breath. He fingered the bandage on his temple. The cut to his head and two days of bed rest still had him a little tired. Granted, spending his first day home turning half the house inside out wasn't the greatest help.

The door to Bobby's room stood ajar, and Roland could hear Monica moving around inside. Before going in, Roland reviewed his directives from Angelica: Keep a keen eye on Detective Steele. Be wary of attempts to remove anything from the house. Right. Yes. Straightening his spine, he tugged the ribbing around the bottom of his cardigan and stepped through the door.

The contents of Bobby's closet were spewed across the area rug. Included in the miscellany were shirts, shorts, and trousers—their particular cut and pattern having gone out of style in the nineties—stacks of books, and a surprising variety of toys and games that dated to the seventies: Connect 4, Star Wars action figures, an Etch-a-Sketch, and Hungry, Hungry Hippo.

Sitting on the floor, legs criss-cross, the holster of her gun occasionally bumping the hardwood, Monica Steele removed more items from the closet and added them to various piles, each labeled with sticky notes. As was her way, she'd made swift work in the few moments Roland had been on the phone.

At the sight of every asset of Bobby's childhood, put on display all at once, something rose up in Roland's throat, threatening to choke him. The loss hit him as freshly as it had seventeen years ago, and he suddenly remembered why he'd never disturbed this room. Hurriedly, he brushed away a tear.

Monica looked up, and with one glance, her expression shifted from laser-sharp focus to sensitivity. She dropped her gaze to the object in her hands—a box containing the game Battleship.

"I always loved this game," she said, obviously grasping for conversation. Turning the box around, she cocked a smile and a rare sparkle entered her eyes. "I used to whoop my brothers' asses. God, they sucked."

Roland forced a grin. "I'm afraid I couldn't tell you whether Bobby was any good at it." Slowly, he crossed the room and eased onto the bed. He raised his brows ruefully. "I was always at *the bank*." He looked at Monica wanly and made the decision to let her see into his eyes, to see the heartbreak there. The tale of his relationship with his son—left to shrivel like a forgotten houseplant—was nothing new to her. At this point, Monica Steele knew a great deal more than where Roland kept the coffee beans and the mugs. Despite Angelica's admonitions, there didn't seem much point in hiding things from her anymore.

Goodness, he was already losing his resolve. Perhaps Angelica should choose a better lieutenant for her missions.

Monica dropped her gaze, as if unsure what to do with Roland's statement about his son, the confessions of one workaholic to another. She glanced over her carefully organized mess. "It'll all go back exactly the way it was," she promised. Clearly, she understood this room was a shrine, and that disturbing it was to disturb the dead.

Roland glanced over her sticky notes. They were labeled with such things as UPPER SHELF, MIDDLE SHELF, LEFT FLOOR, et cetera.

"Your organizational skills are impressive," he said. "But I should hardly make you bother. There's absolutely no reason to keep any of these things." Perhaps the shrine had stood here long enough.

Monica shrugged. "You have the space for it. This is Bobby's whole life. Why not keep it?"

"Well, I didn't know half of it was here. And now that I see it..." He threw a hand weakly. "It pushes knives into my heart. I was a terrible father. I gave him the allowance to buy whatever he wanted—but I didn't give him... me. I always assumed there'd be time tomorrow."

Monica stared several moments at Roland, her expression an unreadable blank. Then she added Battleship to the LEFT FLOOR stack, got up from the rug in a single, smooth movement, and joined Roland on the edge of the bed. She leaned her elbows on her knees and stared out the windows toward the lake. "There's no use living in the past, Roland."

"Living in the past?" He sat up a little straighter and glanced around the room, noting the gas lamps converted to electric, the door to the water closet that was added in the twenties, the iron-frame bed they were sitting on. The closet Monica had just dis-engorged was as modern a feature as the house possessed—an exciting new development of the 1950s. He cocked a smile. "It's like you haven't *seen* my house."

Monica slanted her eyes at him. "You know what I mean."

He nodded. He supposed he did. Whatever his relationship with his son, or lack thereof, there was no changing it now, and very little point in harboring regrets. It wasn't as if they could bring Bobby back.

Roland turned to face Monica. "Do you know, I've never fully expressed my gratitude—"

She waved his words aside. "Just doing my job, Roland."

"No, no. Not the investigation, though I suppose I should thank you for that, as well. What I meant was... Well, I know you think very highly of Wade. He was, in many ways, your mentor. And yet, here you sit letting me go on about Bobby as if... as if nothing had happened between the two of them." As if Wade hadn't killed him.

She looked at him through slitted eyes. "I might suck at people skills, but even I know that if I want your cooperation, I shouldn't beat you over the head with the most painful part of your past."

Roland shook his head knowingly. "Oh, I think it's more than that. You know, Angelica's wrong about you. Beyond that tough exterior, there's a woman who genuinely cares about the people around her."

Monica squinted, bobbing sideways to stare at the side of his face. "Hang on, there's something between your ears. Oh." She grinned. "I think it's cobwebs."

Roland slanted his eyes at her and reached for a witty comeback, but she slid back onto the floor and vanished head-and-shoulders into the closet before he could.

She stacked one more pile of books onto the rug, then grabbed a flashlight from her belt and shone it into every corner of the closet—floor, walls, and ceiling. With her knuckles, she rapped on every inch of plaster and every floorboard. Apparently, they all sounded as they should. She sighed and sat back on her heels, staring at the hollow interior as if it had just beat her at Battleship and she couldn't understand how.

"Let's pick up tomorrow, shall we?" Roland suggested. "You look exhausted."

"I'm fine," Monica insisted, moving the first stack back into the closet.

Roland twirled his thumbs. "Yes, well, I go to bed at nine..."

Monica looked at him over her shoulder. "How late is it ?"

"Eight."

"Christ, Markham, you could have said something." She stacked items more quickly, yet just as precisely as promised, as if Bobby himself were the last one to have touched them. In a matter of minutes, she was done. She stood up, brushing her hands together. "We can start on the guest bedrooms tomorrow."

"Your enthusiasm for the mundane is truly inspiring."

"My partner says I have an unhealthy addiction to rock turning."

"I'm sure you have no shortage of rocks to turn these days."

Her eyes drifted to the floor. She looked worn. Defeated. "To be honest, leads are drying up. Whoever's behind all this—he's still out there." Working her jaw, she stared at the ceiling and clapped her hands on her hips, as if burning off her frustration. "We're no closer to catching him now than we were five weeks ago when we found Fritz Geissler's body at the end of your pier."

Roland lifted his brows. "Five weeks? Is that all it's been?" He shook his head. "It feels like longer."

"A lifetime," Monica agreed, looking like someone who had slept very little in that span of time.

Roland rose, tucking his hands into the pockets of his cardigan. "You'll find him, Monica. I promise you."

Her eyes were dead. "You can't promise what you don't know."

"Well, I know you. And I know you won't give up, regardless of the circumstances." He squinted and smiled. "Have a little faith."

Monica rocked on her feet, indecisive, then cracked a grin and brushed Roland's arm affectionately. "Thanks."

"Of course." He cocked his head toward the door. "Now get out. Shoo. If I have cobwebs between my ears, it's because you won't allow an injured old man his rest."

Monica lifted her hands. "I'm leaving. I'm leaving," She scooped her portfolio and digital camera off an end table and breezed out the door. "Is eight o'clock too early tomorrow?"

Roland followed her down the grand stair to the foyer, resplendent with its tiled map of Geneva Lake, done in white marble and aqua blue glass. "Hardly. I'll have the coffee ready, now I know what you like."

She raised a warning finger. "No cream, no sugar."

"I expected no less of you. It'll be served black and as hot as the Devil's pitchfork." He opened the paneled door for her.

Monica stood on the white portico, the sky beyond blushing with the shades of sunset. "I appreciate all your help, Roland. I know none of this is easy."

"I confess, I look forward to not having my doors beaten down in the night."

She smiled. "I'll do my best. I promise. I won't stop until everything's back to normal again." She gave him one last smile. "Good night, Roland."

"Good night."

Roland watched her descend the stairs to the circular driveway and climb into her unmarked car. He waved as she drove away.

Back to normal, she said.

But what was normal anymore? He'd lost any sense of normalcy the night Bobby died.

# Chapter Seven

# MONICA

I grabbed the break room coffee pot, sloshed the brown stimulant of the gods into a Styrofoam cup, and tossed it back like it was hard liquor. It was just hot enough to burn, and I embraced it.

Roland was right. I was exhausted. Had been all summer. But I kept going, kept pushing myself, because what was the alternative?

I squeezed my eyes shut and tried not to cry like a toddler who'd missed her nap. Were we ever going to solve this case? I thought of the deaths and the close calls. The remaining known members of Bobby Markham's ring—Fritz Geissler and Jason Thomlin—were murdered. Someone had made an attempt on Tommy Thomlin's life—or was it two now? A sixteen-year-old boy had set off a bomb, killing himself, one of my fellow officers, and our police chaplain, Bill Gallagher. And now someone had attacked Roland Markham.

I couldn't stand watching this happen to my hometown, to people I knew. It was eating me alive, and I was scared there'd be nothing left of me by the time it was all done.

But of course, as a cop, I had to swallow those fears down. Burn it with scalding coffee. Pretend the feelings weren't there. Keep my head up. Because if I wasn't there to run into the fray when shit got real, who was? Who would stand between my town and the danger that threatened to destroy it?

I turned around to lean against the counter, stare at the empty break room, and nurse my coffee. That's when I noticed the lights on in the report room. Staring through the door, I saw a well-muscled cop, forty-odd, with dark hair going gray at the temples. Ryan Brandt sat at his computer, burning the midnight oil as if he were me. Somewhere between the case's need for manpower and his past experience and training, he'd gotten the job of investigating Bailey Johnson's abusive foster home. Trying to work patrol and an investigation simultaneously had to suck. No doubt, he was just as tired as me—more, maybe.

Seconds crept by, and I told myself to quit staring, but failed. There was something both comfortable and comforting about soaking him in, like I could have happily stared at him all night. Like I could picture the two of us going home together at the end of watch. Like I could feel his arm around my shoulders as we tried to take in a movie before bed, only to fall asleep together on the sofa.

I lifted half a smile. What had happened to me? When Ryan had shown up again at the start of the summer, I'd wanted nothing more than to feed him through a woodchipper. After cheating on me ten years ago and ruining our marriage, it was better than he deserved.

But something had changed the day the bomb had gone off. I couldn't stop picturing the flash of light, the starburst of shrapnel—the way Ryan had grabbed me, thrown me to the pavement, and covered me with his own body. I could still make out the scar over his left eye where a ball bearing had come *that* close to having his name on it.

Given nanoseconds to act, his most basic instinct had been to protect me.

He was sorry for what he'd done to our marriage. He'd told me as much. Repeatedly. He was still in love with me. That part, he'd never said out loud, but it was obvious. And with every passing day, my screams for justice lost volume, shushed by deepening curiosity. He had changed in the years we'd been apart. Or perhaps I was witnessing the transformation before my eyes. He was done being the player and the traitor. Every time I found myself wishing for a shoulder to lean on... I turned around and there he was.

At this point, I was almost getting used to having him around again. I was almost looking forward to those little moments when our paths would intersect. I almost wanted to sit with him right now and commiserate about a long, hard day.

But, of course, Monica Steele would never do a thing like that.

I swayed back and forth, chewing my lip, staring.

Oh, hell.

I grabbed a second Styrofoam cup, filled it with coffee, and walked into the report room.

I plunked the coffee down next to his hand, pulled up a chair, and straddled it backwards. Sipping from my own cup, I let my teeth sink into the rim a little and wondered why I'd gone for such an aggressive entrance. Why I'd put the back of the chair between Ryan and me, my arm across the backrest.

His gaze dropped from his screen to the coffee, then lifted to me. I could see the hint of a question there. Monica bringing Ryan coffee just wasn't a thing these days. I met his eyes, brown and liquid and deep, and kept chewing on my cup. Yeah, I really didn't know what to say about this, either.

He smiled, creases forming at the corners of his eyes. Those were new. I liked them. I couldn't look away.

He picked up the coffee. "How'd you know I was too lazy to get this myself?"

This was the part where Monica Steele would stab him with some fresh, new barb. *When are you NOT a lazy, half-assed bastard?* Something along those lines. But for some reason, those weren't the words that found their way to my lips.

I stared at the pencil beside his keyboard and mumbled around the rim of my cup. "You aren't lazy."

His coffee paused midair. Served the perfect opportunity to rip him a new one, I'd passed it up, and he'd noticed. In fact, I'd paid him a compliment. His brain was probably short-circuiting right now. If my response had brought him hope or joy or the giddy sensations of a silly schoolboy, he didn't let it show. Just brought the coffee the rest of the way to his lips and drank. He set the cup down with the calmness and poise of a boat with the perfect amount of wind in its sails. My insults really didn't affect him anymore, and neither did my compliments. This level of self-assurance was new to him, too. Another thing I liked. Envied, maybe.

I set my coffee on the edge of his desk. "What're you working on?" Work was a safe topic.

He sighed heavily. "Oh, you know, just getting to know Bud Weber far better than I ever wanted to." He rubbed his hands over his face. "How can a man who reeks that bad come off so clean?"

"He had to have made a mistake somewhere," I assured him.

He shook his head. "I just want to get Bailey out of his house. Why is that so much to ask for?"

"Hm," I said by way of agreement. This had become more than a case to him. In fact, his instinct toward the girl was... father-like. I searched for a better word, but there wasn't one. It felt so strange, considering how indifferent he'd been to the notion of having kids back when we were together. In fact, he'd been such a loose kite in the wind, he would have sucked at being a father.

His care toward Bailey was making it impossible to share the one thing I'd never told him. We would have had a child together. But when I'd caught Ryan cheating, I'd terminated the pregnancy—and never told him a word. And now, as I watched him transform into a new person before my eyes—one who literally worked overtime for the benefit of some homeless child—telling him the truth was only becoming harder.

Who was this new Ryan?

"You really care about that kid." A sterile observation. My voice masked any hint of real interest.

Ryan crossed his arms over his body armor and leaned back in his chair, his eyes distant and haunted. "Do you know, I had a talk with Bill Gallagher a few days before... before the bomb."

I nodded. Bill had thrown himself over the bomber and no doubt saved countless lives—but ripped our hearts out in the process.

"We talked about Bailey."

I lifted my brows. If Ryan had been talking to the chaplain about Bailey, he really *was* serious about taking care of that kid.

"Did you know Bill and Peggy were foster parents?"

I nodded.

He stared vacantly at his coffee cup. "He said, after so many years bouncing around in the system, a foster kid learns not to trust anyone. They learn to push everyone away—even those people trying to help."

I could see how that would happen.

"Bill said what Bailey needs is... 'relentless' love. A love that pulls her in close, even when she's pushing you away. She needs someone to prove to her that they're not going to leave her this time, no matter what."

A familiar pang twisted through my belly, reviving guilt-ridden questions about whether I'd abandoned my own baby—whether I had, in fact, sacrificed her for the sake of revenge against her father. In a cruel turn of irony, was Ryan a more faithful parent than I was? Bailey wasn't even his kid...

I frowned and shrugged. "So, what's this mean? You gonna adopt her or something?" I said it sarcastically.

But Ryan's response froze on his lips, his mouth open.

What, he wasn't taking that seriously, was he? Jesus Christ, nothing in my world made sense anymore.

Words finally formed on his lips. "I'm not leaving her. Not until I see her safe in a good home. Not until a judge signs her adoption paperwork."

I shook my head. "And what if that never happens? She's sixteen. The system's going to kick her out in a couple years, anyway."

Ryan worked his jaw, his eyes distant and intense. In the crook of his elbow, one hand balled into a fist. "Then she can call *me* when her car breaks down. She can call *me* when she's trying to choose her college courses. She can call *me* when she's got three great job offers on the table—because, damn it, she will."

I stared at him, speechless.

He glanced at me. "You don't think I've got that kind of reliability in me, do you?"

I shifted my head sideways, reaching for words that eluded me.

Ryan focused again on his coffee cup, as if knowing that he'd put me in an uncomfortable corner and was giving me space. "She's fully half the reason I decided to stay when Wade offered me the permanent position. I'm not giving up on her."

I blinked, words of some variety finally finding their way to my mouth again. "And what's the other half?"

For a drawn-out moment, his gaze remained fixed in front of him, and I thought it was probably out of place for me to ask.

But the next moment, he lifted his eyes to mine pointedly and simply let them rest there. He said nothing. But I felt pulled down into the pools of his eyes, submerged into his soul, and in some sunken treasure chest in the deepest corner of his heart, I saw... me.

He was staying for me.

Even though, like Bailey, I wasn't giving him a single damn reason to do so.

He looked at me with zero expectations, only an openness. An offering. If I needed anything, he was there for me. He would welcome any little excuse to help me, no strings attached. And if I could never love him again, that was okay.

But the open door was there, and he would keep standing there holding it open until I either walked in or walked away.

The decision was mine.

My stomach churned. I reached for my coffee and threw back a swig.

Ryan straightened in his chair, reached for his mouse, and clicked through his screens. "There was something else Bill told me."

"Yeah?" I focused on the bite the black coffee left in my mouth. My chest was tight. I could barely breathe.

"That I don't have the full story about you and me. That I never got to hear your side."

Oh, God. My arms and legs began to tremble.

"I know I hurt you. I'm sorry. And I'm ready and waiting if you ever want to tell me the rest."

Not pushing. Not demanding. Just holding the door open. He stood just inside with his chest bared, and he was offering me a knife. *Stab me*, he said. *I can take it. The only way to fix a badly-healed wound is to bleed.*

He didn't get it. He wasn't ready. If I took that knife and nicked his flesh, no matter how gently, he'd bleed out. He'd be devastated.

If he felt this strongly about some kid he'd met this summer, how'd he feel about his own child? His own flesh and blood?

He would hate me. He'd leave me.

I wasn't okay with that. I was only okay with the version where I was the one leaving *him*. That scenario put me in the pilot's seat. My shattered heart couldn't tolerate any other arrangement.

His offer was hanging: to tell him the rest. I chewed the edge of my cup, shredding it.

Then I swung my leg over the chair and left the room. "See you in the morning."

I felt his eyes follow me. "Good night, Monica." He said it like I hadn't just slammed the door in his face. Did nothing I said hurt him anymore? Who was this man?

I dumped the rest of my coffee down the sink, slammed the tattered cup into the trash, and stormed out of the station.

## CHAPTER EIGHT

# RYAN

Bill had been right—there was something she wasn't telling me. Something big. I mean, I *could* be wrong; it was hard to tell the difference between Monica feeling pissed at the world in general and Monica trying to cage the beasts of her own inner fury. But I *had* been married to her for a decade. I was pretty sure I was reading her right.

I wanted her to open up to me about whatever it was. For her sake, not mine. Whatever she was holding back, it had the scent of a creature big enough to crush her if she didn't turn it loose. I was used to her flirting with danger, but short as I was on details, I had no idea if this was a battle she could win.

I turned back to my computer, shaking my head at myself. Smiling, even. All summer, I'd been desperate for her to forgive me. For *my* sake. I could barely stand the scorn—not when I already beat myself up on a daily basis for the colossal mistakes I'd made.

But now I'd reached this strange new place of just... acceptance. She might forgive me. She might not. Whichever way the tide turned, I'd probably remain afloat. At the end of the day, I didn't need her forgiveness before I could forgive myself and find a way to move on. To become a better version of me.

For the first time in my life, I felt like I knew who I was. Not the young jokester, prankster, and class clown—hoping desperately that my classmates liked me. And not the hot catch, the Casanova, that "one night in—" name a city of your choice—breaking hearts while fighting like a tiger against ever having mine broken again.

I was just... me. Ryan Brandt. Strip away the unfounded fears and the menagerie of behaviors that had followed them in like the circus train rolling into town, and the truth about me was as clear as a map and a compass.

I'd shown up on this planet with one job to do: to help people where it looked like they needed it. It was the only version of me that felt real. Authentic. Like a clean summer wind. And maybe I screwed that up desperately sometimes—like pulling away from Monica when she needed me to pull close. But where things didn't go to plan, you looked at your compass, leaned into the helm, and tried again, fighting wind and wave and whatever sea monsters rode in on them.

Maybe my relationship with Monica would never follow the nice dotted line to the X that marked the island paradise overflowing with lost treasure. But that was okay.

At least I saw the possibility of that glittering sunset—her hand in mine, the sand between our toes—and I tried.

All I wanted was to say I'd tried.

# CHAPTER NINE

# MONICA

*"You see, I know everything. I even know how to exploit your children. Yes, Monica—YOUR children."*

Two and a half weeks after the bombing, the unearthly voice of the person calling himself The Man Upstairs still grated through my memory. If there was anything worse than not knowing how to tell Ryan about our child, it was the thought that the man behind this summer of violence implied *he* knew. But how was that possible? There was only one person I'd ever told, and I trusted her completely.

I surfed the FBI's National Crime Information Center database while sipping a glass of pinot noir. The pairing was a first for me, though working from home wasn't. My house was on the opposite side of the lake in the little town of Fontana, just twenty minutes from the LGPD. Curled up on the sofa with one of the department's laptops balanced on my knees, I plugged in one name after another. Murdoch, Sandra. Callahey, Dana. Pennington, Aubrey.

I glanced at my legal pad. My list wasn't complete; just the names I'd pulled out of my records from the abortion clinic I'd gone to in Madison. There was a nurse here or there whose name never made it into the records; receptionists who simply worked the front desk but had access to plenty of confidential information.

Still, this was a start. Depending what I found here, I could call the clinic later and ask who else had worked there at that time.

But my current list was an intelligent place to start before diving in head-first and blind.

I ran each name through several searches. Criminal history. Past arrests. Warrants. Apparently, one of the nurses was habitually late to work; she had three speeding tickets. The other two names didn't appear in the database; their records were clean.

I glanced at my legal pad and sighed heavily. There was one more name. Brenda Holstadter, the doctor who had actually performed my procedure. I didn't want to think it was her who had leaked my records. While I'd marched into my appointments with complete conviction and determination, I had actually been a total mess inside. But tenderness and sympathy only would have inspired me to vomit. So while I had no doubt her shoulders were available for a good cry for any unexpected mother who needed it, they had remained square and professional for me, and I appreciated it. Whatever regrets I later developed about the abortion itself, I'd always look back on this woman as a kind and sensitive soul.

I bit my lip, typed her name into the search field, and hit enter.

A single result came back. My heart pounded. No, I hadn't wanted her to be in here. But there was still hope. It could be something small and irrelevant.

Gnawing the nail of my left thumb, I opened the page and read. Ten years ago—about the same time as my abortion—someone had raised a complaint that Dr. Holstadter had violated patient confidentiality.

I groaned out loud and stared out my window, leaning my forehead in my hand and my elbow on the back of the sofa. I glowered at the dark and empty street. I hadn't wanted it to be her. I waited until my breathing calmed down, then grabbed the wine glass off the coffee table, swallowed a generous mouthful, and read on.

But the report was brief. More of a footnote than anything. All it said was that, due to an absence of evidence, Dr. Holstadter had been cleared of all charges. I scowled at the screen. I needed more. I reached for my phone on the coffee table and dialed Tara Slater—the only person I'd ever told about my abortion. She and I had been close when we worked in the detective bureau in Madison.

"Hey, lady," she said.

"Tara, I need a report from MPD."

"You're on to something?" She was more or less up-to-date on my little side project.

"Maybe. Can I give you a case number?"

"Hang on. Let me log into my laptop. I brought it home to type a report."

My heart soared. I hadn't expected to get anything until tomorrow at the earliest. She booted up her computer and I read her the case number.

"Okay, found it," she said. "Wow. There's a lot of paperwork here. Looks like this dragged on for a while."

For several seconds, I heard nothing but the clicking of her mouse. I closed my eyes and counted my breaths, impatient to hear her speak again. To get my hands on a clue. A scrap of information. Anything.

Tara's voice finally returned and my eyes flashed open. "I don't know if this helps you much, actually," she said. "A patient accused Dr. Holstadter of telling her boyfriend about her abortion. The entire staff at the clinic agreed that the boyfriend showed up asking questions, but they also agree none of them shared information or even so much as acknowledged that his girlfriend had been there. They told him they couldn't discuss patient information and sent him away. In the end, nothing could be proved against Dr. Holstadter or the clinic."

I chewed my nail again. "Was that the end of it?"

"Yeah, looks like it. I could check with city records tomorrow and see if any civil action was taken against the clinic or Dr. Holstadter."

"That would be great."

Her laptop clicked shut. "How you doing, anyway, girl?"

I eyed the long-stemmed glass on my coffee table and shifted a brow. "I'm drinking wine."

Tara laughed. "I would be, too."

I closed my own laptop and set it down next to the wine, then grabbed a cable-knit afghan off the back of the sofa and snuggled into it. "I'll feel better when I know who this creep is and how he knows about me."

"Have you said anything to the task force yet?"

I twirled a piece of yarn fringe around my finger. "No." I knew I should. If I found information leading to the identity of The Man Upstairs, it would be hard to justify the fact that I hadn't told the task force that he had access to deeply personal information about me. But he had tread on sacred ground. On top of that, there was no doubt in my mind that I'd lose Ryan the moment word was out. I grasped at a straw. "You know there's nothing to what The Man said. I'm just being paranoid. There's no way some rando knows about my abortion."

"Yes, but he does know your name and your phone number. He might know other things, too. The hours you keep. Where you live. The road you take home."

"I've been taking a different route every night," I said.

"Good. Look, I know it's hard, but you should really tell the task force. Or someone other than me. Just for your own safety, you know? So if you go missing or some shit, they'll have a clue what happened." She backpedaled. "Not to jinx you. Sorry. But I'm serious."

I grinned wanly. As cops, we watched our backs every moment of every day, on duty and off. But since that phone call, I'd lived permanently in Condition Orange—the stage of situational awareness where I'd identified a specific threat and expected something to happen any moment. I tugged the yarn. "The task force knows someone claiming to be behind the murders called me. They have the audio file I recorded. If I go missing, he'll be the first person they think of."

"Okay, but..." Tara sounded unconvinced. "They should know the whole thing."

"Noted." I eyed the wine again. I didn't want to talk anymore, especially about this. I wanted to drown my woes until the morning. "Thanks for the info, Tara."

"Sure. Keep me posted, okay?"

"Will do."

We said goodnight and hung up. I exchanged the phone for the wine and sipped deeply. It was bitter and full-bodied. The alcohol vibrated warmly down my throat and through my nerves. A pleasant, if hollow, embrace. Sometimes what a woman really wanted was a shoulder to cry on.

I glanced around my living room. Since my mom's passing, I'd completely remade the place, saving it from the 'shroom-inspired 1960s designs I'd grown up with. After painstakingly stripping the wallpaper by hand, I'd painted the walls a soft, warm gray. The moldings around the ceiling and doorways, original to the house, had been sanded clean, primed, and painted a bright white. I'd taken a gamble when I went to town on the orange shag carpet and was ecstatic to find a hardwood floor underneath. After a good stripping and refinishing, it gleamed. I'd rolled out a maroon oriental rug over the top, then moved in the furniture, a mix of old and new. I'd gotten the sofa on clearance—a minimalist piece that felt like flopping into a marshmallow. But the rocking chair in the corner had traveled with my great-great-grandmother, Ingrid Stahl, when she homesteaded in Wisconsin. According to the story, she'd threatened to stay in Germany if the rocker didn't come with. The rocker stuck with the family. The spelling of our name didn't. Someone down the line changed it to Steele.

This was the most TLC I'd ever poured into a home. Maybe because this was where I meant to stay for the rest of my life. Maybe because I'd grown up here and was delighted to finally rip out the parts I hated. Maybe because I'd always planned on fully renovating a house—even if I'd originally planned on doing so with Ryan grunting the appliances into place and one of the kids accidentally putting a foot in a paint can and ruining a floor. Maybe breathing life into an old home was the one part of my dream I forgot to give up on.

I twirled my glass and wondered if Ryan had made it home yet. I wondered if he was thinking about me right now, like I was thinking about him...

*"I'm ready and waiting, if you ever want to tell me the rest."*

Maybe Tara was right. Maybe I should just tell him.

I eyed my phone. It wasn't too late to shoot him a text. Throw together some prosciutto and Brie sandwiches and pour another glass of wine. Maybe we'd talk. Maybe we wouldn't. Maybe for now, we'd just get used to being around each other again.

The thought was thrilling and terrifying at the same time, like the way I felt in high school when we first started calling each other. Every time the phone rang, there was a chance it could be him. This was the way I'd felt between classrooms when I caught his glance in the hall. When we smiled secretly at each other. When our friends started whispering about us. Whatever they said, I doubt it was what I was thinking. *I'm going to grow old with that man.* But once Ryan and I started dating openly, they started saying it, too. We were like two souls who had already lived many lives together. Maybe we'd had a bit of a tiff, we'd spent a few years apart, and now we'd found each another again. That was all there was to it.

My eyes traveled over the room. He had sat at that dining room table, his shirttails neatly tucked, when he first met my parents. He had kissed me for the first time on that front porch with the fireflies glimmering under the trees. He had climbed a tree to my bedroom window when he'd gotten himself banned for keeping me out too late the night before. My parents never knew it, but I lost my virginity in the upstairs shower when they were gone for the weekend. I don't know why, but that ugly old shower was one of the things I kept when I gutted the house.

I pulled the afghan closer, brushing the nubby fabric against my cheek. This house felt empty. Lonely. I'd carried on with my dreams without Ryan. But they were empty dreams. I wanted him. Right now. I wanted to pull him into the upstairs shower and start over again where we began. But I wanted all of him this time. More than we'd ever had before. I didn't want any secrets between us. Including my own.

But every time I tried to wrap my mouth around the words I needed to say—every time I envisioned telling him about our baby—my throat froze. My mind went blank. My soul fell out of me and tumbled into an endless hole.

Why did everything have to be so hard?

I turned my head into the marshmallow pillows and cried.

# TUESDAY JULY 22, 2014

## CHAPTER TEN

# TOMMY

Relying on countertops and various articles of furniture for navigation, I ventured from Wade Erickson's living room to the kitchen—wincing with every other step, but gaining steadily on my target. To be frank, until someone had put a bullet into my left side, I'd under-appreciated how the core muscles were sympathetically related to just about everything—from walking to sitting to lying down. True comfort had grown elusive, but I didn't mean to let that stop me.

The kitchen sink attained, I pulled a glass from the cupboard and filled it with water from the tap, leaning what was now my good side against the counter. Sunshine poured through the window and created hundreds of points of light in the tumbling water, drawing my attention, reminding me of something strangely familiar... the sunrise glinting on silver studs in a black leather vest...

*The man grabbed my shoulder. Rolled me over. Through waves of pain, I barely registered what he looked like. Tilting his thick head, he regarded me studiously, as if admiring his handiwork.*

*"Gut wounds are hell. I could put you out of your misery."*

The voice forced its way into my memory. My eyes crossed on the tiny lights, twinkling over and over...

Behind me, the lock snicked open on the door to the garage.

I roused myself and shut off the water moments before it spilled over the rim.

The door swung open, followed by abrupt silence. I could practically hear the look of surprise and disapproval on Nancy Erickson's face. "Sebastian Thomlin, what do you think you're doing?"

Well. I really was in trouble if she was using my given name.

I eased around and leaned back against the counter. Nancy, Wade's wife, stood in the open door, her arms laden with reusable shopping bags, one strand of blond hair falling into her eyes.

I raised the glass. "Keeping hydrated," I defended myself.

She toed the door shut, then hefted the bags onto the peninsula counter with a small grunt. "You're supposed to be keeping off your feet, you stubborn old codger." She planted her hands on her hips. "I swear, I'm going to have Wade handcuff you to a chair tomorrow."

"Funny. I remember the doc saying he wanted me to walk some every day." I lifted the glass to my mouth and savored my hard-won refreshment.

"Yes, *some*." She waved an exasperated hand. "If you're on your feet every time I turn around, you'll only set yourself back." She sighed and dug through her bags. "For Pete's sake, I was barely gone an hour. You couldn't wait that long?" She rounded on me, wielding a pair of zucchinis. "What if you'd fallen? What if you'd hurt yourself?"

I shrugged and noted the obvious. "I didn't."

Nancy muttered aloud as she breezed between counter and fridge, freezer and pantry. I had to fight the instinct to help. But I wouldn't be able to keep up with her, and it was clear any further attempts at physical activity would only provoke fresh rebukes.

"I'm impressed how quickly you're recovering and all," she rattled on, "but I'm worried you might be pushing yourself too hard." She wagged a finger at me. "Your physical therapist thinks so, too. I can tell."

"She's a professional. She can tell me herself what she thinks." I hid my scowl behind another mouthful of water.

Nancy narrowed her eyes at me. "Oh, but you know how to walk that line, Tommy." She wavered her hand in the air, palm-down, and wrinkled her nose. "Maybe you're pushing too hard, or maybe you're progressing nicely. But you can't fool her forever. You mark my words, she's going to say something about it." She frowned and shook her head. "What's the rush, anyway? You know you're welcome to stay here. It's no trouble."

Yes, but it was. After the attempted break-in not long ago, Nancy had ended her season early as a docent at Black Point Estate, a 19th-century mansion-turned-museum that dominated an overlook on the South Shore. Her job as a tour guide only demanded a few hours out of her day, but now even that was too long to leave me alone and unguarded.

And now that I'd been caught taking too many liberties with my freedom, there were good odds she'd curtail her trips to the grocery store, too, pushing that responsibility off on Wade, who was already burnt out from working the investigation. Wonderful.

I swirled my glass. "I just want to get back to work. The summer's slipping away."

And I did. I'd been driving the Mailboat every summer for forty-eight years, seven days a week, counting the newspaper deliveries on Sundays. The routine was ballast against the many waves that had tried to capsize my life. Nothing had sunk me yet. Regardless what happened, it was a comfort to shed the flotsam and jetsam of my life on the gangway and know that something in my world was reliable.

Even more importantly, I wanted to get back to Bailey. But I couldn't say that part out loud. The only reason I knew Bailey was my granddaughter was thanks to a conversation I'd had with my son Jason the same night he was killed. It was a conversation I should have reported to Wade immediately, but never had.

Besides, I didn't think it was right to broadcast the news that Bailey was my granddaughter until I knew what she herself felt about it. Telling her was the first thing I'd done when I'd come to in the hospital and found her keeping watch at my bedside. But try as I might, I couldn't remember her reaction to the news.

Frankly, a month of silence was pretty telling.

"Work, work, work," Nancy complained as she put butter and eggs in the fridge. "I swear, you're married to that boat. Is work your answer to everything?" She glanced up, eyes accusing. "You know, you were like this when Elaina died. And when Jason disappeared. I don't know what you do out there—bundle up your feelings and throw them overboard?"

My mouth flinched. No. More like stow them in the hull and carry them with me. Thoughts of my wife Laina and my son Jason—and now Bailey—were never truly that far from me.

Nancy closed the fridge door and leaned against it. "Tommy, I think you should go to therapy. And I mean for more than what happened this summer. I don't think you've ever really processed what happened with Jason and Elaina. You just keep—" she threw a hand "—shoving it all down somewhere. Well, someday, there won't be anywhere left to shove it."

I shifted my weight uncomfortably. "You know I'm not great at talking about myself."

She spread her hands dramatically. "That's the point! I don't give two pennies about your excuses. I think you should go to therapy, and I think you should take the rest of the summer off so you can recover fully."

I sighed—or maybe growled—and turned to splash the rest of the water down the sink. I thunked the glass on the counter when it was empty. "I'm worried about Bailey." There, I was out with it. Or at least part of it. Was Nancy satisfied? I braced one hand on the counter behind me, the other going to my side where the wound bit, aggravated by moving too abruptly. "I was the one reporting her bruises. Who's keeping an eye on her while I'm gone? Her foster dad could be doing anything to her, and no one would be the wiser."

Even as I said it, I wondered, as I often did, why the bullet wound itself was the most sensitive, while the surgical scar running the full length of my abdomen seemed to be healing fine. Was the discomfort purely psychological?

Nancy looked at me blankly, as if surprised I didn't already know what she was about to say. "Oh, Ryan's been checking in with Bailey. Ryan Brandt, one of the patrol officers." She glanced at the hand over my side, then lifted her brows significantly. "There's chairs, Tommy."

I ignored her hint and narrowed my eyes in memory. "Ryan? He used to jump mail for me." I'd seen him back in town earlier this summer.

"Did he?" Nancy asked, folding her shopping bags. "Small world. Well, with the entire detective bureau tied up with the murder investigation, he's heading up the inquiry into Bailey's foster home. He checks on her all the time. I swear, he's guardian angel to you both." She collapsed her hands over her empty bags, leaned forward, and tilted her head at me. "You should know, he saved your life. He was first on scene when you were hurt."

Ryan? I pictured the dark-haired boy who used to pull pranks on the other kids. Everything was a joke to him, and you had to keep one eye open, especially where your personal effects were concerned. He was perhaps more of a handful than most of the kids, but he always meant it in good fun, and it never crossed anyone's mind to take serious offense. Years later when he donned the badge, I'd never particularly doubted his efficiency as a cop.

But neither had I imagined my life in his hands. If I had, it probably woulda made me nervous.

The doctors and nurses had painted the picture pretty clearly—how much blood I'd lost, how few breaths I'd been drawing, how close I'd come. But until Nancy told me, I never would have guessed at Ryan being the one to throw up a wall between me and eternity—between me and never living to see Bailey again. Nor would I ever have guessed at him being the one to watch over my granddaughter while I couldn't.

Well. All things considered, I guess he'd turned out okay.

"He's watching Bailey?"

"Mm-hm." Nancy hung her bags by the door. "No more bruises lately, or so he says. He's keeping that foster father of hers in hot water. I'm sure he'll have that creep's license removed in no time. So, you see?" She smiled and shrugged happily. "Nothing to worry about."

Well, that's where she was wrong. I wasn't about to quit worrying. Not where Bailey was concerned.

Nor was I going to pass up the chance to speak with someone who'd seen Bailey more recently than I had and could verify that she was okay. Maybe he could even provide a clue as to why she'd quit talking to me.

I narrowed my eyes at Nancy. "Do you have Ryan's number?"

# CHAPTER ELEVEN

# RYAN

I popped open the twentieth cardboard box with yet another sneeze-inducing cloud of dust. Dang, I'd only put off unpacking for a month and a half. Did dust really collect that fast?

I sniffed, rubbed my nose on the sleeve of my tee shirt, and reached into the contents of the box—socks, underwear, shirts, dishes. I smiled in appreciation of my own ingenuity. I mean, why *not* stuff the glassware with socks?

I smelled one.

Eh, clean socks would have implied greater ingenuity.

My phone rang. I reached into my pocket, but it was empty. Glancing around my sea of cardboard and randomly stacked household goods, I panicked with every renewed bleat from the phone. What if it was work? Some new disaster could have happened, bringing them to call us out. Or it could be Bailey. I didn't want to let any call from her go unanswered. I started pawing through the piles in the general vicinity of the ringtone.

On the final ring, my eye fell on a stack of jeans balanced on the edge of the sofa. The corner of my phone stuck out from beneath.

I lunged over a collection of empty boxes, stretching like a wide receiver for a football that was just out of reach. My hand closed over the phone.

The box beneath me crunched with the sound of broken ceramic, and I finally realized where I'd packed the coffee mugs. Shit.

Stretched over the broken box, I swiped the screen and brought the phone to my ear. "This is Brandt."

"Ryan? This is Tommy Thomlin."

My heart made a somersault—and it had nothing to do with pulling the handle from my favorite coffee mug out from under me. "Tommy! Man, it's good to hear your voice. How are you?"

Smiling like an idiot, I extricated myself from the mess and plopped down on the floor with my back against the sofa. I hadn't seen him since he was in the hospital. He'd been in rough shape. Really rough shape. I doubted he'd even known I was there.

"Oh, getting on. I hear I owe you some thanks. Wade's wife tells me you were the first on scene."

My arm strung across my raised knee, I twirled the broken mug handle. "Just doing my job, Tommy."

I would have said the same to anyone thanking me for carrying out my duties. But this time, I was lying. It had been more than my job that day. Back when I was a mail jumper in high school, Tommy had been like a second dad to me. His presence had felt particularly meaningful as I'd watched my own father grow ever distant with alcoholism.

To tell the truth, seeing Tommy hurt had shaken me pretty hard. While administering first aid, I might have been mentally yelling at him that he wasn't allowed to leave us yet.

Tommy went on. "I, uh... I also hear you've been keeping an eye on Bailey for me."

My heart skipped a beat. This was why he was calling? I clutched the mug handle and threw a fist pump. I'd been dying to talk to Tommy about Bailey. Tossing aside the handle, I sprang to my feet and slid my hand into my back pocket. "Yes, I have." As much as she'd let me, anyway. "Been trying," I amended.

I picked my way to the outskirts of the circle of exploded boxes and started pacing. Tommy was the only person Bailey trusted. He was the ally I needed to help me get her out of Bud Weber's foster home. I was so excited that we were finally having this conversation, I didn't even know what to say next. Instead, I waited for Tommy to elaborate what was on his mind.

"You seen her recently?" he asked.

"Last week." I'd shared a bag of chips with her after her tour on the Mailboat and tried once again to get her to confess that Bud was abusing her.

"How is she?"

I lifted my eyebrows and nodded. "Good." Perhaps more relaxed and conversational than I'd ever seen her—though she'd clammed up once she realized what I was after. But overall, her mood had been positive, and that was refreshing.

Then I realized what Tommy was really asking and mentally slapped myself. "No new bruises. None that I could see."

Tommy sighed as if the question had been weighing on him for weeks. "Good."

Well, damn. Of course he'd been worried. The only reason I was working an abuse case was because Tommy had reported Bailey's bruises. Come to think of it, I should have called him ages ago to give him an update.

I stopped pacing and pushed my hand through my hair. "Tommy, I promise you, I'm doing everything I can to get Bailey out of that home. I won't stop until I know she's safe."

His next words carried a bite of anger in his tone. "Why is she still there?"

My mind raced through a history of six summers working with him as a mail jumper and confirmed this was the first time I'd ever heard him angry. At the sound of his displeasure, my chest turned to ice, halting my breath. The thought that he could be mad at me was strangely terrifying.

I shook the thought away and reminded myself he might just be frustrated with the situation, same as me. I forced myself to breathe again. I was an adult, for God's sake. It was strangely hard to remember that in Tommy's presence, though. When he was around, you just wanted to be a kid again, looking to him for hints of approval or disapproval, like a toddler who knocked over his tower of blocks then turned to his parents, waiting for their reaction.

"I don't have any evidence where the bruises are coming from," I explained. "Neither Bailey nor Bud are talking, and we don't have any other witnesses."

Tommy growled under his breath. "This is wrong, Ryan."

"I know, sir."

Sir? It was like I was talking to my lieutenant. I let it slide. There were more important things to address. This was my opportunity to explain that I needed Tommy's help.

I started pacing again. "Look, it would go a long way if Bailey would admit that Weber's abusing her."

Tommy voiced the obvious question. "Why won't she accuse him?"

I clenched and unclenched a fist. "I wish I knew. Weber's aware I'm on to him. He could be threatening her."

"Is he?" His question was to-the-point.

Well, it was the scenario with the greatest probability. Domestic violence could turn its ugliest when the victim made moves to leave. But even as I thought about it, something shifted in my gut, suggesting that in Bailey's case, I wasn't quite hitting the truth. There was something more. Bailey routinely defied explanation. She did things for her own reasons, feeling obligated to explain them to no one.

"I don't know," I admitted. "She's afraid of something. I just don't know what. She doesn't trust me."

By the uplift in his voice, I thought he was smiling, as if he didn't believe me. "Even with you coming 'round all the time to check on her?"

"No." I paused and fidgeted with a floor lamp that was poorly put together. It wobbled from the base all the way up to the lamp shade. I shrugged. "You're the only one she trusts, Tommy."

My words were met with silence. Had the line been dropped? I glanced at my phone, but it said we were still connected. "Tommy?" I asked.

"I'm here," he said. But that was all.

Slowly a new realization dawned. In the course of simply going about his life, being the lighthouse to a couple hundred mail jumpers, he might not have realized that the access he had to Bailey's soul was exclusive.

I leaned into my assertion. "I mean it. She doesn't trust anyone but you. In fact, I was really looking forward to talking to you about her. I was hoping you could get through to her. Get her to open up. Convince her to give me the evidence I need to get her out of that home."

Tommy's hesitation weighed like a hundred feet of water pressing down on my chest. What was he thinking?

When he finally spoke, it wasn't what I'd expected. His voice was subdued. "I think you overestimate the relationship, Ryan."

I blinked. Shook my head. How could he believe that? How could he miss how much he meant to Bailey?

I shifted my stance. Lifted a hand as if Tommy were actually in the room with me. "Look. Bailey's had one hell of a summer. And she's been stoic through it all. Finding a dead body on your mail route?" I shrugged. "She was a little shook, that's all. Shooting in the street? She cried a bit. The day she called to tell me someone was going to set off a bomb? She was all business. She is. One. Tough. Kid. But—"

I paused, my breath going unexpectedly shaky as I drummed up the memories of that morning on the Mailboat. The morning Tommy had been shot.

"But when she found you hurt, Tommy, she..." I rubbed the back of my neck, remembering Bailey's face awash in tears. The way she'd bitten the back of her hand, as if desperate for somewhere to funnel the pain. "She fell apart."

Tommy didn't speak, so I went on.

"When the medics arrived," I said, "I tried to take Bailey off the boat so she didn't have to watch. But she was *not* going to leave you. She *screamed* when I tried to take her away."

I could almost feel anew the pain in my shins as she kicked and thrashed, not even caring who she hurt in her desperation to stay near her captain, her anchor.

"She screamed so loud, I thought she was going to shatter the windows. She..." I sighed and tossed a hand. "She loves you, Tommy."

There. I'd told him what I knew, or as much as I could manage to say out loud.

I leaned back against the wall, feeling defeated, and closed my eyes. *Please, Tommy. I've tried everything else. I don't know how to help Bailey without you.*

# CHAPTER TWELVE

# TOMMY

Seated at the small desk in my room at Wade's, I stared at the lines in the laminated woodgrain. Ryan's words mixed with fragmented memories: Bailey kneeling beside me, her knees and hands smeared with blood. The tears flowing down her face like rivers. The terror in her eyes.

I tried to absorb the possibility that Ryan could be right.

But if Bailey cared so much about me, why was she avoiding my calls? Why did it never cross her mind to answer one of my texts? None of this made any sense.

"Tommy." Ryan's voice pulled me away from the precipitous edge of my bottomless questions. "Please. If she won't talk to you, she won't talk to anyone."

I licked my lips and clung to the one thing I knew for certain. "I don't want her with Weber anymore. That's all I care about." I hesitated, a thousand doubts drowning my resolve. But the weight of my previous statement was immutable. I sighed and forced myself to say the rest. "I'll do what I can."

Ryan exhaled loudly. "God, you're awesome, Tommy."

I scrubbed at an old water stain on the laminate. "Well. Maybe hold your review until the results are in." I thought about explaining that Bailey had already been ignoring me for a month—but that led to tricky waters. I didn't feel the need to explain that my concern for Bailey went beyond captain and crew.

"I have faith in you," Ryan said with childlike simplicity.

Grand. And if she never spoke to me again? I needed assurance that she wouldn't go abandoned. "You'll keep checking on her?"

"Can do, Captain." He said it like I was still his supervisor. Well, if it got the job done, that's all that mattered.

I shifted in my chair and eyed the bed longingly, wondering how things like walking from one end of the house to the other, sitting upright, and talking on the phone could be so tiring. I was spent.

"Thanks for your time, Ryan. And... for everything." Well, that covered a lot of ground. Maybe I should have been more specific. Saving my life. Watching over Bailey.

He seemed to absorb my meaning anyway. "Any time, Tommy. I'm here to help."

We said goodbye and ended the call. For several moments, I sat staring at my phone, lost in thought.

*"She screamed so loud, I thought she was going to shatter the windows. She loves you, Tommy."*

I tilted my head, trying to wrap my mind around the conundrum that was my granddaughter. She loved me... but she wouldn't speak to me?

*Bailey-girl, what's going on inside your head? Why can't I get through to you?*

Well. I'd promised Ryan I'd try. I brought up Bailey's phone number. Paused at the sight of our chat history—painfully one-sided, except for a six-week-old conversation confirming a last-minute shift in schedule.

I reconsidered what I was doing.

And then I started typing.

# Chapter Thirteen

# BAILEY

If you wrap a swing around the bar enough times, shortening the chains, you can loop your knees over the seat and swing upside down.

That's what I was doing at Maple Park in the historic part of town—swinging upside down, my hair sweeping the gravel, my hands pressing a book to my nose. From the corners of my eyes, I could see the cute little houses with front porches and shutters on the windows, all of them sticking upside down to green sky with bottomless blue grass beneath them. When the swing ran out of momentum, I did a few stomach crunches to get it going again. The blood rushing to my head, I read about some other girl with some other set of problems.

They say it's smart to get perspective on life.

Maybe hanging upside down from a swing isn't what they meant. Whatevs.

I had the afternoon off, and I didn't feel like spending it at Bud's house, even though he wasn't there. He was at his restaurant, like always. But every corner of his house smelled like him. Felt like him.

I just wanted to get away.

Increasingly, I didn't want to be anywhere. I just wanted to be away.

My phone chimed with a new message. I looked down to where I'd left it on the ground but couldn't tell, as I swung by, who the message was from. So, on the next pass, I set my book on the gravel and picked up my phone. Still swinging, I swiped the notification bar.

The text was from Tommy.

I stared at his name forever. It showed up on my screen the same way I'd typed it when I first started working with him—"Captain Tommy"—and not "Grandpa" or something else like what grandkids called their grandfathers.

I let my arms hang, crossing them over my head—or under, I guess?—my phone pressed into my elbow, and I thought of all the different words for your grandfather. Gramps, Grampy, Papa, Granddad...

None of them seemed right. But maybe that was because suddenly having a grandpa out of a bottomless clear blue didn't seem right.

I was procrastinating. Maybe I should just read Tommy's message.

I dropped my phone next to my book, made a handstand on my next pass, and unlooped my knees from the chains. I let the momentum carry my legs ass-over-teakettle, then flattened myself belly-down on the gravel, the swing flopping crazily overhead. Its shadow jerked back and forth over me like a demon-possessed bird with a broken wing.

Propping myself on my elbows, I opened Tommy's message. It was really short.

*We need to talk.*

Wow, so curt. What made him think being rude would get him any further than his previous messages? I scrolled up and reviewed them all—a bunch of variations on the same theme that he wanted to talk with me. I read each one, trying to remind myself that none of them mattered. That someone finally giving a damn about my existence was no big deal. That my grandfather refusing to let me shut him out was meaningless drivel.

But when the tears blurred the text messages, I put my phone to sleep and stared the other way. The swing was still wobbling off-center, but gradually finding balance. I hated it for so easily reverting to something I'd never had. Didn't it know how much it hurt? To come from nowhere? To be no one? To never be able to close your eyes and let someone else keep the watch while you simply slept or played or ate a goddamn Chicago dog? My entire life had been spent watching my own back, because, seriously, when had I ever been able to rely on somebody else doing it?

The pain welled up in my chest. Expanded like a monster fighting to burst free. But there was no way to get it out. It was lodged there, beating its wings, scrabbling with its claws, tearing me to shreds from the inside out.

When I couldn't take the pain anymore, I got up on my knees. Shoved the swing hard. Let out a soul-wrenching scream.

When the swing came back at me, I stayed right where I was, knees planted firmly in the gravel. I waited for it.

The swing clocked me square in the forehead. Stars burst in front of my eyes. For a second, I felt sick to my stomach. Involuntarily, I threw my hands in front of my face to keep the swing from hitting me again on the rebound. Then I half-sat, half-fell back onto my heels.

Stinging pain set in. And when it did—the monster in my chest vanished. I closed my eyes and sighed with relief. Anything was better than that wrenching agony in the middle of my body. This was the only way I knew how to get rid of it—hurting myself. I wasn't sure why it worked, but it did. I could literally feel the endorphins releasing into my bloodstream, finally bringing me balance. I didn't know how to get it any other way.

I folded over my knees and buried my face in my arms. The relief would only last a few moments. I was bent on appreciating it while it was here. When the pain from the swing faded, I'd have just two options. I could fight really, really hard to quit thinking about the stuff that had sent me over the edge in the first place—but that was like avoiding getting sucked into a tornado because you willed your feet to stick to the ground.

Or I could hurt myself again.

Maybe I should go for someplace less visible next time. Ryan would think Bud had hit me.

As the pain in my forehead began to subside, I turned and peeked at my phone. Maybe hitting myself was dumb. What if there *was* a way to stop the tornado?

I sat up, brushing the tears from my face, and picked up my phone. I woke it up. Messages from Tommy filled the screen. At the sight of them, with his name emblazoned across the top, I felt the monster stir. The wings begin to unfurl. The claws reach out.

*It isn't fair you never got to have a mom and dad. It isn't fair you didn't get to grow up with your grandpa instead. It isn't fair you didn't even know who he was until now.*

*It isn't fair, it isn't fair, it isn't fair…*

I punched the three dots in the corner of the screen, then hit the button saying *block sender*. When it asked if I wanted to delete the message history, I said yes.

And then, for good measure, I deleted Tommy's number from my contacts. As the whirly circle spun, my phone processing the command, I kept my eye on the contact image: a picture of me standing next to Tommy on the rub board of the Mailboat. Until it vanished.

I shifted my eyes, searching the playground suspiciously.

The monster curled up into a tiny little ball, the size of a pencil eraser. It sank way down deep in my chest somewhere. It slept, barely a pinprick of pain. Hardly noticeable.

I'd stopped the tornado.

Tossing my phone aside, I grabbed my book and rolled onto my back. Crossed one calf over the opposite knee. Idly kicked the swing so it jerked around, again, like the demon-possessed bird with a broken wing.

I read about some other girl with some other set of problems.

Personally, I didn't have any.

# CHAPTER FOURTEEN

# BAILEY

Pops of light. Over and over and over. All around me. Bullets flying. The windshield shattering. Car metal ripping. Some part of my brain knew I was dreaming.

Another part of my brain reminded me that once, a few weeks ago, this hadn't been a dream.

Gravel against my face. Asphalt against my knees. I laced my fingers over the back of my head. *Pop, pop, pop.* There was no way I was going to survive a gunfight like this. I shouldn't even be here. I'd just wanted to give some guy from the restaurant his hundred-dollar tip back.

Some guy who, it turned out, was actually my dad.

I twisted my head to peer past my arm. There he was, the man with the wavy brown hair. He was propped up on one elbow, squeezing off bullets. Keeping two armed men busy. Drawing their fire. Keeping me safe. I closed my eyes, too scared to watch. I already knew how this turned out.

The shooting stopped. The silence was absolute, as if I'd been sucked into space. I stayed curled in a ball, too terrified to move.

*Open your eyes. Bailey,* I said to myself. *Get up. Save him. Save him this time.*

This was my chance to do things over. Whatever I'd done last time, it had ended crappy. It had ended with my dad dying. This time, I would ignore everything my dad said—everything that had led to us wasting time. I wasn't going to remove the gun from the other guy lying on the street; turned out, he was dead anyway.

I wasn't going to let my dad grab my hand and shove the silver helm necklace into my palm. It was a nice keepsake and all, but I would a thousand times rather have had *my dad*.

This time, I was going to tell him to shut up and sit still, and I was going to call 911 right away. And then I was going to find a way to stop the bleeding, even though it was coming out of, like, three bullet holes and his mouth.

This time, I wouldn't let him die. I had no idea what would happen afterwards—he would probably get life in jail for all those banks he'd cleaned out and that cop he'd killed while trying to get away. But at least he'd be alive. He'd be alive, and we'd have time to figure out the rest. He'd have me, and I'd have him.

I'd finally have my dad.

But it started with me opening my eyes and running to him and doing everything different than I'd done last time.

In the dream, I opened my eyes.

I ran.

I fell to my knees beside him.

He wasn't breathing. His eyes were still, like two dark lakes reflecting a sky full of stars.

No, no, no. I'd waited too long.

That's how the dream always went—me doing something wrong and my dad dying. Again and again and again...

I draped my body over his and cried. Next time. Next time, I'd do it different...

*I promise, Dad. I'm sorry. I'm so sorry...*

The ground began to rock beneath me, swaying gently back and forth, up and down, the way I'd always wanted my mother to rock me, if only she hadn't been tripping again. The ground beneath me wasn't asphalt anymore, but a polished wooden floor. My dad was gone. I was alone. Water washed against a hull.

I was on the Mailboat. I was still dreaming, but maybe now I could actually sleep.

I breathed and listened to the water ripple beneath me, the sound waves and the tiny vibrations carrying through the deck. If the Mailboat had a voice, if it had a soul, I thought I heard it speak, its tones deep and low like the twin engines below me. *Shhh, Bailey-girl. It's okay. I'm here. I'm always here...*

I sniffed and ground my forehead into the floorboards, trying to get as close to the Mailboat as possible, to soak up the comfort it offered.

And then with a jolt I remembered what always happened next in the dream.

I sat up, and with a flash of déjà vu, I knew I wasn't alone. I looked to the helm. Tommy stood next to it, staring toward the stern. He didn't see me. He looked past me, intent on something—or someone—else.

I turned my head to follow his gaze, already knowing what I'd see.

Bud stood in the middle of the boat, dressed in a black leather vest with silver studs. The butt of a gun stuck out from his waistband. Why was I dreaming him here? Was it because he'd pointed a gun at me the other day? Was my brain confusing the terror of what happened to Tommy with the terror of living with Bud Weber, suggesting they were basically the same thing?

Bud's mouth moved, but the sound came out a beat later, like a video with the audio out of sync. The effect was weird, detached.

"*Bailey says you were the one who told the cops about her bruises.*"

Tommy didn't answer. Just kept staring at Bud. There was no expression to his face. No feeling. No... life. The soul had gone out of him. The same way he'd looked after Jason was killed.

Didn't he understand what was about to happen? Why was he just standing there?

I could stop this. I had to. I held up my hand. "*Bud, no. I was the one who told the cops. I told Ryan about my bruises.*" It was a lie, but I was desperate, and I didn't care how hard Bud beat me. "*I'm sorry. I shouldn't have done it. I'll be a good girl again. I swear it. Please, don't hurt Tommy.*"

But he didn't seem to hear me. Tommy didn't seem to see me. It was like I wasn't even there. I was invisible. What I wanted didn't matter.

Bud spoke again, his eyes on Tommy. "*Bailey's mine, so shove off.*" His hand moved to his gun.

"No, don't!" I screamed. "He's my grandpa! Don't hurt him!"

Bud drew the gun. Dropped into a shooting stance.

I jumped off the floor to push Tommy out of the way—only to realize that my motion was a camera trick, a bunch of stills showing my body flying forward, while I was actually still glued down to the deck. There was no reason. Just the universe telling me to sit there and take it, like I had all my life. I wasn't allowed to have an opinion.

*"Bud, no!"* I screamed, my voice silent, unheard, but my throat going raw. My eyes shot to Tommy. I yelled his name. Why was he just standing there? Why couldn't he see me? *"Tommy, please. Don't leave me."*

That last sentence echoed over and over through the boat, overlapped with three more words I didn't remember speaking, even though I heard them in my own voice.

*"I love you..."*

Tommy tilted his head, as if he'd caught a distant whisper. Then, seeming to realize where it came from, his eyes shifted. Met mine. Came alight. He turned to face me more fully. He finally knew I was there. The connection felt real. Strong. It was going to turn out different this time. I was going to save him this time...

A light flashed out of the corner of my eye. A pop burst in the small space, hurting my eardrums. A tiny ball streaked past me, leaving an angry black trail of smoke that ripped and distorted reality around it.

It punched through Tommy's shirt, leaving a sprig of red. He flinched. Dropped face-forward to the floor.

"No!"

I reached for him, but I was too far away. I still wasn't allowed to move. He lay on the floor fighting for breath, and I couldn't help him. The camera-trick version of me shuddered to my knees beside him and grabbed his shoulder, crying, useless.

*Take it,* the universe said. *Sit there and take it. This is what I'm going to do every time you love someone.*

"No! No!"

Another voice pushed through the chaos and the terror. It rumbled deep and low, like a pair of engines, steady and strong. *Bailey-girl, it's going to be okay. Trust me. It's okay to love him.*

"Tommy!"

I sat bolt upright, my eyes flying open, my brain spinning the way it does when you wake up out of a dead sleep. Images from the dream mixed with snatches of reality. Tommy vanished like mist. The Mailboat melted away. They were replaced by a darkened room, yesterday's tee shirt and shorts thrown over a chair, my book on the corner of the desk.

Moonlight streaked across my denim quilt. It highlighted the little tufts of pink yarn holding it together and the random pockets someone thought would be cute to keep when they cut up the old jeans into patches.

I pushed my palms into my eyes. For God's sake, *why* would you have *pockets* on a *quilt*? To keep change in? Did they think I was going to pass toll roads in my dreams? For several moments, I sat sobbing, mentally screaming at the insanity of everything.

When my breath had calmed a little, I opened my eyes. Wiped away the tears. I followed the moonlight to the window. The threadbare curtains fluttered in the breeze. Cicadas filled the air with noisy whirring. My face was soaked. My throat was raw. I didn't want to think why.

Why was I always trying to fix everything while I slept? It was like, when I wasn't trying to forget everything that had happened this summer, I was trying to fix it.

The sounds of the TV drifted in from the living room. Bud was home. I glanced at my bedside clock. Two A.M. He kept the strangest hours. Aside from watching late-night comedies, I didn't want to know what he did in the middle of the night. Apparently, my subconscious already had ideas: running around killing my real family.

I rolled back onto my pillow, my heart going a mile a minute. Had I screamed out loud? I hoped not, but my throat said otherwise. I especially didn't want Bud to hear me yelling Tommy's name. I didn't want him to know how much I cared.

I stared at the ceiling, refusing to close my eyes. The images were waiting for me on the other side of the darkness. I'd stay up all night if I had to. Or maybe sleep would have pity and somehow find me in my exhaustion and claim me, swift and dreamless.

I thought I'd quit loving Tommy. I worked the Mailboat every day pretending he was never coming back. I'd blocked his number because he meant nothing to me anymore.

Then why did I keep seeing him in my dreams?

*Next time, I won't let it happen*, I promised him. *Next time, I'll do something different.*

A voice in the back of my mind rumbled deep and low. *It's okay, small one. It's okay to love him. So do I. So do we all. Everything's going to be okay.*

I blinked, and another tear slid down my cheek.

## Chapter Fifteen

# BUD

Bailey's scream cut through the dialog of the late-night sitcom, actually vibrating the beer in Bud's glass. Slouched on the sofa, he let his eyes blur on the screen. He was barely tracking the show anyhow.

She'd yelled the boat captain's name. And then she'd gone silent. He waited, but there wasn't another peep from her room. It was like them first few nights after Zayne died—Bud just waking up randomly, the other half of the bed empty and nobody he could share the pain with but a dark, uncaring room.

The kid really loved that old man. Why'd Bud have to go and do that—shoot her favorite person? Was it because he was jealous of Tommy trying to take her away from him, like any decent person would? Bud weren't no kind of guy to be any kid's foster dad.

Why'd he have to go and take all the rage crashing around in his head and offload it on somebody else? Was that any way to get over the demons stuck up in there? By handing them off to people who would be perfectly happy and normal if not for *him*?

Bud leaned his head on his fingertips and stared into his beer glass, feeling empty.

Why'd he have to be so freaking messed up?

# FRIDAY AUGUST 1, 2014

# CHAPTER SIXTEEN

# ANGELICA

California sun beat down on the asphalt as Angelica crossed the parking lot to her car, her phone cradled to her ear.

"Am I catching you at a good time?" Roland Markham asked.

"Yes, perfect," Angelica replied, smiling. It had been a couple of weeks since their last conversation, and it was good to hear his voice. "I was just leaving the office." She unlocked her car and slid into the cab, already cool, thanks to her remote starter. "What's up, Roland?"

"I have news from my friend, the reporter."

Angelica's heart leapt. "Did he get the records from the police station?" She could almost feel the pages between her fingers. She pictured a long, late night curled up on her sofa, her eyes searching hungrily, the long-buried evidence against Wade Erickson leaping from obscurity.

"My dear, I wish I had better news."

Angelica's hopes crashed. "They wouldn't release the reports?"

"Apparently the Markham Ring is considered an open investigation—particularly considering recent events."

Angelica braced her elbow on her steering wheel and laid her head on her palm. Of course. Everything was tied up, safe and sound where the public could never question Erickson's actions.

"Did you ever hear back from the Walworth County Clerk of Courts?" Roland asked.

Angelica sighed and pushed her bangs off her forehead, letting the air conditioning touch her skin. "Yes." She'd visited their offices in hopes of learning something about the grand jury that had determined not to bring Wade Erickson to trial for killing Bobby.

"And?"

"They sent me the record of the grand jury's official verdict. Everything else is confidential."

"Ah," Roland's pause spoke volumes. "Angelica, I know you must be terribly disappointed."

Something rose up in her like a dragon slowly unfurling—neck, then spine, then tail and wings. "And you aren't?" she bit out. Why did he speak of this as if she were the only one affected? She threw her hand. "It was your son he killed."

The other end of the line went silent, and Angelica felt terrible. She covered her eyes. "Roland, I'm sorry. I shouldn't have said that."

He sighed slowly. Angelica was surprised to hear his voice tremble. When he spoke, it was with vast pauses. "I've... struggled for years with the sense that Wade got away with something... *no one* should get away with."

Every word hung in the air between them. Angelica listened, riveted, realizing Roland had never let her so deep inside his heart. By the way he struggled with the words, she wondered if he'd ever let anyone in so deep.

He went on, his voice high with emotion. "I've tried to force myself into making peace with what happened. I told myself the professionals had done their jobs and the law had taken its due course. But—" His voice caught. "This can't be right. No one should lose a son. Not like this."

Angelica pressed her fingers to her lips, choking up. She couldn't help thinking about her own sons and how she would feel in Roland's circumstances. She wouldn't care what her child had done. Nothing could reconcile her to one of them being shot down in an alley. Her mind dredged up unwanted images—her younger son Mason featuring prominently. Kaydon, the elder, took after his father—blue eyes, blond hair, fair skin. But Mason... he was like his mother. Black hair. Brown eyes. Brown skin. Why did that fact make her heart tremble sometimes? Why did she worry more for his safety than for Kaydon's?

She wanted desperately to let Roland know how much she hurt for him, how deeply she understood. She wished she could wrap him in her arms. Why was she two thousand miles away in Malibu? For now, words alone would have to suffice.

"Roland, you know I'm in this with you. I'm not stopping until I have answers. And if Wade Erickson is at fault for anything, nothing will stop me from making sure justice finds him."

Roland swallowed, as if pushing back his emotions. "I know, my dear. Thank you." He drew a deep breath and lifted his voice to a more positive tone. "You know, I'm so glad I stopped to speak with that studious young lady in the Lake Geneva Library."

Angelica laughed, her smile bittersweet and deeply genuine. "Me, too, *mi viejito.*"

Roland paused. "I'm afraid I don't know what that means."

She laughed again, wondering how to explain. *My little old man* didn't sound quite as endearing in English. "It means you're family."

"Oh." Roland seemed startled.

She wondered if he remembered her explaining how central *familia* was to her. It was everything.

Roland cleared his voice hoarsely. "Well, when are you coming back? You promised you'd bring your youngsters to see where their father used to gallivant as a lad."

Angelica bit her lip. "My mother doesn't think I should bring them."

"Really?" Roland sounded taken aback. "Whyever not?"

She shook her bangs out of her eyes and stared up through the windshield at the waving palm trees and the cloudless blue sky. "Kaydon and Mason have been struggling. Not just with Will's death, but..." She stopped just long enough to re-examine her every decision, only to arrive at the same conclusion. "I haven't held anything back from them. They know now who their father really was." A thief. A fugitive. A liar. It had killed her to tell her sons, but to hold it back would be to make herself just as much of a liar. She couldn't do that to them.

"Oh, I see," Roland said, his voice full of understanding.

"They looked up to him," she said. "It's a lot to process." Her voice shook. She was still processing, too. "Bringing them to Lake Geneva, it might be—it might be too much too soon."

"I understand. The invitation remains, regardless. You're welcome on my doorstep any time."

Angelica smiled. "Thank you. When the boys are ready, I'll bring them."

"I am eagerness itself. In the meantime," Roland asked, "what of the investigation? What rock do we pry under next?"

Angelica sighed. "I'm not sure, to be honest." The job was infinitely more complicated from two thousand miles away. "I have to think."

"Well, if you have any epiphanies, you have only to pick up the phone."

Angelica smiled. "Thank you, Roland. I appreciate it." And she appreciated even more that he didn't suggest collaborating with Monica Steele again.

They said their goodbyes and ended the call. Angelica gripped her steering wheel and breathed, a tide of different emotions rising in her chest—the warmth she felt for Roland, her concern for her boys, the tension over her husband's unsolved murder...

And the lingering resentment over the fact that he'd lived an entire life with her, claiming to love her—while telling her nothing but lies about himself.

Her hands trembling, she shifted her car into reverse and backed out of her stall. Somehow, she had to get back to Lake Geneva. All the answers were hidden somewhere in the peaceful town on the shores of the lake.

# CHAPTER SEVENTEEN

# MONICA

I sat in the chair that had become my usual spot in the upstairs training room at the PD. The desks around me were barren, awash in cold fluorescent light, the natural light through the windows slowly fading to something flat and lifeless, something dead at the end of the day.

Mindlessly, I tore strips of paper from the legal pad in my portfolio. With precision, I compacted each one into a tiny ball, then tossed it onto the stack I was compiling on the edge of my desk. By now, it was deep enough to bury a gerbil.

Barely aware of what my hands were doing, I allowed my eyes to rove across the line of marker boards at the front of the room. My partner, Detective Sergeant Stan Lehman, had covered every inch in a rainbow of colors at a dozen angles. On the right-hand side, he'd taped extra sheets of paper to the wall for more room.

Of course, everything we needed was stored in a database, and the members of our interdepartmental task force all had access—Walworth County and the FBI and the ATF and the neighboring departments that had offered a hand. But Lehman's scribblings were a decent visual on just how much we now knew about the Markham Ring—Bobby Markham, Fritz Geissler, and Jason Thomlin. We'd pieced their entire lives together, from their births to their wildly successful bank heists to their deaths.

What we didn't have was a single solid lead on the identity of the individual calling himself The Man Upstairs—the individual claiming to be behind this summer of blood. Like God himself, he was invisible, unknowable... and all-knowing.

And he kept reaching his hand down, casting judgment, gathering souls. I might not have questioned his wisdom, except that he'd seen fit to judge Tommy and Roland, too.

That, I couldn't stomach.

Footsteps paused in the doorway, shoes shushing on industrial carpet. Lehman appeared in the frame and reached for the lights—then pulled his hand back.

"Monica, I didn't see you there. I thought someone left the lights on."

I glanced at my partner, a tall man in his forties, dressed in the same black polo and tan slacks as me. His gray hair was styled in trendy spikes, as if he were clinging to youth that was already long gone. The notch he set his belt to agreed with me.

I went back to ripping paper.

He observed my machinations for a moment, drummed his fingers on the doorframe, then stepped further into the room. He nodded toward the pile I'd made. "Working on the case?" His eyes, light gray like his hair, twinkled with humor.

I gave him a smoldering glare. I didn't have the mental space tonight for cheap jokes.

He leaned against the desk at the front of the room—the same one from which he held court over the task force—and folded his arms over his chest. "How's it going with Old Man Markham? Found anything in that museum of his?"

I hoisted my eyebrows. "Oh, sure, if you like antique coins, silver-wrought spoons, and medications that expired a century ago. Have you ever actually seen a bottle of stomach bitters?"

Lehman pulled his chin into his neck and shook his head.

"I popped the cork. Pure alcohol."

He laughed.

I leaned my face on my palm and stirred my pile of confetti. "We turned the whole place inside out and found nothing. If someone entered Roland's house, they probably found whatever they were looking for, waltzed out with it, and left us completely in the dark. Just one more dead end. Woo-hoo."

Lehman looked down and toed the carpet. "Look, I know the lack of progress is eating you..."

"Eating me? There's nothing left but bones." I slapped my hands down on my desk. "This task force has been meeting for four weeks, and what do we have to show for it?"

Lehman motioned to the marker boards behind him. "A new art installation. Really, I'm wounded you don't like it. It was about time we had a little class around here."

"Lehman." I locked eyes with him. "What we don't have is a man behind bars. What we don't have is any guarantee these deaths and injuries won't keep happening. And if we don't get a lead soon—" I twirled a finger "—this task force is going to fall apart. Other departments can't keep loaning us resources forever."

Lehman dropped his teasing mood and met my gaze with equal sincerity. "You know four weeks isn't a long time for a case of this scale."

I spread my hands. "And while we sit here playing puzzles, people are getting hurt. People are getting killed."

"I know," Lehman snapped, his voice bouncing sharply off the walls.

I quickly shut my jaw. I was the one around here losing my temper left and right—not him. Lehman had the patience of a glacier—one of the things I hated about him.

He shrugged his shoulders, turning his palms up. "What do you want me to do? Wave a magic wand? Pull the perp out of a hat? I'd love to, but you know that's not how this works." He reached his hand toward me, his gesture soothing. "Monica, you are a great cop and a great detective. But you have no patience. And right now, that's all we've got to work with on this case. We just have to follow every lead, no matter how small, until one of them turns up something. That's how the game works."

I looked down, tearing another shred of paper, my blood simmering. I hated this feeling—this *helplessness*. I spoke through my teeth. "This wasn't why I became a cop, Lehman—to stand by and watch good people get hurt."

"I know. I know." He ran his hand over the spikes in his hair and bounced his foot a little, as if distancing himself from his loss of temper and what had come close to an official reprimand. "I need you in this game with me, Monica. I mean, without you, who's going to take care of the rock turning and the paper pushing? You know I hate that shit."

I raised an eyebrow. But it was true. Wherever possible, he took the interviews and interrogations, and I took the haystacks and the rock piles. We played to our individual strengths, even while we cussed each other out to our faces.

"You still here for me?" Lehman asked, his voice shaking a little.

I leaned back in my chair and rolled my head at the implication I wouldn't be. "You know I am."

"You're not going to peel off 'cuz that asshole ex of yours decided to stick around?"

I smirked. Working next to me every day, Lehman knew better than anyone the depths of my hatred toward Ryan. Lehman's sympathy was kind of cute, if a bit outdated. "No. I'm staying."

"Great. Good. Losing you right now is about the last thing I need—even if you have the social skills of a scorpion."

I slit my eyes at him—but little digs like that were our comfort zone. It was the only way we put up with working together.

He pulled at the collar of his polo shirt and twisted his neck. "God, I could use a cold one. You down? First round's on me."

I shook my head. Tonight, I wanted to be alone with my thoughts, dour as they were.

"Suit yourself." He rose from the desk. "I'll see who else I can rope into it." He threw a wave and made for the door. "See you Monday, Steele."

I nodded.

He left. I stirred the tattered pages, thinking about the tatters of the case, our tattering tempers, and my quickly tattering soul.

We needed some kind of break on this case—and soon. I couldn't stand watching this kind of violence happen to my town, to the people I knew and cared about.

## CHAPTER EIGHTEEN

# SKULL

When Angelica Read unexpectedly pulled into a driveway three doors past her own, Skull calmly kept driving, passing her as if he hadn't been following her at all.

Why had she stopped there? Did she know she was being followed? Was she too nervous to go to her own house? A few weeks ago in Lake Geneva, he'd been forced to follow her into the lobby of the police station after learning the futility of dropping a bug in her purse; she rotated between several, and to date, he hadn't seen her with the same bag twice.

During that close encounter, she hadn't merely seen him; she had nearly tripped over him when she left.

Did she remember what he looked like? Had she recognized him now, tailing her a few lanes over and several cars behind? He'd taken precautions to change his look—he was a dark blond now, with a faded undercut and a narrow beard and mustache filling in nicely. And though the California sun was brutal today, he'd hidden his signature rose-and-skull tattoo under the long sleeves of a cotton button-down.

He drove another two blocks and parked, then watched Angelica from his mirrors. Without so much as a glance in his direction, she got out of her midnight blue SUV, leaving the engine running. Then she climbed the stairs of her neighbor's house and rang.

Skull quickly understood what had brought Angelica here. Two boys, perhaps twelve and nine, burst from the door and raced for Angelica's SUV, each trying to claim shotgun. The smaller one—the one with dark skin and hair like his mother—got there first. His hand on the latch, he took the time to stick his tongue out at his brother before claiming his reward.

The older boy, blond-haired and fair-skinned, only gave his brother a silly smile—*Okay, you won*—and got into the back seat. Skull gathered he was more the type to smooth things over than pursue an argument. He also wondered if the younger brother might be the type to take advantage of that.

Skull cocked a smile. So, these were Kaydon and Mason Read.

Angelica stood in the doorway a few minutes more, talking with another woman. A boy Kaydon's age stood nearby. Did Angelica's sons come here to play often?

Skull grabbed his laptop off the passenger seat and typed a note, reminding himself to gather data on the residents of 21845 Allen Rose Drive. Then he pulled up his spreadsheet and notated the time of day when Angelica had picked up her kids—five thirty-six p.m.

This was his first day of surveillance here in Malibu, and his spreadsheet was still a vast swath of white space. No worries; it would fill up quickly. He'd already entered Angelica's house while she was at work, rifled the papers in her home office, photographed the calendar hanging on her kitchen wall, and bugged the entire place. Then he'd made his exit without leaving so much as a trace that he'd ever been inside.

His prior visit to Angelica's neighborhood was also when he'd gotten the code to the gate. He'd buzzed various houses until he found someone at home, then told them he needed to check a faulty meter. It never ceased to amaze him how far you could get with a clip board and the air of someone who looked like they were supposed to be there. When he told the homeowner he had to make a few trips for "parts," he asked for the code to the gate, for convenience.

And they gave it to him.

He had access to everything he needed. Within a couple of weeks, he would be flush with information on Angelica Read—including what would be the most likely thing to bring her back to Lake Geneva as soon as possible.

The Man wasn't done playing with her yet, and his patience was running thin.

# SUNDAY AUGUST 10, 2014

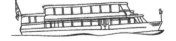

# CHAPTER NINETEEN

# TOMMY

The young hostess, dressed in a red tee shirt sporting the name "Gordy's," grabbed three menus and three sets of silverware, rolled in napkins. "Your table's ready," she said with a bright smile.

Nancy and Wade rose from the bench by the door, and I gained my feet only a moment behind them. A month and a half since the incident, and a twenty-minute drive to Fontana on the far end of the lake finally felt doable. Nancy and Wade had been hopeful to bring me out into the world a week and a half earlier, in celebration of my seventy-sixth birthday—August the first—but I'd managed to dodge that foisted honor by claiming exhaustion. I wasn't much in the mood for celebrations, anyway, regardless of the occasion.

The dining room in Gordy's was packed with the after-church crowd. As we made our way to our table, a hand popped up across the room, catching my eye. I recognized Ron and Anne Kelly. All three of their kids had worked at the cruise line. It was Ron who had waved me down, while Anne blew a kiss. Their faces shone like a pair of lighthouses. Apparently they were thrilled to see me. I smiled and nodded.

It had been the same at church this morning, a dozen people crowding in after the service, eager to express their joy over finding me vertical. I hadn't known I knew so many people. It wasn't even my church; it was Wade's.

Well, you work with everyone's kids in a small community long enough, I guess you get to know a few faces.

The hostess laid our menus down at a corner table, featuring a booth against the wall and chairs oriented with their backs to the room. A bay of windows overlooked Geneva Lake, Gordy's Marine, and, on the shore, an Adirondack chair sized to suit a giant. A couple snapped pictures of their youngsters sitting on the edge, feet dangling, as per tradition on this side of the lake.

"Your waitress will be here shortly," the hostess chirped. She twirled away, her dark curls flying.

Nancy slid into the booth, settling in next to the window. "I'm craving one of their burgers. But they're so *tall*. I can barely fit them into my mouth."

"Cut it up and eat it like a salad," Wade suggested helpfully, scooting in next to her.

"Well, it's hardly a burger anymore if you do that..."

I lowered into the chair across from Wade, noting that, in keeping with his cop instinct, he'd chosen the seat that gave him a full view of the room. His eyes scanned left and right, more attentive than usual, even for him, giving the lie to his otherwise casual body language. I despised his vigilant attitude as much as I did the tan blazer he'd slipped over his blue button-down shirt this morning. The only reason he was wearing it in the August humidity was to conceal a shoulder holster. I ground my teeth. Was this how I was supposed to live the rest of my life now, dragging an armed guard with me to church and Sunday lunch?

For all that, it was a shift in Wade's eyes that first alerted me to someone approaching from behind. Even with the split second of warning, the feminine hand resting on my shoulder gave me a start.

"Oh, Tommy, it's so good to see you. How are you?"

I didn't anticipate the crash of adrenaline in response to the simple greeting. I twisted around to look up, my brain almost too scattered to recognize Agnes Sandvall standing next to my chair. My heart thundered, and I gripped my knees under the table, trying to steady myself. What was the matter with me? I'd never reacted like this before, even if startled.

Agnes, Jason's second-grade teacher, still wore black, horn-rimmed glasses, but her bob had gone from brown to white. Her husband Abe, a lanky lineman who refused to wear anything but overalls, hovered behind her, grinning, his eyes wide, as if permanently windburned.

Agnes scanned me up and down, the way maternal women do when they want to both look you in the eye and make sure your limbs are attached where they belong.

I pasted on a smile, though it was somewhat worn after the crowd from church. "I'm fine, just fine," I assured her.

"You got our card?"

"Yes. That was very kind of you." Actually, I had no idea. I'd received dozens of cards, not to mention enough flowers to fill a botanical garden. Most of the letters still sat unopened in a basket Nancy had helpfully placed on my bedside table. Well wishes had meant little to me when my worries were all for Bailey.

"We literally could not believe it when we heard what happened." Agnes turned to her husband. "Could we, Abe?"

He shook his head. "Nope. Not for the life of us. Not in Lake Geneva. No way."

"Nooo!" Agnes wailed. "And then the bombing? Can you imagine?" She tsked. "I was saying to Abe just the other day, I don't know what's going on around here. It's like being in Chicago."

Abe shook his head woefully, his eyes going even more wrinkled and round. "Murder a day in the Windy City."

"We don't want anything like that around here." She batted a hand at Wade. "Not that you aren't doing your best, Wade. We know you are."

Wade nodded, his eyes meeting hers sincerely. "I appreciate it."

Agnes patted my shoulder again. "Well anyway, Tommy, we're just glad you're okay."

I nodded politely, grateful she didn't ask for details of the incident or my injury, as some people had. Regarding the shooting itself, there was little to share, had I even been so inclined. Wade was running an open investigation, and my own memory of that day remained fragmented. As for inquiries about the nature of my injury and my recovery, I'd hesitatingly obliged once or twice this morning—only to realize how much I despised it. No doubt, the questions arose from concern on the part of friends and acquaintances, and yet I couldn't shake the sense of voyeurism. I just wanted to put the entire event behind me.

"Are you getting back to the Mailboat soon?" Agnes went on.

"Yes," I replied, but caught Wade raising an eyebrow at me. He knew I could barely keep to my feet for twenty minutes at a time. How was I supposed to work a five-and-a-half-hour shift on the Mailboat?

Agnes was ignorant of any trouble brewing across the table. "Oh, good," she said. "It wouldn't be the same without you." She roughed up my shoulder gently. "You take care now, you hear? Tell us if you need anything. Just pick up the phone."

"Will do." At this point, I had dozens of identical offers—and intentions of following up with none of them. What I needed most, none of these well-wishers could give me.

The latest delegates from my fan club walked away. Feeling Wade's eyes on me, I flipped open the menu to study the entrées and made a try at small talk. "Haven't been to Gordy's in a while. Don't tell them over at Chuck's that I'm playing favorites." A friendly rivalry stormed every summer between the neighboring, brother-owned restaurants.

When Wade didn't respond, I hazarded a glance. He frowned and rapped the stem of a fork on the table as if on the verge of telling me to wait in the car if I couldn't behave.

Nancy raised her eyebrows, bit her lips together, and turned to her menu, pointedly staying out of the conversation. She'd seen us argue enough times to know it was best to watch from the sidelines.

I sighed and turned the vinyl-sleeved page. "I packed my suitcase this morning." In for a penny, in for a pound.

"Why? Going somewhere?"

I shrugged. "Home. You know the tap for the garden hose locks shut if you don't use it regular."

"I've been over every week to water your lawn. The tap's fine."

"Oh."

"What's this about the Mailboat?"

I pretended to focus on the beverages on the back page, even though I knew I was having coffee. "The doctor cleared me for work. I called Robb yesterday. He's willing to put me back on, part-time."

"You ready for that?"

"It's just the Mailboat tour. I'm not taking any other shifts." When he remained silent, I sighed and finally looked him in the eye. "It's August. The summer's slipping away. I need to get back to work."

He spread his hands. "The boat'll still be there next summer. Take it easy for once in your life."

"No." I didn't mean to snap like I did, but I was clean out of fuse. "Is this what my life's supposed to be like now? Hiding? Always watching my back?" I waved a hand at him. "Letting you carry guns into churches?"

He visibly bristled. "And I'm supposed to let you walk into an enclosed space—a boat in the middle of the lake, no egress—and endanger hundreds of people, thanks to their proximity to you?"

I shook my head. "That's not the shooter's MO. He chooses his targets specifically and catches them when they're alone." Wade knew a criminal rarely altered his methods.

Wade threw the fork down and looked away. "I hate it when you use cop speak."

"Well then, you shouldn't have become a cop and taught it to me."

His jaw working, his gaze across the room, he spoke more to himself than to me. "I never wanted you to live in the world I live in." He met my eyes again. "Give me a little more time, Tommy. Let me catch this guy first."

I shook my head. "Wade, I don't *have* time." Seeing an objection of storm-like proportions forming on his lips, I sallied forward. "I talked with Ryan Brandt a couple weeks ago." I was navigating straight into the choppy waters I'd hoped most to avoid. Well, Wade hadn't left me a lot of options. "He wants my help on Bailey Johnson's case."

Her "case." I hated sanitizing it like that, as much as I hated calling her "Johnson" when her name should have been Thomlin. Someone was beating my granddaughter black and blue, and Wade wasn't going to keep me away from her a minute longer, even if unwittingly.

Wade raised his eyebrows. "You talked with Brandt?"

I toyed with a napkin. "Yeah. He thinks maybe I can get through to Bailey. Get her to open up about those bruises and where she gets them."

He shrugged, still unimpressed with my insistence on getting back to my job, and stated the obvious. "Have you thought about calling her?"

"I've tried. She won't pick up. She's pretty determined not to talk about it." Wouldn't it be nice if that was all it was? What did she think of having me for a grandfather? My mouth went dry, and I wondered where the waitress was with the water glasses.

Nancy glanced at Wade from the corner of her eye. When he returned the look, she shot her gaze back to the menu, but lifted her chin. Through a vibration in the table, I registered her tapping her toe pointedly. It was her first commentary on our argument.

I read from it that I'd won her to my side. In fairness, how could you argue with a threat that may or may not come after me again, versus a dangerous situation that was unfolding daily for Bailey?

Anyway, I hoped that was how Nancy read it. Regardless, she appeared to be waiting for Wade to hurry up and pass his blessing already.

Wade sighed. He'd picked up the fork again and was bending and straightening it, the tendons in his hands straining. "How about you get a security system at your house?"

I shrugged. "How about you give me the number of the company you use?"

"Done." He dropped the warped fork on the table with a clatter and stared across the room, as if interested in staring at anything but me.

It was clear he still hated the idea of me getting back to my own life—and he probably would until he had a suspect in custody. Well, I couldn't afford to remain inactive. I'd endured a month at his house, watching the sun rise, watching it set, watching one variety of flowers in the garden go out of season, watching another come in. Wade's granddaughter Avery had lost her first tooth. Derry had gotten his first bike.

I needed to watch my own grandchild—not his.

## CHAPTER TWENTY

# BAILEY

Sitting on a stool on the aft deck of the Mailboat, my feet propped on one of the lower shelves of the concessions counter, I popped Cheetos and watched Noah Cadigan make his deliveries. The boat sped past yet another pier. He leapt from the rub board, dashed to the mailbox nailed to one of the posts, and shoved in the Sunday paper. While his hands were still busy flipping up the door, his feet were already changing stride. Fractions of a second later, he was sprinting back for the still-moving boat.

A wave washed against the port side, rocking the boat to starboard. I reached out to grab my soda, stopping it from careening clean over the edge of the counter.

The Mailboat leaned into the pier, wood squealing. The passengers gasped. Noah came to a full stop, the pier shuddering beneath his feet. Then he must have realized, crisis or no, he was about to run out of boat. He jumped, grabbing the last few inches of the handrail. The passengers drew breath again, then gave him a round of applause.

I looked over my shoulder through the rear windows. The pier quivered in our wake.

Facing forward again, I raised an eyebrow and popped another Cheeto. Yup. Just another slipshod day at the Mailboat. The cruise line office would be getting a heated call from the pier's owner sooner or later—a more common occurrence this summer than usual. By now, every pier on our route sported a stripe of navy blue paint, compliments of Captain Brian, Tommy's

replacement. It was safe to say Brian was still getting the hang of it
.

Instead of striding back up the rub board toward the bow, Noah hooked his arm through one of the open window frames and shook his head at me. I shrugged in reply.

We could emote freely back here; the aft deck was empty. Despite assurances that the Mailboat tour ran seven days a week, few people internalized the fact that we delivered the Sunday paper. Those who did come took the main and upper decks and avoided the aft; the engines below were pretty loud back here. Also, the passengers all sat on the shore side for the better view—again, despite assurances that the boat would literally lean starboard, making it even harder for Brian to avoid hitting the piers.

Noah held out his hand. "Hey, toss me a bag?"

Clearly, he was in no hurry to get back to his post. There were no deliveries on this next stretch of shore, and little by way of tour narration. Brian could man the mike for a few minutes. I grabbed a pack of Cheetos from the basket on the counter and threw it by the corner so that it flipped end-over-end. Noah caught it just before it flew over his shoulder into the lake. Coordination came in handy as a mail jumper.

His elbow still hooked around the window frame, Noah ripped open his bag. "Hey, uh... I just wanted to mention..." He kept his eyes on the bag and not on me. "I never apologized for that one day..."

His words trailed off, and I was pretty sure I knew what day he was talking about. My stomach tied into knots, and the Cheetos suddenly lost all appeal.

He straightened his shoulders, as if making up his mind to commit. "That day we were talking with Jimmy... If I came off like I was saying I was your boyfriend or something, I'm sorry. That wasn't what I meant."

"It's cool," I said with a shrug. But at the same time, I wiggled my foot back and forth on the edge of the shelf. *Talking* with Jimmy? It had been a screaming match, and then Jimmy Beacon had set off a bomb, killing himself and two other people.

Ryan Brandt had told me there was more going on in Jimmy's life than our argument, but... I don't know. The argument was the only part I was there for.

Noah lifted his eyebrows, still worried. "We're all cool?"

"Yeah." As if to prove it, I popped another Cheeto into my mouth and crunched it. I didn't want to think about Jimmy accusing Noah of trying to "steal" me.

Noah nodded. "Good."

The space went silent, except for the engines. Noah and I really hadn't brought Jimmy up since the fight. Like, how do you even talk about that—a kid you knew from work and school setting off a bomb? Especially when you kind of felt responsible? Noah had been Jimmy's only friend, and I, his one true crush.

Noah stared at his snack pack as if somewhere in the greasy, mirrored interior, he could find the answers to all life's questions. "I really wish I hadn't gotten mad at Jimmy," he finally said. "Maybe if he felt like he had someone to talk to, he wouldn't have killed himself."

Oh, so we were actually doing this? Talking about Jimmy? Great. But... it was kind of interesting to know that Noah felt the same as me.

"I shouldn't have pushed him away like I did," I said, my voice just loud enough to carry above the engines. "Jimmy wasn't actually weird; he just didn't know how to talk to people."

Noah nodded somberly. "My therapist says we're not supposed to blame ourselves for things we can't control."

I squinted uncertainly. "Sooo... did your therapist ever have a boy crush on them, then try to blow up the town?"

Noah smiled wanly and shook his head. "Probably not."

I nodded, feeling justified, and crunched another Cheeto.

But also... Noah was going to therapy? For Jimmy? I hadn't thought they were that close. But then, did that matter? Maybe Noah was the smart one, and I was the idiot. I had a therapist through foster care, but I hadn't talked to her in months, despite the summer I'd just had.

Staring into his snack pack, Noah shook his head, as if shaking off the conversation. When he spoke again, his voice was more upbeat. "Did you hear the news?" Suddenly, he was smiling all big and crazy, and I didn't think he was that excited about exploded corn flavored with cheese.

"What?" I asked.

He looked up, shaking his blond bangs out of his eyes. "Tommy's coming back. Thursday, I think."

I froze, the bite in my mouth turning to cardboard. "Where'd you hear that?"

"Brian. Tommy's only taking the mail tour, so Brian's still on the second shift." While the Mailboat only made postal deliveries once a day, it took a more normal boat tour immediately afterwards—one that didn't involve getting so up-close and personal with the shoreline. Noah grinned and threw a thumb over his shoulder. "The piers will be relieved."

I pulled half a smile. "I think *Brian* will be relieved."

Noah laughed. Holding the window frame with one hand, he let the forward momentum of the boat swing him backwards and out over the lake. For half a second, it looked as if he were going to vanish clean off the end of the boat. But a moment later, holding his snack in one hand, he started walking up the rub board toward the bow and his next newspaper delivery.

I stared into my little plastic bag, shaking it so the big puffs jumped to the top. But then I just sat there all blank and lame, one word surfacing in my thoughts.

*Crap.*

I'd kind of hoped Tommy wouldn't be back before the end of summer. And then I'd kind of toyed with the idea of not coming back next year. You know. So I'd never see him again.

For most of the season, I'd been able to pretend as if Tommy had never told me I was his granddaughter. As if nothing had happened. Like we'd never even met. Like I was some other Bailey who was still a mail jumper and still lived in foster care, but didn't give a shit. *Ain't got no parents? So what. Neither do frogs, when you think about it. They just hatch and swim.* The lack of internal drama was nice.

Was I ready to go back to things the way they were? To the questions, the doubts, the fears?

Yeah, nope. Why else had I blocked his number?

I'd already made up my mind. This was where Tommy and I were supposed to part ways. *Oh, you're my grandpa? That's cool. I'll probably actually treasure that for always. I mean, seriously, you're probably the least-messed-up person I've ever met. But this is where it ends. 'Kay, it was good. Have a nice life. 'Bye.*

That was kind of all I wanted right now. To treasure the time we'd had. But to run away from it, too. To keep it safe in a little memory box where it would collect a comfortable layer of dust between now and the next time I opened it.

Like, years from now.

I wasn't ready to dive back into the angry ocean. The confusion. The crazy, messed-up feelings. And now I had to magically get it all figured out.

By Thursday.

# MONDAY AUGUST 11, 2014

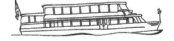

# CHAPTER TWENTY-ONE

# RYAN

I turned off the shower in the men's locker room at the PD and ran a towel over my just-washed hair. My muscles ached in that way I'd grown to love after a workout; it was leg day today. The fact that I had the energy for the gym after my shift—and an organized enough schedule to remember which day was leg day—was testament to how much quieter things had gotten. That fact was an altogether good thing for the town—but the lack of progress on Bailey's case ate at me.

I wrapped the towel around my waist and crossed the tiles to my locker. The room was empty; everyone else from my shift had left long ago. I was one of only a handful of people who actually used the department's gym. But then, everyone else had a home life worth getting back to.

I pulled on a pair of worn jeans and a tee shirt, then eyed my phone sitting on the shelf. It had been a couple of weeks since Tommy had agreed to help with Bailey. Should I call for the progress report? Or was I being too eager? It was probably too early for much to have changed. What did I expect Tommy to do—wave his hand and make miracles happen?

Yeah, actually.

I thought back to when he was in the hospital. He'd been disoriented and incoherent for days, but Bailey had let me drive her every afternoon, just so she could sit at his bedside. And then, just when he'd made a turn for the better, Bailey had ended her visits. I still couldn't think what had gone wrong—what may have passed between them.

And despite that, I still believed Tommy was the answer to unlocking Bailey's soul.

I had to know how things were going.

I picked up my phone and hit Tommy's number in my contacts. After a couple of rings, his voice filled the line.

"Well, hello, Ryan."

I grinned. Why did the mere sound of his voice lighten my mood? It was just the effect he had—and I was willing to wager I wasn't the only one who felt that way.

"Hey, Captain, how are you?"

"Good, good. Heading back to work this week."

He dropped the comment so casually, I nearly missed the significance. "Wait—wow. When?"

"Thursday, bright and early."

I ran a hand through my damp hair. "That's great." I felt like offering congratulations, but something about that same casualness in his tone—like brushing over something relatively insignificant—suggested he wouldn't care for it. So I skipped to the meat of the call. "I just wanted to check whether you've touched base with Bailey yet—but maybe I'm jumping the gun."

"No, no, I, uh... I tried dropping her a line a couple times."

"You have?"

"Yeah. Haven't heard back, though."

Disappointed, I rapped my knuckles on the door of my locker, then paced, staring at the floor. "She's not much for talking, that one."

Tommy chuckled softly. "Until you get her on some random topic."

Really? I'd never seen that side of Bailey. For me, she remained a clamshell, tightly shut. But by the quiet fondness in Tommy's voice, I knew he spoke from experience. I was reminded once again why he was the perfect man for this job.

"You work with her on Thursday?"

"Yeah." He clipped the word into a grunt. "So says the schedule. I have her every day for the rest of the week."

"Well, that's promising." I stopped pacing and filled my lungs. "Hey, thanks again for your help. I really owe you one."

He paused, and I thought he might be as uncomfortable with my gratitude as he was with any attempt at congratulations on his recovery. But the silence lengthened beyond even that explanation. When he spoke, his tone was somber. "No. You don't owe me anything."

I frowned. Was it just me, or was something a little off? I shook the thought aside. I was probably just reading it wrong. It was late. He must be tired. I should let him go.

"Well, good luck Thursday," I said. "You'll keep me posted?"

"Can do."

Our goodbyes were brief, and we hung up. I paced some more, my concern about the tone of the conversation evaporating as overwhelming hope for Bailey's future welled up instead. Everything was going to be fine; I was positive. It was that same sense of surety I used to have as a kid. With Tommy at the helm, what could go wrong? Within moments, I was practically dancing, warm feelings chasing each other up and down my spine.

After several moments, I realized I needed to offload this energy somehow. Share it with someone.

And of course, there was only one person I wanted to share it with.

Would that be a little premature? A little presumptuous? I mulled the question, even while pulling a tube of gel out of my locker and quickly styling my nearly-dry hair. The scent was a little fresh, a little spicy. Monica *had* brought me coffee that one night... Perhaps there was no harm in testing the waters, seeing how warm they were.

I closed my locker and jogged up the stairs to the second floor. It was late, and the station was silent. The day-shifters had gone home, but as I had guessed, a light was still on in the Detective Bureau. Hand on the knob, I took a second to peer through the narrow window in the door and smiled. Seated at her desk, she was still hard at work. There was no slowing that woman down, just as there was no arguing with her clean-cut beauty—her angular features, her straight, dark hair. She was like a new handgun, gleaming, deadly, its own kind of sexy, a little too hot to handle.

Playing with fire had always been my weakness, and Monica was the hottest fire that had ever burned me.

I thought about a comfy sofa and her tucked comfortably beside me. A bowl of popcorn between us. A million Netflix titles to choose from. A few minutes insulting each other's taste. Then us settling on a nice rom-com. A little bit of laughter. Plenty of cuddles. And the slowly dawning realization that a night like this was completely perfect.

Nothing ventured, nothing gained. I pushed the door open and stepped in.

# CHAPTER TWENTY-TWO

# MONICA

For the hundredth time, I clicked through the documents Tara Slater from the Madison PD had dug up. By all appearances, the case in regards to the alleged breach of confidentiality had been laid to rest after the initial investigation; lack of evidence to prosecute. She'd also confirmed there never was a civil suit against the abortion clinic or against Dr. Holdstadter.

Of course, that wasn't enough info for me. I'd kept right on digging, but my research on the complainant wasn't promising. A woman in her early twenties at the time, she had dozens of arrests, from domestic disputes to minor drug charges to shoplifting.

My read on it? A classic self-centered bitch who couldn't stand that her boyfriend disapproved of the abortion. At one time, she'd even raised charges against a shopkeeper and a mall guard, claiming they'd bruised her when they detained her after one of her shoplifting sprees.

How entitled could you get? The girl didn't deserve to be a mother.

None of this either proved or disproved that Dr. Holdstadter could have leaked my own secrets. But if it wasn't her... then who? How did The Man Upstairs know about my abortion?

I planted my elbows on my desk and buried my face in my hands. "God damn it."

"That bad, huh?"

I jumped and looked up. "Ryan—hey." My hand sneaked to my keyboard and hit the shortcut to minimize my windows. "What are you doing here? You working night shift?" One glance at his torn jeans and snug gray tee shirt told me that was bullshit. Either that, or we'd gotten a new undercover division for the male model industry.

Shit. I was never going to forgive him for looking so good after all these years.

He shook his head and leaned an arm over the top of my cubicle wall. "Got off a while ago. Thought I'd pop in and see what you were working on."

I shrugged and opened my mouth to reply, trying to think of something coherent to say about the case I was *supposed* to be working on. But the details of my official investigation—the Markham Ring—were as far away as the other Lake Geneva. The one in Switzerland.

Ryan filled the silence for me. "I heard Klemmens and Hollister weren't at the task force meeting this morning."

I nodded. "Some of the departments are pulling back their personnel. We've been meeting for over a month, and leads are drying up." I leaned my cheek against my palm and scrubbed an imaginary stain on my desk. "I knew the help couldn't last forever."

"You'll get to the bottom of this. You always do."

I pulled a mirthless smile, then went back to scrubbing what I knew was a part of the pattern on the laminated desktop.

"Hey, look, in good news, there've been no further incidents. No deaths, no injuries."

I quirked my head and nodded. God, I hoped it stayed that way.

A smile lifted one side of Ryan's mouth. "Oh, and guess what? Tommy's going back to the Mailboat this Thursday."

The words hit a strange chord inside me—sweet and dissonant at the same time. "Is he?" I turned to look out my window. I couldn't stop my brain from ripping me back to the day Tommy had landed in the hospital, looking like Death's next-of-kin. After the years I'd spent with him as a mail jumper, the sight had shaken me harder than I cared to admit. Tears sprang to my eyes. "God, I'm glad to hear that." My voice went hoarse and shaky.

Ryan's gaze was fixed on me; I could see it by his reflection in the darkened window. He said nothing, but his mere silence sent comfort. The way I felt? He seemed to feel that way, too. Tommy had meant the world to us when we were kids.

Hell, what was I talking about? He still did.

Ryan lifted his chin toward the window, looking beyond our reflections. "Moon's out early."

I wondered what that had to do with anything, but shifted my focus to follow his. He was right. The empty parking lot below was bathed in silver, like a ballroom floor polished to a high shine, just waiting for the guests to arrive in all their finery.

"Wanna go for a walk?" he said, "Work off some stress?"

Work off some stress? He would have invited me to the gym downstairs if that's what he really meant. Pump some iron. Pound out a few miles on the treadmill. Scream some dead lifts. Sweat off our frustrations.

But judging by his damp hair and the aroma rolling off of him—like cloves and ginger and an earthy forest after a good, clean rain—he'd already hit both the gym and the shower.

*Moon's out early.*

The town would be quiet, the lake like an iridescent gem. Maybe, in some alternate universe where we didn't hate each other, we would even hold hands. Feel the warmth of each other's palms and fingertips. Remember that we weren't alone in all this. That we were two very real people who had made very real mistakes but could somehow find forgiveness. For just one night, we could forget everything.

I could quit fighting and screaming and just... *be.*

I made up my mind and changed it three times in a row. It was the final change that counted.

"Sure," I said, and put my computer to sleep—and with it, the loudest of my arguments against such a terrible decision.

My heart pounded as I stood. My legs felt like water. What was I doing? My brain yelled at me to stop and think this through, but my heart screamed to go for it.

The smile that greeted me when I looked up—quiet, yet full of joy—threatened to melt everything hard and bitter in my soul.

## CHAPTER TWENTY-THREE

# RYAN

Yes! I refrained from pumping my fist and instead held the door for her like a proper gentleman—one who still had a brain and an unexploded skull to keep it in. Was this really happening?

We went down the stairs and I opened the outside door for her, too. And the next thing I knew, we were walking down Geneva Street together, side-by-side, like any one of a hundred couples you could spot on a summer night in Lake Geneva.

Or close to it. Monica was in her detective's uniform with her badge and her service weapon strapped to her hip. Not the most romantic date-night ensemble. But with everything that had gone down lately—especially The Man Upstairs calling her on her personal cell—I approved of her remaining armed.

We walked in silence past sleeping storefronts, me hovering about two inches above the pavement, my heart going a mile a minute. What was happening? How did I avoid ruining the whole thing?

And then, as we hung a left and wended our way down Broad Street toward the lake, I realized Monica was eying the store windows—not like a woman appreciating dresses and purses and other shopping delights, but like a cop making sure everything was locked up and quiet.

Hands in my jeans pockets, I leaned in closer. "This isn't foot patrol, you know."

She ripped her gaze away from the windows—but only looked lost and confused, her eyes darting everywhere and nowhere. She laughed nervously. "Then what is it?"

I read between the lines. *If I'm not a cop, then what am I?*

Had it been so long since she'd let anyone court her that she'd forgotten everything that made her perfect? Beautiful? Desirable?

I stood in front of her, holding up a hand, and brought her to a stop. I looked into her eyes, deep brown, bottomless... trembling with fright.

"Tonight is anything you want it to be," I said. "Nothing more, nothing less."

Her gaze centered on mine and went still. The longer I stared into her eyes, the more I felt myself tumbling head-first into their depths, my stomach left behind somewhere, my heart taking wings. I didn't know what I'd find if I ever hit the bottom, but I was pretty sure it would trigger feelings too strong for me to handle.

So I broke my eyes away. Found them drawn upward instead to a massive, pale light.

The moon was huge, magnified. It felt close enough to pull out of the sky and eat like a sugared wafer. Every crater, peak, and valley glittered with incredible detail. A supermoon.

I grinned. "Look at that."

She tipped her face skyward, the moon bathing her features in its glow. Her mahogany hair, cascading over her shoulder, caught the light in long silver blades. Her eyes glittered like stars breaking through the dense canopy of a pitch-black forest. It was the first light I'd seen in her eyes since the day I'd broken her heart.

My breath stopped short. I couldn't rip my gaze away. It was like falling in love with her for the first time all over again. But better this time. The teenager who had originally fallen for Monica Steele had no idea what love truly meant.

Her eyes shifted to mine. Now, they were channeling light and darkness simultaneously, fearlessly, and I felt caught up in the swirl, like being sucked into a sky dancing with Northern Lights.

"Tonight's anything I want?" she said.

I nodded, my mouth dry.

She lowered her voice. "I want to walk with you," she said.

And then... she slipped her hand into mine.

We walked, me in a sort of stupor. Her hand, delicate yet strong, sent electricity up and down my spine. This was real.

This was happening. Everything was unfolding far better—and far faster—than I had dared to imagine. But where to from here? How did I make sure this night stayed perfect? How did I avoid screwing things up, like I always did?

Our footsteps carried us silently down Broad Street until the lake and the Riviera opened on our view. We turned to walk along the shore, and the excursion boats—the Mailboat and her companions—appeared behind the Riv, glowing in their coats of white paint like fallen fragments of stars. The reflection of the moon stretched toward us, wavering across the surface of the water in a magical wake.

With every step, the heat in my veins built and crashed like waves. And with every new trickle of adrenaline, I felt more and more compelled to say the words that had been banging their fists against my heart.

*Monica, I'm still in love with you.*

Giving in to that urge would ruin everything. But my mind was already made up.

# CHAPTER TWENTY-FOUR

# MONICA

We strolled down the sidewalk between the shore and Library Park, the water lapping the rocks at our feet, the leaves on the trees flickering in the breeze. Ryan's hand in mine was strong, warm, and tense with energy, like a horse fighting to mind its bit and bridle, but craving to be given its head to race down a track of its own choosing. My own grip was silent. Patient. Collected.

For the first time in ten years, I wasn't a cop anymore. I was a woman. Ryan had reminded me that I had that permission. It was such an ancient, forgotten part of me, and I meant to enjoy every moment.

When we arrived at the boat slips on the far end of the park, our feet carried us onto the whitewashed planks, our movements synchronized in wordless agreement. We followed the branching catwalks to the very last slip on the very last pier, and there we stopped and stared over Geneva Bay toward the Riviera. The moon and the lake peered into each other's faces, like two wise old sisters with much to discuss, and all night to do so.

Ryan finally broke the silence. "Monica—"

"Shhh." I wrapped my arm around his waist and leaned my head against his shoulder. I didn't want anything to break this moment. Not yet.

As I pulled us together, he started almost imperceptibly. And then, after a pause, he wrapped both arms around my shoulders and laid his head on top of mine. I could feel his heart through his chest. It was going a mile a minute. His entire body quivered.

Soon, there would be no holding him back. Whatever he meant to say, he would say it. I embraced the last few moments of silence, even as I let them go.

When he spoke, his voice was thick with emotion. "Monica, I am so sorry."

My throat constricted. A stab like a knife, surprisingly swift, cut to my heart. But I recognized the sensations for what they were.

They were the final, parting sobs of a woman whose heart had been badly broken; they were the pain of letting go of something old, broken, and useless, the shards cutting my palms even as I let them fall. As I stared at the moon and the lake, like a little sister who had been allowed to sit in on their conversation, they whispered to me that some things were more ancient and enduring even than heartbreak. Things like forgiveness. Love. Second chances.

"I know, Ryan," I said, searching my own soul and finding nothing there but a surface as smooth as the lake. A surface on which we could create whatever patterns we wanted.

He took me by both shoulders and turned me to face him. His eyes were earnest. "Monica, I love you. I have always loved you. You have always been *the* woman. Always." His voice shook, as if in desperation to make me see, to make me understand. "*Always*," he said one last time.

I gently laid a finger on his lips, hushing whatever well-rehearsed argument might escape. In silence, I stared into the eyes of the only man I'd ever loved. Through our touch, through our gaze, I felt the bonds that had always been meant to exist between us reach toward each other and twist together.

"Ryan," I whispered. My lips quivered as my next words fought to form, as they pushed their way past the wounds. For a moment, I feared the words I needed wouldn't come.

But they did.

"I forgive you."

Something rushed from my chest like water. A decade of hatred. Of vengeance. Of pent-up fury. When they were gone, I felt empty. Washed out, but washed clean.

I didn't know I could ever feel this way again. Just... me.

At my words, dampness sprang to Ryan's eyes and a shudder wracked his body. He pulled me close, held me tight, as if afraid I'd vanish. "Give me one more chance. We don't need to rush anything. Just—please. Let me prove myself. I... I want us back together again so *bad*." I heard the tears in his voice.

Ten years ago, I'd shown him the door without so much as an opportunity to explain himself. He wanted the second chance I'd never given him. I closed my eyes and searched for any last, lingering voices of resistance, of hatred. But they seemed so far away now. So small. So unreal.

Slowly, I nodded. The wind over the lake teased the word from my mouth. "Okay," I said.

When I opened my eyes again, disbelief was washing over Ryan's face. He studied me, as if waiting for me to take it back, as if afraid I might. But when I didn't, hope flickered in his eyes.

The inches between us were too great a distance to endure. His hand crept into my hair. Mine cradled the back of his head. Our lips met, hesitant at first, then long and sweet.

We broke apart, and he looked down at me, eyes searching. "We're really doing this? We're trying again?"

I gave him half a smile. Cocky. Sexy. Playful. And yet brutally to the point. Like we used to be. "Yeah. Why not?"

After everything that had happened this summer? Seriously. *Why not?* If there was ever a time to be a little daring—to grasp at the things we really wanted—that time had to be now. If there was ever a time to overthrow the specters of the past and drag them out into the daylight to watch them burn—that time had to be now. Besides, this Ryan was a new man from the one I'd banished.

And slowly, one falling shard at a time, I was realizing... I could be a new woman.

I breathed deeply, warmth filling my chest as I stared into a pair of glittering brown eyes, more complex and fascinating than I remembered. More warm and comforting than I could ask for. I wanted this. I wanted us.

But then a voice I'd forgotten to quell rose up screaming.

*You haven't told him.*

I froze like a deer in the headlights, fear exploding in my stomach. I sank into Ryan's chest, tearing my eyes away from his so he wouldn't see the terror in mine. What was I doing? I hadn't told him...

Ryan stroked my hair. "Are you afraid?"

I closed my eyes and nodded, knowing he could feel the movement. We were talking about two different things. It didn't matter. Fear was fear.

He held me close. "Me, too."

*You have to tell him.*

What if he walked away the minute I did? Could I even blame him? I had shoved the fault for our failed marriage squarely on his shoulders, and he had biddably carried the burden all these years. He'd played the devil, and I the angel, even as I'd cold-heartedly robbed him of fatherhood and marched away, chin in the air, as if I'd done nothing at all.

But the thought of building our new relationship on secrets and a lie twisted my very soul. It would only lead to another breakup down the line. Worse. Harder. Uglier. And then there would be no redemption and no one to blame but me.

If I was going to do this at all—if I was going to allow myself to fall in love with Ryan again—I had to do it right. A clean slate or a clean break. There was no other option.

Tears rolled down my cheeks and soaked into Ryan's tee shirt. Slowly, I felt another brittle old thing break, the pieces piercing my hands as they fell. I let my resistance bleed out of me.

He nuzzled my hair. "What's wrong?" he whispered.

I rotated my head and gazed out over the lake, still clinging to him. The black water was suddenly unfeeling. Distant. The moon a blank disc. I was alone. Afraid. "There's something you need to know," I said, my voice choked.

He spoke into my hair. "Tell me anything."

*Anything?* He didn't know what anything meant.

I pulled away and looked into his eyes. They searched me, open, inviting whatever I was trying to say.

*Don't do it now. Wait a day. A week. Let it be beautiful for just a moment.*

I pulled the words up from somewhere deep inside, feeling as if I were ripping out my soul along with them. "When we divorced..."

I was resurrecting the past. Inviting it to hurt us again, just as it was finally slipping into the shadows. But Ryan's gaze didn't flinch.

"When we divorced, I... I..." My throat constricted. Fresh tears welled up. I forced the words through. They slipped out in a messy whisper. "I was pregnant."

Ryan's eyes narrowed in confusion, then darted, searching mine. His brow went heavy. Did he even believe me? We'd tried so hard for so long. We'd accepted that we were never going to have a child.

I didn't allow my gaze to flinch from his, even as my voice faltered, rising several octaves, abandoning dignity, staggering like a soldier too drunk to know she was wounded. "I was pregnant, and I... I had an abortion." All of a sudden, I was ugly-crying, and I didn't even care. The words were coming. They were finally coming. "I'm sorry. I... I was so angry. I did it to punish you, Ryan. Oh, *God.*"

The aching emptiness in my belly filled every inch of my body and threatened to explode outward, ripping me apart. I squeezed my eyes shut, my mouth open in a silent cry. My fingers dug into Ryan's arms. My baby wasn't here. The child I'd wanted like nothing else on earth... *wasn't here.*

"*My baby*," I cried, the pain visceral. "*My baby...*"

His arms pulled me close. Held me tight. Held me together. What did he think of me? I didn't know. I didn't care. I was far beyond that now. I was reeling through the void I'd created in my own soul, carved out with the weaponized shards of my broken heart. I'd built a Wall around that black hole to keep people out. To save me from slipping through. But it was too late now.

The shattered pieces falling everywhere were me.

# CHAPTER TWENTY-FIVE

# RYAN

I held her tight, afraid that if I didn't, she'd scatter a thousand directions, the pieces lost beneath the waves. I'd never seen her like this. I didn't know what to do. What to say. I groped for words. They were all pointless.

And slowly, past her explosive tears, the meaning of what she'd said sank in.

She had been pregnant?

Her head tucked beneath my chin, I stared into the inky water, as if an explanation would arise from its depths.

She had been pregnant. She had been pregnant while I'd been off ruining our marriage. She'd been pregnant while we started the divorce proceedings. She couldn't have been pregnant much longer after that. I would have noticed. I would have seen.

That thing she'd wanted so badly for so long—to be a mother—it had finally been hers.

And like everything else in our lives... I had ruined it.

Bill Gallagher had been right. I hadn't known the full story. Not even the half of it. I'd been bumbling along without so much as a clue to all the wrong I'd done. Cocksure bastard that I was, I'd convinced myself I could toy with a single, tantalizing thread—only to unravel entire tapestries I hadn't known existed.

As the sobs wracked Monica's body, the depths of her grief burned away the layers of my soul, revealing a black sludge that oozed through every corner of my being. I writhed in disgust. No wonder she hated me. I'd robbed her of everything.

Monica should have put a bullet through my brain the day I'd blithely sauntered into her life again.

# Chapter Twenty-Six

# SKULL

A burger in one hand, Skull balanced his laptop between his knee and the steering wheel of his parked rental car and typed with his free hand. His windows were open to a cool breeze, his windshield pointed toward the final striations of a red and gold sunset, crosshatched with electrical wires and towering palms. The burger was thick and juicy, stuffed with crisp lettuce and tomato and the kind of ketchup that was actually worth writing home about.

Hands down, Angelica's boys knew the hidden gems in Malibu's local cuisine. Parked across the street from the restaurant in question, Skull had an excellent view of the patio table where Angelica and her sons enjoyed their own burgers. Angelica had finally picked up the same purse in which Skull had placed a bug a full month ago in Lake Geneva. Voice-activated, it still had battery life. And disguised as a fully-functional pen, Angelica would probably never recognize it for what it was, even if she wondered where she'd picked it up. Thanks to the bug, Skull knew the kids had begged Angelica to go out for dinner tonight at what was apparently their favorite burger joint.

He licked mayo off his thumb—the condiment an incredible balance of creamy and tangy—and attached a spreadsheet to the email in his secure client portal. For the past ten days, he'd been monitoring Angelica, her home, her office, her sons. His spreadsheet was now bursting with information, everything referenced and cross-referenced. As was outlined in their contract, it was time to submit his initial report to The Man Upstairs.

He hit "send," then set his laptop on the passenger seat and enjoyed the evening and the rest of his meal while listening to Angelica and her kids chatter. They mostly conversed in English, occasionally Spanish. Skull was fluent in both, so it didn't matter. When they said anything of particular note, he added it to his spreadsheet.

Fifteen minutes later, his phone rang. He recognized the number as his client. That was fast. He crumpled his empty wrapper and answered.

"Good evening, sir." Skull's presentation was always professional, especially for The Man. As a rule, most of Skull's clients were abysmally petty in their complaints—ex-lovers, business agreements gone bad—and their plans for revenge were woefully unsophisticated.

Not The Man. His plot unfolded like the movements of a sonata—first the introduction, furious as a storm; then the slow and careful exposition, which was where Skull felt they were now; and finally the recapitulation, which he could hardly wait to witness.

Of course, Skull only ever heard a few bars of the entire composition, like living in the apartment next door to the maestro, listening to his creations through the wall. But what he heard stilled his soul in absolute worship. No doubt, this would be the most sophisticated job of Skull's career. The Man paid well enough, Skull could consider retiring afterwards. But would he? Or would he continue to pick up crass jobs, vainly hoping one of them would reach the same highs as this?

"I've received your report," The Man said. "I have a favor to ask of you."

"Name it."

He did.

The burger turned sour in Skull's stomach. He pinched the phone between his ear and his shoulder and carefully cleaned his fingers on a paper napkin. "Sir, you understand that's outside the bounds of our contract."

"Yes, I do. I wouldn't ask if I weren't in such a bind. I've canceled my contract with Weber, and I won't have Baron Hackett's services again for a few weeks."

"With all due respect, sir, can this wait a few weeks?"

"I'm afraid not. I've already waited far longer than is optimal. Everything hangs on bringing Angelica back to Lake Geneva as quickly as possible."

Skull glanced across the street at Angelica and her sons, ignorant of the two men discussing their fates over the phone. "We could accomplish that with far less risk if you permitted me to complete my surveillance. One mistake could ruin months of work."

"I understand. However, at this point, I'm afraid we have no other option than to move as soon as the opportunity presents itself."

"If you insist. But that's still not something you should rely on me for. It's outside my skill set, and if I reveal myself, I'll be useless to you as a tail."

"Skull. Once this job's done, I'll no longer require you to tail Angelica or anyone in her circle, unless I *want* her to know she's being followed."

"You'd leave yourself with more options if you contracted someone else. I can recommend three good people off the top of my head in the greater Los Angeles area."

"You understand, the more people I bring into my confidence, the more risk I assume. No, no, Skull. I'd much rather it was you."

Skull rolled his head uncomfortably. He was used to putting his foot down with unreasonable clients, but until now, he had never considered The Man unreasonable. Skull flourished as the man in the shadows, the one who saw all, yet went unseen.

"I understand your hesitation," The Man went on. "Let me be clear, I'm asking for no bloodshed. Far from it. And if you'll permit, I'll say only one more word on the subject, and if that doesn't move you, I'll let it go."

Skull sighed. "Go on."

The Man let the silence linger between them, then uttered the one word he'd promised. "Rosie."

Skull's blood ran cold. Involuntarily, his eye went to the tattoo on his left forearm—the skull with the rose blooming from the crack in the bone.

So, The Man knew. About the one occasion on which Skull had bloodied his hands. Well, wasn't that a flex? This whole time, The Man had never needed an intelligence expert; he merely hired Skull because he *could*. No doubt it offered him extra security, distancing himself from his own dirty deeds.

Skull licked lips suddenly gone dry. "Should I interpret that as a threat, sir?"

"I'd prefer you didn't. In fact, I should hope you'd take it as a compliment. You see, I learned long ago the fine art of delegation; letting you focus on what you're good at permits me to focus on what I'm good at. I think it speaks volumes of your skill that I choose to rely on you."

"Then why are you asking me to do something I'm not good at?"

"*Au contraire*," said The Man. "You're *very* good at this. Rosie proves it. You got away with your deed."

Yes, but he very nearly hadn't. At every moment, the threat of a life sentence—or worse, a death sentence—had hung over his head.

"You're afraid," The Man went on. "You're afraid of your own strength. I'm asking you to spread your wings. Shed your fear. Be everything you were born to be. You flirt with the darkness inside you, but refuse to let it blossom."

Skull ground his teeth and shook his head. "You're wrong. I am not Bud Weber." Sweat broke across his brow. Why? The sun was going down, and the evening breeze through his open windows was cool.

"Bud Weber? Hardly. I would say you're far better. You appreciate the finer points, the details, the intricacies. You understand that everything I'm working towards is so much more vast than a hit job here and there." He paused, as if to give Skull room to think. "It's such a small thing I'm asking of you. No blood. No real harm done. I'd like you to deliver a message for me, that's all."

Skull sighed, closing his eyes, and when he did, he saw Rosie. So beautiful. So sweet. Everything he'd thought he ever wanted in a woman. He saw the way she looked at him, confused, betrayed, moments before she collapsed, moments after he struck her on the skull with an alto flute. *His* alto flute. And yet he'd managed to pin the murder on her father, the orchestral conductor, thanks to the wealth of information he had on the man. Skull had always found people so fascinating...

He'd also sworn he'd never bloody his hands again. But... The Man's task didn't involve bloodshed. It did involve furthering the Plan. Listening to the sonata unfold, for just a few more bars...

"When?" he asked.

"Good, good," The Man said, his voice filled with approval. "At your earliest opportunity. There'll be a bonus in it for you."

"That's appreciated, sir. I'll report to you as soon as it's done."

"Excellent. Good luck."

They hung up. Skull stared at his phone, then gazed across the street at Angelica and her sons.

No blood. Right. There'd better not be.

# CHAPTER TWENTY-SEVEN

# KAYDON

Twelve-year-old Kaydon craned his neck as the soccer ball sailed clean over his head, clean over the top of the goal net, and clean over the hedge into the neighbor's yard.

He closed his eyes and sighed. "For the millionth time, Mason, the Belgrades' yard is not the goal."

But Mason, nine, was already doing cartwheels, falling all over himself in the grass, and getting up to run loops. "Goooaaal!" he yelled, and followed it up with several victory whoops.

Kaydon shook his head and pushed through the gap in the hedge into the neighbor's front yard. The only reason the gap existed was because Mason kept launching balls that direction. Fortunately, the crabby old couple next door hadn't discovered it yet.

Kaydon scanned the yard, dark except for the light pouring from the Belgrades' picture windows. Through the glass, he noticed Mrs. Belgrade sitting with her feet up in front of their big-screen TV. But instead of watching the show, she looked like she was working on her laptop, glasses perched on the end of her nose. Mr. Belgrade was filling a tumbler at the wet bar, his rings and his Rolex watch glinting.

Kaydon finally spotted a splash of white—their ball—nestled in the middle of a fern bush. He dashed through the shadows and grabbed the ball. Two fronds were broken off the fern. Those would require an explanation later. But that was tomorrow's problem. For now, he'd yell at Mason for kicking the ball into the Belgrades' yard. On purpose. Again.

The ball under his arm, Kaydon pushed back through the hedge. To his surprise, Mason wasn't doing cartwheels anymore. Bits of grass stuck in his shaggy black hair, he stood on the edge of their own yard, facing a mid-sized black SUV that had pulled up to the curb. He was apparently talking through the open passenger window to the driver. With the headlights in Kaydon's eyes, he couldn't make out who it was. But the guy's voice sounded angry, and Mason was actually standing still, slowly shredding a clump of grass, his head bowed but his eyes on the man in the car.

Kaydon ran up beside his brother and stared through the open window, catching the end of the driver's tirade.

"If we've told you once, we've told you a thousand times. Keep out of our yard."

Mason nodded sheepishly and dropped tatters of his shredded grass.

But Kaydon frowned. "You're not Mr. Belgrade." Their crabby old neighbor was at home. He'd just seen him through the window.

The man's eyes—dark, hawk-like—shifted to Kaydon. "I'm his son, Adam."

"Oh." Kaydon had seen Adam Belgrade once or twice. Didn't he have dark gray hair, though? Not a sleek undercut with dark brown highlights. Wasn't Adam Belgrade heavier? And... nicer? He sure as heck didn't remember him having all those tattoos...

"How many times have you been in our yard tonight?" the man who definitely wasn't Adam Belgrade demanded.

Mason twisted the grass in his fingers. "A lo-o-ot?" He dragged it out, as if he weren't really sure.

Kaydon rolled his eyes. Of all the times to be honest...

"How many times?" the man asked again.

"Twi-i-ice?"

Kaydon frowned at his brother. Did he really have no idea just how many times he'd kicked the ball over the hedge? Or had he finally found the wisdom in lying?

"What did you break this time?"

"Nothi-i-ing?"

Kaydon thought about the bent fronds on the fern bush but decided not to say anything. The guy actually looked really mad—whoever he was. Maybe Kaydon should go get their mom...

The man drummed his fingers on the steering wheel. "All right. You know what?" He grabbed the door latch, got out of the car, and rounded the hood. Kaydon and Mason edged backward as he came closer. But he grabbed the handle on the rear door and swung it open. "Get in the car. I'm taking you next door, and we'll have a look. I find *anything* broken, and I'm calling the cops."

Mason's brown skin went ashy.

Kaydon shook his head. "We're not supposed to ride with strangers."

The man flipped a palm. "I'm your neighbor. We live in a gated community. Get in the car."

Something writhed in Kaydon's belly like a snake. He put a hand on Mason's shoulder and started to pull him back toward the house.

The man reached under his untucked shirt. His hand came back pointing a gun.

Kaydon froze, forcing Mason to a stop, as well.

The man held the weapon near his hip, between himself and the still-open door. The only way to see it was if you were looking right at it, like Kaydon and Mason were.

The man's voice shook, as did his gun hand. Under the street-lights, his face had gone colorless. "It's real—do you understand me?"

The boys nodded.

The man shifted the gun to Mason and his eyes to Kaydon. "I will shoot your brother first, and then you, if you do not get in this car."

The snake in Kaydon's belly turned into a rock. It was the only thing he felt. The rest of his body went completely numb. He stared at the gun, pointed at his brother, and for a moment, he thought he was dreaming. He had dreams like this nowadays, but they mostly involved diving underwater, swimming down, down, down, grabbing at the rope tying his dad, trying to save him from drowning, while his dad thrashed and struggled.

And every night, he never saved him in time.

He pulled Mason closer. Now that Dad was gone, he needed to keep his brother safe. His mom, too. That was his job now.

There'd been a police officer who talked about this in school once—what to do if someone pointed a gun at you and told you to get into a car. He'd said to run, hadn't he? He said it was hard to hit a moving target. But if you got in the car, you'd probably run out of options.

Meaning you'd end up dead.

Kaydon tightened his grip on his brother's shoulder and got ready to yell at him to run.

"Wait," the man said, beads of sweat breaking out on his fore-head. "I work for the man who killed your dad."

Kaydon froze and narrowed his eyes. This guy knew who killed their dad?

The man shook his head. "I'm not supposed to hurt you, and I don't want to. But I have my orders. I need you to come with me. Just for a little while. And then I'll let you go home. I promise."

Kaydon tried to read the man's face, but the shadows were too sharp. They hid his eyes. "You'll tell me who killed my dad?" It was all his mother wanted. Wasn't that why she'd gone to Wisconsin this summer?

"Yes," the man said. "I swear it. That's why I'm here. But I need you to come with me."

Kaydon thought it over. "Take me. Leave my brother."

Mason stared up at him, close-mouthed but wide-eyed.

The man shook his head. "It has to be both of you. I have my orders."

Kaydon chewed his lip. "You'll tell us who killed our dad?"

"Yes."

"And you'll bring us home afterwards?"

"You can go home as soon as it's done."

Kaydon took a deep breath. His mom would never agree to this, and she would probably be right. But he could find the answers she wanted so badly. The answers *he* wanted so badly.

And the guy looked genuinely scared. Stupid as it sounded, Kaydon believed that he didn't really want to hurt them. That he'd bring them home, like he promised.

He clamped his jaws together, dropped the ball and herded Mason toward the car. As soon as he did, the man lowered his gun, justifying in Kaydon's mind that maybe he was making the right decision.

He whispered in Mason's ear. "Do exactly what I say."

Mason nodded and crawled into the back seat.

Kaydon followed him with a sinking feeling. When did Mason ever do what he said?

The man closed the door behind them.

# CHAPTER TWENTY-EIGHT

# ANGELICA

Angelica pushed open the glass door to the front yard. "Kaydon! Mason! Time to come in!"

In the glow of the street lamp, she saw the goal net and the soccer ball, abandoned in the grass, the boys nowhere to be seen.

Barefoot, Angelica walked down the steps into the cool grass and rounded the house to the sloping backyard. The water feature poured over flat rocks into the swimming pool. Squirt guns and pool noodles lay scattered over the brick patio. She picked them up and put them in the plastic bin where they belonged, then scanned the yard.

"Kaydon? Mason? I made sopaipillas!" She felt like she was bribing them—which she was. They never wanted to come in for bed.

Angelica planted her hands on her hips and turned a slow circle. The yard was empty. Silent. A thread of fear began to weave its way up her spine.

It had been weeks since Roland Markham had been attacked. All had been quiet since then, and she'd finally convinced herself she was just paranoid. She and her boys were fine. Lake Geneva was thousands of miles away. Whatever terrible things were happening, they were confined to a small town in Wisconsin.

She entered the basement through the walk-out patio doors; maybe the boys had come in already and she hadn't noticed. But the playroom was abandoned, light sabers and RC cars littering the floor, a pair of Xbox controllers lying in front of a set of bean bags.

Her pace quickening, she scoured the rest of the house, all three floors, the bedrooms, the bathrooms. Finally, she grabbed her phone off the kitchen counter. Dialed. Hugged herself tightly while the phone rang.

"Hey, Angie," her neighbor said.

"Jessie, are Kaydon and Mason at your house?"

"I don't think so. Hang on." Jessie's voice was muffled as she called. "Bryce! Are the Read boys up there with you?"

Angelica could just make out Bryce's reply, shouted in the background. "No."

She closed her eyes. Her heart pounded harder. Her hands shook. It was hard to keep the phone next to her ear. *It's okay. They're okay. Keep calling the neighbors...*

"They're not here, Angie," Jessie reported. "They're not at home?"

"No." She waved her hand. "It's fine. I'll try the Stanleys'. Maybe they're playing with Zak and Kaysi."

"Mmmm..." Jessie's tone was doubtful. "They haven't been to the Stanleys' in ages. Not since Zak and Kaysi started high school. I guess they're 'too cool' to hang out with our kids anymore."

It was true. But Angelica shrugged. "I'll try anyway. Just in case."

"Of course. Call me back when you find them, okay? I'll let you know if they show up here."

"Thank you."

Angelica hung up. She called the Stanleys. Then the Murdochs. Then the Perrys. Jessie checked in again. When she heard the boys were still missing, she promised to head straight over. Angelica started to call neighbors she didn't even know very well, rechecking every corner of the house and yard while she held her cell phone to her ear. With each call, her stomach roiled worse and worse, and the truth slowly dawned.

The boys were gone.

Angelica was pacing the living room, wracking her brain for where to look next, when Jessie rapped on the glass of the front door, then let herself in and kicked off her flip-flops on the rug.

"Any news?" she asked. Her narrow face looked even longer than usual, her green eyes intense with worry, her dark red bob hanging in straight lines to her shoulders.

"No." Tears pricked Angelica's eyes.

Jessie pulled her into a hug. "Tim's driving around the neighborhood, looking for them."

Her neighbors' generosity was overwhelming. Angelica finally just broke down and cried.

Jessie stepped back and looked at her. "Have you called your parents?"

Angelica wiped her eyes, careful of her mascara—then realized what she was doing. God damn it, why did she care about *mascara*? She pushed the heels of her hands into her sockets. "No," she answered.

Her friend's practical gaze sized her up in a moment and apparently concluded—correctly—that Angelica was a wreck.

"I'll call them." Jessie loosed the phone from Angelica's limp hand, then steered her toward the sofa and pushed her down into the white leather upholstery. "How about the police?" she asked, her fingers tapping the screen. "Have you called them?"

"The police?" Angelica muttered.

She stared over the glass coffee table to the chair where, two months ago, a female police detective with a long, dark brown ponytail had sat and offered cold condolences on her husband's death.

Afterwards, and just as coldly, she had informed Angelica that the love of her life was a criminal. With the precision of a surgeon, Monica Steele had cut out even the beautiful memories Angelica had of Will—the last thing she could cling to—and thrown them in the dirt.

The image in Angelica's mind spoke—knees crossed, leather portfolio hanging carelessly in one hand over the edge of her chair, opposite fingers resting casually against her chin and cheek. "*Yeah, sucks that your husband was murdered. By the way, he was an asshole.*"

And then her mind accepted what her soul had been screaming at her all along: That if Wade Erickson had lured and murdered her husband, he could just as easily have taken her children.

The life drained out of Angelica's soul.

Jessie's thumbs paused on the phone screen. "Angie?" She repeated her earlier question. "Have you called the police?"

Angelica stared into a void, where everything was meaningless, except for one thought. She forced it through lips made of stone.

"No police."

Jessie dropped her chin and raised her eyebrows.

# Chapter Twenty-Nine

# KAYDON

In the back seat of the stranger's car, Kaydon kept thinking how weird it was that Mason wasn't yelling random ideas at the top of his lungs, or bouncing in his chair, or poking him in the arm just to be annoying. Instead, Mason sat with his hands on the thighs of his cargo shorts, his eyes wide, his whole body trembling.

Kaydon slid his hand across the center of the back seat, reaching for his brother. They hadn't held hands in a really long time, 'cause they were both too old for that stuff. But instead of fighting him off, Mason grabbed his fingers and held on tight.

The stranger had put his gun back in his belt, but Kaydon could see the sweat beading on the side of his face and the back of his neck. As he gripped the steering wheel, the muscles in his arms were tense. Kaydon found himself staring at the tattooed image of a skull with a crack in the temple, a rose blooming from the fracture. It made his stomach churn. Why was this guy wearing a picture of something so beautiful coming out of something so dark and scary?

He shifted his eyes away, out the window. He should pay attention to where they were, just in case the stranger *didn't* take them home and Kaydon had to figure it out himself. As he watched headlights and taillights swarm around them, he felt as if he should know where they were, but he couldn't even think how long they'd been in the car or what direction they'd taken out of the gate at the head of their neighborhood. It was all a blank.

Panic began to rise from his belly to his throat—until he realized what so many cars going so fast meant. There were four lanes, and he could see the ocean to his right. They were on the highway—the only one. The Pacific Coast Highway. They were driving toward LA, or maybe one of the suburbs.

He knew where he was. The thought brought a degree of comfort. Pushed the panic back down. It was just like driving to visit Abuela and Abuelo. Right? After all, the stranger had promised to bring them home when this was done. They couldn't be going far.

He took a deep breath, like Abuelo had told him to do if he woke up from another nightmare about his dad. After several breaths, his stomach felt quieter. He glanced at the stranger again. The guy was still really nervous, the muscles in his jaw and neck strung tight. Maybe he didn't have a grandfather who taught him what to do when he was scared.

Kaydon screwed up his courage and opened his mouth. "Where are you taking us?"

The man's gaze flicked from the road to the dash to the views out the windows. His voice was low, tense, distracted. "I don't know. Anywhere."

Heat rose to Kaydon's face, anger pushing out the fear. "You don't even know where you're going? Then why'd you take us?"

"Because, I need you to deliver a message to your mom."

"You could have given it to us in our front yard. What's the message?"

The man glanced up to the rearview mirror, meeting Kaydon's eyes in the reflection. "This is the message."

Kaydon frowned. What did—?

Then he got it. This man was proving he knew how to get to their family. He was proving he could hurt them any time he wanted. Kaydon kicked himself. He never should have agreed to get in the car. He should have done a better job keeping Mason safe. Their mom would be worried sick.

"You'll take us home again, right?" Kaydon asked. "You promised."

"Don't worry. You're going home. Soon as this is done. You just do as you're told, and I promise you won't get hurt." He looked into the mirror again. "Okay? I don't want to hurt you."

Kaydon stared hard into his reflected gaze. "You stick to your end of the deal, we'll stick to ours."

The man thought about that, then nodded. "Deal." He focused again on the road. "You're a good businessman."

"I got it from my dad." Kaydon wasn't sure what made him say it. But his spine felt a little straighter, a little longer, just from thinking about his dad. Maybe this guy's boss had killed his father—but he couldn't kill everything his father had meant to him.

The man glanced at him in the mirror again, then nodded, his expression one of respect.

They stayed on the PCH so long, Kaydon began to lose track of time again. When he heard the blinker, he realized they were finally getting off. He scrambled to find street signs. Santa Monica... Ocean Avenue...

Only a few minutes off the highway, the driver pulled into the empty bus lane just outside the big, blue arch over the ramp to the Santa Monica Pier. Mason let go of Kaydon's hand and pushed himself up in his seat to see. His eyes reflected street lights, traffic lights, carnival lights. The ramp dropped down the hillside to the vast wooden pier, which stretched across the beach and out into the ocean. At the end of the pier, the amusement park lit up the night in ever-changing colors, the towering Ferris wheel dominating the view.

The driver looked into the mirror again. "You know where you are?"

Kaydon nodded. "Santa Monica Pier. So, this is where we were going?"

"Sure. Why not?"

Mason's eyes were still on the Ferris wheel. "Are we going on the rides?"

The man only snorted, then turned in his seat and looked at the boys. "Listen carefully. This part is important. There's something you need to tell your mom. I need you to say it to her exactly as I say it to you. Understand?"

Kaydon nodded.

"'Are you enjoying playing detective?'"

Kaydon frowned. "That's the message?"

"Yes. Remember, you have to give it to her word-for-word. You got that? Say it back to me."

"'Are you enjoying playing detective?'"

The man's eyes shifted to Mason. "You, too."

He made both boys repeat it correctly several times, then nodded to himself and sank back into his seat with something like a sigh, something like a shudder. "Okay. Good. That's it."

Kaydon frowned. "No, it isn't. You promised you'd tell us who killed our dad."

The driver looked at him again over his shoulder. "You really want to know? He's powerful. He gets people killed. He gets little boys kidnapped."

Kaydon thought it over. But really, what was the danger in knowing? He was already stuck in a stranger's back seat. He squared his jaw and decided the risks he and Mason had already taken tonight weren't going to be for nothing. "It's *all* I want to know."

The driver nodded. His eyes went quiet, as if he were looking inside himself and not the upholstery of the seat next to him. "They call him The Man Upstairs."

Kaydon frowned and pulled his chin back into his neck. "God?"

The driver laughed. "Yeah. Sure. He may as well be. He knows everything. He knows things you thought were dead and buried. That's why he's dangerous. He knows where your pressure points are—where to lean on you. How to get you to do things you never thought you'd do."

Kaydon stared into his hollow eyes and wondered if he was talking about himself right now—about kidnapping him and Mason. He was clearly scared about it. But somehow, The Man Upstairs had gotten him to do it anyway.

"All right," the driver said, "that's it. I've told you. Now get out of the car."

Kaydon stared at him, confused. "You said you'd take us home."

The man gave half a smile. His eyes narrowed like a clever fox. "I said you could go home when it was over. I never said how you were going to get there."

Kaydon's mouth dropped open in shock. "We're at the Santa Monica Pier. That's an hour from our house."

He glanced through the window, and his eyes landed on a man who slouched cross-legged against the trunk of a towering palm tree. His jeans were torn at the knees, and a scraggly beard nearly obscured his face—except for his eyes, unnaturally blue. They stared straight back at Kaydon, and yet were as hollow and empty as if they saw nothing at all.

Chilly fear slithered up Kaydon's spine. He glanced over the rest of the park that stretched up the shoreline away from the pier. He spotted another man curled up on a bench, a plastic garbage bag tucked under his chin like a blanket. A woman with long gray hair pushed a shopping cart down the sidewalk, her eyes on the ground.

Kaydon blinked. Was this what this place was like after dark? The stranger *couldn't* leave them here.

But the driver shrugged and shook his head. "You never read the fine print."

Kaydon felt the barb. *You're not a smart businessman like your dad,* he seemed to say. *You're just a dumb kid.* Devastated, all Kaydon could do was gape. How were he and Mason going to get home?

The man nodded toward the pier. "There's a police substation down there. You give me fifteen minutes to put distance between me and you, and then you go find one of those cops and ask them to take you home."

Kaydon found his anger again, and after that, his tongue. "You're not leaving us here."

The man shook his head. "Sorry kid. I know your mom. I've been watching her for weeks. I'm not showing my face anywhere near her." He reached into his belt and pulled out the gun, aiming it between Kaydon's eyes. "Now get out of my car."

Fear spiking up his spine, Kaydon grabbed his brother's hand and shoved open the door. They tumbled out onto the sidewalk together. No sooner had their feet touched the pavement than the black SUV pulled onto Ocean Avenue and sped away. The force of its own acceleration slammed the rear door shut. Kaydon strained to catch the license plate, but only got the first two numbers.

He glanced at the man slouched against the palm. His blue eyes stared back, but he didn't move from his spot. So Kaydon turned to Mason. "You okay?"

Mason nodded. He glanced at the homeless people, then looked down the ramp toward the pier. The carnival lights danced in his eyes again and his nostrils seemed to twitch at the lingering smells of hot dogs and burgers and buttered popcorn. "So-o-o... do you think the arcade's still open?"

Kaydon did a double take. Had his brother already put the whole thing behind him? They'd just been *kidnapped.* They'd been abandoned in a park full of people potentially even more desperate than the man they'd just escaped. He grabbed Mason's arm and tugged him toward the blue arch, away from the park and its nighttime residents. "We're not going to the arcade. We're going to find a policeman."

"It hasn't been fifteen minutes."

"Yeah." Kaydon clamped his jaw tight, rethinking every minute they'd spent with the man with the skull tattoo and deciding he hated him. "He didn't tell us who killed our dad, either."

CHAPTER THIRTY

# ANGELICA

Angelica's home was chaos. At one point, she had written a list of friends and neighbors to call and assigned sets of names to every family member. But the list had gotten scrambled, and increasingly her siblings, her cousins, her mamá, and her tía and tío were talking to the same people—sometimes one after the other—while others were going uncontacted. Meanwhile, she'd heard nothing from those family members assigned to search the neighborhood and surrounding areas by car and by foot.

She wanted to believe the holy mess in front of her was like dinner after midnight mass on *Nochebuena*—Christmas Eve—the table getting set and tamales pulled from the steamer at just the right moment and a glass of wine in the hand of every adult—all as if by magic, no one knowing exactly how everything was accomplished.

But as she scrolled through the tablet where she was keeping her notes, all she saw was a smattering of disjointed information, gaps in logic, and fractured storylines.

Betty Murdoch swore she had seen the boys playing soccer in the front yard at nine fifteen. But Angelica had started looking for them at nine, so that couldn't be correct.

Wes Belgrade thought he'd glimpsed someone sneaking through his yard after dark, but he hadn't been sure, and he couldn't say what time that had been.

For as long as a week or more, the Stanleys had seen a car rolling slowly down the street around the same time of day every day, but Kevin was confident it was a blue sedan while Sarah said it was a black SUV.

And Mrs. Perry helpfully reported that a very nice young man had been over to fix a broken gas meter a week or two ago.

Angelica scowled at that last note. Why had she even bothered to type it in? She deleted it.

Pacing across the terracotta tiles of her dining room floor, Angelica scrunched her hair with her free hand, as if doing so would help her think. But the words blurred together on her tablet. Her boys were out there somewhere. It had been close to two hours since she'd realized they were missing. They could be anywhere. They could be hurt. They could be...

They could be dead like their father.

As the possibility crossed her mind, the room began to tilt and spin. The voices of a dozen people became muffled. Meaningless.

A headline flashed across her memory. *Lakeside Resident Attacked in Home.*

"*I'm fine, my dear,*" Roland's words echoed next. "*It was just a bit of a mishap.*"

But it wasn't. Roland had been attacked just after she had left Lake Geneva. Just after Monica Steele realized that the two of them had been speaking together.

Angelica stared through the open patio doors to the yard beyond, the pool area dimly lit by solar lights stuck in the ground. Her vision went to static, and suddenly she was staring through a service window at the Lake Geneva PD into the dispatch center. Police Chief Wade Erickson—terrifyingly tall when he was more than a name in the newspapers—stared back, his eyes crystalline blue, piercing, all-knowing. He saw her. He knew what she was doing in Lake Geneva. Thanks to Monica Steele... he even knew where she lived.

Where to find Kaydon and Mason.

"Angelica...? Angelica...?" A voice nagged at the outskirts of her mind.

The train of her thoughts broke like an iron cable snapping in two, the razored ends slicing the air. She rounded on whoever had interrupted. "¿Qué?" she demanded, her voice grating on the word.

Her Tía Carolina looked up at her, trembling from her ballet flats to the gray-and-black bun pinned to the top of her head. She gripped a tray piled with small, square pastries, dusted with powdered sugar and glistening with honey. The sopapillas. Tía

Carolina had re-heated them. They steamed, filling the air with the scent of warm, deep-fried comfort.

Carolina's voice trembled. "You should eat, *mija.*"

Angelica leaned forward. "Why would I be hungry? Why?"

Before Carolina could respond, Angelica struck the bottom of the tray, throwing it from her tía's hands. Sopapillas exploded across the dining room. The metal tray clattered to the floor, bouncing from one edge to another, filling the room with a noise like a cymbal. Carolina raised her hands to her face, as if afraid of what Angelica might do next.

When the tray finally reverberated to a stop, the room was deathly silent. Her breath heaving, Angelica glanced from one family member to another. Her mamá, seated at the dining room table next to her papá, stared with eyes as severe as her ruby red lipstick and nails. Angelica's brother Rafael stood in the kitchen, one hand in the pocket of his faded jeans, the other holding his phone, his thumb hovering mid-dial, his eyes wide and confused. Her Tío Alberto leaned on his forearms on the island counter, his thick palms pressed together, his lips silent about Angelica's outburst against his wife, but his eyes showing sadness and disapproval. Angelica's neighbor Jessie stood in a corner of the dining room, her narrow fingers pressed to her mouth, her eyelids fluttering.

The only one not looking at Angelica was her papá. Javier sat at the dining room table, his wife's arm strung through the crook of his elbow. Silver head bowed, he stared at his hands, folded in front of him.

Angelica bit a trembling lip. The fact that her papá wouldn't so much as look at her hurt worse than the stares from every other person in the room.

Angelica turned again to her tía. Carolina's initial shock had faded away, replaced by a hint of uncertainty. But behind that wall of fear, armloads of sympathy were clearly desperate to break through, begging to be accepted by her *sobrina*, like always.

"I'm sorry," Angelica said under her breath.

Carolina offered a watery smile and nodded. She wrung her stubby fingers as if to wash away the incident.

Angelica cast her eyes around the room, meeting the looks from her family. "I'm sorry," she said again, this time to everyone.

Heads nodded. Eyes dropped downward in embarrassment. Tío Alberto set his jaw and scratched behind his ear.

Angelica's papá didn't stir. But she saw a muscle in his temple flinch. The thought that she'd disappointed him shamed her.

Jessie took a hesitating step forward with an awkward bob of her head. Seeing that no one stopped her for intruding, she cupped a hand on the back of Angelica's shoulder.

"Angie," she said, "honey. Listen to me. You're stressed. Of course you are. It's been—what?—two hours since the boys went missing? You and I both know they're not hiding for the fun of it. It's unfathomable they just ran away—not with everything happening. They wouldn't do that. And they were fine this afternoon when they were at my place." She fluttered a hand to make her point. "They were happy. They were fine."

Angelica flexed her jaw in response to Jessie's babbling. Did her neighbor really think she didn't *know* that her sons had been kidnapped?

Jessie held both of Angelica's arms and dipped her head to look her in the eyes. "Angie? Angie. Their father was *murdered*."

Angelica wanted to snap back that she was well aware of the fact. But she bit her teeth together. After upsetting her tía, she would let her friend make her point, even though, by now, she knew what Jessie was getting at.

Jessie glanced uncertainly around the room. "Now, I know there's nothing your family won't take on together." She flashed them all a smile, as if hopeful they'd accept her words as a compliment, rather than take offense to the point she was ever-so-slowly working toward. She turned again to Angelica. "But, honey, this whole thing might just be a little over your heads. You have to think of the boys. You have to bring them home by whatever means necessary."

She looked for a moment like she might go on. Like she might finally put words to her implications. But at the last moment, she decided against it. She sucked in her breath and bit her lower lip, awaiting a response—or even a backlash—from Angelica or her family.

Angelica worked her jaw again. Jessie didn't have to say it out loud. Her neighbor thought they should call the police.

Angelica found her gaze fixed on the pendant hanging from a chain around Jessie's neck—an American flag made of sterling silver, red rubies for the stripes, diamonds for the field of stars. Angelica's vision blurred. Her family had come to this country believing beautiful promises. That they'd find a better life here. That they could work hard and enjoy the rewards of their labors.

In such an idyllic world, things like peace and security could be taken for granted. Couldn't they?

Why was she learning at every turn that safety was merely an illusion?

In fact, why had she married Will in the first place? Because she loved him? Or had she seen how the system here really worked? That safety and freedom were only guaranteed if you were wealthy? If you were white?

Tears streaming down her face, she closed her eyes. No, that couldn't have been the reason. She tried to picture Will. Tried to hear the sound of his voice. Tried to remember the feel of his heartbeat against her ear.

But all she could feel was the sting of his betrayal. The fact that he had built an entire life with her—and never told her who he really was.

All she could see was Monica Steele sitting jauntily in a white leather chair, cocking a smile, shaking her head. "*You poor bastard. He really played you hard, didn't he?*"

All she could see were Wade Erickson's blue eyes—piercing through her skin into her soul, damning her for interfering with his personal vendetta, his power trip.

Angelica opened her eyes. She could barely make out her neighbor's face past her own tears. "No police," she whispered through clenched teeth. In the silence of the room, the words carried to every corner.

Jessie stared at her dumbfounded, as if sensing for the first time the distance that secretly existed between them. They lived only two houses away—but in two different worlds. Her hand dropped away from Angelica's shoulder.

Only a few short months ago, Angelica might have agreed with her neighbor that any differences between them were superficial. But perhaps she had been wrong. Perhaps she had been naïve. Perhaps to join Will and his world had been to betray her family, their struggles, their story—everything they had come from.

She'd been trying so hard to forgive Will this entire time. Perhaps what she really needed was to forget him.

"*Mija.*" Her father's voice—low, warm, unflinching—cut through the tension in the room the way a spring rain overwhelmed the desert. He had barely spoken all evening. Barely moved. As if the thought that his grandsons were gone had completely drained him. Tonight, the smiles were nowhere to be found. The laughter. The little opportunities to make someone else grin. It was unsettling—frightening—to see him so serious.

He lifted his head and met her gaze. The scar Angelica knew so well cut across his left brow, parting the eyebrow in two halves, continuing in a furrowed scar across his left cheekbone. His right eye stared at her, a warm brown in color; the left, a cloudy white.

"You are afraid," he said, the observation simple, the undertones vast. "You are afraid to call the police."

The muscles in Angelica's neck and jaw were painfully tense. "And you aren't?" she demanded. How could he, of all people, ask such a question?

"Sí," he said. "I am afraid. And because of this fear..." He paused and filled his lungs slowly, as if the act were old, forgotten, rusty. "I have not breathed freely in twenty years."

Teeth clamped in silence, Angelica returned her father's gaze, focusing her attention on his good eye, like she always did. After all this time, she barely noticed the one that had been blinded, the pupil and iris a bluish cloud. She tried to tell herself it was because she was used to the scars that marred her father's face.

But she realized now that her excuse was a lie. To look at her father's scars was to look into a past that terrified her to this day. A past she had fought valiantly—and successfully, she thought—to put behind her.

It had been a case of mistaken identity, the police insisted. Her father had been in the wrong place at the wrong time. He had matched the description of their suspect, a man who had held up a convenience store at gunpoint. But even so, Javier shouldn't have resisted arrest, they said.

And so the scars he lived with were his own fault, when he had simply been afraid? Confused? Was that what she was supposed to believe?

The memories of that day boiled back to the surface—that day a policeman had forced her father into submission with a baton; that day she had seen her father in the hospital, his face bandaged, swollen, marred to the point she didn't recognize him. The tears spilled down her cheeks. She'd been young, just a teenager. Her mind had been shattered. It had gotten trapped in a single, circling question she could never answer.

How could one human being *do* that to another? To her papá? Didn't they know how good he was? How much she loved him?

"Tell me, Papá," Angelica said, her voice trembling with fury, "have you learned to forgive them for what they did to you?"

His gaze dropped to his clasped hands as he turned her words over in his mind. Then he smiled, sat up a little straighter, and shrugged. "No."

The too-simple confession, the smile that had unexpectedly returned to her father's face, broke the tension in the room just enough to prompt a low laugh from several of the family members. Others just smiled sadly.

Angelica had no laughter. She waited for her father to go on.

His face turned thoughtful, and he looked at his hand, turning it over. "When I was a boy, my older brother was stung by a bee." He tapped the back of his hand, indicating the place.

Tío Alberto humphed, apparently remembering.

"And he cri-i-ied." Javier dragged the word out comedically, smiling and shaking his head.

The family laughed, especially Angelica's cousins.

"And that was how," Javier continued, "I became afraid of bees." He looked up at Angelica. "I was afraid they would sting me, so I ran from them. I ran from them for years and years and years—and do you know? In all that time, I was never stung by a bee." The smile lit his face again. "But Dios mío, did I run a lot."

Angelica listened, head tilted but arms folded, wondering what this had to do with her boys. There was no better storyteller in the family, but this time, her father's story only made her stomach roil. They didn't have time for this. They needed to find Kaydon and Mason.

But her father went on, his pace unaltered. "And one day—I was so tired—and I stopped running. And I asked myself what exactly I was afraid of." He shrugged his shoulders, lifted his eyebrows. "And I didn't know. I had a lot of pictures in my head of angry, evil bees chasing me down and stinging me until I couldn't see, couldn't breathe. But where did those pictures even come from? I didn't know. And then I saw how I didn't actually know the first thing about bees. I didn't know the first thing about the thing I feared. I just had a bunch of scary ideas all built up in my head. I feared..." He paused, searching for words. Then, appearing to find them, he leaned forward and tapped the fingers of one hand on the table, his gaze fixed on Angelica. "I feared what I did not understand."

Angelica's eyes narrowed, her thoughts beginning to follow his.

"And so," he went on, "to make the fear go away, I decided to understand. I read books. I used to look at anything with black and yellow stripes as if they were all the same. But then I learned that there's bees and there's wasps and there's bumblebees. Bees make honey and they make plants grow, and they're hard workers, and if they sting you, they give their life to do it, because they're just protecting their home, their colony, their *familia*. Wasps?" He scowled. "Wasps are assholes."

More laughter. This time, it sounded a little freer, a little easier. Even Angelica allowed a fraction of a smile.

"They're like cats," her father said. "They're curious, and they get all up in your business, and then they get angry, because everything is *your* fault." He drove a forefinger into the table. "And they can sting you again and again, and suffer no consequences. And then there's bumblebees." He chuckled. "It's a good name for them. They run into you, and then they go end-over-end, and they bumble somewhere else." He traced a drunken path through the air with his finger.

Angelica could sense the entire room listening, giving her father their full attention; hungry, perhaps, for whatever wisdom he was unraveling for them, one thread at a time. Angelica pressed her lips together and waited, as well.

"Once I understood bees and their crazy relatives..." He shrugged. "I wasn't so afraid anymore. You respect the honeybee. You let the wasp have your soda so you can eat your burrito. And bumblebees?" He humphed another laugh and waved a hand. "You drive them home. They're drunk."

More laughter.

Javier grinned and tilted his head, taking Angelica in. "What I understand, I no longer fear. And what I fear..." His smile wavered. He pulled in a deep breath. "What I fear, perhaps I do not understand."

A knot formed in Angelica's stomach. What applied so simply to insects couldn't possibly apply to men. To monsters.

"And do you know?" he went on. "The man who hurt me, he didn't understand me, either." Shaking his head in disbelief, he held his hands like an open book on the table. "He didn't even... *try*. And I cannot make him understand me, even though that's all I want. Even though, to this day, I wake up in the dead of the night, and I storm up and down my own house, and I say to him, 'Why won't you stop what you're doing and listen to me?' That's all I want. I want him to *listen* to me. To understand. But I can't, because—" He searched for words again, stuttering, then finally shrugged and made a lop-sided grin. "—good news, he's not actually in my house in the dead of the night."

The family laughed out loud this time. Angelica tried to hold it back, and failed. Biting her lips together, she looked at the floor.

Javier let his gaze drift downward again. "You asked me if I have learned to forgive him. No. I haven't. I'm afraid of him." He shrugged. "I don't understand him. And I don't want to, because the fear is so strong." His face contorted with the words, and Angelica could see in his gaze the depths of that fear. "But fear is exhausting. And so... I pray." He blinked and lifted his eyes upward, as if he might find the Blessed Virgin above the ceiling fan. The crucifix on his chest caught a glint of the light. "I ask for the fear to go away. I ask forgiveness for the anger. I ask, if it isn't too much, if I can one day feel what it's like to breathe again. And God answers in my heart, 'When you learn to understand, you will be free of the fear.' And I told God—"

Javier paused, choking up. He had to fight to get his next words out.

"I told God, 'You give us back our boys, and I will learn to understand. I will walk toward the thing I fear. I will try to understand the man who hurt me—whether or not he is man enough to understand *me*. I swear it.'" He clamped his jaw, stared at the table, and crossed himself, as if sealing a pact.

A hot tear trickled down Angelica's cheek. Tossing her hair, she stared toward the darkened skylights overhead and turned over her father's words. This whole time, investigating her husband's murder, had she allowed the past to cloud her judgment? Had her suspicions turned toward a cop because she feared cops altogether? She didn't want to think so. But now, she was more confused than ever.

In one thing, her father was unequivocally right: Fear was exhausting. And Jessie was right, too; her family was getting nowhere on their own.

Angelica moved toward her father and knelt on the floor beside him. He turned in his chair to face her, and she took both of his hands in hers, studying them. "I'm not good like you, Papá," she confessed. "I don't know how to be a saint like you."

He slipped his hand under her chin and lifted her face so they were looking at one another. Pride radiating from every wrinkle of his face, he whispered to her, *"Tú eres mi ángel. Mi Angelica."*

She smiled through her tears. She didn't feel like an angel; but she would accept that she was her papá's. His blood ran through her veins. Perhaps she could find strength in that.

"You will find your way," he promised. Then he breathed deeply. "We will all find our way."

Angelica nodded.

He shifted his jaw and glanced down uncertainly. "Should we call?" he asked, his voice low.

She stared into her father's eyes—the brown one deep and full of love, the white one shallow, clouded, and unseeing, reminding Angelica daily of hurt, of fear, of confusion. Exhausted, she nodded, then touched her forehead to her father's chest. He bowed his head over hers, smoothing her hair.

Her mamá stirred uncomfortably, then patted Angelica's back and pushed her chair away from the table. She harrumphed importantly—the way she did when there was work to be done. "Well, then, somebody better pick up the phone. Carolina, I'll clean up that mess. You find something else to warm up."

Angelica laughed into her father's shirt. Food. It was her tía and her mother's cure for everything. That and Vicks VapoRub.

The house came to life again, her tía and her mother bustling, Jessie scuttling to the broom closet to help, other family members feeling at liberty to stir once again. In the middle of it all, the phone rang on the island counter. Rafael, standing the closest, picked it up.

"Read residence," he said.

A voice hummed on the other end. Rafael's spine straightened. He clutched the phone in both hands. "Where are they?"

Electrified, Angelica lifted her head. She stared at her brother, listening, and quit breathing.

"Yes. Yes," Rafael said into the phone. "We'll be right there. Thank you." He hung up and turned to Angelica. "That was the Santa Monica Police. They found the boys."

A sob exploded from her chest. Her father held her close and rocked her. Past the flood of her own tears, she barely heard him choke out, "*Gracias, Jesús. Gracias.*"

# CHAPTER THIRTY-ONE

# ANGELICA

Angelica pushed through the front doors of the Santa Monica Police Department and spilled into the tiled lobby, Rafael and her parents on her heels. Her eyes scanned the room—the glass window, similar to the one at the Lake Geneva PD; the night dispatcher listening to her headset...

Then her eyes zeroed in on a pair of boys—*her boys*—sitting in two metal chairs. Swinging their feet, they spoke with a tall, thin man, thirty-something, dressed in a dark blue uniform with a bulky vest under his shirt. He stood over the boys, his weight casually shifted to one leg, his hands resting on a thick belt. It sounded like they were talking about soccer... the World Cup... their favorite teams...

At the sound of the door, Kaydon and Mason turned their heads. Their eyes locked with Angelica's, and they sprang from their chairs.

"Mom!" Mason yelled.

Their feet pummeled the tiles.

Angelica dropped to her knees, arms wide, hands reaching, heart pounding. Rafael and her parents made various exclamations, but their words became irrelevant, distant noise. She grabbed her sons and held them tight, her fingers tangled in their hair, one head gold, the other black. They smelled like cold night air and exhaust fumes and a hint of Febreze, like a car that had been professionally cleaned, and inexplicably, they smelled like buttered popcorn.

The police officer was mumbling something to Rafael which, for the moment, was unintelligible and unimportant—he found them walking down the Santa Monica Pier—a detective was on his way to interview them—words, words, words. Her sons were hugging her back, their faces buried in her neck. They were talking, too, the sounds barely registering. *It's okay, Mom. Don't cry.* Her family's hands rested on her shoulders, on her sons' shoulders. None of it mattered. Her sons were here, and they were alive, and she had them in her arms.

Slowly, as if someone had turned a dial, the room returned to normal volume, normal color, normal time. Angelica finally pulled back and examined Kaydon and Mason from head to toe. "Are you okay? Are you hurt?" There had to be something wrong. Something for her to fix. Some way to comfort her sons. To comfort herself.

"We're fine," Kaydon replied.

Angelica looked into his eyes, blue like his dad's, as serious as if he were chairing one of his father's board meetings. He'd grown up so fast since his father died, as if, at the age of twelve, he felt the family were his responsibility now. Who had told him such a thing? Where was her little boy?

"What happened?" she demanded.

"We were playing in the front yard," Mason volunteered. His brown eyes were round, like a drawing from a comic book. And yet, he spoke with animation, as if he'd been on some adventure no more dangerous than the third-grade books on the shelf in his room. "We were gonna come in for bed on time, honest."

Angelica shut her eyes and shook Mason's shoulder. "*What happened?*" she demanded again, terror overtaking patience for her son's ramblings. She immediately regretted raising her voice, even as she felt relief for letting the emotion vent.

"It was my fault," Kaydon volunteered.

Angelica looked askance at her older son. He often stepped forward to shield his brother, sometimes claiming far more fault than was his due. But this time, she felt compelled to believe him. The seriousness—the maturity—in his tone unnerved her.

"Tell me," was all she said.

He met her eye as he spoke. "A man in a car pretended to be Adam Belgrade. He acted like he was mad at us for letting the ball go over the hedge again." He shook his head. "But he didn't look like Adam Belgrade. And then he told us to get in the car so we could look at the yard together and see if we broke anything."

Horror shot through Angelica's bloodstream. Her grip tightened on the boys' arms. "You got in his car?"

Kaydon shook his head. "We weren't going to. We were going to run back to the house. But then..." He blinked, as if some unpleasant memory had flashed across his mind, momentarily interrupting the flow of his words. "He... he pulled out a gun—"

Angelica's mamá drew a sharp gasp. From the corner of her eye, Angelica saw her papá put an arm around her shoulders.

Kaydon went on. "And he... he pointed it at Mason, and..." Kaydon blinked again and shook his head in a tiny, sharp gesture, as if his brain were literally fritzing out.

Angelica couldn't stand to see what tonight had done to her son. She laid a finger on his lips. "Shhh, that's enough for now. You can tell me the rest later."

Tears gathered in Kaydon's eyes. "I couldn't let him hurt Mason."

She pulled him close. "It's okay, *mijo*. You're safe. You're home." She rocked him back and forth as she held him tight.

As if to give her a moment with her sons, the policeman offered his hand to Rafael. "I'm Officer Damon, by the way. They found me on the Santa Monica Pier."

Angelica's brother shook the man's hand as if the cop were any other client at his graphic art studio—and the casualness Rafael managed to put into the gesture was a wonder to her. "Rafael Morales," he said.

Damon tilted his head toward her brother. "And you must be...?"

"Their uncle," Rafael said. Then he motioned to Javier and Martina. "These are their grandparents."

Damon turned to Angelica's father—and the officer's glance went first to Javier's scarred eye. The cop's own eyes narrowed, sharpened, questioned. Angelica thought he studied Javier a beat longer than necessary.

The fear crept into her father's face again, and he shrank away, though the movement was almost imperceptible.

Angelica bristled. She knew her father's scar made him look like some desperate character. Well, who's fault was that, anyway? Granted, Damon didn't know the history. He didn't know his own people were responsible for how her father looked now.

A moment later, the policeman shifted his attention to the normal eye, and in response to whatever he saw there, he seemed to shelve his questions. He extended his hand. "Good to meet you, sir."

Javier filled his lungs, then leaned forward and took the man's hand. "Thank you for finding our boys," he said.

The officer assumed a position that looked like the military "parade rest," but with his hands clasped in front, and shrugged. "They found me." Then he squinted and jabbed a thumb at Kaydon and Mason. "So, they really are brothers?"

Angelica wondered if he was aware of the tension he'd unwittingly introduced when looking at her father's scar, and if he was trying to make amends with light conversation.

Javier grinned in response to the question the family received all the time. He nodded at Kaydon. "That one takes after his father."

The cop shook his head. "Son of a gun. I thought they were pulling my leg." His face turned more serious, and he looked at Javier again, seeming to make an effort to meet his good eye. "They told me about their father, by the way." His gaze shifted to Angelica, who was still kneeling on the floor, and he nodded respectfully. "I'm very sorry for your loss, and that you don't have closure on the case yet."

Angelica breathed, wondering if the officer's politeness in any way made up for the split second in which he'd misjudged her father. She wasn't sure. But she permitted a nod in return.

"When will the detective get here?" Rafael asked.

The cop flicked his wrist, checking his watch. "Any minute. We appreciate you waiting. The faster we get this ball rolling, the faster we can catch the guy who took them. We've already contacted the Malibu PD, the highway patrol—everybody's looking for this guy and the car the boys described."

Rafael nodded. "We appreciate your being so prompt."

"Of course. After what happened to their dad—it sounds like what happened tonight could be connected."

Angelica frowned. *Could be?*

She let it slide and turned to Kaydon. Holding him at arm's length, she smoothed his hair. "*Mijo*, how did you get away?"

"He let us go," Kaydon said.

Angelica scowled in confusion. "Let you go? How? Why?"

"He just dropped us off at the Santa Monica Pier. He told us we were supposed to give you a message."

Angelica looked into his eyes and felt herself begin to tremble. She braced herself, trying not to let Kaydon see it. "A message?"

Breath frozen, she waited to hear what it was that the man who killed her husband wanted her to know.

Mason piped in, as if reciting lines for a school play. "We're supposed to tell you, 'Are you enjoying playing detective?'"

The words echoed back and forth in her head, her mind scrambling to derive meaning from them—if possible, more meaning than the originator of the message had hoped for her to find. Obviously, they were a threat. Her husband's killer knew she was investigating, and he was warning her off. That's why he'd taken her sons. That's why he'd given them back again with the message.

He never would have risked so bold a move if she wasn't on the right trail. Would he?

And those words... *playing detective*? They were belittling of her efforts. They accused her of being a wanna-be. They implied that the speaker knew far more about detective work than she did, and she should keep her nose out of places she didn't belong.

The image of Wade Erickson filled her mind once again—that cool glance he'd given her through the glass window at the Lake Geneva PD. His eyes seemed to read so much while saying so little.

She closed her eyes and bit her lips together, trying to remember her father's advice. Was she allowing her fears to cloud her judgment? Or did she finally—*finally*—have ahold of the truth?

A thick, warm hand rested on her shoulder, and she knew her papá was following her thoughts, too. Though what conclusions he was drawing, she couldn't tell.

"Mom?"

Angelica opened her eyes at the sound of Kaydon's voice. His blue eyes were serious again and all-too-grown-up.

"He told us who killed Dad," he said.

Every atom in her body ceased vibrating. Her father's hand tightened on her shoulder.

"Who?" she asked, barely able to force out the sound.

"His boss. He called him The Man Upstairs."

Angelica's nostrils flared in disappointment. A code name. Nothing more. But still, even that information might be useful.

"Do you know who that is?" Kaydon asked, his voice almost daring to be hopeful.

Angelica shook her head. "No, *mijo*. But I will find out. I promise you." She pulled him toward her and touched his forehead to hers.

"I promise, this will never happen again. You'll be safe, do you understand? No one will ever hurt us again."

# THURSDAY AUGUST 14, 2014

# CHAPTER THIRTY-TWO

# TOMMY

My Navy-issued haversack slung over my shoulder, I made my way past the Riviera and under the corner breezeways, marveling that walking was now something I could do unaided. What I had taken for granted my entire life was now a novelty to be wondered at and appreciated, as if the past two months were somehow more real than the foregoing seventy-six years.

I emerged onto the pier, and my eyes went immediately to the bow of the Mailboat, where Bailey often waited for me, her feet swinging lazily over the water.

She wasn't there.

My steps slowed. I told myself I'd simply arrived first. We both trended early to work, and on your average summer's morning, I was as likely to beat her as she was me.

All the same, I couldn't help thinking how empty the Mailboat felt without her there.

I breathed deeply and squared my shoulders. She'd be here soon enough. Most likely, she'd arrive before Noah Cadigan, whose schedule was perfectly reliable, though ten minutes behind the true time. In the interim, there would be opportunity for Bailey and me to finally sit down and get our overdue talk out of the way—or at least to get it started.

I shifted my attention to the Mailboat's windshield, as if peering into the boat's eyes. Unblinking, serene, she stared back, and I could almost be convinced that she knew I was here. That she was glad to see me returned.

I stepped forward and rested a hand on the frame that encased the windshield. Layers of anxiety I hadn't known I was harboring broke their moor lines and drifted lake-ward, and for the first time in nearly two months, I felt as if I could fill my lungs fully again.

Nancy Erickson was right; the Mailboat was my answer to everything. At what point had this boat and her routine ever failed to be there for me? After Jason vanished, she remained unaltered. After my wife passed, she was unchanged.

And now, after forty-eight years, every fiber of wood, every scrap of steel, every layer of paint, was as much a part of me as it was of the boat. When her engines rumbled to life, my heart beat. When she dipped through the waves, I breathed. So long as she stayed afloat, so did I. The days of my life were counted by the number of times I'd circumnavigated this lake. This boat had been a part of me for most of my years, and I had missed her.

Pulling my keys from my pocket, I moved further down the boat and unlocked the doors, then secured the latches in the floor that held them in the open position regardless of wind and wave. As I leaned down, the ache in my side remained manageable; I grimaced but didn't groan.

Placing a hand on the door for aid, I rose, then took in the length of the boat: the black-and-white photos of bye-gone days that hung in the stern, the white plastic chairs lined up in stacks, the row of windows along the port side that gave a panoramic view of the northwest shore of Geneva Bay, the water smooth as glass.

Lastly, I turned to my helm and my captain's chair, both facing me as if awaiting my return. The stool for the mail jumper sat beside and yet a little removed from them, alone, somehow profoundly empty.

I shifted my jaw. Bailey would be here soon.

Placing my haversack on the floor, I stepped up to the helm and scanned my workspace. Nothing on the front counter was quite where it belonged—the cancellation stamp, the stash of rubber bands, the cheat sheet correlating every shoreside address to a lakeside pier number. The binder containing the script for the tour narration seemed to be missing altogether, and that was a problem of no small proportion. Not every mail jumper had it fully memorized, including Bailey.

I began to put everything back where it belonged, keeping a particular lookout for the binder, when my eye fell on something even more incongruous.

A small round hole in the lip of the counter, filled in with sawdust and glue and sanded to a smooth finish.

*Lead hit wood with a sickening, splintering sound, as if the slab of pine had pulled in a sharp gasp.*

Adrenaline spiked through my body, tensing every muscle. My eyes transfixed on the patch in the wood, and the scar in my side throbbed. It was the pain—and the uncanny fear that it might spiral into something unbearable—that triggered the sweat breaking across my back in waves.

I told myself to look away, to look at anything else, and instead, I stared as if mesmerized, as if I were hungry for the sight and for every dark memory attached to it: Bailey leaning over me crying... The blood on her hands... The pain in my side intensifying into something excruciating...

That day felt more real than the past two months, which felt more real than the previous seventy-six years. And in that light, what was the point in looking away? Of giving my attention to anything else?

"Tommy!" A voice barked my name, and footsteps pounded toward me down the pier.

My head snapped up and my heart hammered. My legs tensed as if to run.

It was Noah Cadigan sprinting toward the boat, smiling brilliantly, his blond hair catching the breeze created by his own movement. Behind him trailed an entire cadre of delegates from the cruise line—mail jumpers, other boat captains and crew, office staff. Robb Landis, my boss, maneuvered a flight of navy and white balloons down the pier.

Some part of my brain was still toying with the dark memories, the one day of my life that was real. I had no idea what this crowd of merrymakers was, or why they were closing in on me.

Noah grabbed the door frame, swung through, and gave me a cheery salute—left-handed. "Welcome back, Captain!"

He hopped aside, and our co-workers filtered in, descending on me with exclamations and open arms. I forced a smile, even while my heart was still pounding out of my chest. I fought the urge to throw up my hands and fend them all off, to beg for a moment I needed but couldn't explain. My mind was doing somersaults, and my chest was constricting, making it hard to breathe.

Somehow, at the last moment, old habits kicked in and carried the day. I accepted hugs and made what I hoped were appropriate comments in response to well wishes.

With the fraction of conscious thought available to me, I scanned the crowd for Bailey.

She wasn't there.

And now, whenever she *did* choose to put in her appearance, there'd be no chance for us to talk.

Well. Today was going just fine.

# Chapter Thirty-Three

# BAILEY

They told me to come early for Tommy's welcome-back party, so I came late instead.

By the time I arrived, the boat was full, and Noah Cadigan and Celeste Jones were tying balloons to every other window frame all the way down the inside, and everyone was talking and laughing like it was a party boat.

Past-me would have scanned the lower deck, the upper deck, and all the piers until I knew exactly where Tommy was. The minute I knew, everything would be right with my world.

Today, I noticed a whole press of people up front by the helm, and I really didn't bother to verify whether Tommy was buried in the middle of it.

The minute I was through the door, I threw my backpack into a chair, grabbed the window cleaner out of the closet by the bathrooms, and headed to the rear deck to start cleaning the windows.

# CHAPTER THIRTY-FOUR

# TOMMY

Brian was candidly enumerating a list of minor repairs I'd likely have to enact on the Mailboat this winter, when I saw her—a petite girl with wavy brown hair making for the aft, her head hanging, her eyes on the floor.

My heart pounded and my throat went tight. Bailey.

I was hemmed in by people, by conversations criss-crossing me like netting. I was just devising an escape route, when I saw Bailey sling her backpack into a chair, open the cleaning closet, and grab the window spray. She headed to the aft deck and began scrubbing windows as if a celebration weren't in full swing. As if she were the last maroonee on a desert island, carrying on her shipmates' traditions, surrounded by nothing but their ghosts.

My shoulders sank in response to the snub. She wouldn't so much as look at me.

# Chapter Thirty-Five

# NOAH

Noah scooted around a cluster of chatting co-workers, trying not to tangle anyone with the balloons Robb had handed off to him. He tied another balloon to a window frame, making sure to alternate navy and white down the length of the boat.

Needing somewhere to share his grin, he glanced across the aisle to Celeste, who was securing balloons along the opposite side. She'd tried out for mail jumper once, and decided flinging herself at a moving boat wasn't her jam. But she often ran concessions on the Mailboat during regular tours, and she'd worked with Tommy often enough in that role. Noah laughed as the balloons tried to stick to her curly African hair with static and she beat them off.

He moved to another window, tapping his foot to a soundtrack inside his head. He would have put the music on the sound system, but there were too many people crowded around the front of the boat, talking to Tommy. No matter; everyone was happy, the lively chatter created a rhythm of its own, and when the party dispersed and he, Tommy, and Bailey started prepping the boat for the tour, he could plug in the music to keep the good vibes going.

He couldn't begin to say how great it was to have Tommy back. Brian was swell and all, but it wasn't the same. Noah looked forward to knocking into fewer piers and being dumped into the lake less often. Brian had a little too much confidence in Noah's speed, and had put him in the water more than once.

Besides, Tommy was *the* Mailboat captain. This was his forty-eighth summer working the tour. Noah was positive Tommy was angling for fifty—a full half-century delivering the mail. It would have been a little devastating if he'd fallen short of that landmark.

But all of that paled in comparison to the comfort of knowing bad things weren't going to win out in the end. Whoever had tried to take Tommy away from them had lost. The family that was everyone here at the cruise line had won. Everything was right with the world again.

Noah turned to see if he'd missed putting a balloon anywhere—and was hit by the breeze of Bailey Johnson dashing by. She snapped open the cleaning closet, grabbed a bottle of window spray as if she meant to choke it, and flew up the rear stairs two at a time.

Noah stared after her, his balloons drifting in the wind Bailey had created.

Was she... Was she seriously cleaning the windows? Now? In the middle of Tommy's party? Robb Landis had said they were only going to pop in, decorate the place, welcome Tommy back, and pop out again so the Mailboat crew could get the boat ready for the tour.

Noah looked across the aisle to Celeste, whose own balloons were gradually drifting toward the ceiling behind Bailey's wake. Wide-eyed, Celeste jerked her head toward Bailey and shifted a flabbergasted brow. Her expression asked the obvious question: *What is she doing?*

Noah shrugged, then glanced toward Tommy. The captain was conversing with Brian, but his eyes flickered more than once toward the aft, and when they did, they looked profoundly sad.

Good. Noah wasn't the only one who thought this was weird. Celeste and Tommy did, too. But... what was he supposed to do about it?

He looked one more time at Bailey—yep, she was legit cleaning the windows—then went back to tying balloons.

He tried to think through everything that had happened this summer. His mind rewound to the day the Mailboat had returned from the repair docks after the shooting. Bailey had been closed off that day, silent, on the verge of tears every other second. Noah didn't have to stretch his brain to understand why. She'd been the one who found Tommy hurt; by all accounts, she'd saved his life.

Noah couldn't imagine what that must have been like. Personally, he would have lost his mind.

So, why did it look like Bailey was ignoring Tommy now? It made no sense. It was unfathomable she didn't care about him. *Everybody* loved Tommy. And if she didn't care, she wouldn't have been such a wreck after he got hurt.

The soundtrack in Noah's head had vanished. The imagined rhythm had left his feet. Something really weird was going on here. He was going to keep an eye open and see if he could piece together what it was.

# CHAPTER THIRTY-SIX

# TOMMY

Thirty minutes after the cavalry had invaded, I was actively shutting down conversations and chasing people off the boat, insisting I was delighted by the whole thing, but that my crew and I had work to do. As people sneaked in final hugs and words of joy, my eyes sought out Bailey, who was cleaning windows as if to set a speed record. Time was dwindling before the arrival of the tourists and the departure of any opportunity to talk.

I hadn't worked this hard to get back to the Mailboat—back to her—only to be balked at the final step.

I at last emptied the boat of extraneous co-workers, except for Noah, my other scheduled mail jumper for the day, and Celeste, whom Robb had instructed to stay and help after the time lost to the gala.

Noah commuted between the concessions stand on the aft deck and the store room in the office barge, which berthed at the next pier over. So, on and off, he was out from underfoot.

But Celeste was tidying up on the main deck—finishing the organization of the front counter, then sweeping and mopping the floor. The only good thing I could say was that she'd somehow found the binder with the script.

Growling under my breath, I grabbed the engine checklist and made for the hatch in the middle of the deck that covered the engine compartment. I eased onto one knee and lifted the hatch. Bailey was down to her last few windows, a mere yard away from me, but with her back to me—so close, yet a world apart.

Outside, the ramp to the aft deck rumbled as Noah trundled an empty handcart down. He glanced inside the boat, and his eyes seemed to briefly take in Bailey and me. Then he looked to Celeste.

"Yo, Celeste," he called through the open doors.

"Yo?" she replied.

"Can you give me a hand with the snack bar? We're out of, like, everything."

"Yo," she repeated. She parked her mop in the bucket, leaning the handle against the wall, then stepped off the boat and followed Noah up the pier toward the office.

One hand on my knee, the other on the open hatch, I closed my eyes and sighed. At last.

I glanced up at Bailey. She blasted each pane with a single squirt, then swiped it with a sheet of paper towel, leaving streaks. I swallowed the urge to comment on her shoddy workmanship and licked my lips. Now that the moment was here, where did I even start?

"Bailey? How are you?"

"Fine," she said, her back to me, and sprayed the next window.

Fine? What kind of answer was that, after the summer we'd been through? Why was she ignoring me? I set my jaw. "We need to talk."

She shrugged. "Then talk."

I shook my head in disbelief. "Will you at least do the courtesy of looking at me?" An uncomfortable thought in the back of my head remembered arguments with her father when he was a teenager. This felt eerily similar.

She whirled, arms crossed, the spray bottle in one hand and the wad of paper towel in the other. She looked at me—her eyes an Arctic smolder. The sight took me aback. I'd never dreamed her capable of such cold fury.

At my stunned silence, she shrugged impatiently. "Well? You gonna talk, or what?"

I tried to remember the last time we'd spoken, back at the hospital. My memory of the incident that had put me there and the early days that followed were still blurry. What had been her demeanor? Not this, surly. But neither could I name precisely what it was—how she had even responded when I told her we were related. When was the last time she had been happy in my presence? Before I was shot? What had I done between then and now to earn her distaste?

My joints and the wound in my side protested that I couldn't maintain an entire conversation on my knee. Beyond that, I didn't like the way she was looking down at me. Yet I feared that by rising, I'd reveal just how uncomfortable I was with the current arrangement. And so, by the laws of convoluted logic, it was the greater part of dignity to remain where I was and suffer the consequences.

I took a steadying breath. "Why haven't you returned my calls?"

She shrugged. "Why should I?"

I frowned and shook my head. "Because I'm your grandfather."

"Yeah? Big whoop."

That cut. For the past two months, all I'd wanted to know was how she felt about having me for a grandfather. Now I knew. And it was everything I feared. "You, ah... You're not interested in your biological family." It was a statement, not a question.

"Why should I be? They've never been interested in *me*."

I clapped my hand on the edge of the hatch, frustrated. "I have been calling you for weeks. You never answered."

She spread her arms in a dramatic shrug. "What do you want from me?"

"What kind of a question is that?" I gestured vaguely in the direction of the Geneva Bar and Grill. "I want that animal who calls himself a foster dad to quit sending my granddaughter to me covered in bruises."

She scowled and shook her head. "No. There's always *something*. Everyone who ever took me in always wanted *something* out of me. Maybe I make them feel good about themselves 'cuz they took in a poor orphan girl and now they're the local charitable celebrity. Or maybe they couldn't have their own kids, and now it's *my* job to love them like I was theirs, when they're just gonna dump me in a few months anyway. Or maybe they like having me 'cuz they can boss me around and I have to *eat it*." She bit the word out, and it echoed in the empty boat.

I shook my head. "I don't want anything from you."

She squared her jaw. "Look me in the eyes and say that again."

I prepared to repeat myself, then pulled up short, the inquisition of her gaze demanding I examine my own motives. Was there anything she'd seen in me that I hadn't?

I wanted her to accept me. If she did, it might suggest I wasn't an utter failure as a parent. It might suggest everything Jason had done—committing crimes, killing a man, forsaking his mother and me—wasn't ultimately my own fault.

It might suggest his death wasn't my fault.

I clamped my mouth shut. She'd known all along there was something I wanted out of her. I stared at her, but couldn't answer her question. Not with honesty.

Something in her eyes shattered, and I realized I'd failed her test—and in the same moment, broken her heart.

Water gathered in her eyes. "Yeah, that's what I thought." She threw down the cleaning supplies, grabbed her backpack out of a nearby chair, and slung it over her shoulder. "Have a nice life." She walked off the boat.

"Bailey—" I pushed to my feet, but as I did so, the wound in my side twinged. I clenched my jaw and kept going. But by the time I reached the door, she was breezing far ahead of me down the pier. I braced a hand on the frame and watched helplessly. I'd never be able to catch up with her.

Have a nice life? What was that supposed to mean? Where was she going?

As I stood watching after her, the discomfort in my side slowly intensified, until I couldn't ignore it. My hand went to the wound, and I leaned harder on the frame, bowing my head and breathing through the pain. I'd worked hard to get back to work—back to Bailey—and for what? To chase her away?

Was this the curse I was doomed to repeat—to chase my own children away?

# CHAPTER THIRTY-SEVEN

# BAILEY

I stormed down the pier, clutching the strap of my backpack in a death grip, the tears gathering in my eyes. The words I'd just dished up soured on my tongue like the chunks that stick in your mouth after you puke.

I only glanced back once—and when I did, Tommy was leaning in the doorway of the Mailboat with an arm across his belly, head bowed, looking like he was in a lot of pain.

My God, if he was still that hurt, why was he even coming to work?

I looked where I was going again, but my eyes were so blurry, I almost walked into a brick pillar. Yeah, I probably deserved that. I dodged the pillar and broke into a run, putting distance between me and the Mailboat, the tears falling hot and messy.

When had I become such an asshole? Why was I being so mean to him?

The answer was obvious. To make him leave me.

I'd always known it was better to lose him sooner rather than later. I already knew keeping him wasn't an option. Keeping the people I loved never had been.

I couldn't stand it anymore—the infantile longing just to have someone care about me. The fury over feeling that way. Every other kid my age was looking forward to busting out on their own, getting their first car, going on school trips, finally stretching their own wings.

Not me. I was trapped forever looking backwards. Still wanting someone to sing me to sleep. Knowing that every song, once started, ended in a blood-curdling scream. My own—as I watched yet another person who'd promised to watch over me vanish. How many horrors could one girl endure in a lifetime?

I ran through the archways of the Riviera and past the fountain with the angel on top. Where was I even going? I wasn't sure. All I knew was that I couldn't stay here anymore, where the world promised everything and gave me nothing.

Running the mail with Tommy used to be the carefree days. Now the carefree days were when I had run the mail without him.

And it dawned on me I was never coming back.

# CHAPTER THIRTY-EIGHT

# TOMMY

Wheels clattered across the pier. I lifted my head and saw Noah and Celeste pushing a pair of hand carts, piled with snacks and beverages. The kids chatted together. Smiled. Laughed. Until they looked toward the boat and saw me, leaning in the doorway. I had no idea what they observed in my demeanor, my expression, but the banter instantly died on their lips.

I swallowed the last of the pain and straightened, letting my right hand fall to my side. The other remained on the doorframe, as if seeking both physical and moral support from the Mailboat. I spoke before the kids could voice the questions building in their eyes.

"Noah, I need you to do me a favor."

He parked the hand cart and brushed his hands together, his eyes wide with concern. "Yes, sir?"

"Go to the post office and see if Bailey's there."

A frown creased his brows. "What?"

It was a bizarre request. Sorting the mail was Bailey's next task. With the windows done, where else would she be?

The fact that I had to ask someone to spy on my own grand-daughter rankled me. But I went on. "And if she isn't there, I need you to gather the mail." Regardless what had passed between Bailey and me, we had a job to do: mail to deliver and a tour to run. As captain, it was my duty to see that those things were accomplished.

Noah blinked. "Yes, sir. But what about—?" He motioned to the hand carts.

I turned to Celeste. "I need you to stay and fill concessions until we know whether or not Noah's sorting mail. If Bailey—" My voice caught on her name. On the way she had walked out on me. My hand gripped the doorframe. "If Bailey's not running the tour today, I need you to come with and watch the concessions stand." I turned to Noah, "You'd be making all the mail deliveries."

Noah nodded, his face a wondering blank. "Yes, sir." He turned and began to head in the direction of the post office, then stopped and looked to me again. "Sir?"

I couldn't stand being *sir'ed* that many times in a row, but I let it pass. I had worse problems to hand. "Yes?"

He paused, head tilted, his eyes trying to push into mine. "Is everything okay?"

"No," I replied bluntly, squaring my chin. "I think it's safe to say it isn't." I gave him a hard stare that warned against further unwelcome questions.

He broke eye contact, nodded, and hurried away.

As if to avoid treatment of like kind, Celeste grabbed the handles of her cart and pushed it up the ramp to the aft deck.

My personal space cleared, I returned to the engine compartment and eased down the short ladder. Darkness enveloped me in the crawlspace, along with a stifling warmth, thick with the smell of oil. Running tours all day every day, the engines never fully cooled. Not until winter, until another season was dead and gone.

Alone in the heart of the boat, it occurred to me that I was actively chasing away my crew. Distancing them from me. I should have been ashamed that I was okay with that.

Forcing myself to focus, I breathed deeply and started my way down the engine checklist.

Fifteen minutes later, my phone vibrated. I pulled it from the holder on my belt and read the incoming text. It was from Noah. It was brief.

*I'm sorting mail.*

I grated out a sigh, casting my eyes around the small compartment. She was really gone, then. She'd walked out. It angered me that my own granddaughter would shirk her responsibilities in such a fashion. Granted, I hadn't had the opportunity to raise her better. And yet, I liked to think I'd passed along better genes to her than that. After all, in forty-eight years, the only thing that had successfully kept me from my duties was a bullet to the gut.

I holstered my phone and completed the final items on the checklist. I needed to inform Celeste that she was staying for the duration of the tour. Worse, I had to inform Robb that one of his staff was now abruptly off the schedule.

Based on Bailey's last words... there was no reason to believe she would be back. Like her father seventeen years ago, she was simply gone.

## CHAPTER THIRTY-NINE

# ROLAND

The marble interior of Roland's house reverberated with the echoes of his doorbell. With a book under one arm, he made his way down the grand stair to the foyer while tucking stray wisps of yellowed tissue paper back into a shoe box. A month after the break-in, he was still sorting through the museum that was his house. Well, he'd promised Monica Steele, had he not?

While he'd still found nothing worth breaking in for, his home had never been better organized—thanks to the book that had become his guiding light. It had been a gift from a friend in the publishing business. When said gentleman heard the daunting task ahead of Roland, he forwarded an advance reader copy of the book scheduled to release later that fall: *The Life-Changing Magic of Tidying Up*. It had proved a faithful companion. Roland foresaw its young Japanese author making the *New York Times* Bestseller list, if he didn't miss his mark.

Arriving at his back door—the one that faced the street, not the lake—he pulled open the heavy wooden slab. To his surprise, Angelica Read stood on the portico.

"Why, Ange—"

She clapped one hand over his mouth, planted the other on his chest, and pushed him backwards into the foyer. Then she kicked the door shut behind her and released him, putting a finger to her lips.

"Ange—" he tried again.

"Shush!" She grabbed him by the arm, steered him into the kitchen, and from there—straight into the pantry. She closed the door, plunging them into blackness. "Are you okay?" she asked in a breathless whisper.

Roland felt the wall for the light switch and clicked it on. "I'm fine. How are you?"

"Is your house bugged?"

Roland raised his eyebrows, surprised, but shook his head and replied with simplicity. "No."

She frowned as if confused by the speed and certainty of his response. "How can you be sure?"

"I've just finished turning it upside down." He pulled his book out from under his arm and eyed its cover. "I believe the final chapter is a congratulations on confirming that your home cannot possibly be bugged." He motioned with the shoe box to the shelving. "How do you like the labels, by the way? I got one of those little printers—"

Angelica closed her eyes and her fists. "¡Cállate!" she yelled, her voice echoing off jars of pickles and cans of tomato soup.

Roland wasn't sure what the word meant, but it was clearly intended to shut him up. He closed his mouth.

Angelica opened her eyes. They glittered with tears. "Someone kidnapped my boys."

Roland stared at her, his mouth falling open.

Before he could speak, she lifted a hand. "They're fine. They're home."

"Shouldn't you be with them?" Roland asked. "Are they safe?"

"Yes. They're with their grandparents. I just—I had to come. I don't know who I can trust. I can't—" She bit her lip and closed her eyes, but not before Roland caught the glimmer of tears. She looked at him again, her brown eyes sincere and pleading. "Please, Roland. I need to talk with you."

# Chapter Forty

# ANGELICA

"The Man Upstairs," Roland mused, pouring two cups of hot tea as he stood by the stove in the island counter, the vast copper hood suspended above him by chains.

Angelica sat at the kitchen table—butcher block—her feet tucked up on her chair as she hugged her knees. Her own skin felt cold to her. Bloodless. "I feel like the answers are so close," she said, her mouth moving woodenly. She shrugged. "They *must* be. Why else would he warn me away? But whoever he is... he's playing with me." She frowned, shaking her head. "He's just playing with me."

Roland twitched his mouth as if in acknowledgment of her words, then crossed the flagstone floor and set a china teacup in front of her, the rim gilded. He sat down across the table from her with his own cup and lifted the lid off a small china bowl. "Sugar?"

She shook her head.

Roland dropped two cubes into his own cup, using the delicate metal tongs. Far from appearing disinterested, his careful motions suggested his mind was hard at work. "You know, there was a day and a time not long past when you were quite sure of yourself. I seem to recall you chided me for not seeing that Wade could have been Bobby's secret partner." He paused, with the lid hovering over the sugar bowl, and met her eyes. "You're questioning your own judgment. Is it because of the conversation with your father?" He set down the lid and swirled his tea with a silver spoon.

Angelica watched his movements, slow and articulated like a well-made watch. Chin on her knees, she sighed. "He says I'm allowing the past to prejudice me."

Roland tapped the spoon on the edge of the cup. "Are you?" The question was so simple, the answer so complicated.

Angelica felt something in the middle of her chest waiver. Falter. "I don't know," she admitted. "I don't know what to think. I don't know what to believe anymore. I don't even know if I can trust my own mind." The sense of instability was growing. Morphing. Engulfing her. Turning to full-on panic. The story she had so carefully researched and pieced together—was that all it was? A story? Was she that desperate to find peace after her husband's murder? Did she secretly crave vengeance for her father's scars? Was she so blinded by terror that she'd lost her ability to reason?

Roland stared at her as if reading her mind. He nodded to her cup. "Why don't you try some of that? You may find it'll help."

Mechanically, Angelica reached for the cup. Lifted it to her lips. Sipped. It tasted of wildflowers, petals, and nectar. It warmed first her tongue, then the back of her throat, then her chest. It seemed to wrap comforting arms around her soul.

She rested the cup on her knees and grinned at Roland. "Chamomile," she guessed.

"Good for what ails you," he playfully intoned. He lifted his own cup to his nose, breathed in the steam, then drank. He settled the teacup back onto its saucer and folded his hands in front of him. "My dear, whatever happens, do not doubt your own mind. Your feelings. Your senses. Without those, what do you have left? Sheer madness. And what good will that do to you and your sons?"

Angelica gave him a half smile and drank more tea.

He shook his head. "No, come what may, you must trust your instincts."

She lifted an eyebrow. "And what do your instincts say about Wade Erickson?"

Roland parted his lips and drew in a small breath. He thought on her words, then turned uncertain eyes on her. "I'm afraid my instincts on the matter may not be of much help. You've observed yourself that I seem capable of holding multiple opinions simultaneously." He chuckled quietly.

Angelica lifted one side of her mouth in a grin. It was true. Roland had never forgiven Wade for killing Bobby—and yet couldn't find it in himself to pin more blame to the man's chest than that.

Drawing a deep breath, she slid her feet to the floor and sat in the chair properly. Despite his own uncertainty, and armed with nothing but a teakettle and a handful of words, Roland had somehow managed to bring peace and clarity to her own mind, which had been nothing but frantic since her boys had gone missing. Coming back to Lake Geneva had been the right decision.

She cradled her teacup in both hands and stared into the golden liquid. "Perhaps my papá is not wrong. But—" She met Roland's blue eyes. "Perhaps neither am I. And in fact, perhaps neither are you."

Roland gave her a questioning look.

She nodded. "Perhaps I need to hold both thoughts, one in each hand, until I find the truth. Erickson *might* be The Man Upstairs. Or I might be judging him too eagerly."

Roland grinned his approval and nodded decisively. "And that, I think, is a very wise way to proceed."

Angelica smiled her appreciation.

"So..." Roland lifted his teacup, blocking his mouth. His eyes darted between Angelica and a corner of the kitchen. "Does this mean you're talking to Monica?" He muttered the question and followed it up with a harrumph to clear his throat.

Angelica scowled. "No." Roland should know that was asking too much too soon.

He shrugged defensively. "Had to ask, had to ask." He sipped his tea with a look of innocence.

Angelica couldn't help smiling at him. Then she breathed deeply and ran a finger along the rim of her china saucer. "I'll think about it."

Roland hoisted his eyebrows, then broke into a grin. "That's more than I could have hoped for."

Angelica nodded. Before she could decide on whether to trust Monica Steele, she wanted to know more. About the woman *and* her boss. The question was merely how to do that.

# CHAPTER FORTY-ONE

# ANGELICA

Angelica rolled her suitcase down the hallway of her hotel, read-ing room numbers. She'd been lucky to find a room at all; the streets of downtown Lake Geneva were filling with some sort of event—a carnival?—and she'd only gotten the room thanks to someone else's cancellation.

When she found the correct door, she parked her suitcase, then reached into her handbag and slid out two items. Her key card—

And a matte black handgun with a simple textured grip.

She understood now why Will had owned this gun. Why he had a concealed carry permit. Why, during their early days of dating and marriage, he had actually carried it everywhere. She'd thought he was paranoid. He was.

So was she now.

She glanced up and down the hall—it was empty—then slid the key card into the lock and threw open the door.

She checked behind the door first, then inside the bathroom, then behind the bed—feeling like some sort of actress on TV. But the gun was real. So were the bullets inside. So were her intentions of never being caught off guard again.

The room was empty. Of course it was. She had told no one where she was staying. Not even Roland.

She went back to the door. Pulled in her suitcase. Threw the deadbolt and slid the chain. She drew the curtains closed so no one could see in through the window. Then she tossed her suitcase onto the bed and unzipped it. Amongst her slacks and blouses sat a spare magazine and a box of 9mm rounds.

Angelica turned her handbag upside down and dumped the contents onto the bed. She needed to downsize to make it easier to slide the gun in and out and to fit the spare magazine. She'd only brought one purse this time—the small white one with the gold buckles. That way, she'd never forget which purse the gun was in. On this trip, her life was more important than having the correct bag for every outfit. She began to sort the contents into two piles, one to keep, and the other to store in her suitcase.

She had thought it was silly, those times Will had taken her to the range, insisting she learn how to shoot. It wasn't silly anymore. Not when the image of Will's casket being unloaded from an airplane was still burned on the inside of her eyelids.

He had dragged her and her sons into this mess. Whatever happened next, she would be prepared. She would keep the gun with her until her work here was done. Until The Man Upstairs was unmasked and brought down.

And then she would go home to her boys.

No matter what, she would go home to her boys.

She tended to keep each of her purses stocked with the essentials: One tube of go-with-anything lipstick, a packet of Kleenex, a twenty-dollar bill, Band-Aids for a pair of boys who could never seem to keep their skin intact. Over time, a random assortment of other items had filtered in. A small notebook. A bottle of hand lotion. And no fewer than three pens, one of which was ridiculously heavy.

She hated clunky pens. How did you even write with them? She chose a sleeker, brushed-metal pen to keep in the purse.

She moved on with her sorting, but found her eye returning to the over-weighted pen. Where had she even acquired it? It wasn't the sort of thing she'd keep.

She picked it up. What was it made of, lead? She screwed the two halves apart to look inside.

A plate of electric circuitry stared back at her, tied to a small, round watch battery.

A bomb was the first thing that sprang to her mind. She cried out, threw the pen down on the bed, and backed away, holding up her hands to shield her face. Had she activated it?

She waited, but nothing happened. Perhaps it wasn't an explosive. But in that case, what was it?

Slowly, she crept forward. Picked up the half of the pen with the electronics. With a flick of her thumbnail, she popped out the battery. Whatever this thing was, it was dead now. She narrowed her eyes on the device. The black and silver pen was sleek, featureless.

Until she looked at the top. There was a tiny divot in the surface. It didn't look stylish enough to be part of the design.

Following a theory, she grabbed her mobile and compared the divot in the pen to the microphone in her phone.

They looked the same.

Ice poured down her back. She needed to tell Roland that a bug could look like an every-day pen. How long had this been in her purse? How many conversations had it overheard? Had someone been listening to her speak with Roland earlier today? Did it merely record audio, or did it transmit it, too? She didn't know electronics well enough to tell.

So she did the next best thing. She screwed the pen back together, took a photo, and used it for a Google image search.

After several minutes of scrolling, she found a match.

According to the website that sold it—advertising it for general note-taking and interview recording—the pen was a voice-activated audio recorder. And it could transmit the audio to your phone via an app, the data traveling over cell signal. There was an option to buy a model that included a GPS tracker—so you would never lose your pen and its data, of course.

Fury built up in Angelica's veins. She set down her phone, grabbed a shoe from her suitcase, and prepared to smash the thing on the floor.

Mid-swing, another idea crossed her mind, and she stopped.

She might have a use for this thing.

# CHAPTER FORTY-TWO

# TOMMY

Noah managed the seventy-odd deliveries without complaint. It probably helped that he had fewer jumps than he would have normally; news of my return had clearly gotten around the lake. I'd never seen so many homeowners lined up on their piers to accept their mail by hand, requiring Noah to merely lean out and pass it off. At any other time, I might have slowed the boat to exchange a word or two with familiar faces. Today, I kept her steady at five knots, smiled, and waved.

Once returned to port, I wagered I was the more tired, between captain and crew. No doubt, Nancy Erickson had been right; I had rushed my recovery to get back to work. After manhandling myself first thing that morning, the lingering tenderness in my side kept me on good behavior the rest of the tour. By the end, I was more than ready to go home.

But before that could happen, I had a distasteful task to get through.

With the passengers disembarked and the boat officially handed over to Brian for the next tour, I made my way to the neighboring pier, where the office was berthed—a barge that housed the ticketing counter, storage, and the entire administrative department.

I walked through the door and found Robb Landis at his desk, his work area cluttered with paperwork, framed photos of several generations running the cruise line, and models of various sailboats and steam yachts.

At the sound of my approach, he looked up and grinned warmly. "Well, ahoy, Captain. How was your first day behind the helm again?"

I rested my hands on the back of the chair that faced his desk, taking some of the weight off my feet and thus some of the discomfort out of my side. As to Robb's question, there was no point idling in the water. "Bailey walked out."

He blinked and shook his head. "Excuse me?"

"She left. Before the tour."

Robb carefully set down his pen and leaned back in his chair. "I'll admit, she was tardy more than once this summer." He wheeled his chair backwards, opened a file cabinet, and removed a manila folder. He flipped it open, scanned the papers, and frowned. "Yeah, that's what I thought. She's due for an official reprimand." He jotted a note, looking none too pleased that it was called for.

My chest fluttered. After everything that had happened this morning, the last thing Bailey needed was a stern talking-to from Robb. That hadn't been my intent.

He leaned back and sighed, puffing his cheeks. "This is so unlike her. What happened today? Why'd she leave?"

I shrugged, rubbing the back of the chair with my fingers. "She's had a rough summer," I said by way of explanation. "I think it just got to be too much for her."

While it was my duty to inform my employer that he was down a crew member, everything else that had transpired this morning was personal and confidential. Bailey had made it clear she found her relationship to me undesirable. I wasn't about to flaunt that information in front of her boss.

Robb looked at me with understanding and nodded. "I'll give her a call."

I drew breath, teeth parted, hesitating, trying to arrive at the right words.

"You think that's a bad idea?" Robb asked.

I exhaled. "It's your decision, obviously, but..." I pictured again the way her eyes had shattered when I failed to answer her question. "I don't think she means to come back."

Robb shifted an eyebrow. "When you say that, do you mean...?" He shrugged. "This summer? Next summer?"

I replayed her last sentiment through my mind. *Have a nice life...*

I squared my shoulders. Shifted weight away from my hands and onto my feet, bearing the sting from the scar. "I came here to inform you of her absence so you could replace her on the schedule."

Robb nodded somberly. "I understand. I'll see what I can do." He shuffled through more papers and unburied a calendar. "A lot of the kids are quitting to get ready for school. I'll get you who I can." He shook his head. "It's a pity. Bailey always worked as late into the season as she could. We really depended on her." He looked up at me. "I'm sorry to hear things aren't going well for her."

I nodded and studied a one-twenty-fourth-scale model of the century-old steamer that berthed next to the Mailboat.

Robb tilted his head searchingly. "Does this have anything to do with...?" He shrugged with his thumbs.

By his lack of words, I understood his meaning. The shooting. Bailey walking onto the boat and finding me hurt. The question raised a lot of memories I didn't care to revive. Eyes looking anywhere but at Robb, I shifted a shoulder. "I don't know."

Well, at least now I was being truthful. I had no idea how much that event had impacted Bailey; whether it could have influenced the hurtful words exchanged this morning. It made no sense, though. I couldn't reconcile the tears I thought I remembered then with the flat hatred she'd offered now.

I filled my lungs. "I should get home. Been on my feet some today."

Robb nodded. "Rest up. Don't worry about all this." He waved his hand over the schedule and Bailey's employee file. "One way or another, I'll get you a second crew member tomorrow."

I nodded, then turned and left the barge.

I'd somehow managed to get through that conversation without revealing more than I was willing. And now, with the schedule crisis addressed, there was only one question left to dominate my mind:

How was I supposed to go on, knowing I had a granddaughter in the world, but that she wanted nothing to do with me?

Well. I'd done it once with her father. Clearly, I could do it again.

Like always, I'd work my routine... until the waves and the passage of time washed away all memory of the pain.

# CHAPTER FORTY-THREE

# RYAN

My hands rested numb on the keyboard at my desk in the report room. The cursor blinked. Blinked. Blinked.

I would have been a dad.

It was testament to my mental density that it had taken the better part of two days for that fact to sink in. I appreciated the notion that Monica would have been a mother. But only now—as I sat typing up a report regarding a break-in at a storage unit—did I realize what that made me.

A dad.

Nothing about our lives would have been the same. We would have hauled all the crap out of the spare room in our house in Madison. We would have painted it in pastel colors, and Monica would have added a bunch of round, bouncy animals by hand, every one an adorable work of art. I would have assembled a crib, and when Monica wasn't looking, I would have painted a poorly-drawn teddy bear in a cop uniform trying to arrest the giraffe. And she would have seen it later and gotten mad, but never gotten around to painting over it.

We would have suddenly found ourselves navigating such exotic purchases as diapers and baby formula, and we would have thrown a child seat in the back of the car. The guys in the detective bureau at the Madison PD would have congratulated me with thumps on the back, and they would have shared tales from the frontlines on the horrors of raising these little bundles of joy.

Would it have been a boy? A girl? Would they have had Monica's looks? Mine? My Uncle Pete's?

And at the end of the day, it wouldn't have mattered. Because at that time in my life, I would have been in no way prepared to be a father. I'd still been full of pranks and hijinks, a full-grown man acting like I graduated high school the day before.

Right down to going out with any pretty girl I felt like.

A shudder raced through my body. I put my elbows on the desk and pressed my hands into my eyes. Thank God the room was empty. I was having a breakdown. My face was wet. I was... My God, I was crying.

I went ahead and let the shudders wrack my body. If Steph Buchanan was watching on the security cameras in the Communication Center, I didn't even care.

This summer, I'd come home to figure out where I'd gone wrong in life. How I'd messed up.

And now I knew.

I'd robbed the only woman I'd ever loved of the one thing she'd truly wanted. And I couldn't envision a world in which she could forgive me.

# CHAPTER FORTY-FOUR

# MONICA

I stood in the doorway of the report room, a cup of coffee in each hand—one for me, one for Ryan. But at the look of frozen devastation on his face, I dared not cross the threshold.

I'd been listening to the radio traffic up in my office, and when I knew he was back at the station, I'd come downstairs hoping maybe we could just sit. Talk. Figure out what the heck we were doing after that bombshell I'd dropped the other night. I had no idea where we even stood anymore. He'd asked if we could restart the relationship, I'd said yes—and then, like the heartless bitch I was, I'd kneed him in the nuts with a confession of the most selfish act I'd ever committed.

And now, here he sat like a statue. Staring at his computer screen. Staring at nothing.

I bit my lip and shrank back behind the doorframe. What should I do? What was he thinking? How badly did he hate me?

The next moment, he pushed his fingertips into his eyes. His shoulders began to shake. He breathed, and it came as a sob.

I turned on my heel, pressing my back against the wall, vanishing. My own chest convulsed with grief. I stared at the fluorescents in the break room and gulped air, trying not to cry, hoping he wouldn't hear I was there.

What had I done to him? To us? I didn't know how to approach him right now. How to convince him I was sorry. I'd never seen him like this, and it terrified me. I'd never in my life felt responsible for so much misery and pain.

Just screw me.

I pushed off the wall, dumped both coffees down the drain, and abandoned the Styrofoam cups in the sink like an asshole. I ran upstairs to my office.

Avoiding Lehman, I slid into my chair and opened random files on my computer like I was trying to remember where I'd left off. But past the water in my eyes, I could barely see my screen. I forced myself not to cry aloud. I didn't need my partner asking questions.

I ran my hands over my face. Rubbed away the tears. I needed to focus. To figure out who murdered Fritz and Jason. Who hurt Tommy and Roland. I needed to figure out who The Man Upstairs was and how in all the seven hells he knew about my baby. And when I found him, I needed to wring his neck out like the damp rag he was.

Lehman's chair squeaked as he leaned back. He called to me over the cubicle wall. "Hey, did you ever upload Fritz Geissler's credit card records?"

"Weeks ago," I bit back.

"Where are they?"

"Where they belong."

His mouse clicked a few times, and I assumed he was looking through the database. "Oh," he said a moment later. Apparently, he'd found them.

I closed my eyes and sighed, low and tense. *For the love of God, Lehman, I can't handle your stupid questions today.*

Lehman cleared his throat in a manner suggesting he was about to open his idiot mouth again. I gripped my mouse like a weapon, ready to throw it at him, if need be.

But instead of lobbing another *Hey, Monica,* over the cubicle wall, Lehman cleared his throat a second time—nervously—and gave his mouse a resounding click.

Music blared. Guitars, drums, fanfare.

I squeezed my eyes shut. What the actual hell? He knew I hated music in the office.

I was on the verge of yelling at him to plug in a pair of goddamn earbuds when the music dropped into a sic beat and Lehman swung around the divider between our cubicles like some kind of rock musician. Sunglasses dropped over his eyes, he struck a pose and strummed an air guitar.

I stared at him in disbelief, my jaw so slack it had to be on the floor. Had he cracked? I knew this case was crazy-making, but...?

Oblivious to my shock, Lehman swiped a speaker off my desk and cradled it like a microphone. The next minute, he was lip syncing. He danced like he was on stage, like he had a full band behind him and a dozen chorus dancers.

Blindsided as I was by the entire spectacle, my eyes wandered to his hair. Something was... off. I was used to the short, spiked-up style he usually wore. But his hair was supposed to be gray. Today it was... black. He'd colored his hair? I shook my head and mouthed, *What the hell?*

As the music crashed to the climax, he dropped to both knees, as if to slide across his imaginary stage. But the short, industrial carpet only let him roll about an inch. The guitars and drums abruptly ended, and there was Lehman on his knees beside my desk, my computer speaker pressed against his sternum, a hand extended toward me, his dumbfounded audience.

I hoisted an eyebrow. Slowly. Precisely. "Stan Lehman, for the love of *God*, what was that?"

"You didn't get it?" he asked, panting. He lifted the sunglasses and parked them on top of his unnaturally dark hair.

"Get what?"

"That was for you." The grin on his face belied the empty skull that had to be behind it.

"Why?"

He rolled his head as if the answer should be easy. "Things have been so tense around here lately. I thought I'd..." He looked into my eyes and must have seen the confused devastation. He wiped the smile off his face. Cleared his throat. Set the speaker back on my desk. Then he lifted his chin and looked me in the eye. "Monica, there's something you should know."

He planted one foot in front of him. So he was down on one knee. Marriage-proposal-style. I hadn't thought my eyes could open any wider, but I was wrong.

I told myself he was just taking the weight off his knee. Of course, that was it. In fact, he was rubbing his kneecap. And yet, a sick, sinking feeling flushed through my entire body. *Oh, my God. No, no, no...*

He lit in before I could find something with which to nail his mouth shut. "You and I are great partners. The best."

Stoically, I tried to maintain the trite tone I reserved for him. "Now I *know* you've cracked." I shook my head as if he were a little boy who needed something simple explained to him. "We're one step away from murdering each other every other Tuesday." I didn't let on that I really just wanted to cry. What was happening? Why was the world such a dick?

He put up a hand and nodded. "Yes, but despite that, we actually work really well together." The sincerity in his eyes made me want to throw up. "We understand each other. We complement each other. You know what I mean?"

I shook my head. "No, never." I let the pun land flat like a pancake. But my heart pounded against my chest. *If you say one more word, I'll cut your head off snip-by-snip with a stapler.*

Were there signs? Had I missed them? Lunches and trips to Starbucks together—that was just because we were partners and shared a car. That time he saved me from a flock of hungry news reporters, then Jimmy Beacon's crazy-ass mother—that was just him being a good partner, right?

What if he thought there was more to it? But, my God, there wasn't. There never had been. I wanted to smack him across the temple with that speaker, knock him out, then call in the medics and say I had no idea what happened.

Lehman lowered his chin and looked me deeply in the eyes, oblivious to my conspiracy. "Monica, you are an amazing woman. You're fascinating. You're strong. I've come to respect you. Admire you."

I ground the heels of my palms into my hands, rounding my back, hollowing out my belly. "No, no," I muttered, not caring how he felt about obvious signs of rejection.

Nothing daunted, he laid a hand on the arm of my chair, his thumb touching my elbow. "Monica Steele, I want you to know that I'm in love with you."

# FRIDAY AUGUST 15, 2014

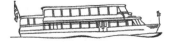

# CHAPTER FORTY-FIVE

# TOMMY

Celeste stepped onto the boat, pushing her masses of black curls into a poof at the back of her head and tying it all in place with a scarf. "Morning," she said through a vast yawn.

I glanced up from the stack of newspapers I was labeling and tried not to frown at Celeste's presence. She'd worked a sunset cruise last night. And now she was up early for a Mailboat tour? No wonder she was tired. Was she really the only crew member Robb could rustle up last minute? Considering she wasn't trained or approved for mail jumping, that meant Noah was working the entire lake himself. Again.

Scowling, I turned back to the newspapers and scrawled the last of the names in the upper margins. My frustrations were eager to find their way to Bailey's shoulders. She'd inconvenienced a lot of people by choosing not to show up.

I threw down my pen, grabbed the clipboard with the engine checklist, and turned toward the hatch.

As I rounded, morning sunlight glinted off the polished metal surfaces of the antique steam yacht that berthed across from the Mailboat. The glare was bright enough to blind me, to force me to blink.

When I opened my eyes again, I found myself *staring at a bulk of a man, the sunrise radiating around his form like an angel, blurring his outline, but flashing strangely with tiny points of light—silver studs in a black leather vest. Eyes I could feel but not see bored into me, burning with disdain.*

*The man reached to his belt. Dropped into a shooting stance. Yanked the trigger. The bullet sank into my side, just below the rib.*

I cried out and grasped the wound. The clipboard clattered to the deck, dropping from my hand as I grabbed the captain's chair to prevent myself from falling.

Celeste stared at me wide-eyed, suddenly looking far more awake, her hands still in her hair. Noah appeared on the stairs in the aft, holding a bottle of window cleaner.

"What happened?" he asked.

I glanced between the two of them. Blinked. Breathed. Searched for the man who had shot me. But there was no one here besides me and the kids. I looked downward and gingerly pulled my hand back from my shirt—terrified to see, needing to know—fully expecting to find blood across my palm.

There was none.

I frowned in confusion. Had it all been in my head?

Celeste shifted a brow, elbows still akimbo in the air. "You need to sit down, maybe?"

I forced my breath to slow, my back to straighten. But there was no slowing down my heart rate. Not yet. "It's nothing," I said, glancing between the two of them. "Just turned wrong."

It was a lie, though I had no idea what the truth was. I touched the scar. It ached bluntly, as if the ghost of a bullet had torn through me all over again.

Celeste tied a knot in her scarf, the ends drooping like a pair of leaves over her left ear. She stepped forward, knelt, and picked up the clipboard. Then she rose and handed it to me.

"Thanks," I muttered and took it.

Noah came another step down the stairs, propping the spray bottle on his hip. "If you need help with anything, all you have to do is ask."

I forced a grin. "You have plenty of your own work." I stepped away from the support of my chair to prove I was all right—to them and to me. "Better get to it. People will be lined up three high and four deep before we know it."

I pushed past Celeste, fearing my usual jocularity fooled no one today. I sensed the kids casting glances between each other before returning somberly to their tasks.

Ignoring them, I grit my teeth and lowered to my knee. The slight stitch in my side was merely the current norm. Nothing was the matter.

And yet, for a split second—for a moment that felt more real than the one I was living now—I'd been convinced the gunman was here. On the boat. That time and reality had warped, casting him forward in time to put a bullet in me all over again, as if to punish me for not dying when I was supposed to—

When I was lying on the deck, in more pain than I knew was physically possible. Bleeding and blacking out. Hearing Bailey scream my name. Hearing my wife's voice again for the first time in ten years. Calling to me. Comforting me. Inviting me to lay aside life and all the ways in which it had disappointed the both of us. To step through the veil and hold her hand again.

My hands shook as I lifted the hatch. I set my jaw and swallowed the tightness in my throat. The powers-that-be had seen fit to keep me here, vertical and above-ground. It wasn't my place to question the wisdom in the decision. That day was in the past—water under the bridge, downriver, and out to sea. There was no point giving it undue attention.

But as I stared at a pair of engines I'd serviced thousands of times, I asked myself what was the point. What was the point in the small, routine machinations of my life, when the fabric of life itself had been torn? When a man I didn't even know could raise a staff and part the entire sea of my existence?

That day, the colors had been sharper. More real. Edged. With glints of silver that tore through the planes of reality to find me, hold me captive, and drag me back.

And when that happened, it was impossible to drag my eyes away. Away from the one day that had been real.

# CHAPTER FORTY-SIX

# NOAH

Half hiding behind a wall, Noah peered down the stairs at Tommy. The captain was kneeling over the engine compartment, just... staring.

Something was so messed up. With Tommy, with Bailey... with everything. And he didn't have the first idea what he should do to help. Bailey was gone, and Tommy kept pretending nothing was the matter.

Celeste climbed the stairs to start stocking the snack bar. Looking up, she caught Noah in the middle of his spying. Instead of acting weirded out, she merely met his eyes, her own as heavy as lead.

Too sad to linger on the glance, Noah turned away and went back to cleaning the windows.

Two hours later, the boat cleaned and stocked, the day's mail loaded, and every seat filled, they left the pier. While Tommy opened the narration, Noah straddled the mail jumper's window, waiting for his first delivery. He hooked his inside foot in the metal stirrup that helped him keep his seat, even if the boat bucked in the waves. A wind that had been growing over the morning rustled his hair.

Beside him, Tommy manned the helm, so close, their shoulders could have touched. But his eyes were as dead as if they were carved from sun-grayed driftwood. His voice was flat and lifeless. He hesitated for words, stumbled over them. He skipped one factoid entirely.

Noah frowned. Tommy never messed up the script.

Setting the microphone down so he could focus on steering for the first delivery, Tommy stole a glance over his shoulder at the passengers. It wasn't unusual for him to check on them—to make sure everyone appeared at home, to confirm there weren't any issues, or even to see if a joke he'd told a thousand times had landed this time specifically.

This glance wasn't any of those things. The mannerism was tense. Anxious. He wasn't checking on the passengers. He was searching them. Noah let his eyes fall to the captain's hands. They shook on the helm.

Noah had to fight the urge to lay a hand on Tommy's arm and tell him everything was going to be okay. That he wasn't alone. That he and Celeste—God damn it, the whole cruise line—were here for him.

But how exactly was he supposed to suddenly grow up and be the anchor for Tommy? For his captain? Badly as he wanted to, he didn't know how to offer to take the watch, wrest the helm from Tommy's hands, and tell him to find his berth so his soul could heal.

Turning away, Noah scanned the shoreline and thumbed the newspaper in his hand, the mail rolled up inside.

*Bailey, where are you?* he asked. *I don't know what's going on, but I feel like your leaving didn't help. You and Tommy are the only ones who were here that day, and I think... I don't know. I think he needs you.*

The first pier approached. Noah sighed, pulled his foot from the stirrup, and swung his leg through the window. He stood on the rub board, ready for his first jump.

A jump that should have been Bailey's.

# CHAPTER FORTY-SEVEN

# BAILEY

Several lawns away from the first pier, I sat in the grass and leaned against a tree beside the Lake Shore Path. A row of shrubs ran between me and the shore, so I doubted anyone on the boat would see me. But I could see them.

I could see him.

Tommy's outline was dimmed by the glare on the glass, but I could still make out his eyes focused on the pier—the pier with a mailbox attached to one of the posts. His hands finessed the throttles and the helm, bringing the huge, two-deck boat alongside as easily as if he were pulling a toy on a string.

Noah leapt from the rub board, landed, and ran to the box. Between minding his footing and exchanging the mail, he had too many things going on to notice me.

I watched, feeling the same way I did when I was thirteen and rode the Mailboat for the first time: fascinated. I'd been with a family from Whitewater then. They had two bio kids they loved more than me. They didn't know the Mailboat sells out every day, even though future me could have told them that. So, they hadn't reserved tickets ahead of time, and when we arrived, there were only four seats left on the entire boat.

My foster parents glanced at each other, glanced at their sunny-eyed kids, then looked at me and told me to stay behind. They said I could explore the gift shops in the Riviera. For two and a half hours. Until they got back.

I mean, frankly, the Riviera isn't that big.

They were pulling out the wallet, buying the last four tickets, explaining to me that I wasn't allowed to go anywhere beyond the Riviera, when an old man in a captain's uniform walked by and apparently overheard. When he realized they meant to leave me behind—when he saw me bowing my head and nodding—his eyes went stormy. He told the girl at the sales counter to sell us five tickets. Then he pulled a chair off another boat and somehow made it fit on the aft deck.

I doubted he remembered that. I never forgot it.

I spent the whole tour staring at him instead of the mail jumpers. That was the day I decided I wanted to be one of them. Not because they were famous and every kid in Wisconsin wanted to be one. No. I wanted what they had. Someone in their lives who cared.

Of course, I knew that was never going to happen. Even though Lake Geneva was where I was born, I'd somehow never managed to end up there again in all my time in foster care. Random neighboring counties? Sure. Lake Geneva? No. Never. Besides, I already knew I wasn't allowed to have the things I wanted.

A few months later, the family from Whitewater decided foster care really was a pain. I went back to the group home. Then I went to Bud Weber. Against all odds, I went to Lake Geneva.

It was the best thing that ever happened to me.

Back then, Bud was still trying to be nice to me. So when I asked if I could apply for a job at the cruise line, he said sure, whatever makes you happy, kiddo. I want you to be happy here, ya know?

And I *was* happy. It was the first time I'd ever had something I truly wanted.

Someone who cared about me.

The mail in the box, Noah turned on his heel and sprinted for the boat. With a well-practiced leap, he landed on the rub board, and the Mailboat whisked him off, the passengers cheering.

I watched Tommy's back as the Mailboat pulled away, until I couldn't see him anymore. Then I watched the boat grow smaller and smaller, until even the wake was a memory of water crashing against the rocks on the shore, and the waves were small and regular, driven by the wind.

A single tear spilled down my cheek, and it cut the inside of me like knives.

A small voice protested that I was supposed to be on that boat. I wanted to yell at it to come back for me, like it always did. Any time I missed my jump. Any time I wound up in the lake. It never left me behind.

Tommy never left me behind.

"*What do you want from me?*" another voice—my own—echoed inside my head. "*There's always something. Everyone who ever took me in always wanted something out of me.*"

*Tommy shook his head. "I don't want anything from you."*

*I bit my teeth together. Hard. "Look me in the eyes and say that again."*

I really, really wanted him to say the words again. To mean them. To convince me they could be true, just this once. That he loved me just because I existed and I needed him. Because I'd always needed him.

Instead, he looked at me... and said nothing.

It was like the universe screwing me over one last time.

Great. Fine. You know what? After this, I wasn't letting anyone screw me over again.

Ever.

All the memories I'd made on the Mailboat—the very memories that used to carry me from one brutal day to the next—were now shredding me apart from the inside out. If I was going to go on at all, I had to go on without them.

So I told myself I'd never been a mail jumper.

I told myself I'd never known anyone named Tommy Thomlin.

I told myself I'd never had a grandpa.

And I said them over and over to myself until I believed them.

One by one, I ripped the memories from my brain like the pages of a book. I held them to the wind, then let them go. They drifted over the lake, fell, momentarily stuck to the surface, then vanished beneath the waves to sit on the bottom forever, like lost diving rings and wedding rings and that one Volkswagen Beetle with the street sign stuck to the front bumper.

When the very last memory had been drowned, I found I was what I had always been. Bailey Johnson. The nothing girl. Random bits of shattered glass glued together with hurt and fury.

I would walk on again. Alone. My footprints leaving blood in the sand, and no one ever noticing.

And no matter what, I would never again allow myself to dream. I would never allow myself to want anything again.

I closed my eyes and leaned my head against the tree, embracing the explosive emptiness that was me.

A twig snapped. I opened my eyes and looked to the row of shrubs along the shore. A branch low to the ground trembled. I narrowed my eyes, expecting to spy a bird or a rabbit.

Instead, I saw matted white fur. A pair of curly ears, stuck with bits of twigs and dead leaves. A pair of small paws with black nails. And two tiny, black eyes, barely visible past the overgrown fur.

A dog? How long had he been hiding there, watching me?

Glancing furtively one direction then the other, shaking all over, he seemed keenly aware of my presence, while being careful never to look at me.

I squinted, but couldn't see whether he was wearing a collar. And it was impossible to tell how skinny he might be, with his fur matted like a feral sheep. He was clearly one of those ever-growing varietals of dog that needed their hair cut on the regular—and that hadn't happened in quite a long time.

I glanced over the nearby houses, each one grand and pristine. I couldn't imagine anyone who lived there leaving a dog in this kind of mess. Other messes? Sure. Maybe. Like, they'd go for the kind where they had their dog professionally groomed once a week, spritzed with canine cologne, and give him his own Instagram—then scream at him for taking a dump on a white carpet, cuz they'd never bothered to house train him.

But not the kind of mess where they let his hair take over like zebra mussels.

Anyway, I was pretty sure this guy didn't belong to any of these houses. He was a stray. And by the looks of it, he'd been on his own quite a while.

I crossed my legs, leaned forward to make myself small, and held out my hand. "Hey, buddy. You okay?"

He jumped at my voice, then glanced left and right in slow motion, as if, by staying as still as possible, he might turn invisible.

"It's all right." I tapped the grass. "You wanna come here?"

His eyes flicked toward mine, the motion magnified by the shifting of his overgrown brows. He must not have liked what he saw, because he immediately looked away, then began to crawl out of the bush in the opposite direction, his tail firmly clamped between his legs, his belly low to the ground.

I grinned at him. "Just cuz you're not looking at me, doesn't mean I can't see you."

He glanced at me one more time. Then, fast as a rabbit, he darted across one of the vast lawns, stretching his little body like Super Man, and vanished behind a house.

Disappointed, I bit my lip. A dog that skittish wouldn't be easy to catch.

On a hunch, I crawled forward and pushed aside the branches of the bush he'd been hiding under. He'd dug a shallow bowl in the ground, and bits of his white fur were stuck to the sides.

I smiled. Just gimme a few weeks and an unlimited supply of chicken...

It wouldn't be the first animal I'd rescued.

# Chapter Forty-Eight

# TOMMY

The wind steadily picked up over the course of the morning. The Mailboat, with its shallow draft and tall profile, caught the breeze like a sailboat. I had to keep her moving fast near the piers so we wouldn't drift into them. Perhaps it was a blessing. The need to focus was the only thing that finally pulled my thoughts closer to the present, and further away from the strangely visceral memories of the past.

Noah kept abreast of the pace without complaint, but was winded long before the end. As Buttons Bay came into view, I knew the majority of the tour was behind us, but the worst of it upon us. Northwesterly winds traversed the full fetch of the lake unhindered, whipping the water into whitecaps. The waves pounded the port quarter, driving us forward and toward the shore. The bow nosed into the troughs and broke through the waves on the other side, washing the windshield and sometimes splashing through the mail jumpers' window, surprising the passengers in the first two rows with the occasional sprinkle.

The scar in my side throbbed, protesting against all the time I'd spent on my feet, the need to see clearly through hazardous conditions outweighing the desire to rest in my captain's chair. Geneva Bay and the Riviera Pier couldn't appear any too soon. I grit my teeth. No way there but through.

I cruised in toward the next pier. Wind and wave disagreed where the boat should be. I kept the helm responsive, both the port and starboard props half-ahead forward, insisting on a straight course. Noah was going to have a long jump and a fast run. I didn't dare get too close with the sixty-ton boat. Noah launched himself off the side and barely landed on his toes on the edge of the pier.

The wind gusted, shifting to the port beam, blowing through the open windows, buffeting the side of my face. At the sensation, I flinched away, blinking.

*His breath was thick with alcohol. He leaned over me as I writhed on the deck. His vest smelled like old leather, old frying oil, and old vomit.*

*"You'll bleed out before she gets here," he whispered in a thick Chicago accent.*

*God, no. He knew Bailey was coming. "Don't hurt her," I gasped through the pain.*

*He reached down. Grabbed my shoulder. Rolled me onto my side, ignoring my groans. I blinked. Focused.*

*I saw him.*

*His arms were covered in tattoos. Sweat dotted his thick neck. His face was strangely round and boyish, yet filled with a darkness that went deep and stirred feelings of terror. A man who had never grown, and yet had grown into a hurricane-like power he had no idea how to contain.*

SCREEEEECH.

Wood squealed. Fibers groaned and cracked. Voices shouted. I felt the boat shudder through my hands and feet.

I blinked.

I was on the lake. Buttons Bay. Water washed over the bow. Sprayed through the window and splashed my shirt. I tried to tell myself it wasn't my own blood, but sweat was pouring down my back.

I looked to the starboard beam. The boat was grinding against the pier. Noah had glued himself to the side of the boat, trying to avoid being swept off by the pier posts. My heart leapt into my mouth. If he fell, he could be crushed.

Bracing my feet, I turned the boat hard to port, pushed forward on the starboard throttle, and shifted the port throttle into reverse, sharpening the radius of the turn. The boat's mass and momentum fought the waves and the wind, which tried to force the boat into the pier. I leaned into the wheel, fire streaking through my side with the effort. I grit my teeth.

At last, I won. The boat fell into the next trough. I pointed the bow into the lake, away from the shore, and shifted both throttles half-ahead to maintain steering. Then I leaned on the helm and breathed, waiting for the stab to reduce to an ache. Around here, I didn't get the luxury of a first mate. A sheet of paper taped under the cutty hatch told the crew what to do if the captain were incapacitated. But the kids had never needed to employ that protocol during my watch.

I needed to know the damages to pier and boat. Long before I was ready, I straightened and turned to look aftwards. My view was blocked by Noah, who had just arrived at the mail jumpers' window.

I rankled at the delay. "Get in here," I barked.

Grabbing the handrail above his head, he swung both his feet through simultaneously and scrambled out of my way. I leaned out and took in the scene. Unsurprisingly, the boat appeared undamaged. A long strip of paint was missing off the edge of the rub board, but Brian had scraped all of that off weeks ago.

The pier hadn't fared as well. Two posts had snapped, the jagged edges entangled together like frayed threads, ready to give. The entire structure rocked in the choppy waves. No doubt, it would soon collapse.

My stomach turned. I'd nicked a pier or two over the years. This was the first time I'd flat-out broken one. If the owners were home, they had to have heard the noise. I imagined I heard the phone ringing in the office barge back at the Riviera Pier.

I growled under my breath and gripped the wheel. Then I noticed Noah staring at me. A second later, I realized I had yelled at my own mail jumper.

"I'm sorry," I said, working my jaw. "I didn't mean to shout at you." The offense was worsened in light of the horrific accident that could have transpired. At the thought of it, I felt the blood drain from my face.

When Noah said nothing, I looked again. His brow was furrowed with concern. Uncomfortable under the scrutiny, I studied the whitecaps breaking beyond the bow instead. What I wouldn't give for five minutes to sit down and breathe...

But as soon as I considered the possibility, I knew it was a bad idea. Fractured images of a black leather vest, of a dark yet childlike face, tried to force their way into my mind.

Drawn by an impulse I couldn't explain, and yet couldn't resist, I glanced over my shoulder and scanned the lower deck. But no one there matched the description of the man in my mind. Instead, I saw wide eyes. Hands only beginning to loosen their grips on the chairs. Feet still braced against the deck. Every face was turned toward me, and I saw fear, doubt, mistrust.

The way friends and neighbors had looked at me the day after Jason broke into a bank, murdered an officer, and vanished into the night. What kind of a man raised a criminal and a killer?

A hand touched my shoulder. I flinched, but it was only Noah. "You okay?" he asked.

He was standing too close. All I could feel was the shooter leaning over me. I brushed off his hand. "Don't—" I stopped when I realized I was about to snap at my mail jumper again. I drew a shuddering breath.

He let his hand fall from my shoulder, no trace of offense on his face. Only that penetrating look in his eye.

I ground my teeth. "Let's get this tour over with," I said. "Have Celeste come up here and help you with the script. I need to drive." I eased into my chair, my side still throbbing.

Noah nodded. His glance lingered on me a moment longer. Then he made his way down the aisle to the aft deck. If anyone wanted a soda or a bag of pretzels during the rest of this cruise, they were out of luck—and I didn't care. I needed to get the mail delivered and get the boat back to port. Nothing else mattered.

And after that... After that, I didn't know. If I couldn't safely operate the boat—if something as innocuous as a breath of wind or a flash of light could utterly shanghai my brain—did I deserve to stand behind the helm?

Interspersed with the images of the man in the black leather vest was now the picture of Noah clinging to the side of the boat, avoiding the pier posts. I couldn't stop thinking what could have happened if he'd fallen. I couldn't be responsible for a thing like that.

The Mailboat had always been my refuge. I'd assumed she always would be. Why did she feel as if she were turning against me now?

# CHAPTER FORTY-NINE

# TOMMY

The moment we were moored to the pier, I stepped off the boat, rucksack over my shoulder. People were already lined up for the next tour. Brian stood at the head of the line, ready to take over the helm.

"Windy out there, isn't it?" he observed, smiling his vague, affable grin.

Offering nothing in reply, I bowed past him, keen on getting to the office barge and speaking to Robb. In the last quarter hour of the tour, I'd been able to think of nothing but the accident at the pier and how close one of my jumpers had come to serious harm.

I stopped and looked back. Noah and Celeste were dropping the gangway into place for the morning's passengers to disembark. I stared at Noah with regret, for both what I'd done and what I was about to do.

I wasn't ignorant of how the kids here looked up to me—however ill-founded that trust.

"Noah," I called.

He turned, his eyes full of the same penetrating understanding as before, and perhaps a touch of hope. After all, I was talking to him this time, not shouting.

I let his optimism roll off me. I doubted he could forgive me for what I was about to do. I doubted any of the kids would.

"I'm sorry," I said, the words covering a great many offenses—but most of all, the one I had yet to commit.

Noah shook his head and lifted a shoulder. "It's just a pier."

As if I hadn't come close to badly hurting him. I missed the resilience of youth, when every problem was simple and had a straightforward answer.

Silently, I gave Noah a nod. Then I turned and made my way to the office.

Robb was on the phone when I stepped in.

"Yes, yes, I understand," he said, his facial muscles tense, pulled back, as if he were being blasted in a stiff wind. The effect was only amplified by the fact that the deck of the barge was sluggishly rolling beneath our feet. "Of course. We'll have the repair crew out as soon as this weather lets up."

A tinny voice rattled on the other end of the line. Robb winced and held the phone away, then, with a pained smile, settled it back against his ear, absorbing the discord from the other end with raised eyebrows. When the voice ran out of steam, he spoke, the smile still frozen on his face.

"Of course. You're very welcome. We'll be in touch... Mm-hm, 'bye." He hung up with a look of relief.

"Zondervans?" I asked. The family whose pier I'd wrecked.

Robb settled back in his chair and sighed contentedly at the sight of an ally he thought he could trust. "Choppy out there today, isn't it?"

If he was giving me an out, I didn't care for it. I'd driven that boat past the piers thousands of times—tens of thousands, for all I knew—in every kind of weather, barring electrical storms. And never had I pushed one of the piers clean off the posts.

I crossed the deck and braced my arms on the chair in front of his desk. The scar was digging like a knife. "We almost had a serious accident."

Robb grinned impishly. "That's not how the Zondervans described it."

I had no room for laughter. "I don't mean the pier."

His smile faded. He regarded me with the seriousness I was asking for.

"I almost swiped Noah off the side of the boat," I said.

"He's all right?" He said it like a foregone conclusion. Of course Noah was all right. Of course the captain of the Mailboat would never allow anything to happen to one of his jumpers.

I ground my teeth together. "He held on."

Robb nodded, and then, seeming to observe that my tension hadn't abated any, he brushed the air with his fingers. "It's okay,

Tommy. Noah's in one piece, and a pier can be repaired. No real harm done."

I stared at him, my jaw tense, my throat going tight for some reason. Perhaps because leaving the Mailboat wasn't something I'd particularly envisioned myself doing willingly. Or ever.

Or as permanently as I was now intending.

"Robb." I rubbed my fingers on the back of the chair. Shifted my feet, searching for a position that involved less discomfort in my side. "I'm sorry. I don't think I was ready to come back to work."

He shook his head, blinking rapidly, adjusting to my words. "If you need more time, that's not a problem. Brian's flexible."

I nodded and licked my lips. For what I had to say next, I found myself unable to look at him. "You might wanna tell him to practice some."

Robb tilted his head. "Why?" When I didn't go on, he shifted in his seat and spoke to fill the silence. "You can have the whole rest of the summer, if you need. There's only a few weeks left. We'll get along without you."

Head bowed, I merely lifted my eyes and stared at him. He was getting warmer.

My meaning sunk in. His head straightened. He leaned back in his chair, palm flat on his desk. "Oh. This is it?"

He said the word *it* as if this moment were some long-foreseen, yet long-dreaded eventuality. Well, obviously it was going to happen someday. When he was born forty-odd years ago, I'd already been well-practiced at the job.

Robb's gaze dropped to the desk. "Well," he said, then laughed emptily. "It's not like you haven't earned your retirement." The smile immediately faded. "I'd try to talk you into staying, but..." He looked up at me again. "you've already been with us far longer than we ever had the right to ask." He licked his lips and bounced his hand on the desk. "Right. Okay. I'll get the paperwork sorted." He gave me a smile, the mirth entirely forced.

I nodded. "Thanks." I pushed away from the chair and began to turn toward the door.

Robb sprang to his feet, the motion reminiscent of a seaman recruit coming to attention. "Tommy?"

I paused and looked back.

"I just wanted to say..." He halted and bounced his hand, his eyes glinting with emotion. He worked his jaw, and when he finally spoke, his voice was husky. "Thank you."

However I'd envisioned myself feeling in this moment, it wasn't this. Hollowed out. Empty. Wondering what it had all been for.

I nodded. Then turned and left, closing the office door behind me for what I believed to be the last time.

I walked off the Riviera Pier, stride stiff but purposeful.

Behind me, a familiar horn blasted three times rapidly. It sounded like a cry, and it went straight through my heart. I knew it was merely Brian signaling that the boat was reversing from the pier. But in my soul, I felt the Mailboat backing away from me. I knew every chair was filled, every face smiling and eager for the fresh new experience on their horizon...

An experience that future generations would now have without me.

Whatever I'd expected this moment to feel like... it wasn't this.

I walked on without looking back.

# SATURDAY AUGUST 16, 2014

# CHAPTER FIFTY

# NOAH

Noah walked toward the Riviera, deep in thought. He'd been awake half the night, rehearsing things he could say to Tommy this morning, none of which were probably right. After all, Noah had no idea what it was like getting shot, what it was Tommy was going through. For all he knew, anything he tried to say or do would simply make everything worse.

But it was asking a little too much of him to pretend as if he didn't care.

"Yo, Noah!" Footsteps jogged up behind him.

He turned and found Celeste running across the brick courtyard that spread in a circle in front of the Riviera.

"Morning," he said with a smile.

She fell into step beside him. "Dude, I went to the carnival last night."

Noah glanced beyond her toward the barricades blocking off the east end of Wrigley Drive. The street, running parallel to the shore, was filled with rides—the kind designed for catching air and throwing your stomach into your mouth. Dominating the skyline was a Ferris wheel, some seventy feet tall. This early in the morning, the carnival was quiet. But by afternoon and long into the evening, the entirety of Flat Iron Park would be alive with tourists, music, and delighted screams.

"I haven't been yet," Noah said.

"I won a goldfish at the fishbowl game," Celeste reported. "And then I took it with me on the Ferris wheel. Bro, you should have seen his eyes!" She cupped her fingers around her own eyes like goggles, making her mouth into a panic-stricken O. Then she cackled and slapped her thigh.

Noah laughed with her, trying to imagine the poor fish staring down at Geneva Lake from seventy feet in the air. He wiped a tear from his eye. After everything that had happened here lately, it felt good to laugh.

They emerged from under the Riviera towers onto the pier, and found Brian unlocking the Mailboat. The smile faded from Noah's face. He glanced at Celeste. Her expression mirrored his.

"Hey, Brian," Noah called by way of greeting.

Brian turned and grinned. "Well, good morning! Ready for another day full of adventure?"

Noah quirked a grin. "Yeah, sure." He glanced up and down the pier. "Hey, where's Tommy? Taking a day off?"

Brian turned the key 'round and 'round in his hand and briefly bit his lips. "Nope. He quit."

Noah gawked. Had he heard right?

"Quit?" he asked. Tommy would *never* quit—would he? "Just for the rest of the summer, right? He'll be back next year?"

Brian sighed and leaned on the side of the boat, one hand still turning the key. "I don't know. Robb suggested I practice going easier on the piers. I got the impression he wanted me next summer, too." His eyes, light as wisps of smoke, looked sad. "I don't think Tommy's coming back."

The words hung emptily over the pier. Noah sensed Celeste shooting another glance his direction, but he didn't have the heart to return it.

At last, as if the silence were too much, Brian shook his head and walked into the boat.

Noah knew there was work to be done, yet he couldn't shift from the spot. Tommy had captained the Mailboat for the better part of forty-eight summers. He was as much an institution of Geneva Lake as the Mailboat itself. A part of the landscape, like the Narrows and the Lake Shore Path; as ever-present and quietly visible as the Riviera. His leaving felt like the end of an era.

Obviously, Noah had known it would happen eventually. He'd just hoped it wouldn't happen until he was done with high school, done with college, done with being a mail jumper. He'd hoped it wouldn't happen until he was somewhere else, working some other job, maybe even married with kids. And the news would trickle down. His mom would mention it on the phone. Or he'd bump into another veteran mail jumper and they'd drop it into the conversation. They'd be like, *Hey, did you hear Tommy retired?* And he'd be like, *Oh, wow, good for him.* And then they'd share a million memories of jumping mail all those summers long ago.

It would have stung less that way.

Beside him, Celeste straightened her shoulders and tilted her head thoughtfully. Staring at the boards beneath their feet, she spoke in a tone that was low yet clear, as if she were delivering a monologue in the theater back at school. "'I wish it need not have happened in my time,'" she said.

Noah laughed under his breath—not only because Celeste was thinking what he was thinking, but because she was quoting Tolkien.

"*The Lord of the Rings*," he said.

"Book One," Celeste added.

"*The Fellowship of the Ring*," Noah specified.

"The Mines of Moria," Celeste intoned nobly.

Noah raised a finger. "That was in the movie. In the book, it was Chapter Two, right after Gandalf throws the Ring into the fireplace at Bag End."

Celeste looked embarrassed. "Aw, dang, really? I guess I need to read the books again."

Noah merely smiled. Even if her Tolkien lore was off—and misplacing Frodo's famed line was an easy mistake—he hadn't realized she was a fellow nerd.

No doubt, they were being way too dramatic, quoting works of epic literature at a time like this. And yet, he couldn't help thinking of Gandalf's reply to Frodo, in light of so much despair.

Noah said the words aloud. "'All we have to decide is what to do with the time that is given us.'"

Gazing downward, Celeste nodded. Then she suddenly looked up, shaking her head. "Good God, none of this crap is right." She gestured with her hands. "Bailey leaving, Tommy leaving, neither of them talking to each other... I haven't the foggiest what's going on, but it's not right."

Hope exploding in his chest, Noah grinned. "My thoughts exactly."

"Great. So." She brushed her hands together conspiratorially. "What are we going to do about it?"

Noah turned to face her more fully, feeling a fire in his belly. "I'm not sure yet about Tommy. I really don't see him much outside of the cruise line."

"Me, neither," Celeste agreed. "Let's come back to that. What about Bailey? That girl spends way too much time by herself."

Noah turned up his palms. "We'll see her in a couple of weeks back in school."

Celeste pointed a finger. "We can figure out what classes she's taking, and sign up for as many of the same ones as we can."

Noah shrugged. "You take one half, I'll take the other?"

Celeste grinned, her teeth white against her brown skin. "Deal! No sitting in the cafeteria alone for that girl—not anymore."

They bumped fists on it and blew them up. Shoulder-to-shoulder, they stepped onto the boat, brainstorming ideas, their words flowing fast and furious.

# CHAPTER FIFTY-ONE

# WADE

Wade sat at his desk at the PD, working his way through a stack of papers, his mind somewhat further away. It had been a week since Tommy had moved back into his own home, two days since he'd gone back to work. It took all Wade's resolve not to pester him over the phone. Concerned as he was that Tommy was pushing himself too hard—and risking his own safety—Wade knew the welfare check wouldn't be appreciated.

He promised himself he wouldn't call until tomorrow.

Holding back was hard. Wade still got a knot in his stomach every time he thought about what had happened—that his life-long friend, whom he loved like a brother, had been shot and could have been killed. Knowing that the man responsible was still at large sickened him.

A rap sounded on his door. Stan Lehman stood in the opening, wearing his black polo shirt and tan slacks. His sidearm sat on his right hip, along with his badge.

"Chief," he said, "did I hear you were headed down to the carny?"

Wade took off his readers. "Yeah. Just for a quick tour. See how the event detail's doing." Studying Lehman, he thought something about him looked different, but couldn't put his finger on it.

"Any chance I can catch a ride?" Lehman asked.

Wade grinned. "Why? Where's your partner?" He glanced at the clock in the corner of his computer screen. Lehman was scheduled to take command of the event detail in twenty minutes, and he was aware that Monica had taken a shift on foot patrol, as well.

Lehman jabbed a thumb over his shoulder. "At the carny. I was wrapping up some things in the office, and by the time I was ready, she'd already left—unit and all."

Wade chuckled. "She doesn't let the grass grow under her feet." He slipped on his readers. "I'll be just a minute."

Lehman nodded and tweaked a dial on a radio he had clipped to his belt. "I'll let Burns know I haven't saddled him with the command post all night." Stepping away from the door, he adjusted his earpiece. His voice faded with distance as he gave his call sign and asked for Sergeant Burns.

It finally hit Wade, just as Lehman vanished. He'd dyed his hair black. Interesting. The man had been comfortably gray for years now. Why would he dye his hair?

Wade's phone rang, a light on the base blinking to indicate that the telecommunications center was calling.

He picked up and cradled the phone on his shoulder. "Yeah?"

Steph Buchanan's voice came over the line. "Someone here to see you, Chief. Angelica Read?"

Wade lifted his head at the name. He put a hand over the receiver and called through his open door. "Lehman."

The detective re-appeared in the doorway. "Ten-four," he said into his radio mic. Then he gave Wade his full attention.

Wade held up a finger, asking him to wait, then spoke into the phone again. "Did she say what she wants?"

"She wants to talk to you specifically," Steph said. "Regarding the investigation."

Well, that was obvious enough. She was the wife of Fritz Geissler, alias William Read, a young man Wade had known personally.

Fritz had also been body number one in this long summer of murder.

Monica had mentioned that Angelica was in town a while back—maybe a month ago? Why was she here now? Why did she want to speak with him in particular? When was the last time anyone had updated her on her husband's case?

He glanced at Stan while speaking into the phone. "I'll have Lehman show her up."

Lehman lifted his brows in curiosity, privy as he was to only half the conversation.

"All right, Chief," Steph said. "I'll let her know."

Wade hung up and looked at Lehman, frowning thoughtfully. "Angelica Read's here. She wants to talk with me."

Lehman pulled his chin into his neck. "Geissler's wife? She came a long way just to chat."

"When's the last time we gave her an update?" Wade asked.

Lehman shifted his jaw and searched the ceiling. "I'd have to ask Monica."

Wade squinted. "Monica was giving her updates? I thought she didn't like Angelica Read."

Lehman scratched his hair, then shrugged. "I don't know if she was or not. To be honest, chief, we were pretty swamped for a while, and there's nothing new to tell Mrs. Read, other than there aren't any developments."

Wade nodded and lifted his brows. "I guess I'll be the bearer of that bad news. Will you show her up?"

Lehman smirked. "In exchange for you being the one to tell her we don't have anything? Deal." He walked toward the elevator.

Wade returned to his paperwork. In the back of his mind, he rifled the possibilities for why Angelica Read would come all the way here again. It couldn't be just to talk to him, upset as she probably was over the lack of communication. And then three facts fell into place in quick succession.

Monica said that Read had been an uncooperative witness.

She also said she'd seen Mrs. Read in close communication with Roland.

And shortly after that, Tommy had reported Roland purporting some wild theory about Wade himself being behind all the violence this summer. That he was the fourth member of the Markham Ring.

In other words, that he was The Man Upstairs.

Wade lifted his head from his paperwork, deep in thought. What had put the idea into Roland's head? Some combination of loneliness and bitterness would be enough to explain it; Roland had never forgiven Wade for shooting Bobby.

But the traumatized imagination of a young widow desperate for answers could certainly add fuel to the fire.

Or Monica could even be correct: that Angelica Read knew more than she was letting on. Perhaps Angelica was trying to blow smoke in everyone's eyes.

Wade glanced at his duty belt, slung onto one end of his L-shaped desk. His back wasn't what it used to be, so he often took the belt off when he was in his office. He slid his sidearm out of the holster and placed it in an open drawer for easier reach.

A moment later, a knock sounded on the doorframe. Wade looked up just as Lehman waved in a petite Hispanic woman wearing a flowy, peach-colored blouse and white capris. In both hands, she gripped a small white handbag. She walked into the room stiffly, her mouth set, her eyes severe.

No wonder she and Monica didn't get along. They were two peas in a pod.

Be that the case, he was more inclined to like Angelica Read.

With Monica, he'd known he liked her straight off the bat. He'd met her when she was just a college student, taking an internship at the LGPD. Her duties had ranged from washing the patrol cars, to training in the telecommunications center, to riding along with the uniforms. But somehow, she'd managed to insert herself into his office in the detective bureau with surprising frequency, where she reveled in combing through reams of data in search of the tiniest of details. She'd even accompanied him on investigations, where she'd proven sharp-eyed and street-smart. She'd shown her worth, and he'd known from the start that she was cut out for the badge. In all the years since, she'd never disappointed him.

Shelving the memories, Wade rose and extended his hand to the woman who reminded him so strangely of his protégé.

"Mrs. Read," he said. The woman barely reached his bicep, and he wondered if he'd been over-thinking the matter when he put the gun in his drawer.

She approached, appearing nervous but determined, and took his hand briefly—a passing touch and nothing more. "Chief Erickson. Thank you for seeing me." She spoke with a light accent.

"Of course. One moment." Wade glanced to Lehman. "If you need, you can grab a unit and head downtown."

Lehman appeared to give it a thought, his foot tapping the industrial carpet—an oddity for him. In a job full of people wired for action, Lehman typically stood out as a man who could wait indefinitely. So, why was he anxious to be moving now?

Despite his signs of impatience, Lehman shook his head. "Burns isn't in a hurry. I'll give it a few minutes." He jabbed a thumb over his shoulder. "I'll just wait for you out here."

Wade nodded. Perhaps the detective felt compelled to listen in on a conversation related to the Markham Ring. Lehman closed the door—but didn't latch it, supporting Wade's theory.

Wade shifted his attention back to Angelica Read and quickly lowered into his seat. He was aware it was rude to sit before his guest did, but he felt self-conscious about the way he towered over her. While his height had been useful in the days when he'd worked patrol, he didn't feel the need now to dominate every person he met. He motioned to the chair in front of the desk. "Please, sit down."

The woman lowered her eyes in a nod of acknowledgment. "Thank you." She slid into the chair, resting her purse on her lap with her hands clasped on top. She sat with her back erect.

Wade folded his hands on the desk. "What can I do for you, Mrs. Read?"

Her dark brown eyes shifted and met his. Her words were polite, but her gaze as ferocious as a tiger. "Chief Erickson, my husband was murdered in this city two months ago, and aside from being made aware of that basic fact, I have heard nothing from your department. *Are* you even still investigating?"

Her accusation cut deep—and he instantly regretted his department unintentionally putting her into a position where she felt the need to ask.

"My apologies, Mrs. Read. As a matter of fact, the case which began with your husband's murder has consumed not only our entire Detective Bureau, but an investigative task force made up of numerous regional agencies. The only reason you haven't heard anything from us is that, regrettably, we still have nothing substantial to report."

Angelica pursed her lips. "Chief Erickson, I need closure—and not just for me. I have children."

Wade nodded. "I understand, ma'am. You and your family have my deepest sympathy. I wish there was some way I could accelerate the process. But I hope it'll bring you some comfort to know that I hold myself and this department to the highest professional standards. One day when we have a name to release, you can rest assured that it's the right name, and that the individual in question will be prosecuted to the fullest extent of the law."

Angelica lifted her chin, her eyes scrutinizing. "Hm. I'll hold you to that. I wouldn't like to feel as if I had to resort to playing detective myself."

Wade found the comment unusual—particularly in light of Monica's report that Angelica seemed to be pursuing some line of investigation of her own.

He merely nodded. "Yes, ma'am."

He thought Angelica's eyes narrowed briefly, but he couldn't be sure.

She went on. "Until you have my husband's murderer in custody, is it too much to ask that someone from this department keep me updated more regularly?" While her chin remained square, she blinked rapidly, and her eyes went glossy with dampness.

"That's not too much to ask at all," Wade assured her. "The Detective Bureau was working non-stop to keep up with the caseload for quite some time, which is our best excuse for going derelict on the duty of updating you. But we should have made a greater effort to keep in touch." It dawned on him that Monica was the wrong person to put to that task. "I'll assign Detective Sergeant Lehman, whom you just met. He's head of the Detective Bureau."

He imagined Lehman's ears perking at his own name—and perhaps his stomach plummeting at the new duty. Until they had more to report, it would be a joyless task.

"May I leave my contact information for him?" Angelica withdrew a pen from her purse.

"Of course."

"Do you have paper?"

Wade removed a legal pad from the same drawer where he'd put his gun. The more he talked with this woman, the more he thought his paranoia had been uncalled for. He couldn't blame Angelica Read for wanting to know more. Though he still wondered why she'd come all this way.

He laid the pad down in front of her. She wrote her name, phone number, and email in neat handwriting, then laid down the pen and slid the legal pad back to Wade.

"I appreciate this," she said.

Wade tore off the sheet with her info. "I'll give this to Detective Lehman."

"Thank you."

She rose, and Wade followed suit. He rounded his desk and opened the door for her. Lehman sat on the edge of the receptionist's empty desk, scrolling his phone—still bouncing his foot.

"Lehman."

He looked up.

Wade handed him the sheet of paper. "This is Mrs. Read's contact information. I'd like you to develop a reasonable schedule for getting in touch with her regarding updates."

Lehman pocketed his phone and took the paper. "Can do, Chief." By the lack of reaction, he'd already overheard and resigned himself to his fate.

"Would you mind showing Mrs. Read out?" Wade motioned to Angelica. She still clutched her purse in both hands, but held her chin high, perhaps in response to accomplishing her mission.

"Sure thing." Lehman carefully folded the paper and slipped it into his pocket. He motioned Mrs. Read ahead of him toward the elevator. "Ma'am?"

Wade held up a finger to Lehman. "I'll be down in a minute. I'm almost done up here."

Lehman nodded.

Angelica paused before going, and turned to look up at Wade. "I have to say, it was reassuring to meet the man who runs this department. Thank you for inviting me upstairs to your office."

Wade nodded, "My pleasure, Mrs. Read. If you need to speak to me again, just call the front desk and they'll put you through."

She nodded, gave him a polite but cold smile, and turned toward the elevator, Lehman in tow.

Wade watched after them a moment, considering the woman thoughtfully. At the very least, he had to agree with Monica that Angelica drew a hard line and was a little difficult to read. But by her accent, English was likely her second language. While she was perfectly fluent, a fear of being misunderstood could explain her unease.

He frowned. His gut said there was more to it. The way she gripped her purse the entire time, holding it in front of her like a shield. She was uncomfortable. The question was, why? Was she really the one behind the idea that he was The Man Upstairs? Perhaps Monica was right to keep an eye on her. There were things Angelica Read kept close to her vest.

Wade returned to his office. Sliding into his chair, he finished his paperwork, grabbing the first pen that came to hand. When the papers were done, he slid the pen into his pocket, strapped on his duty belt, holstered his sidearm, and strode to the elevator to join Lehman downstairs.

# CHAPTER FIFTY-TWO

# ANGELICA

Angelica exited the police station, swearing under her breath. Wade Erickson was annoyingly hard to read. He hadn't flinched at the mention of her children—and while she'd waited for him to let slip that he knew she had two sons specifically, the words had never passed his lips, nor anything else that would suggest he knew more about her boys than he should. He hadn't reacted to the words "playing detective," either.

As for namedropping The Man Upstairs, she was proud of how she'd slipped it in at the end. But had she been too subtle? Had he even noticed? If he really *was* The Man Upstairs, how could he have missed it?

Angelica slid behind the wheel of her rental car and turned on the AC, then leaned her head in her hand and bit her lip. Was she obsessed over the wrong man? Was her papá right? But Erickson's office was *upstairs...*

She closed her eyes and laughed at herself. Roland would say she was reading too much into that.

Well, if Wade Erickson *was* The Man Upstairs... she'd challenged him to his face—not only by returning to Lake Geneva, but by marching straight into his office and throwing his words back at him. Whatever she did with the rest of her night, she should remain in public. Just to be safe.

Her stomach churned. Her papá wouldn't approve of what she'd done.

Or maybe he would be proud?

*Dios*, she didn't know. She didn't know what she was doing anymore.

At least one thing was for sure. She'd managed to plant the pen in Erickson's office.

She pulled out her phone and opened the app that went with the pen. It had taken a call to customer support, but she'd managed to convince them that she'd given her phone to a cousin, and forgotten to disconnect the app. It probably helped that the person on the other end of the line was a native Spanish speaker and thoroughly understood helping *familia*. In a matter of moments, the helpful customer support person had disconnected the pen from the original phone and even helped Angelica set it up with her new one.

Now, as she sat in her rental car, she watched the app refresh. To her delight, it showed a new file, time-stamped to the moment she'd stepped up to the front desk of the police station and activated the pen with her voice.

She was about to tap the file to review her conversation, when a new file popped onto the screen. Instead of displaying a green check mark, the icon showed a moving graphic of vibrating sound waves.

The pen was recording.

Angelica drew a quick breath... then tapped the new file.

Chief Wade Erickson's voice filled her cab.

# CHAPTER FIFTY-THREE

# WADE

Wade navigated an unmarked vehicle through the crawl of downtown traffic, a mix of bumper-to-bumper cars and swarming pedestrians. As he waited for the light at Center and Main, he glanced at Lehman. The head of his detective bureau stared out the passenger window, absent-mindedly bumping his fist against his mouth. His gaze seemed infinitely further away than the crowds of tourists on the sidewalk.

Wade shifted an interested brow. Stan Lehman acting keyed up was an anomaly worth noting. Normally, the detective was so laid back, Wade wasn't sure how he managed investigations as efficiently as he typically did.

"You're awfully eager to work the carny tonight," Wade ventured.

Lehman turned his head, eyebrows arched as if he were catching up with the conversation. "Hm?"

"I thought you hated anything that didn't involve sitting behind a desk," Wade teased.

Lehman cocked a mirthless grin and looked away again. "Cruel, Chief. Cruel."

Wade laughed under his breath. "I know I'm in a glass house over here. I'm pretty friendly with an office chair myself."

Lehman only grunted and bounced his foot.

Wade slanted his eyes. While work-life balance was a joke in law enforcement, Wade still wasn't keen on letting one of his officers manage an event detail while he appeared this distracted.

The light changed and traffic inched forward, the cars in line waiting for a break in the crossing pedestrians. Wade reviewed what he knew, trying to think what could be eating Lehman tonight.

One thing seemed fairly obvious.

"So, your partner dumped you," Wade commented.

Lehman snapped his head around, eyes wide as if panicked. "What?"

Perhaps Wade should have chosen better words. He hoped he hadn't triggered Lehman into thoughts of his ex. Was that what was on his mind?

"Monica," Wade clarified. "She headed to the event without you."

Lehman shook his head, the trace of a dismissive sneer across his face. "You know her. Five minutes from now is too late." He bounced his foot even more aggressively.

Wade didn't miss the signal of heightened agitation. Ah. So he was on the right track; Lehman's distraction likely had something to do with Monica. He finally completed the turn onto Center Street. He had the equivalent of two blocks—and as long as five minutes—to figure it out.

"The two of you fall out, or something?" Wade asked. He knew Monica could be hard to get along with. Lehman was a saint for putting up with her like he did. "Should we have put her on vehicle patrol tonight? Kept her out from under your feet?" Sergeant Warner was managing the black-and-whites out of the station.

Lehman's eyes shot to Wade. "No." He said it too swiftly to sound natural, and seemed to know it. Heat rose to his face and his eyes darted awkwardly, as if he were seeking something else to say.

Wade scrutinized his detective sergeant. Suddenly, the truth sunk in.

Wade arched his brows. "Oh-h-h." That's why Lehman had dyed his hair.

His thoughts shifted to Ryan. Poor bastard had competition now. That boy might want to get a move on. Did he even have any idea? Wade repressed a nervous smile. Things were about to get lively around the PD.

"How long's this been brewing beneath the surface?" he asked.

Lehman tapped his fist against his mouth again. "Long time."

So, Ryan's return hadn't precipitated the development. But maybe it had helped Lehman focus his resolve?

"Does she know?" Wade asked.

"Yeah," Lehman said. "I told her."

By the tension evident in his every movement—and by the fact that Monica had abandoned Lehman at the station—that conversation hadn't gone well. Better luck for Ryan, if that was the case. Or possibly, she would disappoint them both. Monica Steele needed no man, and was a famously brutal heartbreaker to anyone who tried to court her. Kudos to Lehman for even working up the nerve.

As they crawled down Center Street, the detective shifted in his seat and filled his lungs. "I've been worried about her, Chief. She's not been herself lately."

"How so?" Wade asked.

"I walk into the office sometimes, and I catch her listening to that phone call over and over." He looked at Wade seriously. "It's happened more than once."

Wade furrowed his brow. That part *was* concerning.

Lehman shrugged. "I mean, I get it. I'd be paranoid, too, if that creep had my personal number and was contacting me with weird messages. But knowing Monica, I just... I wouldn't have expected her to let it get to her like this, you know?"

"Hm," Wade replied. If he'd known Monica was reacting so badly to that message, he might have handled a few things differently.

Realizing he'd fallen into a silence, he glanced at Lehman. The man was staring at him quizzically.

"You know something, Chief," Lehman said accusingly.

Wade rolled his head with a smirk of disappointment in himself. He'd shown his hand. "Well, I was *going* to tell you, but your getting into a relationship with Monica complicates things."

"I guess it's a good thing we're not in a relationship, then," Lehman shot back, the bitterness over Monica's rejection apparently drowned out by frustration that Wade wasn't shooting straight with him.

"The principle stands," Wade replied.

Lehman squared his shoulders. "Sir, is there something I need to know about one of the officers under my command?"

Wade rolled his eyes skyward and groaned. "This is why we should have a policy against relationships within the department."

Lehman's gaze went stern. "With all due respect, if you enacted such a policy, you'd find yourself short a detective sergeant." He slow-blinked and shook his head. "And a lot of other officers." He began to count on his fingertips. "Steph and Asher, Piper and Lange—"

Wade lifted a palm. "I know, I know." He sighed deeply, then bumped the heel of his hand on the rim of the steering wheel, fingers splayed. "All right. Fine. Things being such as they are—yes. There's something you should know about one of your officers." He skewered Lehman with his gaze. "I'll leave it to the lover-boy to figure out how he wants to tell her that he knows this."

"Understood," Lehman said. But his unflinching gaze flinched.

Well, good. The man had a proper fear for how complicated this was going to be.

Wade studied Flat Iron Park as it came into view, flashing with carnival lights and throbbing with music, the entire area a sea of humanity. Beyond, the last light of the dying sun colored the surface of the lake in stripes of blue, with the towering Ferris wheel dominating the sky.

He bit the bullet and spit it out. "Monica had an abortion ten years ago."

Lehman gaped as if Wade had socked him in the bread basket. Clearly, he had taken the news as the lover-boy.

Well, Wade had warned him.

"You breathing over there, buddy?" he asked.

"Ten years," Lehman muttered. "That's when she broke up with Brandt. Oh, shit." His hand went briefly to his mouth before he looked to Wade. "Was the baby not his?"

Wade smirked. "Nice theory, Sherlock. But considering she's never been seen with another man—before or since—the baby was almost certainly Ryan's." He flicked his eyes over Lehman. "Good luck getting an in with her, by the way."

Lehman waved the comment off. "She hates Brandt."

By the distant look in his eyes, he was still processing her abortion, oblivious to the obvious: She had never loved anyone *but* Brandt.

Wade studied the head of his detective bureau critically. "You processing this all right, Detective Sergeant?" He emphasized Lehman's rank. After all, the man had only extracted the information by demanding disclosure on one of his subordinates.

"Uh..." Lehman blinked then looked at Wade sheepishly. "I'll admit, Chief, that wasn't anything I was expecting."

"Hm," Wade grunted, feeling justified. Traffic had come to a complete standstill again, giving him space to think. In the coming weeks, he'd have to keep an eye on his detective bureau to make sure it was still functioning properly—particularly considering that Mark Neumiller, the third detective in the department, would soon be returning to his winter role as school resource officer at Badger High. The workload at the end of the tourist season didn't justify having more than two detectives on duty. And now those two detectives would be Monica and Lehman.

"So, that phone call," Lehman said. "That *was* personal." He ran his hand over his mouth. "My God, no wonder she's been freaking out." He shot his attention to Wade. "Wait, how'd *you* know about the abortion? She told you?"

Wade could understand why Lehman would assume so. "No," he said, sadness in his voice. It pained him that Monica had never come to him with that information herself. "Even as her mentor, I didn't earn that privilege."

"Then...?" Lehman shook his head and turned a palm up.

Traffic remained frozen. Wade tapped his fingers on the wheel. "Ten years ago, I was working a case involving a breach of patient confidentiality. The complainant was from Lake Geneva, and the facility in question was an abortion clinic in Madison. I ran up to conduct some interviews."

"And?"

"And Monica Steele was sitting in the waiting area."

Lehman thought it through and shook his head. "She was working at the Madison PD then. She could have been investigating, too."

"She was in civvies, and a nurse called her name and led her to an exam room."

Lehman shook his head, then ran both hands down his face. "My God, why didn't you tell me before? Why didn't you tell the task force? This is a lead."

Wade turned up a hand. "How was I supposed to out Monica when she'd never even told me? Protecting her privacy was important to me, as well—particularly if this turned out to be a false trail."

Lehman scowled at him. "So, you've just been sitting on this information?"

"Of course not. I've been re-examining everything about the patient confidentiality case. But I've only confirmed the same thing I found then: That there was no breach of protocol. That's why I wanted to bring it to you, so you could go over my work, see if I missed anything, see if you could knock anything loose." Wade lifted his chin indignantly. "But, of course, you had to go and complicate things, Mr. Don Juan."

Lehman sighed. "Look, I'm sorry I'm human."

Silence settled over the interior of the cab. Wade drummed his thumbs on the steering wheel. Lehman was right. Wade couldn't begrudge him the longing for companionship again. Someone to share a life with. Someone you trusted to have your six—on the streets as well as at home.

"Been a while since you and Becky broke up," Wade observed.

Lehman turned to stare out the passenger window—but not before Wade caught the way his eyes went flat and lifeless, a contrast to the carnival lights splashed across his face. "Yeah, don't remind me."

After years of putting up with unpredictable schedules, over-ruled plans, and unfulfilled expectations—not to mention the insane stress anytime she knew her husband was putting his life on the line—Becky had decided being married to a cop was too much to ask of any healthy, well-adjusted human being.

Maybe that was why Lehman had his heart set on another cop this go-around.

They finally rolled up to the Mobile Command Unit, which was parked at the southern corner of the upside-down triangle that was Flat Iron Park. The command vehicle could have passed as an RV—and in fact, it was, complete with a slide-out and an awning—but every inch of it was built to accommodate the concept of a miniature, rolling police station that could be parked wherever they needed it, whether for an event detail like tonight, or an unfolding emergency. Prominent "Police & Fire" decals marked the sides of the vehicle, and a fifteen-foot telescoping camera tower jutted into the air.

Wade parked beside the Command Unit and shut down the engine. A cluster of officers stood under the awning.

Lehman took a deep breath. "We've got to talk to Monica. And the whole task force. Well... what's left of it. Frankly, this could be the best lead we've got right now."

Wade nodded. "I agree. I'm sorry I didn't share it sooner."

Lehman shrugged. "I guess you're human, too."

Wade lifted a wan smile. Truer words were never spoken.

He lifted his eyes and picked out Monica Steele standing amongst the officers. She was looking smart in a patrol uniform, her dark hair twisted into a tight bun at the base of her neck. That girl had been like a daughter to him since the day she inserted herself into his office and said, "You need an intern—me," then plunked a coffee down on his desk.

# CHAPTER FIFTY-FOUR

# ANGELICA

Angelica listened to Erickson and Lehman's conversation, not daring to breathe, even though the transmission came through crystal clear.

Whatever she'd been expecting to hear... it wasn't this: A lot of workplace drama, like a telenovela. Steele's partner, Lehman, was in love with her—something the chief hadn't known. But Lehman hadn't known that Steele'd had an abortion ten years ago—something the chief *had* known.

What confused Angelica the most was how they both agreed that this detail from Monica's personal history had bearing on the case they were working on. What case? Will's murder? That made no sense. Will and Steele had nothing to do with each other, besides Steele's investigation. No, Erickson and Lehman had to be discussing something else.

The pen picked up the sound of car doors opening and closing, then a lot of loud music, the murmur of a crowd, a jumble of nearer voices. Erickson's, being the closest to the microphone, came through the clearest, but he only spoke now in brief expressions, as if exchanging greetings. She couldn't identify the other voices. None of them sounded like Lehman anymore.

Overwhelmed by the chaos of the transmission, Angelica turned off the player. The app assured her it was still recording. She'd try to review it later, perhaps in the quiet of her hotel room.

For now, she had some thinking to do. She got out of her car and started walking, still remembering her decision to stay in public places—just in case. In good news, the entire town was bristling with people. Erickson wouldn't dare move against her while surrounded by witnesses.

# CHAPTER FIFTY-FIVE

# MONICA

Hands on my duty belt, I scanned the carnival while half-listening to the banter of the other officers. I tried not to think how petty it had been of me to abandon Lehman at the station. We'd had a perfectly comfortable, passive-aggressive relationship until now. I was just beginning to realize how that relationship had been one of the pillars of my life. Why'd he have to go and ruin it?

I forced the thoughts aside and focused on the carnival. In front of me on Wrigley Drive, vomit-inducing rides flung carnival-go-ers bodily into the air. Popcorn littered the ground like a spring skiff of snow. The air smelled of hot dogs and hamburgers, the grease hanging as heavily as the lake humidity. The live music coming off the stage at the north end of the park rocked the very air, and I knew that the beer tent next to it, separated from the rest of the event with paneled fencing, was at peak business.

I watched for open containers that may have found their way out of the twenty-one-and-up area, for celebratory attitudes devolving into tightened fists, for anything less innocent than candy bars passing hands.

So far, all was good. Young couples strolled hand-in-hand, pointing out the next ride or game they wanted to try. Gaggles of teens navigated the crowd blindly while sipping sodas and staring at their phones.

But repeatedly, I found my eye drawn to the young families.

Kids ran through the carnival holding clouds of cotton candy and stuffed toys as big as they were. Their parents juggled strings of tickets and a jumble of childhood accoutrement their small ones had handed off to them, as if the adults were the personal attendants of the children.

I couldn't look at the kids long without the wrench returning to my belly. I forced my eyes away and kept scanning.

Then I realized what I was really looking for: Ryan. Even though I knew he was on vehicle patrol tonight—north of the bottleneck of downtown and nowhere near the carnival. Still, I wanted him to appear out of the morass. I wanted to see his confident stride, his warm eyes. I wanted him to wrap me in his arms. Tell me everything was okay. That he forgave me. That he still loved me and still wanted us to start over.

But we hadn't spoken in days. Perhaps, subconsciously, I was avoiding him as much as Lehman. I was terrified that Ryan hated me—and it was better to live in ignorance than to risk confirming the truth.

A black SUV pulled up next to the Command Unit. Wade stepped out from behind the wheel, Lehman from the passenger seat.

Lehman's eyes went to mine immediately. Rather than expressing sarcastic indignation that I'd left him behind—the way he would have looked at me in the good old days—his eyes were concerned, searching.

Jesus Christ. The last thing I needed from Lehman was empathy in response to my being an asshole.

I turned and walked away, even while the rest of the security detail was greeting Lehman and the chief. I'd finished my last circuit of the grounds two minutes ago, so it was clearly time to start again. I didn't even wait for my partner of the night, Owen Pratt.

Footsteps jogged up behind me. "Monica." Lehman fell into step at my right shoulder.

I pasted on a cold smile and stared away from him, toward the less-insane rides for the little kids. "Lehman. So glad you could make it," I intoned.

"Yeah, I'm your *partner*," he replied. Apparently, he was a little stung I'd dumped his ass at the PD.

I bounced my eyebrows. "Really? I thought you'd gotten tired of that designation."

"Come on, Monica, you're the best partner I've ever had." He tried to find my eyes with his. "But now you know where I stand."

I rounded on him. "Yeah. With your head up your ass, and your foot in your mouth." I shifted an eyebrow. "Pretty impressive, really."

"Monica—"

I grit my teeth and pushed my finger into his sternum. "I *trusted* you, Lehman. And you *ruined* it."

Tilting his head, he cast his eyes down and gently caught my hand in his, stopping me from digging him in the chest. "Wanting you to open up and live a little is 'ruining it'?" When he looked at me again, his eyes were painfully sincere.

I snapped my hand away, the touch too intimate for my comfort. His words too close to the vacuum of my inner existence, the emptiness in my belly that I'd built my Wall around.

"I don't give a damn what you want, Lehman." I got up in his space, tilting my chin so I could look him in the eye. "Just because you work on the other side of a cubicle from me, you think you know anything about me? Well, you don't. So keep your damn feelings to yourself. We have a job to do—a serial killer to catch. Or have you forgotten about that?"

Undaunted by my tirade, he took me in with that look of undying patience that I hated about him. His gaze was understanding. Penetrating. With a surge of panic, I realized he was staring straight into the void in the middle of my soul—the place even I never visited. The sacred space where I kept thoughts of the child I could never hold. Involuntarily, I stepped back. I was reading too much into that look, wasn't I?

"You keep trying to forget," he said, "that there's more to you than the badge."

I shook my head, fighting to hold back the tears. "You're wrong," I said. "There isn't."

Not since I'd lost Ryan. Not since I'd given up my child. Everything besides the badge hurt too much to even think about.

I stalked away. This time Lehman didn't try to stop me, and he didn't try to follow.

I ran my hands down my face, as if to wash away the feelings. The hurt. The rage. I really had counted on Lehman. As my *partner*. Without that, how was I supposed to finish this case? Why was life such a dick? Was it too much to ask that the men in my life value me the way I wanted them to? To be loved by the man I'd spent ten years hating, and supported by the man I tormented daily yet relied on?

I bowed my head and laughed and cried at the same time. Life was merely giving me everything I deserved. Your soul couldn't be as warped as mine without a comeuppance eventually.

I wove my way through the carnival, northwards towards the concessions, the beer tent, and the concert. The sea of humanity parted around me, avoiding me. Whether they were put off by my uniform or by the ice that rolled off my shoulders, I didn't know and I didn't care. To them, perhaps it was one and the same. I was just grateful to be left alone.

Perhaps it was my hyper-awareness to averted eyes that alerted me to the sensation that one set of eyes was openly staring. Lifting my head, I scanned the crowd. Flashing carnival lights washed the shifting sea of humanity, and in the middle of it all, a woman stood frozen, her eyes delving into me.

Angelica Read. Her black hair hung loose around her shoulders and her delicate hands clutched a small white purse. What was she doing back in Lake Geneva? Why was she staring at me?

I thought back to our interview in her house in Malibu, two months ago. She'd sworn she didn't know her husband's real name. That he wasn't from Lake Geneva. That he'd never involve himself with a criminal ring.

But she was wrong. He had.

I narrowed my eyes and felt myself shaking my head subtly. It wasn't possible a man could change his whole identity and live a lie so effectively that his own wife didn't know. It was impossible she was as ignorant and innocent as she claimed. And if she knew her husband's criminal past—it was altogether possible she knew The Man Upstairs. Why else did she keep coming back to Lake Geneva? Why else had she been talking to Roland? What did she have to do with the break-in at his house? With him getting hurt?

I began to move forward, closing the distance between her and me. Roland had insisted Angelica and I should talk. And he was right. The talking could start now.

# CHAPTER FIFTY-SIX

# ANGELICA

Angelica's body stiffened as Monica Steele strode toward her. It had taken Angelica a moment of concentration to confirm that it really was Steele; she'd never seen her in uniform before. The bullet-proof vest and gun belt altered her figure, and she'd pinned her hair up, as opposed to wearing it in the long ponytail Angelica had seen previously.

In hindsight, perhaps she shouldn't have stared. Steele looked none too pleased.

Trembling, Angelica told herself to stand her ground and let Detective Steele approach. She grasped her purse in both hands, but held it low in front of her. She was aware she was hanging onto it like a lifeline. She wouldn't touch the gun inside unless desperate—unless truly afraid for her life. In the meantime, it was no doubt best that Steele didn't know she had it.

Angelica's mind spun with personal details she suddenly knew about the detective. She was divorced. She'd had an abortion. Her partner had told her he loved her, but she didn't love him back.

Perhaps knowing such intimate details should have helped her see Monica Steele in a more generous light—regardless of the bizarre and unfair methods by which she'd acquired the knowledge. But at the same time, each of these facts only helped to paint the detective as the unfeeling woman Angelica had met in Malibu. Looking into the woman's eyes, all she could see was ice.

Roland was positive Steele could be trusted. That she was the cop they needed on their side. If Angelica walked away now, when it was clear Steele meant to talk to her, she would handicap any opportunity to open a conversation later. Roland would be disappointed.

But Wade Erickson was Steele's mentor. Roland had said so, and Erickson had repeated it only minutes ago. The two of them were so close—and had been for so long—that Erickson was hurt Steele had never told him about her abortion. Would Steele really believe an accusation against such a mentor? Angelica still had no proof.

As Steele closed the distance, Angelica wavered back and forth, questioning everything the other woman might be thinking and doing. And then her papá's wisdom echoed through her memory.

*We fear what we do not understand.*

Her papá would tell her to speak to this woman. To understand her. At the very least, to try. She was his *ángel*, and he expected no less of her.

But another thought seared across Angelica's mind: What if Steele already knew that Angelica had spoken with Erickson? What if the police chief *was* The Man Upstairs, and he was incensed at Angelica's return? At her brazenly confronting him with his own words? At her planting his own bug on him?

What if he'd sent his protégé after Angelica to finish off his little problem?

The carnival lights strobed across Steele's face, momentarily painting the left red, the right blue, looking eerily like police lights.

Angelica blinked, and a memory painted itself across the inside of her eyelids: A sterile, gray emergency room. A gash across her father's brow and cheekbone. Blood bathing the left side of his face. His eye swollen shut.

When Angelica looked again, the police detective was mere yards away, her eyes hard, piercing, her footsteps driven. Angelica thought of how easily her two boys had vanished from her own front yard, and feral panic gripped her body.

She turned on her heel and ran.

# CHAPTER FIFTY-SEVEN

# MONICA

As I strode purposefully toward Angelica Read, I watched a dozen emotions cross her face. What was this woman's problem? What was she hiding? Her odd behavior only made me more determined to speak with her.

Angelica's fingers worked nervously along the upper edge of her purse, white with short straps and gold clasps. I narrowed my eyes on the handbag—

And noted an odd bulge pressing against the inside of the leather. Boxy. L-shaped. A handgun?

The next instant, she whirled and ran pell-mell through the crowd.

I took after her, grabbing the radio mic clipped to my shoulder. "Forty-four twelve, foot pursuit. Hispanic female, possibly armed. Westbound toward Wrigley."

# CHAPTER FIFTY-EIGHT

# LEHMAN

Lehman stopped in his tracks as Monica's transmission fed through his earpiece. Twisting his head in concentration, he strained to hear past the noise of the carnival.

"Copy," another voice said—Piper Lange. Lehman knew she was working dispatch for the event detail from a small room in the back of the Mobile Command Unit. "Can you describe what the suspect is armed with?"

"Negative." Monica's communication was garbled by her own heavy breathing and her radio mic clunking against her ballistic vest. And then, contradicting her previous statement, she clarified, "Handgun."

Adrenalin spiking, Lehman jerked his head around, gazing toward the place where Monica had vanished into the crowd. He deliberated only a moment—

And then he ran south, away from Monica and toward the Mobile Command Unit. Tonight, his assigned duty was the entire event detail. To help Monica bring her suspect in safely, it was his job to coordinate the overall response.

Besides, he knew better than to try riding in on some white stallion and "saving" her. She wasn't the kind of woman who appreciated being saved. And right now, the sight of his unwelcome face would only distract her from her work.

Like always, he could best support her from a distance—however much the distance hurt him.

# Chapter Fifty-Nine

# ANGELICA

Angelica dashed past games and concession stands, her heart pounding. She didn't even know where she was going, where she was.

One thought pounded through her head over and over: *I must come home to my boys... I must come home to my boys...*

Through the treetops, she spied a massive wheel, slowly turning, lights chasing each other in shifting patterns along the rim and down every vein. The Ferris wheel. She'd seen it before, dominating the skyline right beside the lake. The shoreline, she was familiar with. She could follow it toward the Riviera, which was somewhere to her right. From there, she thought she could find her car—blocks away, and thankfully out of the thickest part of the tourist traffic.

Angelica glanced over her shoulder. To her horror, Steele was gaining on her, running as swiftly and smoothly as if she trained every day.

Panic rose to her throat. Angelica didn't have blocks. Steele would catch her within moments.

She looked again to the sky, to the slowly turning wheel, desperate for a strategy, for help—

A man with blond dreadlocks stepped out from behind a brightly colored concession trailer, carrying two bags of ice. Angelica didn't see him until it was too late. Gasping, she threw her hands in front of her and ended up ramming straight into his chest.

He exhaled sharply, the air knocked from his lungs. The bags slipped out of his hands. They hit the ground and exploded. Ice spilled across the grass. The cubes chilled Angelica's toes through her sandals and turned the grass slick.

Angelica and the man rotated around each other like dance partners, the man looking shocked and justifiably angry.

"I'm sorry! I'm sorry!" Angelica said, palms out—and kept running.

She glanced back long enough to see Monica Steele round the same corner—

And wipe out on the ice. It looked like she went down hard.

*Gracias, Madre Maria,* Angelica prayed, even as she felt a twinge of guilt for taking pleasure in someone else's pain. But now, she had more time, even if it was only a moment.

# CHAPTER SIXTY

# MONICA

Angelica Read vanished around the corner of a trailer, its signage proclaiming hot dogs, corn dogs, sodas, and other carnival fare. Piper Lange's voice came over my radio.

"Forty-four twelve, we have foot patrol units moving toward your location. Can you provide more description of the suspect?"

Breathing hard, I reached for the button on my mic. "Hispanic female. Mid-thirties. Five two, a hundred and twenty pounds. Wearing a peach blouse and white capris. Carrying—"

I rounded the corner of the concessions stand. A man in a Hawaiian shirt and dirty blond dreads stood there, staring in the opposite direction from me, hands in a shrug as if he were processing something unbelievable.

I adjusted course to dodge him, only for the ground to slide beneath my feet like ball bearings.

I went down. Hard. Landed on my left elbow and hip. Plastic snapped underneath me. My hands and forearms swam through something cold, wet, and hard.

I blinked, waiting for my vision to quit tilting. Suddenly, the man with the dreads was leaning over me, offering a hand, asking if I was okay. Piper's voice nagged in my earpiece. "Forty-four twelve, please repeat?"

I shook my head like a dog, blinking away the last of the dizziness. God, that was embarrassing.

Ignoring the young man's offered help, I sprang to my feet and scanned the crowd.

"That way," he said, pointing toward Wrigley Drive and the shore. "She went that way."

I spotted her, dodging through the crowd, toward the Ferris wheel, as if she were fleeing toward some magical gateway that would transport her to another world.

"Thanks," I said to the young man, and took to my heels again. My hip and elbow weren't sore—not yet. But they would be tomorrow, along with random other parts of my body I hadn't realized I'd jarred.

I reached for the mic on my shoulder and clicked the button. "Forty-four twelve, westbound toward Wrigley."

A moment later, Piper replied, "Forty-four twelve, do you copy?" with the voice of someone who was still waiting to hear from me.

I scowled at my mic, as if it were Piper herself. What the—?

Then I remembered the sensation of snapping plastic. Shit, no. I reached for the actual radio unit, clipped to the left side of my belt. My fingers found a jagged edge to the casing.

God dammit.

# CHAPTER SIXTY-ONE

# LEHMAN

Lehman swung open the door on the side of the Command Unit and bolted up the stairs into what was, hands-down, the most tech-savvy RV in the city. He pulled out his earpiece and un-clipped his radio from his belt. There were enough mics mounted all around the walls in here, he wouldn't need his personal set anymore.

He stepped into the main room, which opened up to his right, and threw his radio down on the table that could serve as work area or meeting room. The slide-out across from it housed a pair of screens which any retiree would have loved to watch "the game" on; but these were drawing their feed from the camera tower mounted to the roof of the vehicle, giving a bird's-eye view of the south side of Flat Iron Park.

Lehman gave the screens a cursory glance, half-wishing he'd simply spot Monica in the middle of the chaos of the carnival. But he had more work to do besides monitor the cameras. Turning, he followed the narrow hallway past a kitchenette featuring a coffee pot and microwave—just the essentials. Beyond this, the tiny room in the rear of the truck was plastered with more screens. If the Command Unit was a mini police station, this area was its tiny dispatch center.

Headset parked over her red pixie cut, Telecommunicator Piper Lange typed furiously at her keyboard as Monica's voice came over the radio speakers.

"Hispanic female. Mid-thirties. Five two, a hundred and twenty pounds. Wearing a peach blouse and white capris. Carrying—"

The transmission ended abruptly with an explosive clatter. Piper startled and pulled the headset away from her ears. She shook her head, settled the headset back down, then spoke into her mic. "Forty-four twelve, please repeat?"

Her request was met with silence.

Lehman squeezed into the small room behind Piper's chair and alongside the only other occupant—the chief—whose head nearly brushed the ceiling. Peering over Piper's shoulder, Lehman read the description Monica had provided. Wait, hadn't he literally just escorted that woman to the chief's office and back? Wasn't that Angelica Read?

Lehman glanced at Wade. "You catch that description, Chief?"

Wade nodded somberly, by all appearances thinking the same as Lehman.

"What the hell happened?"

Wade only looked blank, his blue eyes hauntingly cavernous.

Piper pointed toward a map on one of her screens, which she'd centered over the upside-down triangle of Flat Iron Park. "Foot patrol units are making toward her location."

"Vehicle units notified yet?" Lehman asked.

"Not yet."

He unhooked one of the radio mics mounted under the cabinets and switched it to channel one. The black-and-whites were supposed to be under Sergeant Lisa Warner's command tonight, but he was officially borrowing a few. Studying the map, he could envision the perimeter he wanted around Flat Iron Park, and thanks to the GPS on the cars, he could see who was already close to those locations.

He depressed the button on the mic. "Forty-three thirty-two, all units: Be advised we have a foot pursuit in progress in Flat Iron Park. Suspect potentially armed with a handgun." He repeated the description Monica had provided. "Closing channel three for incident. Stand by for assignments. Forty-four ten, Center and Main, switch to channel three. Forty-four thirteen, Wrigley and Center, switch to channel three. Forty-four o-six, the bridge on Wrigley, switch to channel three."

Lehman found himself pausing before calling out the last assignment. Forty-four thirty-seven. Ryan Brandt. A small voice in the back of his head was annoyed that Brandt had the closest unit to the northwest corner of his perimeter.

Lehman blinked and shook his head. *Monica hates him. It's fine.* Selfishly, he would have been all right if Brandt had left at the end of the summer, like he'd originally intended.

Lehman clicked the button again. "Forty-four thirty-seven, Broad and Main, switch to channel three."

Lehman turned the knob back to channel three himself, planted his hands on the countertop, and sighed, shifting his weight. Feeling eyes on his back, he glanced over his shoulder. Wade leaned against a cramped desk in the corner, arms folded across his chest as he studied him curiously. Lehman returned his attention to the monitors. He shouldn't have hesitated before giving Brandt his assignment. Not much got past the old man.

"Let me check with Steele again," Piper said.

Lehman nodded, letting her use the channel.

She spoke into her headset. "Forty-four twelve, do you copy?"

Her question was once again met with silence.

She and Lehman exchanged glances, silently asking the same question. What had happened to Monica?

Brows heavy, Wade Erickson turned around to the monitor that was mounted above the desk he'd been leaning on. With the click of a few buttons, he brought up the feed from the camera tower. Navigating the controls, he began to sweep the park, trying to get a visual on Monica or Angelica Read.

Lehman bounced a fist on the counter in front of him, then pushed off and began pacing the tiny room—barely two steps in each direction. "Ask the foot patrols if they have eyes on the pursuit yet." Arguably, it was more efficient for him to do it himself—but he was hesitant about putting his voice in Monica's ear after their argument. Whatever she was doing, he didn't want to distract her.

Piper activated her mic. "Foot patrols, does anyone have eyes yet on 4412 or the suspect?"

One by one, the teams reported back. Negative. Negative. Negative...

Nerves mounting, Lehman stared over the chief's shoulder at the camera feed. Trying to spot two individuals out of a crowd of thousands was like playing "Where's Waldo?"

*Monica, where are you?*

# CHAPTER SIXTY-TWO

# RYAN

I hit my lights and sirens and sped toward downtown, several blocks south and east of my current location. Meanwhile, I kept my ears glued to the radio.

Piper asked 4412—Monica—to report. I waited for Monica's response, but there was only silence. Why wasn't she responding? Piper went on to ask the foot patrol units if any of them had visual on her.

No one did.

My stomach went into a knot.

I rethought the past several days, asking myself why I hadn't made a better effort to talk to her. I'd told myself that a bomb like the one she'd dropped necessitated time for us to mutually process. That I was giving her space and time as much as I was myself.

And then I remembered that we were cops, and tomorrow wasn't necessarily a given—and that I was just an idiot.

Tightening my hands on the steering wheel, I breathed deeply and let the air out slowly, even as I sped toward downtown. Monica was fine. She was a professional. Maybe she was grappling the suspect and couldn't stop to report. A brief tussle in the grass—Monica was always down for a wrestling match—and she'd slap the handcuffs on, no muss, no fuss, just a little bit of cardio.

Or perhaps the suspect had pulled the gun and gotten the drop on her.

I ignored the trickle of sweat under my arms. Monica would be fine.

# CHAPTER SIXTY-THREE

# ANGELICA

Frantic, her lungs beginning to feel as if they might explode, Angelica kept running. She wouldn't be able to outrun this woman. Her best hope was to confuse her. To disappear. Perhaps she could hide—just long enough to gain distance.

Angelica ran across the street that paralleled the shore. It was alive with people, feet treading pavement that was bisected by rubber mats covering the network of cables that fed life to the carnival. The Ferris wheel was directly in front of her. The entire shore-side of the street was lined with dizzying rides, lifting people into the air, dropping them almost to the ground, flinging them skyward again, filling the street with screams. People stood in long lines, waiting their turns for a near-death experience.

There were too many people here, nowhere she felt she could disappear.

To the left of the Ferris wheel, Angelica spied a funhouse. At the moment, it was receiving less love than the air-born rides. Surprisingly quiet, surprisingly sane. A young man was managing the attraction, his dark hair undercut with sporty horizontal lines shaved across the sides of his head. He was chatting casually with just one small family as he counted out their tickets.

Angelica sprang over the low fence meant to keep delinquents like herself out and ran to the doorway that led into the funhouse.

She paused only long enough to glance back. The ticket taker and the small family were staring at her, surprised.

Beyond them, beyond lines of ride-goers and waves of milling pedestrians, Angelica spied Monica Steele. The policewoman was running toward the funhouse, her brow heavier and angrier than ever.

Angelica bit her lip and slipped through the door. As she turned to take in her new surroundings, she realized her mistake.

A dozen women stared back at her, their dark hair long and loose, all of them dressed in peach blouses and white capris, leather purses with gold clasps clutched in their left hands. Their faces all stared back, brown eyes wide, terrified.

It was a maze of mirrors. This... this was a terrible idea. But she was out of time. She glanced over her shoulder. Steele was approaching the fence.

Angelica moved forward into what looked like a long hallway—and ran smack into glass.

She put a hand to her throbbing nose and lip and stifled a cry. What had she done? Why had she made such a stupid, *stupid* mistake? She was never getting out of this.

Her mantra ran through her head again. *I must come home to my boys... I must come home to my boys...*

Putting her hand in front of her, she felt her way forward into the belly of the maze—just as she heard Monica Steele's running footsteps approach the funhouse.

# CHAPTER SIXTY-FOUR

# MONICA

I leapt the barricade past a confused carny and a young family and charged through the door, just as a sandaled foot disappeared in front of me.

I reached out to grab her—

And stubbed my fingers on glass.

Moments later, the rest of my body crashed into the mirror, my hands catching me. What the actual—? I stared into my own confused face.

Glancing to my left, I saw the real hall leading deeper in—and Angelica, whirling and running away with a panicked shout.

I sprang off the mirror and lunged for her, going for a grapple—only for the image to be replaced by mine at the last moment. I body-checked yet another mirror.

I stopped to breathe, then turned slowly, eyes wide. It was a maze of mirrors. The mood lights along the floors brightened and dimmed, adding an eerie effect to the place. Where was Angelica? I drew my gun, countless copies of myself mimicking my movements.

Of everywhere on earth, why would Angelica run into a place like this? I shouldn't be in here. I turned and looked behind me in the direction I'd come—and couldn't make out hallways from walls. My heart began to pound.

Piper's voice came over my radio. "Vehicle units, any sighting of 4412 or the suspect?"

"Yeah, that would be a negative," I whispered. Obviously, no one knew where I was. I didn't know where I was anymore. And by my best guess, the closest person to The Man Upstairs was hiding in this house of insanity.

Ryan was the last of the vehicle units to report. "Forty-four thirty-seven, negative."

At the sound of his voice—the first I'd heard it in days—I rocked forward and bit my lip so hard, I thought it would bleed. Where had he been all this time? Why hadn't he talked to me? I needed him now the way I'd needed him my whole life. I needed to let him know that I hurt, that I was afraid, when I didn't dare show that side of me to anyone else.

Piper tried to reach me again. "Forty-four twelve, please report."

I backed up against what I hoped was a mirror—found that it was, in fact, a mirror and not an opening—and reached for my radio mic. I called in, even though I knew I wouldn't be heard, keeping my voice low so I wouldn't be heard by the wrong person. "Forty-four twelve, I'm inside the maze of mirrors next to the Ferris wheel."

Once again, I studied the way I thought I'd come from. Extending one hand, I felt for an opening. Found one. Hoped to God it was the way out.

Several twists and turns later, I knew it wasn't. I turned back—what I thought was the way back.

My own reflection appeared out of weird places, throwing my heart into my mouth, triggering my instincts and muscle memory to aim my gun at what turned out to be me, over and over again.

I clamped my teeth together to keep myself from either screaming or vomiting. I relied on my senses to get me through my job every day. But in here, nothing was real. Everything was an illusion. Who the hell designed a place like this? Who the hell ran into a place like this in the middle of a pursuit?

Again and again as I discovered my own pale face, my own hollow eyes, I felt as if, for the first time in ten years, I was seeing myself the way I really was: A ghost of the woman I used to be. A shell who pretended she wasn't afraid, pretended she wasn't hurt—when hurt and fear were all she knew anymore.

# CHAPTER SIXTY-FIVE

# ANGELICA

Finger-length by finger-length, Angelica sought her way through the maze. There had to be another way out. The lights kept shifting colors, brightening and dimming. But even when she could see, open corridors turned out to be twists and turns, and what looked like solid walls were unexpected openings.

At last, the hallway Angelica was following came to a dead end, two panes of glass simply joining in a forty-five-degree angle. She felt them over three times before believing that the designers of the maze would force her into a trap like this.

Heart trembling, she turned. Maybe it wasn't too late to go back...

The lights shifted from red to deep blue, casting the maze into near-darkness.

A footstep scraped the gritty wooden floor, the sound carrying far too clear, far too close.

Angelica froze. A whimper escaped her throat before she could stop it. She clamped a hand over her mouth.

The footsteps stopped. Silence.

The lights went to black.

Angelica slid to the floor, knees bent in front of her. She grabbed her purse and pried open the clasps. Pulled out Will's pistol and pointed it down the hallway. Waited, hands shaking.

# CHAPTER SIXTY-SIX

# MONICA

I crept forward, one hand on the mirrors, the other trying to keep my gun low, trying not to brandish it at every shift in movement. What if there were civilians in here?

The lights shifted to a blue so dark, I could barely see. Mid-step, I hesitated, my foot dragging the floor.

A tiny cry broke the silence.

I froze, my ears straining. The hairs on the back of my neck stood up, screaming at me that I wasn't alone.

For the love of God, I wanted this to be over. To get out. To breathe.

The lights went to black.

# CHAPTER SIXTY-SEVEN

# ANGELICA

Angelica waited for a light that never came. Why didn't it come? Why was it still black? For effect? To make people scream? It was working. Angelica bit her teeth together to force the scream to stay inside. She kept the gun pointed straight ahead.

The sounds of the carnival echoed distantly, muffled through the walls of the funhouse. Rock music. Cheers loosened by liquor. Voices. Laughter. A huckster promoting a game. "Just shoot the target—take home any toy you want!"

The inside of the maze was as silent as a coffin.

Her mind jolted from one panicked terror to the next—her father hurt, her husband pale and dead, her boys vanished, Monica Steele trying to murder her—

*I must come home to my boys... I must see Steele before she sees me...*

The lights blazed white, blinding her. She blinked—

And Monica Steele was standing squarely in front of her, gun aimed at her from the hip.

Angelica let the scream out and pulled the trigger.

## CHAPTER SIXTY-EIGHT

# MONICA

The lights sprang back on, dazzling.

A petite, Hispanic woman was curled in a ball on the floor, ashen-faced, the barrel of a gun aimed at my head. Fire flashed from the muzzle.

Mechanically, hours of practice taking over, I shifted to the side to throw off her aim. Dropped into stance. Brought both hands to my weapon, weapon front and center, lining up my sights. I squeezed the trigger, my focus narrowing to center mass and nothing else.

# CHAPTER SIXTY-NINE

# LEHMAN

Through the thin walls of the RV, above the noise of the crowd, the music, the rides—Lehman could have easily missed the sound. But after two decades of training, of target shooting, of firearms qualifications—Lehman knew the sound inside and out.

The gunfire pierced the air. High-pitched. Sharp. Rapid.

Feeling the blood drain from his own face, he glanced to Wade. The chief's eyes stared back, intense as gunmetal.

One of the foot patrol officers shouted over the radio. "Forty-three ninety-one, shots fired! Shots fired! It's coming from Wrigley Drive, somewhere near the Ferris wheel."

Wade turned to his screen and panned the camera toward the huge wheel. Some kind of funhouse sat beside it, half-obscured by a string of rides. Tourists who'd been traversing the street or waiting in line were looking around apprehensively, no doubt wondering if the oddity they'd heard was just carnival noise, maybe an airsoft rifle from one of the target shooting games, maybe balloons bursting, maybe someone shaking up soda bottles and popping the caps. Other fair-goers were less trusting, already deciding to migrate away from the area. Some walked. By two's and three's, others began to run.

Lehman grabbed the radio mic, no longer caring if Monica heard his unwanted voice. "Forty-four twelve, report."

Silence.

His knuckles went white on the plastic casing as he stared at Wade's screen. "C'mon, Monica, where are you?" he grated between his teeth. "What the hell's going on?"

# CHAPTER SEVENTY

# RYAN

"Forty-three ninety-one, shots fired! Shots fired!"

My fingers gripping the steering wheel like a vice, I pushed through the thickening traffic. In response to my lights and sirens, cars found ways to clear me a path. The drivers seemed willing, but their options were limited—and that was only going to get worse the deeper I pushed into downtown. I thought of alternate routes I could have taken—but odds of them being any better would have been a hope and a prayer.

Lehman's voice came over the radio, ordering Monica to report.

When she didn't, I had to breathe deep, the sandwich I'd eaten an hour ago threatening to come back up, the words *officer down* wracking their way through my brain like a collapsing carnival ride.

# CHAPTER SEVENTY-ONE

# ANGELICA

Angelica watched as Detective Monica Steele turned into a spiderweb of cracks, chunks falling to the floor. What was left of the woman fired back. Mirrors to Angelica's right broke. Glass rained down, showering her face, knees, and feet. Angelica screamed, covering her head.

She'd shot a reflection. So had Steele. But where was the woman really? For the love of God, Angelica didn't want to stay around to find out.

She leapt to her feet, desperate to either find or create a way out.

# CHAPTER SEVENTY-TWO

# MONICA

I watched as the woman sitting on the floor smashed into a thousand pieces and fell in chunks to the floor. My brain shattering, short-circuiting, I pulled back behind what I hoped was cover and glanced twenty directions. Whatever I'd shot, it wasn't Angelica. Where was she? Where the goddamn hell was she?

Glass smashed. Through my shoulder, which was propped against one of the mirrors, I felt the entire structure tremble. Oh, God, what now? What was this madwoman doing?

# CHAPTER SEVENTY-THREE

# ANGELICA

With the butt of her gun, Angelica struck the glass behind her. Chunks fell from the panel and shattered at her feet. Thin plywood stood behind it, already cracked by the blow from her gun. She stepped back and kicked it the way Rafael's kids did in their martial arts class, rotating on one hip, coiling her leg close to her chest, and driving it forward. She ignored the jagged glass, the rough surface of the layered wood, and the fact that she was wearing sandals.

To her shock and relief, the entire panel snapped free of its fastenings and fell into the next passage, the mirror on the back side of it crashing and flowing outward like so much spilled water.

She stepped through the hole she'd made, the panel a bridge over broken mirror. *Dios*, she was done with this place. She'd get out of here if she had to break every wall.

But only a few turns later, her hand flowing along the glass, the lights happily swirling between every color of the rainbow—she saw an opening that framed greenery. She saw a wheel slowly turning. People riding in the seats. People standing in line. People staring toward the maze of mirrors. Staring toward her.

Her heart stopped. Was this real? Was she through, or was it another illusion?

Angelica shoved her gun back into her purse, hooked the straps over her elbow, and pawed her way forward. Her hands broke out into clear air. It was real! It was a side entrance to the maze, opening onto a small porch and facing the Ferris wheel. She was out. She'd made it.

The park was devolving into chaos. Carnival-goers had clearly heard the gunfire. People were glancing around wide-eyed. Herding their children away from the maze and the nearby rides. Running.

Angelica jumped down from the funhouse platform and vaulted the fence around it. She took to the sidewalk which ran between the shore and the unadorned backs of the rides, their rear facades spilling cables into the grass like entrails.

She had to get out of here. In the dispersing crowd, she could look like just another fleeing figure. Monica Steele was still lost somewhere in the maze. This was her chance.

# CHAPTER SEVENTY-FOUR

# MONICA

Wood splintered. Glass crashed like a cascade. My God, she was tearing the entire house down. Was she trying to get away? Was she trying to get *to me*? Heart in my throat, I sucked three quick breaths to brace myself, then peered out once again from cover, my gun pointing the way.

In what remained of the broken mirror I'd shot, I saw an image of a panel busted flat out from the wall.

What the—? Where was Angelica? I scanned every direction. Somewhere, there was more than a reflection; there was an actual broken panel, and Angelica Read had escaped through it.

Toeing my way forward—kicking walls this time instead of gently bumping them—I turned a corner and found what I dared to believe was the actual busted panel. Reaching out, I found empty air. My God, something in this madhouse was actually real.

Better yet, I thought I felt moving air. Smelled lake humidity laced with sugar and butter and deep-fryer oil.

Placing a hand along the wall, I stumbled forward, then ran. My heart pounded. Bile tried to push its way into my throat, and the edges of my vision kept turning black, as if I were going to pass out. This was panic like I'd never known before. I couldn't trust my own senses in here.

Suddenly, the pulsing black frame of my vision was filled with the sight of trampled grass and the flashing lights of the Ferris wheel. A full-on lake breeze brushed the side of my face. Stumbling out onto a side porch of the maze, I gulped the air, then braced my hands on my knees, trying not to puke.

I heard the voice of Aaron Lange through my earpiece. "Shots fired! Shots fired!"

"No shit, Einstein," I screamed, "ya think?" I scanned the park for him and his partner, Chad Rauch, but couldn't spot either of them.

Some voice in the back of my head yelled at me to pull myself together—and instead, I was running my nose along the back of my hand—because I was crying.

*Shots fired.* The words kept running through my head. This was my fault. I shouldn't have kept chasing her inside. I should have realized immediately it was a maze of mirrors and that I was only seeing reflections when I thought she was just inside my grasp. I should have waited outside. Figured out how to flag down my partners. Someone other than Angelica or me could have been hurt. Maybe someone *was*. Those walls were paper thin. Those bullets could have gone anywhere.

God, I was headed for Wade's office after this.

I looked up and scanned the park. Where was Angelica? People were trickling away from the maze and the adjacent rides. Parents were calling for their children. The young lady operating the Ferris wheel took one glance at me, then shifted the towering ride into slow gear as if to start getting people off. Bless her, she was the only human in this carnival with any frickin' brains.

And then I spotted her: A petite form with flowing black hair. She was jogging down the sidewalk that ran behind the rides.

Lehman's voice hummed in my ear. "Forty-four twelve, report."

*I've BEEN reporting, you asshole,* I mentally replied.

Then I leapt off the platform and gave chase. My idiocy aside, I had to keep Angelica in sight. I was the only one who knew where she was.

# CHAPTER SEVENTY-FIVE

# LEHMAN

When Monica still didn't report, Lehman wiped a sweaty palm down his thigh. Some part of his consciousness registered his heart hammering—the same part of his brain that was picturing Monica bleeding out in the grass on the backside of some carnival ride. But he couldn't stop now to address his own stress. That wasn't how the job worked. Deal with the crisis now, deal with the fear later. Compartmentalize. Focus.

Staring at the map of Flat Iron, he clicked the button on the radio mic. "Forty-three ninety-one, report your location." Unlike the cars, there was no GPS for the foot patrols. Lehman counted on them reporting in, then had to be able to visualize their locales.

Aaron Lange replied, his voice stilted from running. "Passing the visitor center. Forty-four thirty-one is with me."

Good. Lange had arrived at the general area where the gunfire had come from, and he was still with his partner, Chad Rauch.

Lehman crossed the room and leaned over Wade's shoulder. The chief had dropped into the chair in front of his desk—though his feet were pointed toward the door as if he were ready to jump up any minute and take more aggressive action than clicking buttons. He panned the camera toward the visitor's center on the east side of Wrigley. The Ferris wheel stood across the street from it, filling the left side of the screen.

Wade pointed at the screen. "Got 'em."

Piper rotated in her chair to see, as well, her face pale. It had been seven years since she and Aaron Lange had tied the knot. This certainly wasn't the first time she'd supported him from the other end of a radio while some variation of hell was breaking loose. While Lehman read the worry in her eyes, the rest of her demeanor remained expressionless, focused. She knew she had work to do.

Lehman turned again to Wade's screen, filling his lungs, a wayward thought flitting through his head: It would have been nice if Becky could have found a way to support him, too.

On the monitor, Lange and Rauch emerged from alongside the visitor's center and dashed into the street, dodging tourists who were drifting, wandering, fleeing. The two officers' heads were on a swivel, scanning the area, trying to locate Monica, Angelica, the source of the gunfire they'd heard moments before...

Lehman's fingers twitched toward the radio mic. He needed to know how close his other foot patrols were. He needed to clear the area of civilians and build an inner perimeter around the area. He needed information on where exactly the gunfire had come from. And to accomplish all of that, he needed more boots on the ground.

Then, on Wade's screen, he saw a carny run from the gate of the funhouse that was almost eclipsed from the view of the cameras by the lunging, whirling rides that stood between them. The young man was dark-haired, the sides close-shaved, maybe some kind of design going on.

The kid ran up to Lange, actually grabbing his arm, and gestured wildly toward the funhouse.

At the same moment, the rest of the foot patrols poured in from various points along the right edge of the screen—Natasha Doyle, Nick Asher, and Owen Pratt, who was supposed to be Monica's patrol partner that night. They all gathered around Lange, Rauch, and the carny.

Silence enveloped the dispatch room as Lehman, Wade, and Piper all stared at the screen. Lehman twirled a dry-erase marker he didn't remember picking up.

A moment later, Lange was directing the foot patrols toward the funhouse. Lehman's view was blocked by the intervening rides, but he thought they were forming a perimeter.

Static finally broke the silence, and Lange called in. "Forty-three ninety-one, I just spoke with an employee who reports seeing forty-four twelve pursue the suspect into the structure, then hearing shots fired. Establishing a perimeter now and proceeding to clear the area."

Without taking his eyes from the camera feed, Lehman turned his head toward Piper. "Acknowledge. Ask if there's anyone else inside the funhouse."

Piper activated her mic and transmitted to Lange. "Copy that. Anyone in the structure besides 4412 and the suspect?"

Over the camera feed, Lehman watched Lange talk to the carny, then turn his head toward the mic on his shoulder. His voice filled the tiny room. "That would be a negative. He was just about to send a family in when 4412 and the suspect entered. It should be just the two of them inside."

Lehman sighed and pushed his fingers through his hair. "Well, that's the first good thing that's happened tonight."

Wade grunted agreement.

Lehman twiddled the marker, thinking rapidly. The suspect was contained, there were no known civilians inside, and there was currently no live gunfire. In that case, his next priorities were moving people away from the area and trying to figure out what exactly was happening inside that funhouse. He ran down a mental list of his resources.

"We could get Warner to bring us the drone," he thought aloud. While the drone itself was at the station, one of its operators, Lange, was on-scene. "Fly it in. See what the hell's going on."

Wade leaned sideways in his chair, leaning his head on his hand. "With traffic? It'll take her ten, fifteen minutes to grab the drone and get here. Another five minutes to get it assembled and in the air."

He didn't have to say it out loud; if Monica was hurt, she could bleed out long before then.

Wade turned and studied the map on one of Piper's screens. "Looks like Franklin and Serrano are at their posts with the black-and-whites. They've got riot shields, tac vests. We could be inside that structure in five minutes."

"It's to risk more officers," Lehman pointed out. Given the option between sending in tech versus sending in live bodies... he generally liked tech better.

Wade nodded somberly.

Lehman pressed the center of the marker with his thumbs as if to break it. He met Wade's eyes, deciding there was no point in not being honest. "I don't like that we haven't heard from Monica."

Wade shook his head, the motion minuscule but sharp. "Me neither."

Lehman turned to Piper. "Do they have contact with her at all? Visual? Audio?"

Piper activated her mic. "Forty-three ninety-one, have you established visual or audio contact with 4412?"

Lange radioed back. "Negative."

Lehman grimaced, his stomach flip-flopping. He didn't like this at all. Why the hell did Monica go inside that structure?

Wade rotated his chair, facing Piper. "Where's the ambulance?"

Piper zoomed out the map, and a grin lit her face. "They've been listening to the radio. They're only a block away—Baker and Wrigley."

"Do you know who's on duty?"

"Garner and Myers."

Wade lifted his eyebrows at Lehman. "We have a tactical medic."

David Myers was a SWAT team member, trained and prepared to deliver medical aid even with live gunfire going off around his head.

Lehman pressed into the middle of the marker with both thumbs, the plastic digging painfully into his finger pads. "All right. Fine. Let's do it. I'll get them organized. You alert the SWAT team in case we screw this up."

Wade quirked his mouth grimly and reached for the phone in his shirt pocket. Since their local SWAT was made up of personnel from multiple departments all over the region, it would be a good forty-five minutes before they had a functional team on the ground. SWAT would be their Plan B if the quick-reaction team went south.

Lehman's hand was on the radio mic when static alerted him to an incoming transmission. Lange's voice came over the air again.

"Forty-three ninety-one, I have additional information from the carny regarding the interior of the structure."

Piper clicked her mic. "Go ahead."

"He says it's a hall of mirrors. He can turn on the lighting inside to make it easier to see, but... it's gonna be a little confusing inside."

"God damn it," Wade muttered, laying his phone face-down on the desk.

"How bad is this?" Lehman asked, not quite following.

"I took the grandkids last summer," Wade said.

"And?"

He narrowed his eyes at Lehman. "You ever pointed two mirrors at each other?"

Lehman recalled doing it when he was a kid—and watching the reflection vanish into literal infinity, countless pairs of his own eyes peering over the tops of innumerable hand-held mirrors. "Oh, God."

"They're set up at all angles in there," Wade went on. "You never know what's a door, what's a wall, if you're looking at another person or just a reflection..."

Lehman began to pace again, raking his hands through his hair. This time he said it out loud. "*Why* did she go in there? Damn it. We can't send a team into that."

They'd have to get the drone—and Monica would have to wait. She'd better still be alive when they got there.

His phone vibrated in his pocket. A sixth sense told him it wasn't just the ex calling to continue their argument over who got the kids next weekend.

He pulled his phone out, glanced at the screen, and exclaimed out loud. The name above the ringing bell icon read, simply, *Steele.*

He swiped the screen and set it on speaker phone, holding the device in the middle of the room so everyone could hear. "Monica, where are you?"

Wade and Piper turned to face the phone, eyebrows high.

Monica's voice exploded over the tiny speaker. "Lehman, you ass, we're not in the goddamn funhouse anymore. We're northbound on Broad, past Main. Where the fuck is your outer perimeter?"

Lehman rested a hand on his belt and smiled unashamedly, never more delighted to be cussed out by his partner. He glanced at the map on Piper's screen and noted that Brandt was still working his way toward his assigned post. Monica's pursuit had blown past his intersection before he got there.

"Sorry," he said into the phone. "Probably stuck in traffic."

Piper was already on the radio, alerting both the foot and vehicle patrols of Monica's new location. Wade shot from his chair to lean over her shoulder. He pointed out a new perimeter for the vehicle patrols, and Piper transmitted the assignments to the units on the street.

Lehman backed away from the live radio mic in hopes his conversation with Monica wouldn't muddy the transmissions. He had a lot of questions right now—but most of them would have to wait. Contain the threat first, sort the rest later. "You okay, Monica?" he asked. "We heard gunfire." He could completely picture Monica Steele ignoring personal injury to continue a pursuit.

She paused before answering, and all he heard was her measured breathing as she ran. "I'm fine," she finally said. And then her hard, steady breathes turned to a sob. "Lehman, I'm sorry. I don't know why—why I went in there—"

Oh, God. She couldn't fall apart now. He turned his back more fully toward Piper and Wade, as if to shield Monica during her breakdown. "Hey, hey, hey, keep it together. You've got this."

She sniffed. "Okay."

Lehman smiled, impressed how conversational Monica could be while both running and crying. Probably came from jogging every day, the way she did. Personally, he would have panted out his location and died. "What happened to your radio?"

"Broke it," she replied, "I can hear you, though."

"Okay. Keep this line open."

"I'll try."

He paced and rolled his head to release the tension. And then he sighed and just said it. "God, I'm glad to hear your voice." He hoped she didn't hear the catch in his.

# CHAPTER SEVENTY-SIX

# RYAN

My radio crackled to life again, and I divided my attention between it and the road. Piper's voice came over the speaker.

"All units, be advised: 4412's radio is down, and she's established contact via phone."

The ton of bricks that had been lodged in my throat melted into wet sand and slid to the bottom of my stomach. Monica was okay.

Piper continued. "She reports still in foot pursuit, northbound on Broad toward Geneva Street."

My ears perked. Like a baseball to a glove, she was headed toward me. If I could just get through this traffic. I pictured myself blasting out into the middle of the intersection and fishtailing to a stop right in front of Monica's winded and disoriented suspect. Shades dropped over my eyes, I'd step out of the patrol vehicle and slap the handcuffs on said suspect—

Piper was listing new perimeter assignments for the vehicle units. I turned off the daydreams of my own coolness and paid attention. The transmission felt garbled, and I realized the radio was picking up both Piper's voice, as well as others in the background. The effect was like talking to customer support in a call center.

Like a homing pigeon, I picked up one of the voices as Monica's. Listening to it through both a phone—Lehman's, I assumed—and a radio, I couldn't make out her words, just her tones. I smiled anyway, just glad to hear the sound of it.

Past Piper's vehicle assignments, I barely picked up a heavy sigh from Stan Lehman in the background. "God, I'm glad to hear your voice."

I took my eyes off the road long enough to frown at the radio. Wait, what?

Shaking my head like a puppy confounded by an itch in its ear, I returned my gaze to the parting traffic. I was overthinking that. Of course Lehman was relieved. He and Monica had been partners for how many years?

That's all it was—one partner's worry for another. Right?

# CHAPTER SEVENTY-SEVEN

# ANGELICA

Feeling as if her lungs would burst, Angelica threw a glance over her shoulder. Damn it, Steele was still within eyeshot. The hall of mirrors—horrifying as it had been—had bought her almost a block of distance, but Steele was the better runner. Angelica's lead wouldn't last.

Tears stung her eyes. God, what was she going to do?

Past her own frantic breathing, she thought she heard a familiar voice in her mind. *Mi ángel, this is wrong. Stop running.*

*I can't,* she replied. *She'll kill me.*

And then she pictured her papá sitting at her kitchen table, head bowed, weeping as he made the sign of the cross, vowing to understand those he feared in exchange for God restoring his grandsons.

God had kept his side of the bargain; her papá would shift heaven and earth before abandoning his.

And what of Angelica? Her father's disappointment when she'd struck the tray from her tía's hands still stung her memory. How was she ever going to tell him that she'd fired a gun at Detective Steele?

Tears coursed down her cheeks, making it hard to see, hard to breathe.

*Papá, help me,* she said, wishing her thoughts could reach him on the coast. *I don't know how to reverse this. I'm sorry. I'm not your ángel.*

She blinked and lifted her eyes. A red brick church filled her vision, occupying the corner across the street from her. Gothic, stained glass windows decorated every surface, and a square bell tower reached for the sky.

Fresh tears burst from her eyes. Had her papá actually heard her? Had God?

She dashed across the street and flew up the stairs, throwing herself on one of the glass-paned doors.

It opened.

*Gracias, Madre de Dios, gracias,* she prayed. *Help me. I don't know what to do.*

Angelica slipped through the door and let it fall shut behind her.

Only to find that nothing was what she expected.

There were no pews. No alter with candles. No pulpit. No tapestries or piano, no organ or hymnals.

The room was barren but for dirty remnants of industrial carpet thrown over the dusty wooden floor. Haphazard rooms had been annexed along the sides, carving space out of the open sanctuary, their walls unequal, few of their ceilings reaching as high as the central cathedral arches. The added rooms created a smaller, weirdly-shaped sanctuary, grotesquely short on square corners or anything else that made sense.

Angelica's eyes traveled to the right, where the added rooms had been finished with paned windows and exterior siding, as if they looked out on a tree-lined street and not the hollowed guts of an abandoned church. Her eyes transfixed on a bay window—*a bay window*—and the real estate agent inside her wanted to scream. Who had thought any of this was a good idea? She thought she'd left the carnival behind her.

Nervous, she glanced around the bizarre surroundings. Monica Steele would be behind her any minute. Angelica bowed her head, pressing her fingertips to her temples. What was she even doing? How had all of this happened? She wanted to stop running. She—

She wanted to talk to Steele.

She closed her eyes with a sigh and a shudder. Roland had told her all along to talk to Steele.

She opened her eyes again. The rising moon hit the stained-glass windows on the south and east walls, spraying rainbows of light on the worn floor, casting her shadow in front of her, solitary and alone. She breathed, watching the dust motes swirl in the slanting, pale light.

In her mind, she felt a warm, calloused hand on her left shoulder. Her papá's. On her right, she felt another, strong but refined. Will's. The man she had loved with all her heart. The man who had grown up in Lake Geneva, Wisconsin, a place she'd never heard of before this summer, much less imagined herself visiting.

She looked at the floor again... and could almost believe she saw three shadows across the worn boards instead of one.

She blinked back tears and scanned her surroundings again. She didn't want to be in the open when Monica Steele entered.

To her left, one section of the haphazardly arranged bump-outs created an alcove full of doors to the various rooms. That would do. She slipped into the nook, chose a pair of French doors, and slipped through to the next room.

Shelves full of books lined every wall. A table in the center overflowed with more volumes. They weren't even hymnals or books of prayer. They were best-sellers, science fiction and fantasy, romance, mystery, historic volumes, local interest. The countless pages filled the room with a warm, comforting aroma, bespeaking long winter nights with candles, hot tea, and warm blankets.

It was a bookstore, tucked onto the side of the church in what once may have been the sacristy.

Angelica shook her head. This building was beyond her understanding, the church that was not a church. But between the shelves full of stories and the fleeting sense that something holy still lingered in this largely untouched part of the building, at least she didn't feel alone.

She slid the door to within an inch of closing, knelt next to a bookshelf, and peeked back into the strange sanctuary.

*Madre María*, she prayed, *help me now. Help me not to be afraid. Help me be my papá's ángel.*

# CHAPTER SEVENTY-EIGHT

# LEHMAN

"She's gone into the church!" Monica's voice blared over the phone in Lehman's palm. "The old Baptist church," she said, as if Lehman knew which one that was. There were a couple churches in the vicinity of her pursuit, and he had no idea off the top of his head what denomination they were, only that one of them wasn't even a church anymore.

"The Geneva Village Shops," Monica clarified. "Get me some backup, Lehman!"

Right. The one that wasn't a church anymore.

He crowded next to Piper and Wade and pointed at the screen. "Outer perimeter—Geneva and Broad, Broad and the alley, alley and Center, Center and Broad. Inner perimeter on the church." The map showed that Ryan Brandt and Shelby Serrano were already close, thank God. "Where are the foot patrols?"

Piper glanced at him, adjusting her headset with both hands, her eyes a little wild, as if she were stressed over too many voices in her ears at once—his, Wade's, the patrols, even Monica over the phone. Her elbows held aloft almost seemed designed to clear Lehman and Wade out of her space.

"The foot patrols have just left Flat Iron," she reported, answering his question. "Northbound on Broad."

"Damn it," Lehman breathed. They were two blocks behind the pursuit. He backed away from Piper, giving her the space she seemed to want. He spoke into his phone. "Monica, we're getting there as fast as we can."

"Peachy. It isn't like she already tried to kill me once."

He stared at the desk Wade had abandoned earlier and drummed his fingers on his belt. While he'd secretly worried over Monica for years—it was different, now that he'd finally told her how he felt. His stomach churned painfully. He was known as the patient one, but this was eating even him.

Wade pushed away from Piper's desk and motioned for Lehman to clear a path. Lehman stepped aside, letting Wade through the door to the hall beyond.

"Chief?" he asked as Wade put his hand to the outer door.

Wade paused long enough to look back, and Lehman couldn't miss the depths of worry in the old man's eyes. The reasons weren't hard to guess. Wade had practically taught Monica everything she knew.

"I'm heading up there," the chief said. "I'm not sure what kind of... *game* Angelica was playing this whole time—" His upper lip curled on the word *game*.

Lehman nodded, understanding. How did Angelica Read's simple request to be kept updated on her husband's case lead to all *this*?

Wade swung the door open. Lingering carnival music filled the Command Unit, drowned now by the sounds of people shouting, running.

Wade closed the door behind him, and Lehman found himself jealous he wasn't going with.

He raised the phone to his mouth again. "Monica, we're coming for you. Hang in there." Looking to Piper's map, he saw the icon representing Wade's car pull away from Flat Iron Park.

# CHAPTER SEVENTY-NINE

# MONICA

My back pressed against the bricks on the exterior of the church, my gun pointed toward the ground, I peered through the glass-paned doors and scanned the large, empty room inside. I'd finally quit crying long enough to see straight, though my lungs were still working hard. It looked quiet inside. Either Angelica was hiding, or she'd already found a way out.

I lifted my phone to my mouth and spoke softly. "Lehman, I might need my hands."

"What are you doing?"

"Nothing. I'm watching from outside. I just want my hands free."

"Okay. But leave your phone on."

"All you're gonna hear is the inside of my pocket."

"I don't care."

"Fine."

I was about to turn off the speaker feature so Lehman's voice couldn't give away my position, when he spoke again.

"Monica? Be safe."

I shifted my jaw. Was that a reprimand for running into the funhouse earlier? An expression of affection? Both? I tried to remember if I'd ever cried in front of him before. I hadn't. Only Ryan. I was still mad at Lehman for upsetting our partnership. Seriously, how was I even supposed to interpret words like that anymore?

I put it out of my mind. "Yeah," I said. "I will."

I turned off the speaker phone while leaving the call itself intact and dropped my cell into the pocket on the front of my vest. I cradled my gun in both hands, still pointing it toward the ground. Leaning out a scant inch, I peered through the glass doors, visually sweeping the room. There were a lot of bizarre angles in there. It was going to be a hell of a building to clear, if it came to that. The original congregation had sold the structure decades ago, and the current owner had subdivided it for shops—most of which stood empty, other than a bookshop that could be accessed from its own door on the side of the building.

I caught movement from beyond a French door in an alcove on the left side. From the multi-colored light filtering through the stained-glass windows, I thought I could make out the top of a head at doorknob height. It bobbed slightly, a shift so minute I could easily have missed it.

It was her.

# CHAPTER EIGHTY

# ANGELICA

Angelica leaned her head against the soft book spines. Across the sanctuary, she could just make out a sliver of Monica Steele's navy blue form, the side of her face, the silver moonlight reflecting off the barrel of her down-turned gun.

Steele wasn't following her in this time. Why not? Because everything had gone so badly inside the hall of mirrors? Because she was afraid? Did cops, with all their weapons and armor and technology, even feel fear?

Her papá's voice ran through her head again. *We fear what we do not understand.*

Angelica and Detective Steele had never, for a moment, understood each other.

She ground the side of her head into the book spines and prayed again. *Madre Maria, how do I reverse this?*

There was only one gesture Steele was likely to understand and accept right now: Angelica giving herself up. But the mere thought of it pained her to the core. Like her papá so many years ago, her greatest wrongdoing was to be afraid. Everything she had done tonight, she'd done from fear. The reasons for her every action screamed through her head—but would anyone listen? Did the police even care? She closed her eyes, a hot tear slipping down her cheek. Would she be arrested? Would she ever see her boys again?

She thought again of running—and even of becoming a fugitive, like Will. If he could do it, so could she.

And then she asked herself: If her papá could go back in time, but know everything he knew now—that he would never see from one of his eyes again, that the fear he'd felt that one afternoon would never end—would he still have chosen to run? Or would he give himself up?

She heard his voice again. "*I will walk toward the thing I fear. I will try to understand the man who hurt me—whether or not he is man enough to understand ME. I swear it.*"

Angelica bowed her head, the tears running down.

She lifted her hands, fingers splayed, the very movement abasing. It ripped her soul out, her pride, the self-confidence she'd always tried to teach her sons. She moved into full view of the French doors and placed her hands against the glass panes.

*Talk to me*, she said to Monica Steele. *Please, understand me. I am so afraid.*

# CHAPTER EIGHTY-ONE

# MONICA

I watched the slip of Angelica's form like a hawk, my heart pounding, and counted down the seconds until my backup arrived.

Angelica shifted, and I flinched further behind the brickwork, tightening my grip on my gun. I felt my focus narrowing, my pulse racing—

Coming into full view of the windows in the French doors, Angelica bowed her head and laid her palms flat on the glass.

I blinked. What? Was she turning herself in? A flood of relief washed through my chest.

I pulled my phone out of my pocket and put it to my ear. "Lehman?"

"Yeah?"

"She's got her hands up. I'm going to try to take her in."

He sighed, and I knew he was questioning whether he should instruct me to wait for my backup.

But God, I couldn't afford to let Angelica change her mind. I couldn't afford to let her get away.

"No bullshit this time," I told Lehman. "I promise." For the love of Christ, I knew how to take in a suspect.

"I appreciate that."

I decided I was taking that for a yes. Still leaving the phone on, I dropped it back into my pocket. Then I studied the distance across the sanctuary between me and Angelica, the awkwardness of trying to prop the front door open and cover her from my current angle, the fact that my current position provided very little cover for *me...*

Scanning the interior, I spied the corner of a wall, bumping out into the center of the sanctuary. It was only a few feet away from me, and some thirty feet from Angelica, putting comfortable distance between us.

I reached for the door handle, popped it open, and flowed toward my chosen cover. Gun trained on Angelica, I called across to her.

"Angelica? I don't want to hurt you. Why don't you come on out?"

## Chapter Eighty-Two

# ANGELICA

Angelica said nothing. Only sat there trembling from head to foot, soaking in the sensations running through her body as if she were detached from this moment. So, this was how her papá had felt, twenty years ago, with a policeman's gun pointed at him. At any moment, Monica Steele could slip her finger over the trigger—a movement so minuscule, so meaningless—and rob her sons of their only remaining parent.

She understood now why her papá had run. Why he had fought. Why, when the officer had grappled him, he'd grabbed the barrel of the officer's gun—and received a baton instead. She knew what he'd been thinking in that moment.

He'd been thinking of her. Of her brothers and sisters. He'd been telling himself that nothing mattered. Nothing mattered but coming home to his children.

And now, he was telling her she should trust the person who could kill her, contrary to her every instinct—not least of which, her instincts as a mother.

Gritting her teeth, she stared at her purse, on the floor by her knees. She wanted to scream—but cried silently instead.

## Chapter Eighty-Three

# RYAN

Far from swerving into the intersection in front of Monica's suspect, I arrived in front of the red brick church to the sight of any typical corner in Lake Geneva—the street thick with traffic, the sidewalks full of tourists.

I couldn't see Monica anywhere. God damn, where was she now? I just wanted to clap eyes on her and know she was okay.

I parked my unit smack in the middle of the intersection, reported to Piper that I'd arrived at my assignment, then hopped out and began directing traffic, turning motorists away from the street we were trying to block off.

Moments later, Shelby Serrano arrived at the next corner over and did the same. The foot patrols came next, winded from their jog, but still faster than our remaining vehicle units, which finally arrived a few minutes afterward, completing the perimeters.

Last of all, the chief rolled up in his unmarked SUV, the light bar hidden on the inside of his windshield flashing red and blue. He climbed out and approached me, looking stern. "What have we got?"

"I think we have them sealed in. I think. I hope." I rested my hands on my belt and squared up to my boss honestly. I wasn't short by any means, but even I had to tilt my chin to look my superior in the eye, and it made me feel like a schoolboy. "I don't know, Sir."

Looking like he had no patience for either chaos or incompetence, he leaned through the window of his unit and grabbed the radio mic from its hanger. Stringing the cord back through the window, he lifted the mic to his mouth. "Forty-one eighty-five to Incident Command. Do we have an update on the location of 4412 and the suspect?"

I filled my lungs slowly and waited for the answer. *Monica, you'd better be okay...*

# CHAPTER EIGHTY-FOUR

# MONICA

Angelica didn't move. Was she hurt? Had one of my bullets actually hit her, back in the hall of mirrors? Had the glass cut her? Why didn't she move?

"Angelica, slide your gun out the door, and we'll talk."

Nothing happened.

God damn it, where was Lehman when I needed him? He was the trained negotiator. The only thing I was good for was rock turning. You needed a soul to talk to people, and the last time I'd caught sight of mine was—

A few nights ago. On the shore of the lake, under a vast moon, my hand in Ryan's. It was on the night I told him about our child, and the thing I'd done out of pure spite.

I shook my head and refocused on Angelica. I couldn't think about that right now. I'd promised Lehman no bullshit. I had to compartmentalize. Deal with the feelings later. Why was I failing so badly at that these days?

Maybe because, ten years ago, I *had* decided to deal with my feelings later—every last one of them—and the rent had finally come due. With a single phone call, The Man Upstairs had slipped the bill in the mail.

"*I know how to exploit your children. Yes, Monica, YOUR children.*"

I bit back the tears. Who was he? How had he known?

I shifted my shoulder against the wall, trying to keep my hands on my gun steady. "Angelica, I want to talk." My voice shook, but

I tried to pretend it didn't. "I have a lot of questions, and I think you can answer them. Please, slide your gun out."

She still didn't move. Didn't lift her head. But her fingers flexed on the glass. Her shoulders trembled. Was she crying?

I just wanted this to end—everything—this entire horrible summer. Angelica could help me. I *needed* her help.

God, Roland had told me that ages ago.

"I just want to ask you who he is," I said, my voice actually shaking. I blinked hard, trying to keep the tears out of my eyes so I could see. "Angelica, who's The Man Upstairs? I just want to know—" My throat went tight, constricting my voice into a whisper. "—I want to know how he knew about my baby."

Angelica's hands went still on the glass. Her shoulders stopped shaking. Was she actually listening? Had I somehow gotten through to her?

Wade's voice unexpectedly sounded in my ear. He was on the radio. "Forty-one eighty-five to Incident Command. Do we have an update on the location of 4412 and the suspect?"

I waited for Lehman—the Incident Commander—to reply, but several moments passed in silence.

I suddenly remembered that my phone was in my vest pocket, and he was listening to every word I said. I'd just told Stan Lehman that I'd had a baby; a baby I clearly didn't have anymore, let him make of that what he may. I'd just confessed that the phone call from The Man Upstairs *had* been personal; that it could lead to the identification of the perpetrator behind this summer's crimes. And I'd just confessed that I'd been sitting on that information for weeks.

God, I was in a world of trouble. Someday, when I got out of the current mess.

# CHAPTER EIGHTY-FIVE

# LEHMAN

Lehman stood in the doorway of the dispatch room, phone in his palm, staring at nothing. Piper was twisted around in her seat, looking at him, hand hovering over the switch to activate her mic. She was ready to send the status report for him—as soon as she knew what it was.

But Lehman was still processing the way Monica's voice had trembled. Her decision to end her pregnancy had been nothing minute. She'd been hiding that pain for as long as he'd known her—longer. God, no wonder she was making questionable decisions tonight. She was falling apart. The Man Upstairs—whoever he was—had completely gotten under her skin. Gutted her.

For the first time, all he wanted was to reach out and hold her hand. Remind her how strong she was. Help her pull herself back together.

"Lehman?" Piper asked.

"They're both in the church," Lehman said—surprised that his voice was hoarse. He cleared his throat, hoping Piper wouldn't notice. "The suspect showed signs of compliance. She's trying to negotiate."

If you could call this a negotiation. Snakes crawled through his belly. *Keep it together, Monica. Keep it together.*

# CHAPTER EIGHTY-SIX

# RYAN

I continued to direct traffic, all the while straining to hear the update on Monica's location through my earpiece. Standing near me, Wade stared toward the doors of the church.

Incident Command finally deigned us worthy of information. Piper's voice came over the radio. "Ten-four. The suspect was showing signs of compliance, so she entered the church to negotiate."

I ground my teeth. God damn her. The suspect had opened fire on Monica mere minutes ago, and now she thought she was capable of carrying out a calm, reasoned negotiation? Either her nerves were made of steel, or she'd completely deceived herself into thinking they were.

I reminded myself that I'd seen her pull off some insane shit—but to be frank, I just needed to see her alive and unhurt right now.

Wade clicked the button on his mic. "Is the suspect still armed?"

Piper replied after a pause, no doubt to check with Lehman, who had to check with Monica. "Affirmative. Forty-four twelve reports the suspect has been carrying a handgun in her purse."

My stomach couldn't take all these cramps.

Wade lifted the mic to his mouth again. "I'm going to try to get visual on them."

"Copy that," Piper replied.

Wade leaned through the window of his SUV and hung up the mic. When he emerged again, he pointed a finger at me. "Don't let anyone past your post."

I nodded sharply. If I saw Monica's suspect, I'd take her to the ground. If I saw Monica, I might just take her to the ground, too, and never let her out of my sight again.

# CHAPTER EIGHTY-SEVEN

# ANGELICA

Detective Steele's words sank in—a desperate plea to know how The Man Upstairs knew about her child. And suddenly, the words Angelica had overheard between Chief Erickson and Detective Lehman clicked into place.

She understood. She understood everything.

Monica wasn't working for The Man Upstairs; she didn't know who he was any more than Angelica did. The tears proved it; the tears were real. She was as afraid of The Man as Angelica was.

Meanwhile, Lehman had talked about a phone call to Monica's personal phone that had left her distracted. Upset. A phone call that implied someone knew about her abortion.

And according to Monica, the person who knew about her child—yet shouldn't—was The Man Upstairs.

At last, she had proof. And Roland had been right—she should have trusted Monica all along. Perhaps they were more alike than they were different. Just as The Man Upstairs had threatened Angelica's children, he had threatened the memory of Monica's child, as well—a child Angelica suspected she hadn't wanted to let go.

She closed her eyes, a tear streaming down. *I understand, Papá. I'm so sorry. I understand now.*

## CHAPTER EIGHTY-EIGHT

# MONICA

Angelica Read lifted her head, meeting my eyes through the glass. Tears streaked her face. Her eyes were brown, like mine.

She removed her hands from the window panes, holding them upright to either side of her face, fingers splayed stiffly. Slowly, she rose from the floor. Toed open the French door. The hinges creaked. Nothing stood between us now. I kept my gun trained on her, remembering my promise to Lehman not to make stupid mistakes again. But my hands shook.

"Turn around—" I tried to say, tried to start walking her through the arrest—but she interrupted me.

"I know who The Man Upstairs is." Her voice bounced off the walls of the empty room.

I stared at her. Waited. Forgot to breathe. Another tear slid down my cheek. Oh, God, was this finally over? Was this whole, terrible summer finally over?

Angelica opened her mouth, her voice whispering across the empty room. "Wade Erickson was in the abortion clinic when you were there," she said. "He was investigating the patient confidentiality case. I heard him say so to your partner."

She couldn't have shocked me any harder if she'd brought the whole church down on my head. I stared at her, gaping. Then I shook my head. Laughed mirthlessly. No, no, no, that had to be bullshit. She was lying. Trying to buy time. The Man Upstairs—whoever he was—had told Angelica about my abortion. That's how she knew.

But that just brought me full circle again: Who was The Man, and how did he know? If it wasn't Wade, then who was it? Angelica's statement contained facts I could verify. Had Wade been investigating the confidentiality case? If so, had it brought him to Madison? On what day? The information would be in his case records. I could cross-reference them with my own calendar.

The thought that Angelica's statement could be true sent ice down my spine. She was implying Wade had murdered her husband Fritz and Tommy's son Jason. Pressured Jimmy Beacon into setting off a bomb that killed one of our own officers and our chaplain and terrorized the entire town. She was saying Wade had attacked Roland.

She was saying he'd shot Tommy, his own best friend.

None of that made sense.

I adjusted my stance. "We'll talk about this," I said, suddenly wishing my face wasn't covered in goddamn tears. "Right now, I want you to turn around—"

Her eyes went hard. Ferocious. "I have evidence." She bit the words out. They echoed in the empty room.

She turned and dove for her purse.

My body went rigid. I yelled. "Angelica—!"

She came up holding something small and black in her hand.

The burst of a gunshot echoed through the sanctuary.

A red starburst blossomed to the left of Angelica's sternum. I watched in horror as she screamed and fell.

The bullet had not come from my gun; my finger wasn't even on the trigger.

I whirled to my left, toward the front door. A tall shadow stood in the opening, backlit by silver moonlight. It highlighted his white buzzcut, the tops of his shoulders, his long, outstretched arms, the barrel of the gun between his hands.

Wade Erickson.

"No!" I screamed, my voice rising to pitches I didn't know it could reach. "*What did you do? What did you do?*"

## Chapter Eighty-Nine

# RYAN

The sound of a gunshot delivered a firm "screw you" to our current containment tactics. So did the screams. Those of us stationed on the outer and inner perimeters abandoned our posts and, weapons unholstered, bolted toward the doors. Lange hit the radio to update both Incident Command and the people stationed on the other side of the building.

"Forty-three ninety-one, shots fired! Shots fired! Move in!"

My deepest instincts recognized the ear-piercing shrieks inside the church as Monica's—even though, in my entire life, I'd never heard her scream like that. My heart pounded through my chest.

Those of us who had been posted near the front of the building converged on the front door. Lange assumed point, and the rest of us fell in behind, careful not to cross our lines of fire.

Even before I'd passed the threshold, I registered Wade aiming his gun toward an alcove on the left. The rest of us trained our weapons in the same direction, toward what looked like a woman lying on the floor—a woman who matched the description of the suspect. Shit. Whatever'd happened to Monica's negotiation? Why had tonight gone so sideways?

I scanned the room for the only person here I really cared about—the woman I'd spent the entirety of this long pursuit losing my mind over. Standing near the corner of a wall, Monica stared at Wade, eyes round, horrified, body crouched as if to protect herself, as if to fall back at a run, if need be. Her hands were tense on her downturned weapon, her arms locked stiff. She screamed at a pitch that had to be shredding her vocal cords. "*What did you do?*"

The team advanced on the suspect, guns trained. I held back, trying to wrap my mind around what was happening right now between Monica and Wade.

"Don't move!" Lange commanded the woman on the ground. "Keep those hands where I can see them!"

From where I stood, I detected no movement from the suspect at all. God, had we killed her?

With his right hand, Wade slid his gun into its holster. He held the left up toward Monica, palm out, trying to soothe her. "She was going for the purse, Monica. She was going for the gun."

"No!" Monica screamed, backing away from him. Did she even realize she still had her gun out? What was she doing?

Wade's eyes darkened. He gestured toward Monica, the cords in his arm and neck going taught. "Monica, you were standing there crying, and she was going to shoot you!"

I heard Lange's voice, both in the room and in my earpiece. "Forty-three ninety-one, requesting an ambulance at the church. Thirty-year-old Hispanic female has GSW to the chest."

Oh, God. Shit. Wade had succeeded in hitting center mass, and if he was right—if the suspect had been about to draw on Monica—then... Seriously, what else did she expect him to do? He'd stopped the threat. He'd done his job—and beyond that, saved the life of the woman I loved.

So, why was Monica screaming at him?

I holstered my weapon and moved toward her. "Hey, it's okay. Monica, you're okay."

"No!" She was still backing away from Wade, staring at him as if she were a rabid animal, as if he were a monster.

Fear slid down my back. I was upset about this, too, no matter which way you sliced it: The fact that this pursuit had ended in gunfire, the fact that we'd shot the suspect—maybe killed her—and worst of all, the idea that Monica may have been just standing here waiting to eat a bullet herself. My stomach was going in knots.

I closed the distance between us and gently but firmly put my hand over both of hers, making sure she couldn't raise the gun. "Baby, listen to me. Put the gun away."

# CHAPTER NINETY

# ANGELICA

Angelica found herself lying on the gritty wooden floor staring at the cathedral ceiling, blinking, feeling as if someone had simultaneously punched her in the chest and put out a burning cigar against her flesh.

The last thing she remembered was grabbing her phone from her purse and whirling around again, ready to show Monica the recording between Erickson and Lehman.

And then she'd glimpsed Erickson himself standing in the doorway of the church, gun drawn.

He'd pulled the trigger, and fire had burst from the muzzle.

In the end, he'd taken care of his problem himself.

Now, staring at the beams that met at a chandelier in the center of the ceiling, Angelica blinked, and a tear rolled down her cheek. *I must come home to my boys...*

A voice yelled at her. "Don't move! Keep those hands where I can see them!"

That shouldn't be a problem. Angelica was quite sure she couldn't move, even if she'd wanted to. The very act of breathing hurt.

A man in a police uniform knelt over her. He was forty-something, maybe, his hair a dark reddish brown. A plate pinned to his chest said A. Lange. He ran his hands over her shirt and waistband, his motions swift, efficient, practiced. Meanwhile, a ring of other officers surrounded them, faces tense, handguns bristling. It was the most bizarre choir a church had ever seen, where hitting the wrong note would send you straight to God.

*You don't understand*, Angelica wanted to say. *The Man Upstairs is standing behind you.*

But Monica understood.

Monica Steele's grief-stricken screams vibrated the floorboards. They were the screams of a woman betrayed by a trusted mentor. The screams of a woman robbed not only of her child, but of the privacy to mourn that child in her own way. Angelica was more convinced than ever that Monica hadn't wanted to give her baby up. Perhaps the woman actually had a heart capable of love.

Angelica wished she'd understood that ages ago.

A. Lange, the director of the deadly choir, spoke into a device attached to his shoulder. He said something about an ambulance. Something about a GSW, whatever that was. Perhaps that's what she was dying of.

Angelica's next breath came as more of a gasp—and remarkably, with very little sensation of actually drawing oxygen. She tried again, with the same results.

Hands grasped her blouse. Tore it open. A. Lange explained what was happening, what they were doing—*You've been shot. Lie still. We're going to help you*—but none of it particularly registered. She felt detached, as if they were pouring out their ministrations on some other person.

And then a woman stepped out from the handgun choir. She had brown skin and black hair, pulled up in a messy bun with strands sticking out in all directions. She looked at Angelica with kind, brown eyes. "¿Hablas español?" she asked. Her nameplate said S. Serrano.

"Sí," Angelica managed to breathe out between gasps.

The woman repeated what Lange had said, but in Spanish. Angelica smiled. Laughed. Her accent wasn't very good. This woman and her family had clearly been in the States for a long time. But the gesture was nice.

It made her think of home.

Not Mexico. Life there had been hard, like a rock around your neck, weighing you down.

It made her think of the little house with red siding and cracked sidewalks where she and her family had crowded in—including Tío Alberto and Tía Carolina and their kids. It was the home where they had all tried to make a new life for themselves. Her mamá had been firm but tireless. Her brothers and sisters and cousins had been wide-eyed with wonder as they discovered their new world.

And her papá, bringing laughter to their crowded new home, had labored from sunrise to sunset, doing his part to take care of them all.

Eventually, Tío Alberto and Tía Carolina had gained their own home, leaving the little house with red siding to Angelica's family. It was still the heart of their *familia*. The gathering place for the Morenos.

It's where she'd brought Will, when they'd first started dating, and thrown him into the center of her big, crazy family. It had been awkward, at first, him being the only non-Latino in the room. He hadn't known their traditions, their culture. But he'd been quiet and polite and asked a lot of silly questions—silly, to them—and eventually won the hearts of them all, not just Angelica.

Eventually, he'd committed to learning Spanish, even though her family could communicate with him perfectly well in English. Will had stumbled through the words, the phrases, depriving them of their natural music with his flat, American accent. He often confused the expressions, to hilarious results. Her papá had never failed to take advantage of his mistakes, dancing a verbal flamenco around him, bringing the house down with laughter and tears.

Will always accepted his father-in-law's teasing in good fun. He swore it helped him learn, warned him against making the same mistakes twice. It had simply been important to him to learn the language the Moreno family spoke at home.

When Angelica had asked why... he'd made a rare reference to his former life, normally shrouded in silence.

"I don't have family anymore," he'd said, staring at the floor, as if staring into a nothingness that stretched to the very center of the earth. At the time, she'd thought he was speaking of his abuse at the hands of his father. Now, she knew better. "There's no one to go home to," he'd said. "No one to visit. No holidays to keep." And then he'd looked at her, his eyes deep, opening straight to the bottom of his soul. "*Tu familia es mi familia.*" *Your family is my family.*

Angelica blinked, another tear rolling down the side of her face.

Through the blur of her tears, past the frantically moving forms of the crowding officers, she thought she saw a light, somewhere up in the cathedral ceiling. It started as a flickering pinprick, but swiftly grew, until it burst into something radiant, something that consumed the entire ceiling. From the middle of the light, a man stepped forward.

Angelica's breath caught. She knew him.

His blond hair was carefully trimmed and combed in a business-like cut. He wore a loose suit of white linen, even though his feet were bare. His blue eyes pierced Angelica's.

She blinked. "Will?"

He reached a hand toward her. His lips moved, and in her mind, she heard the words he'd told her every morning and every night. "Angelica. Eres mi vida."

*You are my life.*

The tears flowed freely down her face.

He had kept secrets from her. Horrible truths.

But perhaps he had done so to grasp at a dream he'd never dared to imagine could be his. Not after everything he'd done.

Perhaps, embraced by Angelica and her family, he had found healing. The man who had broken laws and run rough-shod over the financial dreams and labors of strangers—that was not the man she had married. Fritz Geissler had died and been reborn as Will Read.

And every moment with him had been beautiful. A dream. A gift. She had loved him with every fiber of her being.

"*Mi corazón,*" she whispered. "I understand. I forgive you."

She felt a tearing sensation in her chest. Maybe it was the police officers trying to do something meant to save her life. Maybe it was the feeling that came with letting go of the hurt, the fear, the anger she'd harbored against Will.

Or perhaps this was what it felt like when your soul tore away from your body, leaving it behind forever.

With a whimper, it dawned on her that she would never see her boys again.

She looked around—and to her surprise, she saw herself lying on the floor in the torn remains of her peach blouse. Serrano was yelling at her. Lange began doing chest compressions. She couldn't feel them, though she knew the sensation should be crushing. Her body would be flown home in a coffin, like Will's had been.

She turned next toward Monica Steele. The detective was screaming at Wade Erickson, her hands on her gun, another officer pushing the barrel toward the floor.

*Monica, I don't want to leave—so hear me out. Let this be worth it. I did everything for my boys. One mother to another, promise me this: Stop The Man Upstairs.*

Her final sentiments sent, she turned to Will, placed her hand in his, and stepped into the light.

# Chapter Ninety-One

# MONICA

I saw Wade Erickson like I'd never seen him before in my life: A liar. A manipulator. A destroyer of lives, of trust. I couldn't stop screaming at him. I couldn't stop wishing I could shift time and the universe and force the last few seconds to play out differently.

A firm hand pressed down over both of mine, pushing my weapon toward the floor, and for some reason the touch calmed me. I knew this hand with every fiber of my being. It was Ryan.

"Baby, listen to me," he said. "Put the gun away."

"Ryan," I whimpered through ugly tears.

"Put it away."

"He shot her," I sobbed like a child, wishing he could put a Band-Aid on the whole damn thing.

He closed the last few inches between us. I felt his chest against my arm, his hand on my back. He whispered in my ear. "I know, baby. I know. Put it away. We'll sort it out. I promise." His fingers curled around the barrel of my sidearm.

My eyes remained frozen on Wade, but Ryan's words filtered through. My muscles unlocked. I let him pry the gun from my fingers.

He popped out the magazine. "Come outside," he said.

I let him herd me toward the door, but my focus remained on Wade until the last. He watched us go, his eyes deep and full of pain.

A pain I fully believed to be a well-played act.

# Chapter Ninety-Two

# LEHMAN

Lehman's phone was exploding with chaos—a shot fired, doors crashing, voices yelling. He'd stepped away from the dispatch room, further down the hall, so the noise wouldn't interrupt Piper's transmissions as she brought in the ambulance and tried to direct the officers on the ground. Lehman strained to make sense of the noise coming through his phone. Tried to piece together what he needed to do to restore calm to the insanity.

But suddenly, it was Ryan's voice coming through the speaker phone, his voice soft, intimate. "I know, baby. I know."

*Baby?*

Lehman waited to hear Ryan groan after a swift knee to the nuts—Monica's threatened go-to for any man who treated her like she wasn't just as strong as he was—but Ryan's punishment never came. Instead, Monica whimpered, cried, as if surrendering herself over to the comfort he offered.

Lehman's gaze transfixed on the coffee pot, and the truth sank in.

Oh.

He sighed and bowed his head, planting his hand on the countertop and leaning over it, his gaze narrowing to a single cluster of charcoal-gray dots in the laminate surface. The hope he'd silently cherished for years died with a single, well-aimed dart.

He hadn't realized he could feel so empty inside. Again.

Monica and Ryan's voices were still coming over the phone, Ryan trying to comfort a frantic Monica. Lehman lifted the phone to hang up. This line was no longer vital to keep in touch with an officer in foot pursuit. He was merely listening in on an increasingly private conversation—one he was telling himself he had no feelings about.

Monica's voice broke to a frantic pitch again. "No, Ryan, listen to me! It's him! He's the one!"

Lehman hesitated.

"What are you talking about?" Ryan asked, posing the question Lehman was asking himself.

"Wade," she grated out, a guttural cry that sounded as if it came out from between her teeth. "He's The Man Upstairs."

Lehman frowned.

The Man Upstairs knew about Monica's unborn child.

So had Wade.

Was it possible Wade had been the one who called Monica with a cryptic message only she would understand? Had he been manipulating Monica this entire time, weaving chaos to his own ends? Had he sat here all night waiting for Monica to put a bullet in Fritz Geissler's widow? And when that seemed unlikely to happen—had he left the Command Post to see to it himself?

Ice ran through Lehman's chest. Had he himself been the one making mistakes tonight?

Suddenly, Ryan's words of comfort to Monica were words he desperately needed to tell himself, too. *We'll sort it out later. We'll sort it out later...*

# Free eBook

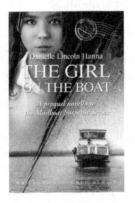

*Her biggest dream was to become a mail jumper, not the key witness to a crime*

**DOWNLOAD YOUR COPY TODAY!**

https://dl.bookfunnel.com/t2jg6baw6d

# Start Reading My Next Book Now!

**Patreon** is a website where top fans can support their favorite creatives in exchange for exclusive benefits. My Patrons get to read my chapters the minute they're out of my pen.

Beyond that, every chapter comes with Book Club Questions, which have prompted some amazing, uplifting conversations. (Good vibes only in my online spaces!) I also post Behind-the-Scenes info, revealing what went into the creation of the story, and the thoughts going through my heart and soul as I write.

My Patrons get a more intimate experience than any other fan. So, come aboard! This is a cruise unlike any you've experienced before.

**JOIN US TODAY!**

www.Patreon.com/DanielleLincolnHanna

# BOOKS BY DANIELLE LINCOLN HANNA

## The Mailboat Suspense Series

The Girl on the Boat: A Prequel Novella
Mailboat I: The End of the Pier
Mailboat II: The Silver Helm
Mailboat III: The Captain's Tale
Mailboat IV: The Shift in the Wind
Mailboat V: The End of Summer
Mailboat VI: *coming soon*
DanielleLincolnHanna.com/shopnow

# THE STORY BEHIND THE STORY

## OPENING A VEIN

I can now say that two scenes in the Mailboat Suspense Series were personally traumatizing to write.

The first was shooting Tommy.

The second was what I came to call The Infamous Chapter 30—the chapter in which we learn about Angelica's past experience with police brutality.

Shooting Tommy was hard because I lost my own father when I was two years old, and a beloved mentor when I was eighteen. I'm not permitted to tell my characters what happens to them in their own stories—and Bailey and Tommy were clear to me from early on that this event was central to theirs, and that it shaped everything that transpired afterwards. Their entire lives.

I wrote Tommy's shooting in nineteen drafts, then really didn't read it again for... four years. Actually, it was extremely recently that I found it in me to read it again for more than quick reference.

As for The Infamous Chapter 30... I have many friends in law enforcement. I also have many friends who are people of color. In fact, my two dearest friends are a former LEO (law enforcement officer) and a black woman. They're like sisters to me. Watching this conflict unfold between police and the black community was like watching my sisters locked in a screaming match. The whole thing turns my stomach.

I think Chapter 30 is the hardest thing I've ever written. It took two weeks just to write that chapter (for comparison, I somehow wrote the entire climax sequence in four weeks), and it stretched me in ways I've never been stretched. When it was all said and done, it weighed in at seventeen drafts, and for two weeks, I came home every night wanting to scream and tear my hair out. My boyfriend Charles will testify that I opened a vein to get that chapter written.

As someone who's been fascinated by law enforcement from an early age, it truly pained me to put myself in the perspective of someone who hates and fears the police. At every minute, I wanted to yell at Angelica and Javier, "You don't get it! You don't know what it's like to be a cop." There were a million things I wanted to explain.

But this was their turn to speak. To express their experiences and beliefs and fears. To be heard. In light of the blood that's been shed in our streets... they have earned that right. They should have had that right before the blood was shed.

To write Angelica and Javier's perspective... I had to *become* them. The same as with any of my characters.

And it *hurt*. It hurt to stretch myself to understand things that were so opposite to my own experiences and beliefs. I hated it.

But I did it.

And I just want to say to the white community and to the law enforcement community... I expect no less of you. If I did it, you can do it.

Javier begged us to understand—with no expectation that it would actually happen.

We need to prove him wrong.

# ACKNOWLEDGMENTS

The experience writing *Mailboat V* was unlike any of the others—first and foremost, because this was the first book I ever released one chapter at a time to a group of truly devoted fans who ate them up as soon as they emerged from my pen. The experience was amazing, and I never want to write a book any other way again. (Check us out on Patreon: Patreon.com/DanielleLincolnHanna.)

So, big thanks to all my Patrons, and especially *Guest at the Captain's Table Barry Fine* and *VIP Passengers Carol Neumann and Pat Nordling.* The excitement of showing my Patrons each chapter as it was finished kept me motivated. I loved taking you way deeper behind the scenes than any other fan has ever gone, I loved our in-depth conversations on the topics of the story, I loved making you an intimate part of the creative process, and I loved hearing what you thought might happen next—and frequently surprising you anyway.

And I cannot wait for our in-person meet-up at Geneva Lake after this book goes to print.

My thanks to the Lake Geneva Cruise Line (CruiseLakeGeneva.com) for their assistance, particularly *General Managers Harold Friestad (ret.) and Jack Lothian,* to the *Mailboat Captain Neill Frame (ret.),* and to *Office Manager Ellen Burling.*

A big shout-out to *Harold Johnson* of Breadloaf Books. Thanks for the wonderful book signings we had there, the fan interactions you hosted, and the fun conversations you had with me and Charles. I miss your shop, and felt it deserved an homage in the series.

A number of Expert Advisers both consulted with me and read my work to check for accuracy.

First, *Alondra Gaspar*. You truly helped me bring Angelica to life through our conversations about Mexican-American life, your suggestions for Spanish expressions, and your recommendations on Mexican cuisine. Angelica and her family are as much your creation as they are mine.

*Dr. Terry Jones*, thank you for teaching me how to damage my characters and how to put them back together again.

*David Congdon*, I never tire of our psychological conversations based on the people talking in my head. Also, thank you for all you do to help those who need it. I'm in awe of the fearless things you do to help people in the darkest circumstances this planet has to offer.

Big thanks and big hugs to my cop bros, *Lieutenant Ed Gritzner* and *Sergeant Jason Hall* of the Lake Geneva Police Department. I can never get over how lucky I am to work with you guys, and I kind of have too much to say about all the cool things we did together to make *Mailboat* V happen. Jason, thanks for your real-time commentary as you read the manuscript during your graveyard shifts when I should have been in bed. Ed, thank you for sending me photos of Geneva Lake when I'm fifteen hundred miles away and you goddamn know it. And thanks to both of you for walking through the climax sequence with me, thanks for letting me hang with you in your shiny new Mobile Command Unit, and thanks for somehow carving out the time to read a very long manuscript cover-to-cover in the middle of your busy tourist season. In a nutshell, thank you for telling me how to do cop stuff right—but but as a follow-up to that… thanks to my boyfriend *Charles William Maclay* for helping me figure out how to screw shit up anyways.

To *Sam Petitto* (ret. police officer, Durango, CO), I can't believe you managed to read and critique my lengthy climax sequence while you were recovering from both jetlag and Covid. I'm amazed by and grateful to you, and incredibly proud of myself for finally earning the equivalent of an A-minus from my strictest teacher.

To my writer's club, *We Write Good*, thank you for helping me see my words through other eyes and pushing me to be the best I can be.

*My Early Reader Team*, you really rose to the challenge this time. I'd hoped to give you more time to read and hunt down my errors, but the end of Book V was the Climax Sequence from Hell. What I hoped to write in a week instead took a full month, leaving you mere days to read one of my longest novels yet. You. Are. Amazing. Massive thanks to *Lisa, Susan Beatty, Stephanie Brancati, Loranda Daniels Buoy, Kathy C, Brenda Dahlfors, Nancy Diestler, Lynda Fergus, Elaine Montgomery, Rebecca Paciorek, Linda Pautz, Pat Perkins, Sanda Putnam, JoAnn Schwartz Schutte, Judy Tucker, Kimberly Wade, Carol D. Westover*, and *Mary-Jane Woodward*.

All my love to my publicists, *Rebecca Paciorek, Susan Beatty*, and *JoAnn Schwartz Schutte*. I'm sure the insane turnaround times had you pulling your hair out. Thanks for keeping me sane and organized, and helping me tell the world I finished another book.

For their unique contributions that resulted in my stunning cover art, thanks to *Matt Mason Photography* (MattMasonPhotography.com) for the imagery, *W. J. Goes* for helping my photographers chase down the Mailboat, and *Maryna Zhukova* (MaryDes .eu) for bringing the images to life. Maryna, I've been a fan of your work for a long time, but this was the first time it gave me chills. I'm pretty sure this is the movie poster, not the book cover.

A heartfelt thank-you to *all my readers* for your undying enthusiasm for this series and these characters. Your imagination gives them life. Wish me luck as I continue to seek a home for them in Hollywood!

And, of course, my heart to those I love most. *Angel*, my German Shepherd, what a noble young lady you've become—while still being utterly hilarious. *Fergus*, my black cat, you are always welcome to chase the thread and the measuring tape from my sewing box. I can't believe you've begun sharing the people-bed with Angel.

And my love, *Charles William Maclay*, your imagination delights and horrifies me in equal measure, and I wouldn't want it any other way. Thank you for never-ending conversations getting to know each other better, and long brainstorming sessions getting to know our characters and stories better—which often amounts to the same thing. It looks like the future has big changes for us, and I can't wait for our next chapter together.

# ABOUT THE AUTHOR

Danielle Lincoln Hanna is the author of the Mailboat Suspense Series. While she now lives in the Rocky Mountains of Montana, her first love is still the Great Plains of North Dakota where she was born. When she's not writing, you can find her hiking with her boyfriend Charles, adventuring with her German Shepherd Angel, and avoiding surprise attacks from her cat Fergus.

Made in the USA
Monee, IL
09 August 2022

11238811R00187